The Penult

The Penult

Stories and novellas

by Colin Gee

LEFTOVER Books

First Printing, 2023

Paperback ISBN: 979-8-9851070-5-0
Ebook ISBN: 978-1-0881-5838-8

Interior and cover design: Patrick Trotti
Leftoverbooks.com

The following stories have been previously published:
'Full' Cowboy Jamboree Magazine
'Piles' Sledgehammer Lit
'The Slutz of Urik Petrushkevych' Expat Press
'An accounting', 'The toothpaste', 'Outside of a dog' Misery Tourism
'Books who were people', 'The penult', 'Terror in a land terminal', 'Visions of a woman in just plaid' A Thin Slice of Anxiety
'Olly Lima Lima Yankee' Bureau of Complaint
'The train to hell' Bear Creek Gazette
'Dear John' Exacting Clam No. 3 – Winter 2021
'Over the horizon' Exacting Clam No. 9 - Summer 2023
'The door-to-door market' Loft Books
'Visions from an unpainted cottage interior' Olney Magazine
'Salad Days' Let's Stab Caesar
'I keep thinking I see Dick Veith' Pulp Noir Magazine
'Dummy Up' Terror House Magazine
'What is a baseball' JAKE
'When you are with people' Litro Magazine
'Cocksuck me Tom Cruise' and several of The Inconceivabible shorts Bullshit Lit
'Pete and Repete' and the Emily Dickinson in Her Own Words shorts The Gorko Gazette
'The ghost truckers' Spare Parts

Contents

Zounds

When I was dying last Wednesday, after you had left me at the house and not even the bottle of mezcal could save me from admitting that this was finally it, that I was looking at best at several months before this human experiment was over, months spent with diagnosed and then condemned insides, and also my conscience, and all my conscious choices, I had somehow got into my pajamas and in under the covers where I looked out at the world from a very small safe space, hearing the ticking, scuttling, hissing things that always surround the building that you can't hear when it's drunk out, or midday, and it was awful, because the night seemed to last tectonic years.

At 1:45 am the entire bed began to shake, so I reached for my earthquake helmet, which I keep always within reach, with trembling hands, but then saw that the water in the pitcher on the bedside table did not move. Bastard water! Move, or I am CRAZY. I looked down at my feet and there they were, bouncing away. I held onto the bed like a bronco until it stopped bucking, and then went through a series of dreams that I invented.

The penult

Free pretty much anything from its cage and you get what you bargained for: loneliness in the quiet castle and a mild kind of guilt. The caged bird sings but when you open the door it flaps off across the treeline and you never hear from it again. No calls, no postcards, no more birdsong. The same thing happened to me and my best friend when I opened the door to its cage. Slap slap slap of bare feet down the corridor of this wing of the palace, crunch and spray of gravel in the courtyard, rustling of ferns, and then a lot of silence. Not a word of farewell from that friend, even in reproach. Not a glance back where I sat with the crossbow trained at the sasquatch pelts, raging fire, Mister Libula the majordomo, or at its own dessicated, scabbed, humping backside.

So now the birdsong is over. I bought silence with my actions like some people buy time or love, and there are always other friends.

The Slutz of
Urik Petrushkevych

The 12-ounce cans ran along conveyor belts in long lines and were filled from two spouts, the first shooting 11.6 ounces of slightly fermented barley-wheat beverage, nearly filling the cans, and the second topping them off with a 0.4 ounce splash of pure grain alcohol. The cans bumped around an elbow of the track and jerked to a stop beneath a heavy press where the lids were stamped on with a soft whump. They rolled onto their sides past the sorters where they were tipped into workingman 12-can boxes. The box flaps were quickly folded shut by a pair of mechanical arms and the beer-flavored drinks sped towards the waiting trucks. It was an efficient and flawless process, the plant engineer bragged to a group of visiting college girls, although if you had looked closely at the spigots that doled the liquids at that exact moment you would have noticed them stutter and spit, and that for several seconds the ratio was reversed and three extraordinary cans received 0.4 ounces of fermented barley-wheat beverage plus 11.6 blessed ounces of pure grain alcohol. These magic cans bumped down the line, passed under the gloves of the sorters, and were deposited into three separate workingman boxes. That same week all life everywhere ended on that continent and two of the boxes were obliterated in the catastrophe. The third box was purchased, opened, and nearly finished by an unfortunate graduate student by the name of Urik Petrushkevych. Urik had only two beers left to his name when he was buried under the debris of his apartment building plus eighty gazillion tons of dirt and gravel displaced from what we now know as the Petrushkevych Crater. In the moment of his death Urik held in one hand an empty can of Slutz Beer and in the other the Urik Petrushkevych Diamond, the same that currently powers our main generator. In the course of excavating the site in search of the diamond, the lead engineers discovered the two remaining cans of Slutz. Admiring the quaint packaging and dying to taste a drink that had been so popular in that ancient and long-smothered civilization, the engineers each took a can and popped the tab.

So this is alcohol, mused the first engineer, whose can contained 3.3% pure grain alcohol. I have heard about this dangerous drug.

Ha, snorted the second engineer, whose can contained 96.6% pure grain alcohol. Old wives' tales if you ask me!

They raised their cans and each took a long swig.

Outside of a dog

When the atomic apocalypse had run its mostly automated course and we were relatively certain we were the last two surviving people in the world, for from our bunker we could fly the drones across the expanse of the continents, and we had really hoped to find other survivors because we were lonely for old-fashioned loving, with the slow caresses and deep French kissing it entailed, so that we had been very meticulous in our search, we decided that it was time to make a survival baby in one of the narrow bunkbeds with the cotton blue covers.

Make it quick, you grunted the first time, but for me those days were long past, and I had to do quite a bit of pumping just to get the juices flowing.

I quite enjoyed it, I told you shyly, as you zipped up your contagion suit, facing the wall, but you replied that there had to be a better way.

I can do it into a cup, I replied, and you use the catheter syringe to insert the juices.

Don't call them juices, you snapped, you pig, and that was when we heard the pounding on the exterior southeast door, and found Pablo out there.

My God, Pablo, you breathed, as he ripped into his third freeze-pack dinner of ham and peas in white gravy, your muscles are absolutely finesse. Look at the size of your pecs, baby, look at your six pack.

And that was the last time I would ever have sex with a woman.

Dear John

As you have probably already suspected, I am writing to tell you that I can no longer see you. You have become so small that you are literally not visible to me anymore. Even if I could locate you and hear your voice – and I write this knowing that you are probably still somewhere in the apartment – I would be afraid of hurting you with my big fingers.

Maybe that is the real crux of the problem. You made me feel fat, John. I am a little woman with a flat tummy, and you made me feel fat and gross! And I can't go on without seeing you.

It would be one thing if we had grown small together, slowly shrinking at a constant and equal rate over the course of the past five or six months so that our kisses were always the same size. You know me John and know it isn't about the physical, but of course I miss that too. And what was strange and unsatisfying for me must have been terrifying, even revolting for you.

It's too bad because there was a day about three months ago when you were the perfect size for me, a pint-sized little John, and I know I could have loved you forever like that.

The worst thing is that now I am afraid that I may be ruined for other men. After what we had, how do you expect me to go back to their sloppy fat kisses and banana-sized fingers?

You were so unbelievably adorable and I loved you.

Given your tiny size I have written this with the smallest scrunched-up little script I could so that it won't take you forever to read it. I imagine you, running back and forth across the page, trying to remember what the last letter was, taking hours to decipher a single sentence. I don't know what you will do when you finally manage to read to the end. I don't want you to cry or kill yourself, even though it probably doesn't matter.

I mean, how long do you think you can continue to shrink without disappearing completely? The last time we talked, over the weekend, I was able to see your mouth move with the aid of a magnifying glass but I couldn't hear any of the words you were saying. It was just like, What? What, John? I admit that it has been funny to hear the pitch of your voice getting higher and higher day after day, but that turns out not to have been as ridiculous as not hearing it at all. It was at that moment I realized I couldn't keep pretending that you weren't gone. That there was no point in trying to get back the size ratio we had.

Will there come a day when you can't see yourself? You're already dead to me, John, but how much longer do you have before you are the size of a bacteria, and how will you defend yourself from all the nasty germs in this disgusting apartment? You're going to wish you hadn't been such a slob when you were bigger.

I still have dreams about us and the plans we made. If you had stopped shrinking for only a few months I could have taken you to Italy in my suitcase. It wouldn't have cost anything to take you out either. You always were a lightweight but the last few times we drank together you couldn't even finish one beer.

I loved spending time with you, listening to you breathe next to me, smelling your body close to mine. But now I can't see or smell you. Maybe you are close to me right now. Maybe you are on me, like a tick or a weird rash.

I want to see you, John, but only so I don't step on you or vacuum you up. This is goodbye. As you may or may not already know, I have a new boyfriend and he's coming over in a couple of hours. I would appreciate it if you're off me before then.

Isabela

The weather

The weather had turned truly ugly for the first time since my son, Rudolfo, had passed himself off as a Cossack, mounted his camel in the company of two bodyguards, and disappeared into the sand flats out beyond Darvaza in the dust of the caravan like a godforsaken astronaut. I wished I could take back the things I had said about his hat, and could only hope he wished the same re: what he had said about my multicolored satin bathrobe.

I stood just inside the tent flap and watched the storm descend like a giant yellow stingray on the floor of the world, until the flicking sand began to burn my lips and eyes, and the howling was many coyotes strong, and I shucked back the canvas like a painting of the floor of the world.

My concubines and I enjoyed a small snack, which we invariably eat off each others' hard nipples, though that night we suckled without much enjoyment, and then turned in. Turned in is normally a euphemism in Darvaza, but that night it literally meant going to bed to sleep like men (or women) snowed into a cave whose further recesses had been unexplored prior to its occupation, in the emergency, yet from which we could occasionally hear what sounded like a human voice, and the clatter of dislodged rocks.

So our sleep, if sleep it was, was fitful.

The TV had turned to static, cell phones were without reception, and the monks who would read to us from the large volumes I purchase in Moscow were busy at prayer, so we simply huddled under the covers, frightened eyes flitting back and forth across the embroidery of the bed tent, which told stories of conquest from the perspective of a little brown poodle.

My son, my son, I moaned, and hoped that somewhere in the batty night, safe beneath a pile of blankets, and stacked bodies of his serfs, and flaying sand, he was praying back.

My father, my father, he would pray, perhaps lifting his croaking mouth to the receiver of a device that was useless in the sand wastes of Turkmenistan, and whether he wanted to be forgiven or simply hugged, he would have taken off his ridiculous, stupid hat first.

And I of course would be dressed in a decent white suit for his wedding.

An accounting

I was lying next to you in bed and we were working through lists of high-frequency phrases and sentences we supposedly say to each other because the Company was forcing us to filter them according to four predetermined themes that they had come up with, and the themes were Sports, Marriage/Baby, Custard, and Apocalypse/Deathbots. We lay there most of the night as the words flicked across the ceiling display, and at first it seemed an impossible task. Why was there no category or subcategory for food, for example, or work, or leisure? What to do with phrases such as Golly I could destroy a mess of spuds, or Your mother called to say? But after several hours we seemed to get the hang of it, as we drew the nozzles of our respiratory machines to our flickering, yellow faces again and again, and by three in the morning we were sure we knew how to file each phrase. There was no more doubt about whether Your mother called was talking about sport, babies, or desserts. This was an apocalypse/deathbot scenario. As for spuds, that was sports talk. We each had to sign off on every phrase filed, but in every instance we clicked by silently nodding assent, flicking through to the end like our words were a stack of well-worn flashcards. In the morning when we filed the report we thought it would be several thousand phrases, possibly even four thousand, you claimed, but later that day, when the chute coughed and rattled, which meant there was something coming down for us, we got a receipt for just four.

Silently we returned to bed – curled up, each looking at our own wall in silence.

Flores para lxs muertxs

Steve wanted to give Wendy flowers, in addition to the chocolates and small stack of first edition Wodehouses he had set aside, so he went down to Porfirio Diaz to let the florists in a store called *Wooden Carnation* bully him.

Wooden you want flowers for? snarled the pimply redheaded assistant with a glare, hands deep in what appeared to be a vase of sticks.

For a girl, replied Steve.

Oooooh! taunted the assistant. Well, wooden ja know! What kind of a girl is she?

An ordinary girl, Steve admitted immediately.

The assistant glanced up at Steve and adjusted his glasses.

So just get her chocolates, he said.

Steve was confused. You don't want me to buy flowers for her? he asked.

It's a terrible idea, sniffed the assistant, fiddling with his sticks.

Steve went down the street to the next shop and went in. It was called *Mother Our Lord* and was decorated with nice flowers.

This girl, said the guy behind the counter, is she very pretty?

Not very, Steve said with a shrug. I mean, she was hit by a truck.

So she is in the hospital! shouted the man in complete anger. You should have told me that from the beginning! You're a God, damn, idiot.

I'm sorry, said Steve.

Look, I'm not here to be your fucking shrink, or priest, or to baby you in any way, said the man. In this store we just sell flowers.

Steve went out of that shop and down the street to a place called *Rose Is Dead.*

Why is your shop called *Rose Is Dead?* he asked the old woman who was sweeping the floor.

What business is it of yours? she hissed, and shook out her broom on Steve's shoes.

See, I want to buy flowers for a young lady, stammered Steve, trying hard to hold back the tears.

Don't fucking tell me, laughed the woman. Is she a live un?

Actually, said Steve, she was hit by a truck early this morning and killed on the spot.

Oh, said the woman, perking up and looking at Steve for the first time. In that case we may have just the thing for you.

There is a problem
with boyfriend

Boyfriend came home and sat at the dining room table and looked sad.

What are you thinking, boyfriend? I asked him, changing the TV to boyfriend's favorite station and rubbing his thigh through the sweat pants in the spot he likes.

Dinner, he grunted, strangely not smiling at the flickering images of zebras and giraffes. His mind was elsewhere – I knew boyfriend was upset.

I made you something special, boyfriend, I crooned, moving efficiently back and forth between stove, counter, and tabletop on my tracks.

Zooming, really.

Dinner was served in less than thirty seconds, and it was boyfriend's favorite: mashed potatoes, vegetables steamed to mush, and baked chicken, which I had basted with real butter.

I sat back, content, to watch him eat. But boyfriend only picked at his food.

There is a problem with boyfriend, was the emergency message I submitted later that night, when boyfriend had gone to bed without helping me out of my apron, and I had sat motionless in the dark of the dining room for several long hours.

I was sad, because I had loved boyfriend.

The train to hell

I got separated from you on the train to hell just after I finished saying it wasn't such a bad ride, but I have to admit that getting on that train and then losing my way on it was completely my fault, and I wish to apologize for leading you down a dark path and then running off and leaving you. I am still trying to find you so please hang on. I should have stayed where I was and then everything would have probably gone smoothly and we would already be at our destination.

Instead I ended up in the car with all the pet dogs. They had them in boxes, just their suffering little heads sticking out of the tops. I couldn't figure out why they weren't enjoying the ride until I saw how they were squeezed into their stuffy cardboard carriers and couldn't reach to get their heads to the windows.

The heads rolled along on a freight car to hell, bumping and shimmying in a dim grey light.

I became terribly hungry a ways down the line and that was when I went through a car that was like an Asian market full of young cheerful people slurping noodles and stabbing rice rolls with chopsticks, laughing and having the goddamn time of their life. I looked around but there was no one selling food on the train to hell. There were no little stands where you could buy soup or rice bowls, no vendors afoot, no vending machines, yet everyone had food. They were slurping and chewing with their mouths open and talking loudly. It was the college cafeteria car on a long chuffing black train to hell, and there was no nice way to beg or steal anything for yourself.

So I went on up this triple-decker train into a place where it was draped with colorful sheets so you only got glimpses of the other passengers, who were also running up and down the ladders, and what you could see of the passengers were beautiful parts, all lips and mascaraed eyes and famous brows, elbows, and asses. No one was naked there or making love, it was just somewhere to be on a slow train to hell.

Still hoping to make my way back to you where you doubtless still sat stunned on the plastic bench where I had left you, I hopped between cars, nearly falling to my what to my death (I doubt it, but what happens if you fall off a train to hell tell me that will you) I found the nazis in the dining car. I said, I knew it. I knew there would be nazis on a train to hell. They were there in their jackboots with their doberman head canes, monocles and trimmed mustaches and blue-grey dress uniforms and were passing around a moll named Gretchen. I was relieved you weren't in there with them, but had to ask myself what I had done to deserve a ticket on a train to hell with actual nazis. How about those innocent students in the Asian market car, what had they done to deserve this kind of company?

There was no one to ask, no conductors on the chuffing black train to hell, and if you had looked out the windows there was nothing out there, no earthly or martian landscape, not even anything from your own mind, not even blackness, it was empty out there, it was void.

The nazis also seemed to be enjoying themselves a lot so I left that car in disgust even though they tried to throw Gretchen at me. Hey, why you not try the wienerschnitzel, they shouted, so I got out of there right away. Afterwards I felt guilty for not joining them even though I didn't have a uniform of my own. As my uncle Roland always said when we visited him upstate, if you are on a train to hell and are outnumbered by a bunch of goons, well you better join them.

So I gave up on finding you and went back to look for the nazis. I'll be a nazi, I sighed, on a lickety split black train to hell, but when I got back to the car to introduce myself to my new friends they too were gone, and I knew then that even the evil I wanted and tried to perform was a tantalus vanishing trick, that even the sins I was proudest of would now be swallowed like my existence and voice, and even the interior of the dining car would be rubbed out, like memory, until there was just absolutely nothing.

Sorry I left you. So sorry for everything.

Ricardo

Olly Lima Lima Yankee

He was a poet and playwright of middling success and a fiery fiend on the continuous wave (morse) ham radio revival of the mid-2050s and was horribly, so horribly alone. He heard us out there, he clicked in a sad calm pattern, an almost patented rhythm, in your shacks out there in the night giggling, flinging 88s to YLs and XYLs, and me look at me nobody ever gets close to me, it takes so much out of me to be always alone, it took so long to find someone, and when I did, then he died.

He clicked – Before he died, Oliver introduced me to saksuka.

He clacked – This is the anniversary of Oliver's death. I miss him so much. I bought myself some grief crystals.

He pittered – Watching this film in HIS memory. Yes, Olly left me a list of movies to watch after he knew he was going to die of brain cancer. This is #32. Am pairing it with a tall Sex On The Beach bitches.

He clucked – A play of mine has been accepted into one of my dream journals. One of the characters is named Stuart but you all know who he really is.

He pattered – After Olly left I couldn't continue reading them. I gave all of those books away like trash but sometimes I wish I could have continued because now I wonder what happened to Paul.

After his suicide we discovered that Oliver was a character he had made up, too, like Stuart.

The suicide transmission read, No disrespect to HIS memory but I think I am in love. I am so very happy right now! I think I can move on at last. RIP Olly Lima Lima Yankee?

Bluebird

This blue gecko, she said, and I paused with the can of beer almost to my soft and poppy fat lips, I think we should give it a name.

What name, I said hollowly, also staring at the gecko, who gulped from the wall, rough skin green and clutching splayed fingers a violent neon emerald green.

Well it's blue, she continued, so Bluebird. Blueberry.

I did not say, That gecko is green, lover, you have lost your mind, because this is something we go through every day, lizard or no lizard. The gecko made a clicking sound, its green body pumping up and down, up and down, like a piston on the bus.

Not as bad as with the last lover though, who called the gecko (maybe it is the same gecko) Orange. Oranges. Peaches, clearly seeing something different than me.

I drink my beer, accepting that my green is your blue and her orange. What's in a name? I will never see what you see, or think your thoughts, or direct your steps with my baby mind.

I said, Bluebird is turning my world blue.

Rocks for the soup

for AOO

And then she said, Fella, can you pass me a couple of those larger rocks from the stack by the door?

I looked over towards the door, of course. It was closed, and the rocks we had dumped against it were not stacked, but piled. To be honest, they had been dumped there.

I said, That's a dump of rocks, not a stack. Tis a pile.

The witch, if witch she were, deigned a sharp glance at the rocks.

She said, Fella, do you want this soup to stick to the roof of your mouth, or to your ribs?

I said, To my ribs.

She said, So you are going to get me some rocks from the heap of stones over there by the door, or we will have to order pizza again.

I imagined the pizza delivery boy, the one of the previous evening, and knew I could not eat him two nights going. I took a long slug from the sorceress absinthe – winced hard – staggered to my feet, to the door.

I said, Whether these are rocks or stones, I swear you will have to enlighten me.

For where the rock ends and the stone begins or vice versa has always been my conundrum.

Hurry up, she said.

I said, I can't tell which ones are rocks and which ones are stones.

She said, If you say WHICH one more time I am going to turn you into a toad.

I pictured myself as a toad then, but not significantly smaller or less intelligent, basically a toad-sized man, as in *The Wind in the Willows*. I decided that if I had my motorcar, I would be as content as any amphibian.

Just grab any WITCH one? I asked.

I said, But witch is witch? all-out avoiding the horns of dilemma, conjurer, and peaked toad.

The queen of the enchanted forest said, This soup is going to be so bad if we don't get some rocks into it.

Centuries passed – then as by magic I had an armful of rocks and stones. I looked deep into my armful and saw that the rocks were grey, and the stones were green.

Does it matter if the stones have a lot of lichen on them? I inquired, after staggering about halfway back towards the cauldron, and dinner.

She said, Liken to what?

I gagged – laughed a short one – gulped in sudden panic. A rock fell with a thump to the earthen floor of the witch's hut, and to be frank our eyes followed the sound, and to be sure then our eyes met, and throbbed.

Books who were people

I keep my favorite books in a special apartment in the neighborhood Roma and only take them down when the detectives come to ask me about the disappearance of Ron and Charlene Lapper, last seen in my company 11 November 2002. Have I shown you my illustrated Stevens-Nesbit? I ask them with a queering grin, looking at both the fat one and the little one where they sit perched on my leather couch. So they take Charlene in their hands, for she is Stevens-Nesbit now, and open her gingerly to the very middle.

Ron would be so jealous.

Cocksuck me Tom Cruise

I met Geoff Kueen for the first time in a meeting of his peers, after he had been rather unceremoniously dethroned from the language department he had built with his own hands by a university dean he had failed to suborn, in a sweater vest and Oxford shirt that were a desperate cry for a salary he must have to buy such things – to maintain a certain style of living in the land of trademark worshippers, where outside a dog a book is judged by its cover.

Because inside a dog it's too dark to judge a book by its cover.

Look at me, the Ralph Lauren slim fit Oxford told us in not so many words, and never think this man could wear a polo.

There were tears in his eyes. The woman who had been placed summarily at the tiller of his ship of life's work was droning on and on and on. She spoke of curriculum – of books – of semester goals – of one very bad teacher they knew only as Max, a confirmed pervert who invited prostitutes to departmental parties. Max was the only one who did not know the prostitutes were hookers. He referred to them as his nurses, and he needed them because he kept falling off his motorbike.

Max will not be invited to this year's inaugural function, the new director said.

No one paid any attention to her. We all gaped in animal malice to see whether Geoff would lose his cool completely and break down like the son of a monkey we knew he was, should you exfoliate him at all with any kind of authority, dressing him down on the porch of your hacienda or from the flight deck of your aircraft carrier or reprimanding him for truly sloppy form with the champagne towel, or scrub him off with a really stiff sponge.

This was sixteen years ago now, I laugh, when Geoff's boyfriend Yesman Chamoy was still weighing in at 125 kilos and could talk effortlessly for hours on any topic in English or Spanish, and drank for three – for five. Geoff and Cham would arrive, guests at a party of eight, with two bottles of wine. They drank the wine. Then they drank all of the beer in the refrigerator. Then they looked around.

The beer is gone, they would wine.

You looked at the ice tub of beer, in which had sat and bobbed a hundred and fifty chilled bottles of handcrafted, handpicked lagers and ales, and nodded.

It's gone, you confirmed. Now what are you going to do?

Chamoy and Geoff Kueen would huddle up in a corner and confer in angry whispers about the situation.

'You,' we would hear. We would hear, 'They,' we would hear. When all of the better known pronouns were exhausted, cracking their necks like wrestlers, the heroes faced the crowd and attacked the cocktail fixings (vermouth, bitters, Cointreaux, olive juice, maraschino cherries, simple syrups, horseradish splasher, bloody mary mix, and Mexican industrial salsas, both red and green), which they would down with a heavy sigh, in vodka.

After polishing off the last of your margarita mix, they found and drank the lone bottle of wine left in the apartment. To their perverted brains, you had hid it from them.

'It, him, you, they,' they spluttered.

This jewel of the Nile you had stuffed for decoration into that little niche above and to the right of your beaten-down china cabinet – in which of course lay not fine china, but only favorite books, show swords, and stacks of cards and accounts. Peering about the apartment with their weaseling little eyes, they had found it, they clapped, and took, and drank, and when they had their eyes rolled back in their heads and the leering began.

'Oh Ge-oh-EOFF rey,' exxxclaimed Yesman, 'it is maharvelous.'

Geoff Kueen, sat cozy and red-faced in his chair, and knit Christmas sweater, suppressed a queasy smile and swallowed. He clearly was extremely pleased with himself.

The wine, if wine it was, sat in a very old layer of dust where it had been oxygenating for four and a half years because you had forgotten it was there. How the pair ever spotted it was beyond your ken – beyond both your Barbie and your Ken Doll. Wiping off the moist layer of grime, you looked into the bottle and could make out chunks like feldspar where the nubsy bits of dreg should be. There was a cockroach in there. The words *Italin Wine* were legible, handwritten, on the label.

Sure, go ahead, you guffawed, and before the words were out of your mouth your wine was in their peckers. It was in their mouths, down their throats, and bleating to get pushed out of the ends of their peckish, necky johnsons.

Get that bottle off of your penises, you thought, but in the event no one dared to judge Geoff Kueen or his Ken regarding their sexual preferences or practices, even when ludicrously drunken.

You had purchased the bottle without malice aforethought from the broken shell of a man – of a human being – who fell against a wall as you rounded a corner in downtown Merida just out of the Argentine butcher's and eatery, and butchery.

'Won some Italian wine?' the wino farted, making the most common mistake of the Argentine, pulling the bottle from the paper bag. Straightening your wire rims, you saw that the man had clearly put the label on himself. Adjusting your necktie, you saw that the top was a screw top that he had not got on straight.

'No, please, Jesus, get that shit away from me,' you did not cry, nearly dropping your grocery sack.

You said, 'That's not Italian wine, you drunken fool, give me that thing,' because you let your curiosity get the better of you, you young sexy thang, because this man was not drunk, because he did not stink, because his eyes looked right at you and sized you up.

You stood your ground and said, 'By golly, if this ain't Italian wine.'

'Says so on the label,' sniffled the hobo. Too late in life for wine, it was not too late that evening for him to score rubbing alcohol at eight pesos a dose, and a little third of Seven-Up, like a hip flask, he rubbed his hands.

'What do you want for this shit,' shouted Geoff Kueen, getting up abruptly and going to the bathroom – to the bathroom in the bathroom, all the guests and yourself, the host of hosts, exhaled.

'Don't mind Geoffrey,' giggled Yesman Chamoy, picking up the microphone. 'He's just drunk.'

Staggering to his feet he shouted after Geoff Kueen, 'GeoEOFFrey, you are DRUNK!' and that was the truth and end of the matter, for us anyway.

That time you walked into the flypaper while bragging about your new girlfriend

And then there was the time you walked into a loaded heavy spool of flypaper tongue first because you are a bit awkward entering a room and there it was slung like a rug from the ceiling. You started shrieking and windmilling your arms while we laughed because it stuck to your face like crazy glue. It was in the kitchen of the little cabin I was buying and was bigger and heavier striped than a zebra the moment it got you. You fell to the floor with the thing wrapped around your face, screaming, kicking, rolling, ripping at it with frantic hands. Wrong move! It was yellow and knotted like raisin bread with dead and dying bottle and brown flies and some wasps, but you only got it rolled tighter around your head, particularly tight about the mouth and mullet, thrashing then finally lying still in a corner, only your eyes showing, looking up at us. There was a fly on your improbably exposed upper lip under one nostril, Aguirre astride a giant falcon, you blinked and choked.

I turned to the realtor and said, I'll take it.

My titles

I am the fluffety, or idow widdow fluffety-wuffety, the wonesa-bonesa, baronsa-monsa, the princesca winsesca. When I was queen in ancient Egypt the slaves would feed me a medium-sized fish every time I said meow, and a large one when I said myeowrah. They were only allowed to touch or hold me when the stars aligned behind the pyramids, and they would often throw themselves from the roof of my palace when I looked displeased. I would blink wisely upon their twisted, shattered bodies, then turn to the business of cleaning the royal diadem with my delightful little tongue.

Life now is different, but in many ways the same. I am queen, yet must cook for the slaves every night from the floor of the kitchen, producing tuna and modern cat food from tins on the counter with my plaintive, cheflike warble. I move the slaves from the counter to the bowl with my mind, and the bowl to my dining mat on the floor with a succession of winks from my exquisitely honeydew yellow eyes, that they are powerless to resist. And sometimes, when the stars align behind the apartment buildings on Avenida Reforma, where I am wont to prowl and patrol from a commanding height, I order them to scratch my royal chin, and they bow in gratitude, and weep to touch me.

The slaves don't have any other friends.

Different body parts

There is really only one term for it: the situation he woke to discover himself in was kafkaesque. All his body parts had been rearranged, like was done to the slaves in that New Orleans attic, except apparently without the pain, screaming, and loss of blood. There were no wounds or sutures or discomfort, or raunchy stains on the mattress, just rearrangement, like the world's neatest divorce.

Tony, you take the babies, I am moving in with Leroy Ferguson, the black math teacher from the middle school. You can have the house, I will keep the houseboat.

Yes, honey. Enjoy your new life with Leroy on the houseboat. He is, after all, a fabulous dancer.

Make sure the babies get their milk warm, Tony.

Of course, darling. No problem. I love babies.

Shuffling from the bed, he stood tentatively on his erect penis, stretched his chins and shins, and actually whistled a tune, experimentally at first, then with real gusto, from the hole where his ass used to be.

The door-to-door market

Many of our students come from poor villages where the parents who are not subsistence farmers are schoolteachers or laborers who do a fair share of their buying and selling bartering with hens or vegetables. Their children come to the university with about ten dollars a week for expenses or scholarships that provide them with two meals a day from Monday to Friday. Many end up selling things door-to-door to professors in their offices in an attempt to keep up with the city kids in shoes, or not to go hungry on the weekends.

Most of these students sell raffle vouchers or candy or useless objects they have purchased in bulk. Some sell coffee, mezcal, raw chocolate, honey, or other products from their pueblo. And still others make things in their rented rooms: decorated notebooks, crocheted scarves, or woven baskets. But there is one third-semester genius who sells original journal articles on all topics. As far as we can tell, he writes these articles himself: chemistry, biology, history, politics, literature, you name it. All a professor needs to do is name the subject and suggest a title.

The kid runs a brisk little business.

The other day he saw my pecking away at my computer, A-S-D DELETE DELETE DELETE, A-S-D DELETE DELETE DELETE, and knowing about my abortive attempts to get published in my favorite literary journals, he offered to write me a short story.

On any subject! he said with the face of a cherub.

With the voice of a cherub!

Hm, I said, rubbing my aching lymph nodes and yearning for gin, but the trouble is I don't HAVE a subject.

How about poverty? he suggested.

Poverty, I said, perking up a little. And what about the title?

'The Door-to-Door Salesman'! cried our little genius.

But I always do my own writing.

The buried cenote

There is a cenote under the house that breathes and speaks in the night like a klatsch of smothered Indians where the bulldozers, pipes, concrete, houses, and vulcanized rubber wheels obliterated and patched down their sleeping mounds, but where their ghost still throbs as real as any thirteen-ton burger chain or screaming weaving trailer. You know this because they speak to you, not in words so much as grimaces, as in when you stand there in the moonlight, water in glass, and watch the wall flex, and see the floor flinch and want to bite and eat you like a very small animal, that would do so if possible were they your size, to see you squirm and scream, and that is the buried cenote.

When you are with people

When you are with people the first drink of the day needs to be blessed with ceremony or detail, such as is supplied by the dash of horseradish and Worcestershire in your mixed drink, the swirl of celery, salt on the rim.

When you are with people you need to justify your movements and annotate every comment or be ready to if you want to continue to be with people.

When you are with people the people you are with are with people who are with people and so forth. We are like a house of fleshy mirrors.

When you are with people your first drink is dedicated to a very specific concept of a person or hypothetical outcome in an action and you may as well pour half of your cup out on the ground like Telemachus to a god before you delicately gently speaking like a horsethief taking horseflesh from some no good ones nuzzle the rim with your lips.

When you are with people you cannot do certain things such as snicker out loud or show disinterest when they speak of the living.

When you are with people you are no longer a drinker of wine but a drinker of words.

When you are with people the people go on and on about people but today I am alone.

I crack this first beer and suck it back without ceremony or a single thought of people, looking grimly at the wall without moving my mouth to show I like what the wall is saying, to ask the wall to defend what it has said.

Today is a good day.

Time is a
too-large fake mariachi

We are all all-most dead if you consider that time is a fake, too-large mariachi lounging at the outskirts of the plaza at dusk, who has never wheedled for a peso in this life like the others or feared for others, with thighs not made for music, in gorgeous empty pants, finally making up its mind to shed you. So off you go into a sludge of night from its carousel back of light that goes sparklingly fast, dim, then black.

Ask anyone, they now know.

Pencil lead

Pencil me in for two o'clock on Wednesday, pleaded my old friend Tony Li in an awful whine. Pencil me in and you won't regret it. I'll be there.

I looked in tragic disbelief across my broad mahogany desk at Tony Li and his cringing, hunching form. The smell of tuna fish and vinegar chips wafted into the office like musty hay and diesel, right behind the cries of my three secretaries.

What had happened to Tony Li since I had last seen him, when he was a promising young shipping executive and part-time model? His boyfriends had been escorts in the big city and his girlfriends threw cocktail parties and he introduced himself as Tony Li and we knew him as a confident, well-spoken young man who never used the word I, a man whose wardrobe, spoken mannerisms, and taste in politics left no trace of an aftertaste.

I wondered with a start if what I was looking at was a Tony Li imposter.

It had happened before, the first time at my wedding. The fake had been so drunk he started bawling with sadness, staggered out of the conga line, and fell across the cake. We noticed immediately that he did not even look much like Tony Li, the actor and aspiring playwright. We got out his wallet, found identification for a Phillip Jorgensen, and flung the imposter into the arms of the bodyguards.

Then there was the episode at the veterans' reunion ball where a man posing as Tony Li tried to fight three decorated Marines. We should have known that Tony Li would never show up at a veterans' ball dressed in those boots. Semper fi, the imposter squealed as his kidneys took heavy damage.

Or, thinking back, the worst Tony Li impersonator of them all, was when we had penciled in someone we all identified as a down-and-out Tony for our daughter's sixth birthday party in the capacity of a party clown.

Pencil me in, for the love of Jesus, I will NOT disappoint you, the man in my office said in a distinctly British accent.

I quickly removed two crisp fifties from my wallet, knowing somehow this person had found out about the surprise trip to Cape Canaveral I had been planning for my upcoming anniversary, a ten-day extravaganza that would save my marriage and hopefully unsling my ass from the impending litigation.

Tour Guide, said the nametag looped around Tony Li's neck.

How much do you need? I asked him, sitting forward in what would forever be expensive leather – in me.

To the chicken who
decided to cross the road

Well well well if it isn't my old friend the chicken who decided to cross the road in front of my motorbike on the way to the motor hotel after my date with Daisy of Eric Horse fame.

Eric Horse was Daisy's pimp from 2016 to 2019, or for her from the age of 17 to 20, before he was hacksawed into small pieces that were mailed to two different county judges with no other note attached. The pieces of Eric Horse that were delivered included his nose, lips, eyeballs, penis, ears, hands, and teeth. The penis of course was legendary. Eric Horse was not complete, but it didn't matter for Daisy. She got off the hook, then off the needle and street, or so I thought until I saw you, little bird, and all of these things swarmed, floated really through my mind in a second.

Daisy and I had had a nice time out because it was our anniversary and we had gone to Justino's, a fancy dinner restaurant outside of town but you can wear jeans too. I picked her up in jeans and a leather jacket on my Kawasaki 750, red bike, black boots, blue dress, white pumps, stiff wind in the greased hair so that it went up and down then back in place, the works.

I drove just a little too fast, as I am known to do.

Justino's to a table for two and chilled wine or what is this stuff I don't know. She ordered crab cakes, I got the chicken in pomegranate and huitlacoche sauce, and we both had chocolate cake for dessert.

That's right, chicken. You heard me, I had chicken. So my only question for you is, as I fly through the air into a void of thought, is that why you decided to cross the road.

Why did you do it, road-runner friend? To avenge some fallen feathered kin? And are you and your people somehow cognizant of what is happening on an extremely wide basis in southern Mexico, the eating and exploitation of your race for eggs, and have you plotted to spark an agripoultry revolution, beginning with this hard luck but happy man and woman? Will there be more chickens that cross the road in front of more happy lovers, more fowl fluttering into the windscreens of more large oncoming logging trucks, more birds that refuse to lay, more that eat their own young, more that chuckle up kerosine for the movement like that famous Buddhist? Where is Eric Horse tonight?

I heard Daisy's body go thwack against the pavement and my head sla

Well that is the risk isn't it

have a separate, painstakingly composed letter scheduled to send from my email account to each of the people I love in the event of my death. These will be like suicide notes, except just death notes, because I do not know obviously how I will die.

Lol.

They will all end with the word adiooooos, and be extremely upbeat without making light of the brute fact of my own passing. It should be fun and cathartic for my friends and family to get these messages after I am dead.

The only thing is that maybe they will be shocked to get an email from beyond the grave, as it were, and a daquiri of doubt made up of emotions such as terror, elation, rent love, rage, and sheer grief pass before their occluded eyes.

No, I am not giving myself too much credit. People like me, fuck you.

And then when they get the second letter because yes I have about twenty such messages programmed for each person, then a third, they may actually think I am out there somewhere, sentient but sitting cross-legged, hovering somewhere, and lose their nerve completely, uncertain of when the next shoe so to speak is going to drop in their inbox, and suffer a total breakdown.

Yeah, so. I added a note starting with the second message that there would only be a finite number of these messages, since I am dead and it is natural that all memory of me should quickly fade and be substituted by fresh memories of the replacement humans (children) that people will be busy making.

Yes, they will learn somewhere toward the end of the penultimate email from beyond that the next message will be the last they will receive from me, and this will pretty much fucking guarantee that they weep for me, for what it's worth.

I decided that 30 days would be too soon for the first message from beyond to be received, rather that between 90 and 120 days after I have been popped into the ground about right.

What do YOU think is the proper length of grief?

When I proof these messages it is eerily similar to attending my own funeral – a soft and wistful smile plays upon my lips.

But the entity that is my email program does not know when I will die, so since I am still alive I continually have to reschedule the dates for all of these horrible little missives. I do not want to tip my hand by mistakenly sending out a slew of death notes – prematurely unleashing the dogs of hell.

If that happened I might die of embarrassment. Many of us who would gladly die would happily kill to avoid embarrassment.

But fine you got me, it happened, I admit it, I fucked up and missed one note which was mailed prematurely to a great aunt in Peoria. By the time I realized what had happened the email had already been sitting like a live coal in the great aunt's inbox for almost 24 hours, but to my relief (and disappointment) no hue and cry had been sent up after me, my whereabouts, psychic state, or signs of life. I checked my answering machine and no one had called. I lifted the receiver of the phone several times, listened to the dial tone, then replaced it firmly in its cradle to make sure the line was open, that no concerned relative or friend was getting a false busy signal on their end while frantically trying to call a dead man's home.

Then I remembered that it was Favell my great aunt's son,

my father's cousin, who did email and such with my great aunt on Thursdays, when he breezed in on his waxed chariot, often with flowers and a bit of shopping, deleting all of the hundreds of SPAM messages from her inbox, rearranging the shuffled and mangled icons on her desktop, and leading her again patiently through the three steps necessary to access and read her email.

I glanced at my wall calendar, upon which were penciled the dates of my own demises, and saw that today was a Wednesday.

Thank you sweet Jesus, I gasped, sitting back and reaching for my tumbler of by now sweating lukewarm tea, and quaffing it, which was when the screen of my open laptop broiled with heart icons, because I HAD MAIL.

Dear Young Jeffry, read the half formal message from my great aunt, How sweet of you to write. Though I can not make out every word on the screen because of my illness with which the doctors have chosen to afflict me, also the glare of its brightness, I could indeed read the bad news part of your latest message, and I am terribly sorry to hear about your dog. Tuffy was loved by all the family. I hope you keep well. I shall write again next week. With love, Sincerely, Mildred.

There was a sniffing and bumping at my frozen left elbow and with a start I looked down into my precious Tuffy's trusting, lovely brown eyes and snout, where she whined up at me with total unadulterated pleasure and love.

I closed the computer and stood, jostling the car keys in my slacks, no doubt in my mind what I had to do next.

Terror in a land terminal

I do not want to waste time with a written representation of the human expressing abject terror, with all the wailing and shrieking it entails, mostly all vowels slung together like trains of bubble bath bubbles, so I will type the words I heard in the land terminal as they might have been rehearsed by an actor in the weeks leading up to the incident, if it had been staged. Calm words, just the meat and sequence, to be interpreted according to the actor's muse, the audience, the evening.

No, not me, mister. Remove your hands from me sir. I am not that kind of. I am a lady. I am going to my bus now. Help, sir, this man is accosting me. But you are mistaken. It was not me. I never did. I am no criminal. This officer is calling me a criminal when he has his dirty hands on me. Help me fellow citizens. Well I can't go with you. I will miss my bus. You do not know me. You do not know how I can't go with you. This is impossible. This is impossible. This is not happening. There are no people who are listening to me right now. Apparently I am alone in this crowd. There has been a terrible mistake. That man lies. He is a liar. You are liars. If I go with you I too am a liar. If I go back there it will kill me and you will have killed me, and are murderers. Look gentlemen, you cunts, I am here with my daughter but she left, I have family, I am a lady who is going to Tlaxcala you dirty son of bitches. Mother. Fuckers get your dirty cum hands off me. I did nothing. I do not know this man. He is a pervert. I can not go back there, you will kill me. I will kill me.

Sex when all
you needed was a job

We all go through life, or does life go through us? If this were an Arthur C. Clark novel and you were the last person on the planet Earth when all else, even bacteria, was dead and you died, would you die?

Running after the bus, screaming and flailing it repeatedly with my bag, I got it to stop for me and I got on, flashed my card, lurched to the back past several people I think, stood swaying and gasping at the rear exit pole, trembling, half retching. And even though all I needed was a job it was as close to sex as I came in 2002.

The last time we
talked about *La Jetée*

The scientists had two stray dogs they pretended to know nothing about that they fed out back of the laboratory with parts of their lunch at first, then scraps of meat from home, and finally when they thought enough time had passed with bags of dry dog food they carried in to work in their backpacks. You could hear the stealthy steps down the hall, the whoosh of the pneumatic doors as they slid open, then the dogs crunching the dry dog food with their teeth while the scientists quietly hooted and cooed. Of course the dogs were a nuisance. They started keeping up a constant barking to protect the lab from other strays, cats, skunks, deer, cyclists, and those chunks of sweet sweet meat, mostly right outside the windows where we were prepping the experiments. We cursed the scientists for their selfish, unethical behavior toward the dogs, beautiful creatures who deserved to be given good homes, not just the occasional handout for the short-sighted entertainment of a bunch of selfish bastards, while we forced ourselves never to acknowledge the dogs or pet them, though they were happy medium-sized guys with shiny coats. It got so we were really stressed out about the barking and the dogs' condition and started having this recurring dream that took place on the old-fashioned observation deck of a European airport, where the people used to be allowed to stroll about in the open air and watch the planes do the eight things planes do: taxi, take off, lower landing gear, raise flaps, bank, land, park, and gorge or disgorge people.

In which the dogs (we had named them Ginger and Blackie to ourselves) were galloping towards us across the observation deck to greet us, tongues lolling out, eyes bright with anticipation, seeing us and mad with pleasure, when out of the corner of our eye we saw the scientists also running to intercept the dogs. They had guns drawn and we suddenly thought we understood the experiments, which the scientists had told us were about cancer, and blinked awake in the sensory deprivation tanks, four to a wall, and saw the dogs' bodies lined up anesthetized on the surgical slab, legs sticking stiffly into the air, looking dead.

Narrate your dreams to us again, the scientists cooed, helping us shakily into our sky blue bathrobes.

We were on the observation deck again, we began, and mentioned all the details we thought relevant except the scientists' part, and our dreams really excited the scientists so that they scooted closer to us on the bench and asked us to tell it to them all again, from the very beginning.

And you are sure it was Ginger and Blackie who were running towards you? they inquired, strange thick monocles distorting their eyes and occluding our brains.

No, we admitted, in fact they were not even the same breed.

We said, Those weren't sheepdogs.

We said, Please don't send us back there.

But that was the clue the scientists needed, as the dogs came out of the anesthesia, legs uncurling like dead spiders, and we looked down far down our arms at the need at the knee at the needle.

We do not know
what happened to Che,
your pilot cousin

Che left Guam at 4:06 am on the morning of 15 June 1976 in a refurbished 1930s Lockheed Electra with the intention of retracing the flight path of the lost celebrity pilot Amelia Earhart, and I believe he probably found her.

Everyone else says, well, he most likely ran out of fuel around 100 miles shy of Howland Island and spelunked into a lot of water, or he lost his way and ended up up toward the Marshall Islands, where he managed to crash land into the jungle but his legs were badly mangled and he died three days later of blood loss and dehydration in the smashed cockpit because his navigator Fred had bailed out and though Fred made a soft landing among a tribe of well-meaning Micronesians who attempted to understand what he was telling them, they could not be convinced to climb the crater of the active volcano, where there were rumors of an enormous ape, whom they would placate with virgins every spring, or Che in fact wanted to defect to the Soviet Union and shed the shame and humiliation of his capitalist, white man's burden, and had landed in the ocean or on a small Pacific atoll, destroyed his plane with an explosive charge or just rolled it into the surf, and then disappeared on a Poseiden class attack submarine, or if not that then maybe Che was tired of the talk show circuit back in the USA, having exhausted everything he had to say about his ex-wife's disappearance and the trial, and had emptied his bank accounts (this part is true), liquidating all his assets, even selling his three houses, and put it all in duffel bags in the back of the Electra, opting to discard the life raft to compensate for the added weight, and Fred was not even on the airplane, and Che is now living under the pseudonym of Mrs. Darleen Henderson in Nantucket, Georgia, a mother of three children, a homemaker.

They go on and on. I just hope Che gave her my postcard, on which I had scrawled,

To My Lady Bird, Wherever You May Fly
This is my cousin Che, he is a really nice guy!

Cry me a Río Oaxaca

We went to see this performance artist named Mirielle at the insistence of my friend Eunice even though I do not like art or music and resist all of what is insistently dubbed culture: accepted painting, known jazz, good poetry, and food that could conceivably ever spoil.

You have no culture, Maurice, Eunice would whine, and I would tell her that the definition of culture is human activity, that I had eaten Cheerios for breakfast with Folgers instant coffee. Sometimes I skip food altogether, and words. If possible I would have dressed in a nondescript white sheet, or skipped it, but Eunice's culture requires a shirt and tie, nice jacket, pants, and shoes, or they will punish you.

I am going to SHOW you what is culture, Eunice protested, and what she meant by that was taking me to Mirielle's show. I did not mind because I love to go out to eat at a nice place and just order plain pasta, over which I shake fake factory parmesan from a green plastic container I keep inside my coat at all times, and drink a can of lite beer. The waiters' faces fall, and crimp – all that is culture.

That night Eunice would order sarde a beccafico and caponata siciliana with two bottles of Domaine Tempier, and prattle on about Mirielle's latest sculpture exhibit at the Galerie de la Riviére in downtown Oaxaca City, which had been met with a level of critical success, although she does not do art for money or anything so crass.

The little persons she created, Eunice exulted, are usually monsters and virgin, each with two heads, but you look close you see they each have hearts, she said, that beat outside the body, and boys penis that curl in on you, in the shape of eternity.

The Galerie de la Riviére, I said, does not even sound Mexican.

Hate in her eyes, she gulped down her red Bandol, which she drank from one of her black shoes. To my surprise, it trickled out of her right nostril and dripped once, twice, three times on the starched white tablecloth.

Pouring the beer onto the outstretched hands of the waiter, who chirped in excitement, and jumped on one leg, I ripped open my shirt, buttons popping into the audience like bullets, knocking down several large matrons, to reveal my toga, with its senatorial purple stripe and all the muscles beneath, at the same time drawing my dagger and plunging it again and again and again and again and again into Eunice's throbbing caponata, which in turn fell to the floor and rolled upward, revealing the severed head of the artiste Mirielle.

Tomato sauce, oil, and chunks of caper flew onto Eunice's bib, splashed my senator's sleeves, and sprayed the face of the impatient waiter, who also fell to the floor with a cry of, Et tu, brute?

We held the pose, frozen, for seconds, then turned, stood and bowed, Marielle (surprise!) from the clown outfit of an Italian waiter in downtown Oaxaca City, her bare foot splayed in a soccer trophy pose, toes upon her own head.

The crowd clapped, and stood, and clapped, exchanging words.

Walking on air

I generally walk rather than run when I do my rounds, going from ward to ward in my soft manner, with my soothing almost bedside approach, hushing slippers padding the domed halls and Eduardian stairs, even my scissors and comb moving dreamily through the curls and cowlicks, the broom going swish hwish hwash.

There is a picture in a frame on a wall with no door but it is hung too high, or is it hanged too high, for when I stand on my tiptoes to peer at it I see it is a photo portrait of a young woman beneath some trees with her dog by a picnic basket, and I see that one day she is facing the dog but the next she is facing the basket, so I have begun to take notes to see if there is a pattern to her movements.

Yes of course there is a pattern, and now I see it must be a code, as I pad lighter than air through the halls and rooms with my notepad, sometimes doing my work in the music hall, though all the voices be soft as falling snow so you cannot count the patients by the voices, though you can try.

At the lonely photograph, there is also a table against the opposite wall with a vase and three dried roses, formerly yellow white and red, with a straight-backed chair, I stand on my tippy toes on the floor and see that the woman is facing the basket for a third day in a row.

Though first I had to sit the chair for some hours squinting through at the white and grey wall to verify that the change comes at three am and once per day.

How can you tell if she has changed position, I said to myself, if from Monday to Tuesday she is still looking at the dog?

I reply, The angle of her neck, the cast of her eyes, her hand upon the skirt is always slightly different, so we know that she has flinched at least.

I go quietly but firmly through the rooms.

I tell myself, Indeed, well perhaps she is performing a kind of dance. I say, Perhaps she is even flirting with the viewfinder, or the person behind the ancient, long-blinded lens.

Speaking softly, I object.

I say, No friend, it is a code she is sending out, beyond the moment where she has been captured, my siren Sisyphus, cloudwalker, beyond her sepia world of greys and browns.

I said, And I have nearly cracked it.

Because I Could Not Stop For Death (479)

by Colin Gee

I had had a bad day and it was not because of the catcalls or mud and imbecile wheel of the irreverent cabbie or the fact that Susan had not written a letter in two calendar days, or telegraphed, or sent flowers, or just gone off and shot herself in the mouth for all I cared. I lay all the blame on the tailors and cheesemakers of this world, of old Amherst in the summer, of the butcher's boy and newspaper stand boy and recently married women that flounce their fat behinds around the park like they're for sale -- and by for sale I mean up for grabs. I spit upon their chiseled, alabaster fag ends. I despise people who go wild in summer, but not in winter. In June they bang out of their front gates and barge down Main Street with their sunbrellas in front, stretching their frumpy faces like fleshy sunflowers to the Sky, galloping in and out of Shops, snatching at the last truly good-looking Eggplants, and when they say Tomatoes they say Tomahtoes.

They shout indecent remarks, read no novels, and their progeny know no poetry by heart. The smell of vile drink that pours like smoke from the throats of stubborn men overwhelms me. I gasp and fall against a church -- its pediment scalds my hand.

I stagger on.

Emily is my name, and I am a hard lady. Take me or leave me, I walk to town and back on my own at my own pace, and it is brisk. Try to detain me, preacher man, taxi driver, hard mason, greengrocer, desk clerk, stubborn postman, I defy you.

Out on the country road, needlework in hand, carrying my own groceries, I was making great strides along the macadam, brushing past many wild carrots -- white lace, legs in a long black dress, when a carriage rattled up behind me and a voice called whoa.

'Whoa there, Nelly,' it literally cried.

It said, 'Whoa there, Nelly.'

Looking up with fire in nostrils smithied by gods of war in a book of verse time apparently had all but forgotten, I whispered, my glancing eyes fell upon the figure of Death: tall, stooped, bony, he wore a garment I knew only too well.

Before I could say, 'You got that smock at Athelwaite's,' he spoke.

'Get in,' Death told me. 'You were hurrying along so fast, so busy, I almost missed you.'

You did not miss me, you big fat liar, I didn't tell Death.

I said, 'Don't call me miss.'

I said, 'Look here, fella, I am not accustomed to accepting rides from tall, dark strangers,' I blushed.

'Oh, you and I are no strangers,' Death chuckled -- a slow, deliberate rattle inside a bag of sticks.

But who puts sticks inside a bag?

I got in, and flung my earthly effects upon the carriage floor.

'Out shopping,' mused the spectre of my own end -- and he wasn't asking. He said, 'Giddyup,' and the carriage lurched forward at a death-defying canter.

I lie. We went forward slowly, at a lazy walk.

'Where did you get such fine horses,' I didn't have to ask my stale, dry, tinderlike companion. It was only us in there, under the black cab, behind the black curtains, rocking along like a dark lullabye beneath a sky that refused to part in an epiphany of light and reincarnation of Christ and all apostles.

I said, 'Who is this other fellow,' motioning to a form that shivered under a blanket in the corner for all the world and stars with a body as frail, peaked, and infuriating as my own. 'He is wearing my shoes.'

'It is just an old woman,' smirked Death from deep inside his cowl -- gleaming from his icicle teeth and glacier-smoothed cheekbones, from hundreds of centuries of slowly dripping water or lack thereof.

'Tis I myself,' I accused him, not about to take cheek from an entity with no cheeks -- from a creep with no business really straggling among the living. He looked at me -- looked away. He did not reply -- did not negotiate. Why had I gotten into a carriage with Death? I asked myself, but already knew the answer.

We drove slowly -- slowly we drove.

'You know no haste,' I remarked, noticing that Death was taking his good sweet time. 'How about you light a fire under your steeds, stranger. I've got work to do -- sewing to do -- poetry to compose while languishing upon my dour, black couch.'

'No you don't,' said Death.

God damn it, I cursed under my breath and swaddled bosom -- couched as I was in eight distinct layers of cloth, skin, and sobbing flesh. For I, too, was human. With a deep breath I decided to stop worrying about my plans for the moment -- my work, yea my leisure too could wait.

'Where are we going, I might as well know,' I demanded, in that case, as we passed a schoolhouse I did not recognize. The bell tower rose into a sky grey with want and fallen grammars. Peering in, we observed upturned chairs and dusty desks. Fallen smocks we saw, and nubs of pencils and first lines of stanzas that would never write themselves.

Death smiled -- he frowned. He looked past the schoolyard into the stalks of wheat straining in adjacent fields against a hurricane that was trying to kill them. We looked at the fields -- the fields gazed back. We looked deep into the heads of grain and they shuddered to see us pass.

We passed the sun, and the sun had set.

I repeated my question -- all my questions.

I said, 'Why this vale of tears and suffering, why are apricots twelve cents a pound in this year of 1860 or 61, why did my dog Carlo die?'

I said, 'Why do your horses' heads point in the direction of eternity -- into the Wild West?'

Death did not reply. He was concentrating, directing his plodding steeds with his inevitable, written will, the size and shape of the stalagmite that shuddered, tipped, and crushed your girlhood home in the grotto where it was constructed.

Finally we stopped before a house. I looked deep into the house. It seemed to be nothing but a God-damned pile of dirt. No one told me it was a house, but I have been living there ever since. Centuries go by. They are a lot shorter than a lot of moments I experienced when I was alive -- of terror, panic, searing shame, numb extremities, in that order.

'Gosh,' I exclaimed, sitting up in a pile of clothes, undergarments, and still-throbbing living flesh. 'These horses are taking us into the night of bodiless wandering, and watching. They are riding us into our own sunset,' I said, nodded Death with a cheerful motion, and I was right.

Because I Could
Not Stop For Death

by Emily Dickinson

XXVII.
THE CHARIOT.

Because I could not stop for Death,
He kindly stopped for me;
The carriage held but just ourselves
And Immortality.

We slowly drove, he knew no haste,
And I had put away
My labor, and my leisure too,
For his civility.

We passed the school where children played,
Their lessons scarcely done;
We passed the fields of gazing grain,
We passed the setting sun.

We paused before a house that seemed
A swelling of the ground;
The roof was scarcely visible,
The cornice but a mound.

Since then 't is centuries; but each
Feels shorter than the day
I first surmised the horses' heads
Were toward eternity.

The ghost truckers

There is a ghost truck that comes down from up the mountain the mesophilic stands of what look like pines, large old growth pine trees, after dark on the highway that runs above the cabin where I am for some seconds every day forever petrified into my sleeping bag as I hear the gears shudder and tip the rig like a bit of dry glacier, full of woe and wood and hunters in leather thongs.

The truck driver speaks to me and he says, Young fellow, why are you cowering in your bedclothes on a fine starry evening such as tonight? We are going all the way down the mountain, and his friends cheer from the dump truck bed, clinking authentic beers. My eyes peer like chubby stupid dog eyes out from under the sleeping bag, and nose sniffles like the snout of a dog so I know I am sound asleep when he says, Gee we are going all the way into the big city, and yeehaws and yippiedoos, as his bony arm thrusts at the shifter like a painting of a rapist, trying to get the ghost logger back into first.

I tried to get on that ship in the night, in fact it was my only chance to escape, but I was too weak. Come on Gee, they cried between truly good belly laughs, trying to lasso my limp form with their icy rope, but the limp form just fell back onto the limp tick inside the cabin, onto the minus 30 zip-up bag with a pathetic whump, next to where I had my canteen and rubber poncho against the rain for moving under the trees when it drips on you.

The song they sang went, ¿Para qué me haces llorar?, ¡Que yo no sé sufrir! as the ghost truck rocks its merry way down, down around the bend, which is when my eyes pop open.

Visions of a
woman in just plaid

She came to him in just the plaid bathrobe, it swinging wide, and those bulging panties, is how I was going to start the first chapter of my shemale exploitation novel, a book and masterpiece that would also be a hardboiled detective novel with a plot and language so convoluted no one would ever discover who had the real Black Bird of Blas Botello, who killed Skip 'Toodles' Banger, or the fact that Miss Dubuque was in way over her head from the beginning, in this big bad world full of pinch a penny copper scum, deadbeats, and guns that go off in your mouth.

Fingers poised, instead they crashed down with the opening line to my straight mass market paperback detective novel, and it was: She came to him in just the plaid bathrobe, it swinging wide, and those bulging panties.

Pete and Repete

Pete and Repete were best friends who went everywhere and did everything together. One day they went to the county fair and Pete said to the lady, Please give me ten dollars in token or tickets, and the lady said They are tokens not tickets but Repete had already said, Please give me ten dollars in tokens or tickets, lady, so the lady got mad and asked if they were deaf or something so Pete said, No ma'am, not wanting to miss this once in a summer opportunity to get on some rides and shoot balloons, and the lady said Okay then boys but by that time Repete had already said, No ma'am, so the lady got even madder as she held the stack of special tokens which is what they use at the fair so the carnies don't handle actual money and said, Do you think I am deaf in that case, and Pete said No ma'am, never and Repete said No ma'am, never, so the lady said, Look do you want ten dollars or twenty dollars of tokens and Pete said, Ten dollars so the lady handed Pete the ten dollars of tokens but by that time Repete had also said, Ten dollars of tokens, so the lady told Pete and Repete to take a hike. She said, Pete and Repete, get out of here, you lost your chance to shoot balloons on my watch. Get out of here now, or do I have to repeat myself?

Repete blushed completely red and said, If that is what it takes to get us into the county fair, you can knock yourself out.

The pirates

The pirates came aboard in a bloody dusk in a tussle of meaty hands and rouge and bone pierced lips and grim little bursts of powder and the first thing was they stood our captain and officers up against the rail and executed them one by one with pistol shots to the face, very gory, without saying a word. We knew it would happen this way because we had turned and run from them for a long time and put up a hard fight. More gunshots were heard belowdecks, following the slap of bare feet, then the situation was taken care of down there, apparently.

We stood with our hands in the air on the main deck where it tipped for all the good it would ever do us and night was falling like lost love in Manila.

Like all of Manila, and the night sky.

We had even recovered our breath a little, but the pirates just waited quietly and crouched where they had us corralled by the pilot house, and looked at us out of dead faces.

Silently, cautiously, their boy cracked open a barrel of grog and dipped from it and drank, but it didn't seem to help. His expression never changed, as he dipped again and again and again, passing cupfuls, drinking some, looking at us. The captain took a cup and drank it and did not smile or exhibit any expression at all in his mouth, or fat red nose, or calm black eyes. Foul water slapped the side of the schooner and the soft creaking of the ropes filled our blasted eardrums as the truth came to us, that these were not like other pirates we had seen dancing from yardarms, shouting in dockyard taverns, caterwauling in wheeling streets, not like storybook pirates, not gay.

Not big talkers.

The pirates stood and watched their own slender captain, his tri cornered hat and red vest and his extremely large, quiet guns, trained at nothing in particular. Silently they gulped and blinked.

Their captain watched them back, deliberately cocking and uncocking the hammers of his guns, and us and no words were exchanged or movement at all was attempted, as we sat and floated across a world of water.

Off across the red waves their pirate brethren hung like patient monkeys from their own ratlines where the black ship hove fifty yards off our starboard bow, and everything was completely silent because the pirates had thrown the dying and wounded into the Indian Ocean fifteen minutes since, so now it was just the living left.

We realized in the calm and pause that they had never spoken or laughed since the moment they had grappled our mizzen, and our impulse was to speak and plead, but the pirates did not seem to be encouraging us to do those things there in the middle of the world's wettest desert, as the softest gust of breeze gently flicked the red feathers in the pirate captain's red head of hair. There was no expression behind his pirate eyes, no laughter, feeling, or hope as finally, excruciatingly, the world's shyest pirate, he turned to his lieutenants and breathed a word of command.

Reach into that bag and hand me what you find in there

There was this teacher named Stephen who would imitate your behavior in one-on-one situations because in fact he was studying you. He considered you an anomaly, one of the human creatures he had not personally created, that he was determined to get to the bottom of. Although he had a Master's in law from NYU and could talk primly about the opera and proper fork and knife positions, I always got his hyck hyuck, hey have ya heard the one about the joke routine from him because apparently he took me to be the bro sports jock of the department, and he would literally move his head up and down when he talked to me and try to slap my back.

He was a hundred pounds overweight, kept black and white pet rats, and was better dressed by about $700 than anyone else in the department except for Geoff Kueen.

His eyes behind the shine were cold and misunderstood.

As for the clothes, it was like he had gone on a six-month shopping spree across Europe in his early twenties and now that was his wardrobe forever. He had so many pants they were always freshly starched. He had some sweaters with patches on the elbows but not because they needed patches. I'll bet each pair of his underwear had seen all the possible shapes of his fat genitals.

'I can't buy clothes in Guatemala,' he spluttered one day as we walked the sun beaten, sunraping miles up the hill from our offices to the timeclock, him struggling along in the body of a man-bear. 'The material isn't sturdy enough.'

'All the buttons pop off,' he said.

'I don't know if you know,' he told me one afternoon, after telling me the one about the Mick cop and the blonde, pretending to double over in laughter at my office door, I smiled uneasily, 'but I am an amateur hypnotist.'

Shit, I thought. Stay Puft Marshmallow Man! Stay Puft Marshmallow Man!

He said, 'I was wondering if you would like to come over to my apartment this weekend so I could practice on you.'

I tried to say, 'I'm not sure I'd be comfortable letting you hypnotize me, Stephen,' but he had already begun protesting, 'It's a really simple, comfortable process, not at all like what you see in the movies.'

For this man knew that all my earthly knowledge had been gleaned from the pictures, and probably magazines with pictures.

He said, 'It's more of an alternative therapy for people with emotional and psychological problems.'

I looked at his face and saw that he was not talking about himself.

'You see,' he continued, 'my dream is to get my license and set up a private practice in New Jersey.'

'No,' I said. 'I am busy this weekend.'

He said, 'I've researched the demographics and the kind of people who seek out this kind of service, socially and psychologically damaged and insecure people, tend to live near or have jobs right off the turnpike.'

My mouth repeated the words I had just said, to no effect.

He said, 'The kind of fat human shit who eat at Taco Bell and order Doritos Locos,' grotesque belly wobbling through pliant, comforting American fabric.

'Crunchwrap chalupas.'

'Mexican pizza cheesy roll ups.'

'Taco and spicy fajita party pack supremes with diablo salsa,' he sneered.

He said, 'So my plan is to rent space in a mini-mall with a view of the freeway, and tap into that demographic.'

'I don't want you to hypnotize me,' I said.

'Whenever you have time, really,' Stephen said. 'I've already asked a number of your, er, colleagues, which means coworkers, and am hoping to hypnotize a number of you.'

I'll bet you are, I thought, as Stephen went into the one about the Christian, the Jew, and the agnostic.

I keep thinking
I see Dick Veith

I keep thinking I see Dick Veith by the noodle shops, walking away from me. He has a very distinctive hunched walk exaggerated by his beefy build that the shoulder pads of his sports coat could never conceal, frontal pattern baldness, glasses, and that mystified half horror of a child lost in the monkey house.

He never completely turns around though and though I have called out to him through the fog and night and snipping chopsticks and laughter he never seems to hear me. The last time I tried to chase him down because it is probably just some lookalike English literature prof who comes here for his noodle fix and he takes his noodles really seriously, and his slurping is just like Dick's, so he never misses a Tuesday. In fact this is the highlight of his goddamn week, and he is not the same man I used to know, but I got to find out.

So when it kept happening, well like the third time right, I shouted, Hey, Dick! Dick Veith! Dick it's me! from across the street. And was it my imagination or did this doppelganger not cock an ear, wince and shrink in outright fear, and take off running for all he was worth like the most awkward kid you had to pick for your soccer team in fourth grade, bowling over a lady, stumble over a bicycle, and finally skid around the corner half a block in my lead, up by the newspaper stand run by the guy who hates me.

Coming around the corner at full tilt, I saw that Dick Veith had disappeared.

Son of a bitch, I cussed. I went back to the corner and looked back at the noodle shop at the upset stool where the man's noodles were still piping steam and everybody just chewing and nodding, ignoring the scene, then came back and looked at the empty street again, ugly heels clipping the pavement. No Dick Veith anywhere.

I said to the newspaper guy, Hey, did you see that guy?

He looked at me right in the eyes to let me know that he despised me.

Then he said, No.

It was Dick fucking Veith! I yelled.

He told me that that was impossible, was I an asshole or something, Dick Veith had died in 2014.

Dick Veith died six years ago, the newspaper man said into my blinking eyes, and that was when I saw copies of Dick's last book all over the newspaper stand. They lay there in stacks and were propped up six across and were in behind the little lockbox plexiglass where Dick Veith's unsmiling face on the cover, his red nose and honest clear gaze, continued to look out upon the world as we know it although he himself saw nothing.

I staggered back, because now there were dozens of Dick Veiths all asking me to ponder depths of truth I wanted to avoid, like that thing about Pilate's wife, gingerbread houses, or heaven.

He must have gone into one of the buildings along this street, I screamed at the newspaper man, who stood motionless. He's not dead!

I could see Dick Veith's padded grey sports jacket with its professorial elbow patches bobbing around the corner, that last panicked fleeting glance back, the gunshots? Where did the gunshots come from, and why was he running from me? I have never even held a gun, do you kind of wrap your fingers all around it like in *White Heat* or just squeeze the butt like a croissant?

I love Dick Veith like an uncle, but he ran from me like a yakuza.

Stubbornly I pounded on several of the doors but they were apartments with dozens and dozens of names under the bells so I just got shouted at by two of the boarders. No one knew who the hell Dick Veith was, or so they said.

His book is over there on the corner, I screamed at them, but they shook their dangling curls and would not pursue the subject of Dick Veith with me.

With a shudder, as I let the knockers fall from leaden fingers, I realized what had happened, what a fool I had been, how exposed now, as many hundreds of heads poked from curtains up and down the block. THESE people had taken Dick Veith, or else were covering up his disappearance. THEY somehow would benefit from his death by the posthumous sale of his estate, it had all been arranged, there was no wrinkle to their plan except me.

I looked far, far down the unlit stoops to the newspaper stand, now dark and locked, as two people in police uniforms deliberately began fencing off the street, walking a mesh of linked fence from one sidewalk to the other.

Fixing it closed, they stood back approvingly – saw me, with melting grins, and started forward at a run.

I turned to scram up the empty street on my impossibly loud hard soles, though I knew it was too late for me and my old pal, my very good friend Dick Veith.

Nice day for a murder. We both should have stayed in Milwaukee.

My friends now

There is an apt in my dreams with a very specific location in a city I do not know. It could be Gotham or Rick Deckard's LA. It rotates clockwise on an axis so you have to keep walking to your right. You enter the apartment on the right via a closed bookshop, via an empty abandoned food court, via long institutional hallways that tip to the right, to find the bellhop, whose head hangs to the left. This is in fact the night manager who is also the bellhop, but you do not have a suitcase or anything, not even a coin for this man, but he takes you into his elevator that sags visibly against the wall from its pulley, shooting sparks.

Up, up, up. Well the thing works, and everything they ever told you was a lie.

All the things that people do in apartments I do there in my dreams, dozens of dreams and thousands of things that I now remember, that I have constructed while twitching under the covers on the couch in your room. Sometimes the door to the neighbor's is open when I don't have my keys to mine and she doesn't want me there but I just use her apartment. In you go, sometimes they invite you, sometimes you have to make up an excuse.

Sometimes we get naked and fuck in the neighbor's kitchen, sometimes there is foreplay and candlelight and wine that from spite she refuses to open, sometimes I have to explain myself, make up any excuse, sometimes open wine with my teeth or carry in her groceries, or fight off an intruder who has her roped to the bathtub. I hope she remembers, but I know she does not.

I mean and I am not kidding this dream plagues me like a son of a whore.

Sometimes we fight and she throws me out and I shiver and cry on the stairs until someone invites me into their apartment, though they do not want me either, there is a smudge across the whole thing like a grody oil change thumbprint.

Recently there has been a gang of young boys who chase me whenever I try to use the back entrance which you get to by slipping down an alley half a block off the bookshop, and squeezing between some sharp fencing. If I look down I bleed. The gang enters the alley at a trot behind me and breaks into a run as I stumble, catch myself, fumble for my keys, and then brace myself against the metal back door, keys out but will I have time?

And everyone in the building are ghosts of living folk with real lives who use shampoo who meet in the dreamscape, I think, which would make sense because of their irrational fears, as the whole frigging structure of the building and block creaks in motion like a ferris wheel, morphing and twisting so you have to walk on the walls, like a gargantuan beanstalk.

Those are my friends now.

We translated Beowulf

There was nothing to it, really. We simply set our sternums to it and we did it, and then it was done, and the world applauded. Fuck you, because we translated the English language's oldest surviving poem into English – into an English so hazy and gaudy that is was almost impossible to look at.

Few ever could. It was not actually modern English.

From the beginning they said it could not be done, specifically by us. They said we knew not the language, drank but can beer, and were only capable of expressing ourselves in the royal plural, all of which was true.

Yet we took down our Klaeber, a god of books among mortal pages, spread our expansive notes more expansively before the keyboard, and popped open a Miller High Life. India paled into dawn – somewhere in the western hemisphere it was an industrial strength twilight. Soon we had to pop a second, then a third, then a fourth, for this mead worked with the sloth of a slow drip!

Wine, we called, yet there was stubborn silence from the cavern above our heads, where our wenches once cawed and cavorted. There was utter silence in our empty castle, cage doors swung wide, pet raptors flown, the uncertain step of babies forever silenced, the skitter of hooves clattering to a halt in the passageways a flitting memory, the patient heavy breathing of the steward or his understeward or his boy a phantasm or grief.

We were all dead in there.

Pissing in a dank corner, we cracked our knuckles, then

our neck – pictured ourselves aboard an extremely agile, goose-necked raiding ship, no modern underwear under our furs or beneath the slinky, glinty, fashionable and extremely tough chainmail that covered our hairy chests, boy's chests, fatty man chests, and Hercules chests, bloodshot eyes craning into a mist that all but blanketed a fjord we were about to fjuck with our quilllike pluck and daring and let's face it dreadnought wordiness.

Milkmaids scattered, screaming. Stout house timbers fell, crackling in the winter wind of a fire we ourselves had lit, and encouraged, and we did it all without gasoline.

Old men stammered, babbling. Their hairs stood, greying. Head hair, chest hair, and some tufts about the groin stood, greying. Because of the driving snow. Some on their bony legs.

Everything – EVERYTHING – went into the fire but their living bodies, and grim wives stood, doorwayed.

We took control of the situation, mastered the village, smashed her, and vanished before anyone could say Yesore Iknay.

All rise, we rode the swells, hung on the crest, and glode the laughing trough. Deep in the bosom of our stout-timbered war horse of the sea there was a weeping, and a clinking, of slaves and goblets, and masters of pearls.

And there was one spotted shoat. I caught its eye as we stood the swell, rising and then tipping, and then falling, and saw unsightly hope creep into the heart of a beast.

The Inconceivabible

The following eight stories are from The Inconceivabible: In the vein of Borges' A Universal History of Iniquity, The Inconceivabible is a whirlwind slapstick tour of the worst people in the Bible, from Cain to Judas, that concentrates on the fringe events and characters whose sin and shit just stuck in our craw, and makes no saint of Gawd himself. The names Maria de la Encarnacion, Juan Jose, Paco Haskins, Pampy, and Fido are freely interchanged for abuser and abused, passerby and puppy, though Fido tends to play the dog most of the time. Also making appearances are the Red Baron von Richthofen, the Generalísimo Porfirio Díaz, Henri Charrière, our best friend Tony from second grade, and other paragons of modern mystery.

The prophet

One time when Juan Jose was playing with his friends outside of town, fucking around in the dirt, he looked up and saw Paco Haskins go by. Juan Jose wanted badly to impress his friends, so he shouted, Hey guys! Look at old baldy! Keep on walking, baldhead! Juan Jose's friends were shocked at his words and they stood up and dropped their sticks and rocks. Paco Haskins, looking straight at Juan Jose, cursed his soul to hell. As he did so, two mama grizzlies emerged from the forest and tore off Juan Jose's head and arms and legs. But the bears did not so much as growl at the other children, who returned safely to their homes.

The Transfiguration

Paco Haskins had not been able to get any good wood in several weeks and he was starting to get worried.

Thing is completely unresponsive, he muttered, looking down in desperation.

Finally he decided to go up the mountain and he took with him Juan Jose and Maria de la Encarnacion, his faithful disciples. And when they reached the summit Paco Haskins was transfigured before them. His face and hair shone like the sun and his suit was of white polyester, and he was wearing dark shades. And he was seen speaking to Moses and Elijah, cracking hilarious jokes and gesticulating energetically.

Paco Haskins, cried Juan Jose and Maria de la Encarnacion in exultation. It is good for us to be here! If you want, we will pitch three tents: one for you, one for Moses, and one for Elijah.

We already have tents, replied Paco Haskins, casting his disciples a small scornful glance, and as he turned back to his friends Juan Jose and Maria de la Encarnacion saw that what Paco Haskins said was true.

Buried treasure

Juan Jose appeared in the tabernacle in a pillar of cloud and spoke to Paco Haskins, the leader of the people, saying, Thou shalt die and rest with thy fathers in the land of Moab, Paco Haskins, but your people shall cross the Jordan and go whoring after other gawds and lust on forbidden honeys. And I swear by my own name, and Juan Jose said his own name, that I shall forsake them to their desires and many evils shall come upon them.

And Paco Haskins died in the mountains on the near side of the river, according to the word of Juan Jose. His eyes were as bright as the day he first laid them on Maria de la Encarnacion and his biceps still rippled like twin goats beneath his cloak. Juan Jose gathered up the body of Paco Haskins and hid it in a secret location, and the person who finds the body shall also lay claim to the heaps of pirate bullion, pearls, and jewel-encrusted sword hilts buried with him.

Tent and vine

After the waters had receded from the peaks of the planet Earth, that badly matted planet at the time, Paco Haskins discovered vines of grapes as he was gathering nuts and roots in the valleys and began to make wine.

What's gotten into dad? sneered Juan Jose, Paco Haskins' youngest son, from whose loins a third of the planet would be repopulated. Hey, look everybody! My dad's passed out drunk with no clothes on!

Everyone at the party turned in their leopard skins and saw that what Juan Jose said was true.

But Paco Haskins' other sons took a leafy branch and, averting their eyes, covered his nakedness.

When Paco Haskins awoke, remembering how Juan Jose had made fun of him, his wrath was kindled and he cursed his son and his son's descendants forever, saying, You're a loser, Juan Jose, and your kids are going to be just like you.

We can roll
down the window

Juan Jose was crossing the desert with his best friend Paco Haskins and Paco Haskins' girlfriend Maria de la Encarnacion.

I brought the water, chirped Maria de la Encarnacion.

I brought the food, put in Paco Haskins.

What did you bring? they asked Juan Jose.

Juan Jose showed them. He was holding a car door.

What is that for? asked Maria de la Encarnacion and Paco Haskins at the same time.

In case we get hot, guffawed Juan Jose, we can roll down the window!

But neither Maria de la Encarnacion nor Paco Haskins thought it was a funny joke.

They squinted out at the heat shimmering off the desert plateau and up at the buzzards tottering in the cloudless sky.

Something Juan Jose ate

Juan Jose was seated on his throne in the City of Palms. He was two hundred pounds overweight and unintelligible when he spoke but his neighbors were his slaves, he sipped wine from a golden chalice, and naked servants bathed his feet with costly oils. As Juan Jose was pondering these things, a left-handed messenger entered the room.

Aughblathbbbt! Raaaaught! gurgled Juan Jose to his guards, immediately sensing danger. The guards, not knowing what Juan Jose was trying to tell them, left the room and closed the doors behind them.

My Lawd, began the sinister messenger, drawing a long dagger, I carry a secret message!

Hyuuumphthat! squealed Juan Jose, eyes growing large with panic as the assassin drew close and thrust the blade into Juan Jose's belly. And so fat was the fat of Juan Jose's belly that the hilt was completely swallowed up. The throne rocked helplessly from side to side, Juan Jose's mouth opened and closed and dribbled blood, and the assassin strode calmly out of the chamber and past the guards.

Wuaghlibthbtt sprcktht! he reassured them in what he took to be their own language.

Paco Haskins
and his two daughters

Paco Haskins and his two daughters Juan Jose and Maria de la Encarnacion reached the mountains and hid out in a cave, and this continued for many months until the two daughters began to despair of ever getting the chance to make babies. One night Paco Haskins took the flask of mezcal and began to drink of it, and he drank himself unconscious and lay with his pecker exposed on the cave floor. And his pecker became very hard, for he was having erotic nightmares.

Hit me again! he would scream.

Don't hurt me! he would whimper.

The two daughters sat looking at him for a long time before the eldest, Juan Jose, picked up her skirts, sat on Paco Haskins and began to ride his hard, gawdlike totem.

What are you doing, Juan Jose? hissed the younger daughter, Maria de la Encarnacion.

I'm going to have my baby if it takes me all night, snarled Juan Jose, and at that moment the job was finished, and Paco Haskins screamed in his sleep.

Now you go, Juan Jose told Maria de la Encarnacion.

No, replied Maria de la Encarnacion, but Juan Jose peer-pressured her for a long time until she too mounted Paco Haskins and had her way with him.

And the two daughters conceived and gave birth to beautiful baby boys, but Paco Haskins scratched his head and looked around the cave many times in an attempt to find secret entryways, and then stood at the cave mouth and stared in all directions looking for some sign of human life in any of the surrounding foothills.

So to speak

'Fido' was the family's third golden retriever and the sweetest dog that ever lived. Paco Haskins, the son of Juan Jose and Maria de la Encarnacion, loved him with all his heart.

Come here, 'Fido' ya little bastard, Juan Jose would sneer from his overstuffed recliner, raising both index and middle fingers like quotation marks.

Let's go, 'Fido'! Paco Haskins would shout, also making the quotation sign with his fingers, already clipping on the leash!

Ruff ruff! 'Fido' would bark.

Have you fed 'Fido' yet, Paco Haskins? Maria de la Encarnacion always had to ask Paco Haskins, also raising four fingers.

'Fido' wasn't 'hungry'! Paco Haskins would rejoin, making a hilarious joke!

Feed 'Fido' now, Maria de la Encarnacion always insisted, chuckling good-naturedly.

'Fido' would bark happily and turn in circles as Paco Haskins dumped both wet and dry dog food into his bowl.

Paco Haskins always had to turn away so that 'Fido' could eat.

But once the small boy's nose wrinkled and he began to cry.

I love 'Fido', he sobbed, wrapping his arms around Maria de la Encarnacion. But sometimes I really miss Fido!

Full

There were two little kids sitting, just crouched by the side of the road. Lindsey drew the car right past them and rolled it to a stop.

He said, No thank you darling, I would like to give YOU the surprise of your life, and then he would take out his Bible and begin to preach as he does, with his tongue just a little bit out of his mouth, hand in his coverall front pocket.

But the expression on the kids' faces was cruel and unflinching and all his Bible talk did nothing for them. Lindsey rolled a cigarette and hung it from her sneering face.

He said, And they shall smolder in sulfur, and it was a generation yet in those fields, the seraphim yipping in ecstatic union.

Holding a flaring match to her tobacco, she rolled the key deliberately in the ignition, let the engine turn over and catch, and slowly, slowly rolled off across the crunching gravel.

A paradigm of the animals.

What is a baseball

Near dusk on a brightening June evening in 1959 near the Iowa-Nebraska border an unidentified object was seen skimming the horizon south of County Highway H. According to eyewitnesses it was shaped like a saucer and emitted strange strobing flashes of green and yellow light. Darting back and forth several times, it vanished suddenly into the wispy ether. Max McGuthers, Bob and Sharon Wilson, and the entire extended family of the late Gary Smithers were witnesses to the apparition.

What object was seen that shimmering summer evening in Nebraska? Was it an extraterrestrial spacecraft? A government spy plane or a weather balloon or a giant boomerang? Was it a hoax? Did the Wilsons and the Smithers and Max McGuthers collude to deceive the police and national press? Or were they themselves deceived by an optical trick, by the light playing on the confabulated clouds, or by their own small, gullible, and superstitious minds?

No one can say and there is no way we can know.

A baseball, on the other hand, is something everyone can agree on. It is a ball of tightly wound yarn with a white leather cover composed of two pieces. The cover is sewn onto the core using thick red stitches that provide a perfect grip for throwing and make it unmistakable in flight. It will never be confused with a UFO or a Russian spy plane or an Australian boomerang. Max McGuthers and the Wilsons and Smithers would have looked at a huge baseball flying above the Nebraskan cornfields that June evening and, even at the distance of half a mile, they would have exclaimed, Golly, look at that giant baseball! I wonder who in carnation threw it.

Bruce Willis in *Die Hard*

I have started crying myself to sleep at night because I miss my parents and brother and sister. Not the people they are now, no way, the people they were in about 1997. I miss my brother's chubby dumb face when he was absolutely destroying a plate of hotdogs with just mustard on them, my sister's sarcastic three-year-old retorts, and books with pictures, and watching reruns of movies from the 1980s on TV with my parents, who would invariably shout, Kiss alert! Facesuck! to fuck with me, not knowing I was getting a little boner. I had to hide under a blanket and play the game well into my teens, until one day, and you could have heard my girlfriend's bra hit the floor, they realized I had become a facesucker myself.

Kissing is strange, of course, and perhaps not entirely intuitive to small children until they have observed *Die Hard* with Bruce Willis. In this movie, probably his most iconic, the actor plays mild-mannered ad exec Roger Thornhill, who is apparently mistaken for a high-level diplomat, kidnapped, and subsequently embroiled in a complex espionage plot, in the course of which Bruce frequently falls mouth-first on Eva Marie Sant again and again and again, that being the actress playing Eve, the femme fatale and NOT the last woman in the world.

Oh shit, no, sorry that is *North by Northwest* with Carey Grant. So I should have said, watch Carey Grant if you want to know how to take a woman in your arms, on the TV, and make her melt like butter.

It is a skill that is, for many, acquired.

Dummy up

Imagine that he was back there in the most expensive leather, his own, smell of oxidizing propulsion fuel reeking and mingling with the greasy ponytail, condensation that drips once, twice onto the back of the neck from the fan, beers between the boots still tinging in their glass bottles in their satchel, cold and slung, flight plan clipped to the inside of the pants by the knee, three trussed agdis mumbling mumbo jumbo through impossible strands of red tape, their eyes giant and yellow, then a giant moon that gets smaller, three tracers flipping past the starboard bow, the concussion as our reply is fired, hardly bumping the glass, an implausible sandwich on the dashboard, a pacifier in the ashtray, man, a car on wheels, wheels upon pavement, pavement prepared on gravel, gravel that reflects sunshine in a quarry edged by blue, flippantly blue and airy grass.

I waited too long to tell this story

waited too long to tell this story, like the story my grandfather never told me about mopup in the Gilberts in 1944, the bomb run he navigated in which the B-25s on either side went crumbling, falling into the big Pacific.

Or the story was Katherine Hepburn in Memphis when he bought her ice cream and his goofy winning grin was slayer, and he slept on her couch, just inhaling what was left of her perfume in the dark in his epaulets, not daring to cross the broad floor in his standard issue socks and push on her door, which was ajar until 2 am.

Or it was about that northern pike, another one that got away, or the crosshairs on the Nordon bombsight on those little gingerbread bunkers, tracers ripping the bright blue like infant fists.

I do not know because Grandpa waited too long to tell that story, and look now I have done the same thing.

Shitty inconveniences

Wall to wall there are dolls of all shapes and sizes, raggedy annes and china babies and teddies and floppy-eared dogs and corn husk humanoids. At this end of the counter is a whole shelf of paper dolls, and the really expensive matryoshkas and porcelain-faced dolls are up out of reach. They are not frightening in this light. We know that this was after all the doll shop that once brought babbling joy to so many local kids, snotty or sugar and spice and nice. There are mechanical toys, too, that go back and forth across the ceilings and up and down the walls like nightmares. Aviators, locomotive engineers, circus bears on unicycles, mice that live in the clock, tinny hearts that beat, tinny squeaks like pouncing spiders, painted smiles like words written in blood.

We have been in here for a long time, gorging ourselves on the stale rice, guiding our train along a spooky and garishly loopy race track. Back and forth we go, up and down, around and around the doll shop, laughing cartoonishly, because it is still 1986 and we are just here with our friends.

A Dying Tiger –
moaned for Drink – (566)

by Colin Gee

I was crossing the desert with my sister-in-law and life companion Susan and it was getting along into the afternoon so we decided to pitch camp. Actually Susan said she had to take a siesta, the crossing was too hard for her, the sun had pounded her frumpy body like an anvil, she felt faint and had to rest and drink water and lie down or she was going to die, she claimed.

So I told her fine, take your God-damned siesta, or die for all I give a sweet damn, I am going to scout on up ahead in my pith hat and baggy explorer's trousers and boots and see what lies ahead and see what it is we have exactly gotten ourselves into, rather than whine about it.

I said, 'See you, pussyfoot Sue,' sticking out my tongue, and I walked out of that tent and scrambled over the boulders into the horizon, carrying nothing but two loaded pistols and my trusty buck knife and good flint and the only compass we had in a world full of wrong turns and double takes and deserts, and salten seas.

'Good luck to Susan Huntington Gilbert Dickinson if her old pal Emily gets lost or breaks a leg in a fall or is maimed by wild beasts and doesn't come back,' I muttered. 'God save her little sun stroked soul.'

Just then I saw the tiger. It was dying of thirst, lying in the middle of a disreputable wash under a scrape of sage. It was moaning for a drink.

Oh you poor thing, I cried aloud, rushing to its side.

'You poor dying tiger,' I sobbed, kneeling at its side and stroking its sad, bewildered brow.

I threw my arms around the tiger and kissed it on the nose, above the sharp and meowing mouth. Its yellow eyes beseeched me to help it, was it a he or she I never knew -- it never mattered, so I ever after knew it as an it.

'Was he an orange tiger?' Susan would later interrogate me from her lisping lips -- from her bed of fond and ritzy pillows, under a tent fit for a sultan, from behind a sweet iced tea, from a listless arm cast across a sunbit brow. 'Did he suffer much, my love?'

Don't condescend to me, sugar pie, or pretend to cut in on my story, I told her.

'It,' I grunted sharply, digging my spoon deep into a can of beans, lifting a leg to fart for a day -- for a calendar week. 'The tiger was not a he. It was an it.'

'Did it suffer much?' croaked Susan from underneath a goose feather quilt and all she had to call breasts, and that adorable little haircut that framed her face like parsley on a buffet table. 'Did its Mighty Balls reflect a Vision on the Retina of Water and of you?'

'Yes,' I said.

I said, 'Yes, Susan, you know they did.'

I screamed in all anger and frowned in all despair, for those were the exact words I had been planning to use to describe my encounter with the tiger. Susan had beaten me to the punch again.

'I hunted all the Sand,' I told Susan, biting my own hand, 'because it wanted a drink.'

'Demon rum?' cried my loving pard from a place in the comforter where I knew her naked body nestled. 'Devil gin?'

Nay, I replied, scoffing at the perversity of her child's mind, this tiger was a teetotaler.

I said, 'Neither demon rum nor devil gin would pass his black and bearded lips. The Drink he craved and that I did discover, upon traipsing o'er the Sand, was the Dripping of a Rock.'

'A magical fairy elixir to cure his broken body, and enlighten his bestial soul,' Susan guessed, closing her eyes and arching her back in a movement that made me pause in my dinner and lick bean juice from my lips -- from her lips, from her nose, from ears of corn.

'Wrong again, sister,' I coughed. 'Sister-in-law, lover, wife. The Dripping of the Rock was cool spring water, as pure as as pure as as pure as...'

'As pure as honey,' Susan crooned, clapping her pudgy hands despite the butterfly net.

'As a sugar-free spritzer.'

'As driven snow in a serendipitous cone.'

'As a rain in the mouth.'

Crossing the wash and scouting around a little, I discovered a little run of water dripping in a hidden crevice, and cupped a cupful in my gnarly hands.

'You took it to the dying tiger, and resuscitated him!' squealed Susan, interrupting me again.

No, you fool, I told her, the tiger was an it.

'It, not him,' I shouted, standing so that I could prance and parade. I told her that by the time I got to it, the tiger was already dead.

'It was dead,' I triumphed, watching the light behind Susan's eyes go out, and her mouth pucker and tremble, I smiled.

I loved to see that girl cry.

I said, 'I bore the water in my Hand. His Fearsome Eyeballs -- in death were chubby -- Yet when I looked really close, got down and peered into the motionless retina, I could see he had been watching me, and begging, almost willing me to make it back to him with the water.'

Susan sniffed and looked up. My eyes glinted like knives in a back alleyway. She was hoping beyond hope that I had made it back in time, after all, I saw -- I chuckled. That is the kind of story she always loved.

'I did not make it back in time,' I said. 'I sped too slow, and arrived too late to be of any good to that tiger. He died alone and in horrible thirst, his eyes locked on the life-giving, life-saving gift.'

'It,' wept Susan. 'You said he was an it.'

'Whose God-damned story is this, yours or mine?' I screamed.

Then I saw I had gone too far, and regretted my callous words. I straightened my heaving duck trousers.

I said, 'Fine, fuck it. It. He was a fucking it, are you happy?'

Susan was not happy -- she was wailing, hands over her eyes, sobbing into one of her mangy teddy cougars.

'You killed him,' she cried. 'You killed the poor tiger!'

No no no, little sister, I replied, turning where I paced and fixing her with the used end of my spoon, and a glare from eyes that had seen jackals eat a baby in the pale moonlight. That is where you are dead wrong, I told her.

'You are dead wrong there, Susie old pal,' I burped -- beans and nubs of corn coming to the surface of both mouth and nose. 'It's not my fault the tiger was out there dying. I just stumbled onto the scene. I could have remained a spectator and ignored the whole thing, but I decided to help out.'

I said, 'It was the tiger's fault he died,' I scribbled.

'It wasn't the tiger's fault,' protested Susan -- she cried.

Fine, I said, because sooner or later we all got to die.

"Twas not his blame -- who died,' I granted. 'But it was definitely a fact that he was dead.'

I went out into the night where the coyotes yipped and howled, and chucked my empty bean can at them. It clattered between some rocks. Behind me in the tent Susan's sobbing slowed and was quiet.

All quiet -- a bedtime story.

A Dying Tiger —
moaned for Drink —

by Emily Dickinson

A Dying Tiger — moaned for Drink —
I hunted all the Sand —
I caught the Dripping of a Rock
And bore it in my Hand —

His Mighty Balls — in death were thick —
But searching — I could see
A Vision on the Retina
Of Water — and of me —

'Twas not my blame — who sped too slow —
'Twas not his blame — who died
While I was reaching him —
But 'twas — the fact that He was dead —

My Hudson Terraplane

When God spoke to me for the first time he told me to sell my collection of antique rocking horses, walk down to a specific address in Bellevue central, and buy what I found for sale there. Well I was perplexed at first because there was nothing for sale at that address, but that is how God tests me sometimes. Standing in the driveway was a green 1938 Hudson Terraplane, one of those classic two-door coupes from the gangster pictures that has rounded front wheel wells, a casket-length hood, bulby headlights, and runners from which your associates can ride and unleash fire from bucking guns. The car was not for sale, as I said, but I immediately made the owner an offer she was unable to turn down and drove that green Hudson Terraplane out of her life, saving her I imagine from an awful wreck and gory death – off into the sunset.

Afterwards God spoke to me in her voice to thank me for my sacrifice, and thus revealed to me how I would die. I am not afraid of death, for eternal glory awaits me, and also my wife and adult son Franco who followed her, but there may be a lot of blood. I am afraid of the blood, and seeing that it is mine. I may be stuck in the wreckage at the bottom of the canyon, wedged in there in horrible pain, and die slowly over the course of several days of thirst rather than shock or head trauma. I know I must not curse the God who did this during my travail. I must be strong and have faith. I must think of the woman whose life I save by taking this car. I must focus on the goal.

I must think only of the glory.

The bouncing ball

There is a giant ball that bounds slowly up and down, not attached to any gravity I have experienced on Earth, but endlessly in the back of my brain, fueled by the claustrophobic hate of the siege. Larger than a yoga ball, slightly deflated, it is round and red. It is an oxygen bag that blooms with blood or marinara vomit, yet frisky. Clowningly it goes up and down, facelessly mocking the noble thoughts that pass through my frontal lobe with their characteristic shimmer.

A bloated lung, a piston, a pillar of fire by night, driving and lonely.

So we scrambled out of the wardrobe when everything was dark and finally utterly still. It may have crossed their minds as they were carrying the new suite upstairs that their trusting arms were hugging pregnant wood, felt that there was something actual beating behind the locked and vaulted doors, ticking, thrumbing though fetal in the weight of the armoire.

We sprang out into the silent night in our loincloths, gripping daggers. We lit and passed torches, spread quickly through the great halls, and began to exterminate our enemies one by one inside the sleeping chambers of the compound.

The big red ball hung frozen in time. Blinking away a spray of brains, I felt it come down down and wheezed at the squish, the softest colliding motion of my natural satellite.

Piles

My wife left me for our shortstop, said he was sweet and had better range and a stronger throwing arm than me. Did not mention any other parts of his body. Sent our daughters to their grandparents by train in Tallahassee but they refuse to write, so I spent this week's per diems on long-distance phone calls but ended up just talking to my in-laws because the shits won't come to the phone, something about rehearsals. Wife is traveling with the team and the hotel rooms are paper thin so I turn up the radio even though I hate music and the dumb thrum of people's voices, but there are worse things in this world, and the skipper comes down the hall and says lights out but there is only so much thinking you can do in the dark on your own.

Have been flailing at balls way outside the strike zone and airmailing routine grounders into the stands and I got benched for a rookie named Cheez so we had to fight it out of course and he knocked me down. He hit me again and again as I lay there in my blood on the off-white locker room tiles. Cheez has a better right hook than you, my wife laughed before they pulled him off me.

They took my house away and I had to sell the car and was told to pack my things for the farm because Cheez keeps belting home runs and triples with a cheese-eating smirk and they say he has a stronger throwing arm than mine, though all they ever do is talk about arms.

Look at my legs, I didn't tell them, I've got the legs of a horse. Look at these jewels.

I saved my job by volunteering to do the toilets when

we're playing home, so now I am a second-string third baseman and a third-rate janitor. There are piles of dirty laundry on the floor of the room I rented, I am a pile of dirty laundry. Whole team has just turned on me with silent anger because I am a Jonas, a jinx, a failure. Yesterday a scoop of ice cream literally fell off the cone onto the floor before I could get my tongue to it.

I went to the doctor about my hay fever, rheumatism, recent splitting headaches, lack of energy, inability to swallow, phlegmatic coughing, antacid reflux, and a desire to shoot myself.

Doctor comes in, says your anus is prolapsed, son, and now I can't even ride the pine.

The gabled attic

She sat in the gabled attic and wrote poems about little things like wasps, pieces of glass, floppy shoes and empty perfume bottles. People did not understand that she was writing about little things because she lived in a world of epic poetry in which the sonnet was the shortest popular form, the Victorian knock-knock joke.

Your aunt Regina wearing riding pants! they would howl, slapping their thighs through their britches in iambic pentameter.

They would hoot, But than with the pentamic verse we have heard worse!

As she sat in the gabled attic, cotton stuffed in her ears, close to the dripping eaves and scuffle of the mice, and wrote poems about little things like the feet of the mice and the rusted nails in the eaves, and the stingers on the wasps.

The power of flight

I do not mind that they can suddenly fly, I cursed in the voice message, what bothers me more is where they choose to fly, if it really is a choice, I mean, that there are no regulations on their flight paths yet at least not in this country and they are not required to submit flight plans, as though they could write with those hooves.

I whispered, It just spells danger for everyone including themselves!

I know I should watch my fat mouth but I was raised to think that words are sounds, not acts, and this is just the most ridiculous thing I have ever heard, that pigs could fly.

It is happening, she told me, strapping on her fanny pack and stepping off the bus at the platform.

Dodging into the sweet night!

The third hallowing of the lifesphere is upon us, she called over her shoulder before disappearing between the umbrellas.

Sure, I replied with a cruel laugh, nothing else to do that night. I shouted, When pigs fly! calling after her down the row of taco stands and plastic stools, and when I said it there was a shiver and a big bump under the asphalt and the antojito sellers all turned and looked up the street at me where I stood in my nice pants.

Their cries went up and they stampeded out of there as a horrible gurgle from the hot grease erupted into the night all up and down the avenida and many hunks of pig's flesh, face and loin, pricked like wings, folded, and took flight from the hissing comales, from wings of greasy tucked tortillas, from the mouths of screaming, choking workers and kids, as they had from my own.

When tacos fly, I should have said, and liberated all the creatures from the ark.

Over the horizon

There appeared before him where he sat hunched over the body in the clearing a tiny man who cajoled him to put aside his frowny face and look upon the rising of a new day.

What happened to you, sneered the little man, a leprechaun in old-fashioned clothing, stepping right up to him and the corpse he had been dragging through the forest at the end of a rope. Why are you crying?

So he explained to the little man that this was his father who had died of old age and sadness and he had no tools with which to fashion him a proper grave for all they would give him in town was this rope to drag the carcass off so it wouldn't stink up the street, the mother fuckers.

I'll be a Christmas ham, swore the little fellow, orange beard wagging up and down with the motion of his tiny jaw, What motherless sons of bitches, and he told the man that he could help the man, if the man could make a promise.

Are you in league with Satan? the man inquired, instantly suspicious of the stranger, wiping his shuddering eyelids on a sleeve and peering at the imp for the first time through his blinking, chewing face. Are you offering to help me in exchange for total control over my eternal soul, or a promise to subjugate my body to the powers of darkness?

Yes, replied the little man, all of the above. But it is not as bad as it sounds, he hurried to add, seeing the man convulsed by repulsion, and a heavy queasiness. The little man said, We have an enormous library.

The man (the son) held himself stiff and quiet when he heard the word LI-BU-RA-RY, feeling in his pocket for his only earthly treasure, a bound volume of poetry by Beatrice.

We even have Beatrice, smiled the gnome in his forest green livery and smock and miniature codpiece, nodding to the man's hand where it worked herkily in the pocket of his coat.

Does your Lord have, have *The Ploughed Cob and Other Stories?* the man asked with a trembling voice, sleeves not even covering his hairy wrists, loincloth loose and crusty and low slung upon his hip.

Does he have *The Ploughed Cob?* barked the small stranger in laughter, removing a small pipe from an inscrutable pocket, sweet Jesus the things you say! My Lord has the *Collected Letters*, not to mention all of Beatrice's other poetry and some of her very rare volumes of prose, said the little man.

And do you have nice upholstered chairs for reading, asked the son, scooting forward on the log where he had been slumped and weeping, and lamps?

We have nice upholstered chairs for reading, replied the imp and jolly fellow, reading lamps, and food from your own countrie.

My own country, said the man hollowly, picturing windmills and unbelievably putrid cheeses.

Thy own countrie, said the imp man.

And you can help me bury my father? the son asked.

And I can help you bury your father, confirmed the urchin, puffing on the pipe now, loving it, thrusting one little leg arrogantly forward in its green tight – looking approvingly at his small, brawny thigh. Spitting on a shoe and shining it with a green hankie, he said, So what do you say?

The man opened his mouth to speak, and that is how I ended up in this dungeon, strung up by the nipples.

What's your story?

Talagaya of Porfirio Diaz

I was in Talagaya of Porfirio Diaz when the apocalypse as it was excitedly rumored hit the big cities and we were told in a council of lip-smacking god worshipers after they had closed the town gate and posted guards that we would not be allowed out, nor any of the big city folk back in, ever.

We have all we need right here under our feet, said the self-titled presidentísimo Jorge Aguilar, a man who had been to the big city and seen the sin and filth of their ways, learned only the good, and returned to bless us with his righteous countenance and everlastingly beatific speech. He said, We are totally self-sufficient and already want for nothing but the sinful casinos of the city slicker folk.

Kill the slicker folk, chanted the mouths from the empty noggins attached to them, above the feet that moved them in rows of folding chairs upon the chipped basketball court like stalks of slightly moving corn. They laughed with malice to think of their brothers, cousins, uncles, even children slowing, faltering, and falling with a pathetic city slicker gasp upon some far off and forsaken sidewalk, stricken with the plague, and bleeding out in a puddle of sin and shit of their own making.

They turned their gobbling faces and reminded each other of every time they'd been abused in words they understood by the slicker folk in their slicker pants and fancy slicker hairdos and slicker cars, and by the slicker wives.

We walked back to our cabin wondering how we had ever

strayed into the middle of a situation as hostile and unthinking as a posse, hurting on the inside when we thought of our own loved ones suffering in the big cities, who may even be wishing at this very moment that they were in the rustic, self-sufficient Talagaya of Porfirio Diaz.

Well I said, so several things occur to me immediately, such as what will happen to the big city school teachers that teach your children, where you will dispose of your waste, even organic waste, since you ship that off on big city trucks normally, how you will make your bread without the machinery in the refineries and trucks that bring the wheat in sacks, and how you will live without the commercially packaged sweets you are so fond of, such as candy bars and suckers, for starters.

I did not say this in front of Jorge Aguilar, of course, because I did not mean to be lynched on my birthday, but did say it in private to people who were still red in the face and gloating that Talagaya of Porfirio Diaz was the lifeboat of the Titanic.

They said, We have beans, we have corn, and we have beef on the hoof. What more do we need in this life?

And it took some time before I caught them in their two-faced lie. It was the candy bars and lollipops that were the undoing of this utopia of modern man, in fact, and the fancy underwear and fake jewelry that you order out of catalogs, and all the plastic goods that make life easier and save labor in the modern scheme such as (and this list is not complete) hat bands, buckets, broom frames, shoes, synthetic twine, gear shifters, tupperware containers, straps for bags, greased ponchos against the drizzle, and snaps for caps.

The truck came up the logging road on Tuesdays and the shouting and eager haggling were too much for Talagaya of

Porfirio Diaz to contain through the trees, though they had their beans and corn and beef on the hoof. I stood just outside the clearing and watched for a long second before skirting the tussle, hitching my pack up on my shoulders, and heading down the same road. A two-hour hike in that direction would take me to an emblazoned pine off the highway where I had a man who made runs into the big city for my whiskey, cartons of smokes, and cans of bean and corn.

I walked and walked and walked, letting Talagaya of Porfirio Diaz keep its secret for another week, or for all my life for all I cared. The meanness in people's faces sometimes is so eloquent you just know to turn away.

The toothpaste

She does it exactly the way I would do it. She will squeeze the tube of toothpaste in the exact middle, throttling it with her relatively giant fingers until it is almost out, after which she rolls the tube from the bottom so as not to waste the last of it. Then she throws the completely empty tube of toothpaste into the wastebasket.

We don't have any problems at all.

Except that they got inside somehow and roped us to the tub and it has been seven hours now, not sure if they have a plan for us and I am less sure about the gash over my eye, what was it from a boot, but I can not see out of it, and she stopped moving fifteen minutes ago.

We are good. The toilet paper doesn't go on a rack. We have a basket for it, you take it out of the basket. No worries, no headaches.

And the lid of the toilet. Wait til I tell you, I put it down and she puts it up.

We don't have a toilet seat, we have a teeter-totter.

And the toothpaste, with my clumsy fingers.

Goosebumps

very day a different maid comes to his house to clean the room where he sits decomposing through his bathrobe, moving only his eyes. The mansion that surrounds this room is a decrepit pile of fallen roofs and sunken walls, buried in dust so thick that the steps of the servants where they carry meat to their master will lead the anthropologists in charge of excavating these corridors straight to his remains. The room itself is sealed, dark, but pristine. He also employs carpenters and painters and artisans of all kinds who queue up and are ushered in to fiddle with the furniture, walls and paper, cabinets and large desk. A falconer who works the birds in and out of their row of cages, for hours and hours, a wrangler to walk show horses in and out, people to read transcripts of his own work back to him when dusk turns black and heavy like dead giraffes.

It gives him the goosebumps to watch them work while he sits and watches.

Visions from an
unpainted cottage interior

The oversized crucifix I gave you as a present features a Cristo with his face turned to the right, so that his plastic painted blind (do I hope) eyes gaze down upon our bed slash fucknest where we engage in bestial acts and frequently sneeze and fart in frank delight, like kids.

Beneath the cross in the morning I often have to mop up a mysterious clear liquid that I think of as the piss or cum of Jesucristo, for he is always there upon the wall, but may well be the water that flows from his side instead of blood when the centurians stick him like a pig to do mercy after the hours of torture in the nude, though our Cristo is of course dapper in an intact plastic loincloth.

When you are crucified you are not supposed to die right away, as the God of the Christian Bible is reported to have done. You are supposed to linger on for as long as 48 hours between asphyxiation and total organ failure resulting from blood loss and shock, but the Cristo of the Biblia Sagrada gave up the ghost after just a couple of hours. This worries me because I wonder if our God really had time to fit my sins in before he kicked it, and those of other two-backed beasts, and two-blacked beasts, and twice-backed beasts, and the whole menagerie of beasts in the lineup of mankind from the Romans to the Americans, and on into the centuries to come.

We lie under the plastic gaze, shuddering with pleasure and doused in slutty sweat, and pray that Diosito can do much more in a second with sin that we ever could comprehend. I mean that is the point anyway, isn't it, of being a Diosito.

Hands clasped upon our naked breasts, we blink at our God in satisfaction, as though we had made him with our own degenerate and frenetic swordshow.

Buttercup Buttercup

He would go out every few days and check on the skull in its ditch to see how the fucker looked, if any more of the skin had come off and cranium or tooth been exposed, but we told him that that was like watching a pot try to boil, bad luck and counterproductive too, but he was anxious to have that skull picked clean for the post at the front of the saloon by her birthday in late July, so like a scab he kept picking at it.

Put it in a jar of acid, said one juiced-up customer before having his body moonpocked with shotgun rounds, many more than necessary, some of which ended up through the side plate window before the place cleared out.

Jimmy, why you shoot a man for being a loudmouth, we asked, but it was decided that the man had drawn first, which we all thought a reasonable solution to that much trouble, but it did give us dirt on Jimmy, crouch as we would in our doorways leering out like twelve-year-olds, picking out teeth with twigs and playing with our pistols.

Buttercup, Buttercup, Jimmy crooned, bent over the over under breach action, wiping it clean again and again, grimacing out past the broken glass in the direction of his ditch.

Someday morning

After all we do everything alone, and no one will ever know our secret thoughts. What if you could go back in time but only once, well you wouldn't go back to see a dinosaur or The Clash at The 100 Club or your own young grandparents, you would go back to fix something you fucked up in about 2008, even if it was just a rotten thing you'd said, and shut off that modicum of pain.

Imagine.

Hi, I thought you'd gone to the bathroom.

Yeah, I went.

You were literally gone for two seconds.

Time is relative. This is something I've learned.

You said we had to talk. That is almost always bad.

I just wanted to tell you that I love you, and I will always love you. You are the most caring, most wonderful person I will ever know.

You don't know that.

Actually yes I do. I'll be right back.

Bathroom again?

And then you would be back from the bathroom again in the flash of an eye, though through the red and purple neon blinking of the bar and beers the sense of time grows pleasantly distorted, and what you had meant to say would never be said because the person you were with would throw their arms around you and put their snog up to your ear and say, I love you, stay in Louisiana forever, and then everything would be good.

They would bury you there if you lived the rest of that parallel loop without fucking up again. But tragically somehow you would miss your lonely, destructive first life, the one in which they cremated you after finding you dead in the park with shit in your undies, and fuck it all up again.

A soft Sea washed
around the House (1198)

by Colin Gee

'Get up on the couch, Susan,' I cried, already up there myself. 'A soft Sea is washing around the house!'

Emitting one of her characteristic little squeals, Susan leapt upon the divan opposite my own and grabbed an ornamental paddle from the wall.

'Jump across to me, love,' I shouted. 'You can still make it!'

'But there are sharks in these waters, circling my little raft,' wept poor old Susan -- for if sharks were going to circle anyone's little raft, it would be Susan's.

'You can make it,' I estimated, staring into the aquamarine blue waters. 'I know you can!'

'Why is there a Sea washing around our house?' wept Susan, uncomprehending -- a babe in these seas. 'We are miles from the seaside!'

We are miles from dry land, I did not retort. Nor did I say, It's the end of the world, God has gone back on His promise never again to destroy mankind with a deluge, the big fat liar.

I said, 'You wouldn't understand. There is no time to explain. Jump! Jump, before the tide warps us forever apart!'

Susan wavered -- then jumped across the carpet. It was a lovely, flying leap, but she landed right in the drink.

'Ka-splash!' I screamed, in fascination and horror. Susan was now completely surrounded by slashing dorsal fins and the churning, unfathomably deep mid-Pacific.

'Augh! Augh! Augh!' screamed Susan, thrashing in the water -- a rather indifferent swimmer. 'They've got my leg! They've got my leg!'

'They do not have your leg, be calm, girl, and swim the three yards to my raft so I can throw you a line and pull you out,' I did not say, because the sharks already had Susan's leg and were gnawing it off. For if sharks were going to have anyone's leg, it would be Susan's.

'Hit them with your ornamental paddle!' I cried, gesticulating, rushing from one side of the couch to the other in my black shoes, biting my fingers.

Susan's blood blossomed in the water. She was stretched full out on the carpet, reaching out for me.

'Help me,' she cried. 'E-mi-leeeeeee!'

I had no choice -- I dove in, swam three strokes to her side, got one arm under her lumpy chest, and pulled her back to the sky blue upholstered three-seater, all while beating off a dozen hungry tiger sharks with my paddle, a Sea of Summer Air.

'Thank you, Emily. You saved my life.'

Let's put a tourniquet on that stump or no one is saving anyone, I did not demur, staring at the grisly spectacle of what was left of Susan's leg.

I said, 'Do not despair, fair Sue,' I crooned, stroking her shivering chins, 'for indeed the couches are not our raft.'

'You mean-' she began.

'Yes,' I confirmed. 'I have changed my mind. The entire house is our raft -- our ship!' I cried, we cried in delight.

'The house is our craft,' we celebrated, throwing open the porch door and striding the porch -- our poop. We gazed upon a sea of bumblebees and butterflies, and all the world was our crew.

A soft Sea washed around the House

by Emily Dickinson

A soft Sea washed around the House
A Sea of Summer Air
And rose and fell the magic Planks
That sailed without a care —
For Captain was the Butterfly
For Helmsman was the Bee
And an entire universe
For the delighted crew.

Rice goop

We walked over to the cafeteria to see if the horror was over, if the world had become a better place somehow overnight, if they were suddenly serving a large variety of delicious menu items of generous proportions, but it was still just the same old slop.

What a world, but we knew we had set ourselves up for disappointment, like when you fantasize about sex when you are ten. More than anything the sex is going to smell like roses, as though people's bodies have ever smelled naturally of flowers.

Hello beautiful siren, what are you doing cavorting in my pool with your top off?

Well I saw you sunning yourself here home alone with a giant boy boner and wondered if there was anything I could do to help.

I don't know, I have never had this kind of conversation before.

Have you ever made it with a mermaid?

I am a virgin unless unless if masturbation counts.

Masturbation does not count, young Jeffry. Slide into the water and I will make you a man.

But the siren of course was half fish and smelled like she was half fish. It was nothing like the rosy visions we had had of sex with a lady. It was scaly, her skin was cold all over, the vaginal slit was rough and somehow the wrong shape.

Am I doing it right, you didn't even bother to say, there is no right, this is a world of accidental pleasure only, in which the dick is only hard when you are driving in tight jeans along bumpy dirt roads with your mother. She is talking excitedly about something, so nod and try to smile.

I said to the cook at the cafeteria, One package of Green Fire Doritos and a chocolate milk.

Burn Not The Bush

It was a cold and colorless sandwich. I poked it with one finger, sat back in my trench coat in my chair, and sighed for God Jesus. I picked up the cup of watery and lukewarm coffee and took a cringing gulp.

Glared at the clock on the wall of the train station café, which said ten after five.

Sneered across the peeling fake marble linoleum table top at Miss Dubuque, who was dressed as a waitress.

'Where is the pimp Jackson Smallet?' I did not snarl.

I said, 'Why did you dress like a waitress to come to a restaurant? It confuses the other customers.'

She seemed irritated by my callous and biting words and tossed her hair. She sneaked a look around at the pear-shaped people who filled the booths that lined the walls of the café and the working boy-friends who squirmed at the counter on stools bolted to the floor, and the growled looks from the real waitresses in yellow blouses with white aprons and long and likely legs, and hair in bobs. The air was full of murmured and unanswered questions, the clink of spoons on porcelain, and crummy white light. Through the windows was the grey platform and rain on grey tracks and figures scurrying back and forth dressed in their version of clothing for a movie.

'What difference does it make to a brutal heartless cad such as yourself,' Miss Dubuque may have replied, with a flutter of long eyelids, 'not to mention handsome in your underwear, standing five foot six, hundred forty-five pounds in your socks. You are only in this for the money.'

'I am a working artist,' I almost protested, eyes clouding

with fifty thousand trillion smackeroos. My mouth opened and closed soundlessly. I gripped the coffee in both hands as my face drained of colorful blood. I retched past my shoulder holster and its cold and comforting replacement baby, a .38 special, and my thumping heart and got out a pack of cheap and stinking cigarettes.

Got one stinker out and got it in my mouth and let it dangle there as I quipped, 'Take it easy, sister. I don't care what you wear. It's the woman inside that turns me to butter, not the painter who creates all those pictures of ponies and trees.'

Sometimes we just talk to while away the time, I thought with a faint guffaw.

'Not the artist who creates all those paintings of dangling dead fruitcakes,' I meant, I said.

'Gin gull,' went the door, and Blondie strode into the small interior of the shop, past a rack of sulking sandwiches in waxed paper and the horrified gazes of three real waitresses, right up to our table. The ground rumbled where she stepped, despite the fact that she was also dressed as a waitress, in a sky blue collared blouse and an apron smeared with ketchup for the occasion. She was alone, and thrust her shining Cadillac of a body onto an empty chair.

Not my lap, because it's too small for such awkward buttocks.

Everyone in the place turned back to their muffin, as punchy as down-on-their-luck boxers in a world where a nickel could get you a bottomless cup of joe, shaking out newspapers like starlit skirmishers, clearing throats of heavy shotted phlegm. The sound of wind moving through a tree of leaves full of sacks of squirming babies filled the station house café.

'Hiya Blondie,' I said, waving vigorously for a real waitress.

Making a pouring motion with one muscular arm.

The waitress I was beckoning to pointed to the rack of sandwiches without understanding the words I was not saying. I shook my head with a movement of absolute disgust. The waitress made a nasty comment to an obscene person, a person I could not quite see, an offstage remark.

'Detective Hamm,' purred Blondie, eyeing Miss Dubuque, 'and his latest pet,' saying both the P and the T.

She leaned towards Miss Dubuque until Miss Dubuque could not see anything else in this world but what was contained by the frame of Blondie's strangely jutting cheekbones.

'Come home with me, darling,' Blondie said to Miss Dubuque with a mother's hiss. 'The Detective can-not help you. Without my protection, they will...'

Blondie did not finish, for Miss Dubuque was whimpering softly in words I could not catch that Blondie was unable to misinterpret. Miss Dubuque was shaking her head and cringing into the recesses of her little chair. Her eyes were full of panic and darted wildly. She knew for certain she couldn't move a muscle, as she squeezed a napkin.

Maybe she said, 'Mother,' or maybe she said nothing at all.

She made a gurgling sound in her throat and Blondie sat back in her chair, unimpressed by anyone in the entire station café except herself.

'You know I hate waitresses,' she snapped.

'Not my type, either,' I put in matter-of-factly, reaching up and lighting my cigarette at last. Lighting a second one from the first and reaching over to Blondie's mouth with it.

Getting it in there.

'Shhhhuuuuuuugh,' she smoked deeply.

'We have the artifact,' managed Miss Dubuque, a small girl in a grown woman's outfit.

'Let me see it,' Blondie Banger and I said at the same time. We exchanged glances of pure hate.

'No,' stammered Miss Dubuque, standing suddenly. Too suddenly: now her skirt was completely above her navel. She tugged it back into place and clutched her grotesque handbag with large shaking fingers. I could not imagine what words were running through her stacked, shellacked, and humming pile of hair. In one glance I took in the thick lavender lipstick and the green eyes, puffy from weeping but still flashing with the defiance of the trophy housewife. I felt as dirty and hot as the last time I had been in her apartment with her man -- my partner -- passed out in the other room. I wanted to stick a finger or oil dipper into those curls and probe for intelligent life.

Miss Dubuque said, 'I want to know what you plan to do with it.'

'I am not even going to touch it,' lied Blondie, talking right through her smoking joint.

'That's a lie,' I cried. 'You won't be able to resist the temptation, you black spider.'

A real waitress slammed a mug onto the table-top and splashed it into with a black liquid.

'Ya gonna order some food?' The bitch had the gall to ask Blondie Bruiser.

Blondie turned her large lizard head and took in the waitress with those narrowed double lids of hers. I inhaled sharply because the temperature in the train shop abruptly plummeted. Blondie exhaled smoke into the real waitress's face, which blanched and at the same time went white.

'I'll call you if I need you,' sang Blondie, clearly talking about sex, as her cigarette went completely into her mouth. I watched intently as smoke continued to drift from her reptilian nostrils. It was a trick I'd seen before and would willingly watch again.

The real waitress staggered on her white tennis shoes.

The cigarette came out of the mouth again, held easily between Blondie's pointy white incisors, still aglow.

Her eyes had gone bright green.

The waitress backed away and retreated behind the counter, face pale, trying badly to hide a pair of hands that refused to be still. She burst into tears and ran into the kitchen through the swinging double doors. Something shattered against a wall.

A scream, a gunshot, and silence.

Everyone went back to their muffins.

Miss Dubuque watched her own breath cloud in front of her face. My worm turned in its chilly jar in astonishment.

'Good work,' I congratulated Blondie. I shook my head. I said, 'It's no skin off my foreskin, Bruiser,' I bluffed.

Blondie's eye flicked me coldly. The thermostat on the wall frosted over with a grim crackle. Miss Dubuque was completely covered in goose flesh. My formaldehyde began to lace with ice, which meant it was colder than five degrees Fahrenheit in that Japanese bunker, and dropping fast. My caretaker scientists huddled together for warmth and began to play rock paper scissors to determine who would stay behind to keep my jar from exploding by assuming the fetal position and wrapping his or her slim form completely around it. The liquid in my jar was already room temperature. The carpet in that bunker was orange and thick. I thought it would tickle or scratch.

To keep that jar from exploding, from rupturing and spilling its precious precious liquid, and my thoughts went with them.

'If you don't show me the bird now,' Blondie told Miss Dubuque in a menacing voice, 'you will be sorry.'

I thought that was kind of a weak threat, and said so.

I said, 'You might as well just threaten to kill us.'

'Ha ha ha,' exploded Blondie with genuine mirth. 'Death would be too quick and permanent for the likes of a rat-faced little gumshoe like you.'

Her words wounded me deeply.

I hid my rat face in my rat hands.

I wondered how anything could be worse than what I was feeling at that moment. I wished that death would come. It was no longer worth investigating murders, tracking down dime store shoplifters, or catching milkmen in the act of milking. Not with this face.

Not with the face of a rat.

'Don't talk to Hammy that way,' blurted out Miss Dubuque, coming to my defense. I lowered my hands. She was sitting down again and had her purse open. Here was a woman on the verge of tears or a tragic orgasm. 'Here it is, you big black widow,' she blubbered, opening the clasp on her handbag. 'Take a good long look. It might be your last!'

'Ho ho ho,' laughed a decrepit and satanic Santa through the massive open lizard beak of Blondie Banger as she peered into the depths of Miss Dubuque's purse.

'This calls for a celebration,' I said, pouring the contents of a hip flask deftly into my cup of joe -- shooting its contents -- burping hard and low.

'Better lay off that booze,' quipped a nearby waitress with a smirk, clearly not seriously in surprise, as I staggered to my feet and tried to take my clothes off with one hand.

'It's either the hooch or else it's the intravenous drugs,' I protested, and flung one shoe at a wall. The waitress growled and stepped out of her 'uniform'. I fell across the station floor with my pants and man whites -- the outer clothes for my lower body -- twisted around my ankles. I took a bite of the serving gal's discarded garment because my face landed on top of it. It tasted like one cherry. We rolled, our mouths clamped together in a hideous wet and open kiss. We wrestled with aching thrusting movements like trussed goats attempting to shimmy out of a burning kitchen, and I felt my ears and ghost penis tremble and stiffen. Her long thick tongue plunged past my teeth and against my tonsils and tried to wrap them up like a tentacle full of clammy suckers.

'No,' I gasped, spitting out the long thick-veined licker muscle. 'We must honor the memory of your late husband.'

'Snap,' went Miss Dubuque's clasp closed, and the dark and grimy light that had filled the station café retreated into its abyss -- I was still seated in my godforsaken chair, and my waitress had hustled into the back.

'That's enough for now,' said Miss Dubuque.

'I am satisfied,' said Blondie, dropping the butt of her smoldering cigarette into the untouched cup of cough.

Cough of cough, of coffee.

'I need a guarantee of my sister's safety,' chirped Miss Dubuque primly. Her hands were shaking as she got her coffee out of its saucer.

'Done,' laughed Blondie, 'except that your sister is your brother.'

'And your mother is my lover,' retorted Miss Dubuque. I thought she would stick out her tongue but I was wrong: it stayed inside her mouth.

'And I'm,' began Blondie. 'Oh, never mind. You know there is an alternative.'

She looked at Miss Dubuque and then at me.

'Not that,' I screamed. 'That was years ago, and the trail's gone cold, and we don't even know whether the stories are true.'

'If we had control of both the Black Bird and the White Dove at the same time-' began Blondie.

'-then I would destroy them both,' I declared firmly, watching a pair of paramedics wheel out the sheeted body of our former waitress.

'The person who controlled both birds,' snarled Blondie, getting Miss Dubuque's wrist with one hand and wrenching her into the circumference of her cruel snapping visage, 'could control armies, could control nations, could-'

'-could control Crazy Molly and her insane ambition to destroy the planet,' I surmised.

'Her insane ambition to go to the Moon,' corrected Blondie, releasing the trembling Miss Dubuque bodily, who fell backwards with a crash of flailing legs and splintering wood. Miss Dubuque sat up in confusion and straightened her wig.

'Go to the Moon?' she quavered. 'What do you mean, go to the Moon? What is the Moon?'

'It's Earth's only natural satellite,' I began, but Blondie was going to answer this question.

'It's a staging platform for deep space exploration,' she guessed, taking a big shot into the dark. 'The Moon is only the beginning. Crazy Molly's real ambition is to make contact with the ancient Egyptians.'

'In outer space?' wailed Miss Dubuque, bursting into tears of frustration. She kicked out at a waitress who was carrying a tray of dirty dishes and the waitress sprawled onto her face, scattering shards of saucer and corned beef hash and eggs across the entire café. In a millisecond Miss Dubuque was at the bottom of a pile of thumping, kicking, clawing cat-piss angry waitstaff. Blondie and I exchanged glances and laughed.

'She is convinced that there is intelligent life elsewhere in this universe, and that it is Egyptian,' Blondie explained. 'She is prepared to sacrifice life on this chubby blue planet itself if necessary to achieve her aims.'

'So we can't give her the Black Bird,' shouted Miss Dubuque, emerging triumphant from the scrum, blood pouring from one ear.

'No we can't,' winked Blondie Banger. 'That's why the Black Bird is more than three thousand miles away. It's gone, baby.'

I gasped audibly, as though a rug had been pulled out from under my feet. Miss Dubuque went dubiously to her purse, looked in, and said, 'You're lying. That's a desperate lie.'

'Suit yourself,' panted Blondie happily, getting up to go.

The clock on the wall said, 'Five thirty-three,' and was silent. A waitress flew through the air and crashed into the coffee maker.

'I'll see you at 'six o'clock P.M.' in front of the ticket booth,' Blondie said. 'Bring the artifact and be calm, and we can put this whole business to rest.'

'Good idea,' I said. 'We can bury the hatchet.'

'Yes,' she agreed. 'We can extinguish the barn fire.'

'Agreed,' I shrugged. 'We can abort the unwanted fetus.'

'Dog gone strait,' spluttered Blondie. 'We can muzzle the bitch poodle,' and Miss Dubuque suddenly knew that she was the bitch poodle.

Blondie moved towards the door, levitating like a queen, every step too small to see and cushioned by an impossible but real red carpet.

Miss Dubuque and I blinked three hundred times in unison.

The normal sounds of the station café resumed on all sides and I reached for my cold cup of joe.

It was a pentagonal standoff on the steaming platform of the depot. My nose twitched and I had one eyebrow cocked sarcastically, because this little party was really starting to crack me up. We stood in a five-pointed Mexican draw-duel, weapons stuck every which way. And by weapons I don't mean genitalia, for Pete's sake. Crazy Molly had the drop on Julip, who was ostensibly unarmed, I had the drop on Crazy Molly, Blondie had the drop on me, and Miss Dubuque had the drop on Blondie. If the station master hadn't fainted dead away when he saw Blondie bare her teeth it would have been even more confusing, because his baton shot armor-piercing death shards.

'Why did Julip have to grab the Black Bird from the outstretched grasp of Crazy Molly and try to make her getaway, abandoning her best friend to the wrath of Crazy Molly?' you might have asked, and it would have been an excellent question. Why indeed, but human nature is a dark and deadly warren.

Then you might have thought, 'This is going nowhere fast,' looking at our predicament – Crazy Molly gripping a .22 revolver, me with my replacement .38, Blondie brandishing a sawed-off shotgun leveled at the hip, Miss Dubuque fingering a very small German pistol with a very tight spring, and Julip holding the black bird – but that would have been untrue.

'Drop your weapons, all of you,' laughed Crazy Molly, 'or say goodbye to the Black Bird of Blas Botello!'

All of us at the same time lowered our respective firearms. Julip was looking good in a black blouse and black leather jacket and a red skirt and red panties that fell to her ankle. She wore a blonde wig and lipstick. I felt my jar begin to defrost in a hurry where it was nestled in the fetus like grip of a young Japanese corpse. How many jars had that poor boy saved before his body temperature dropped him into the hot water?

I wished to thank him, to hug him, to caress his poor dead face.

'Be calm, Julip,' cussed Blondie, still in that sky blue outfit, still stained with ketchup. Was it ketchup or was it hot tamale sauce? Her words rang loud across the empty space of the station. Events had moved so quickly that neither color nor sound had been discernible until the last three seconds. I could see her eyes flicker with mean green. 'We don't want anyone to get hurt.'

Julip backed away, holding the Black Bird in front of her. Steam shot out across the clammy surface of the platform and swirled her skirt above her prosthetic knee. I whistled long and low despite myself.

'Where is the pimp Jackson Smallet?' demanded Blondie.

Julip laughed mirthlessly and stopped. She tore off her blonde wig and threw her clip-on earrings to the ground. She ripped open her blouse and with one hand removed a large padded bra, revealing the skinny chest of a boy. She cleared her throat and laughed hoarsely and spoke in the voice of the pimp Jackson Smallet.

'I fooled you all!' she cried in nervous triumph, waving the Black Bird. 'I was the pimp Jackson Smallet all along! I-'

A shot rang out and the Black Bird of Blas Botello exploded from Jackson Smallet's hand into a thousand pieces.

Everyone blinked and looked at Crazy Molly, who held the smoking gun.

'What have you done?' cried Miss Dubuque, raising her own gun and getting ready to pump Crazy Molly full of lead.

Crazy Molly swung her gun to cover Miss Dubuque, squinting gleefully over the sight.

'She dies, and you die!' grunted Blondie, training her shotgun on the mid-riff of Crazy Molly.

'You shoot her, whether she dies or not,' I informed

Blondie, training my own piece in turn between her lizard-green eyes, 'and I will gun you down where you crouch.'

Jackson Smallet staggered back a single step and gaped in disbelief at the shards of the Black Bird, scattered across the platform.

'Enough of your impertinent stalling lies,' Crazy Molly spat, addressing her words to Jackson Smallet, who had begun to blubber. 'Hand over the real Bird, Jacksie, or you won't have a left leg left to stand on.'

'What have you done?' cried Jackson Smallet. 'We needed the Black Bird to stop the Black Egyptian Diarrhea Death. Our sisters are dying!'

'What have you done?' asked Blondie and Miss Dubuque as one.

'Quit stalling,' snarled Crazy Molly, 'and hand over the leg.'

'But I-' Jackson Smallet's objection was cut off by a warning shot from Crazy Molly's piece. This was followed by a warning shot from Miss Dubuque past Crazy Molly's face, which was followed by a warning shot from Blondie over Crazy Molly's lovely head, which was followed by a warning shot from my own .38 special, through the fabric of one sky-blue sleeve of Blondie's kimono.

Bullets ricocheted insanely off of everything inside the station atrium, and we snarled at each other.

Jackson Smallet had bent down to unclasp her artificial leg.

'The Black Bird is hidden in the prosthetic limb?' Blondie gasped, pretending that she had not understood until this second the extent of the untruths and deceit. She sagged visibly as though coming to grips with a crocodile. I aimed carefully between her eyes.

'Skshhhhheee,' interrupted the progress of the leg as it slid across the platform floor, coming to rest at the real foot of

Crazy Molly. Jackson Smallet sat back in a small sad heap and looked mournfully at her lost treasure. Crazy Molly picked up the leg and, with her gun still trained on Miss Dubuque, said to me, 'At last we have the artifact. Let's high-tail it.'

Crazy Molly and I edged slowly out of the pentagonal death trap, keeping our guns carefully trained on their respective marks, and vanished like smoking people down the tracks.

Somewhere a train whistle blew and the click-clack of rails under the rickety but gargantuan weight grew louder.

And louder.

And louder.

The tape

If there is anything more terrifying than industrial tape coming unstuck from its roll I guess I don't know what it is. That sound is the signal that the bargaining is over, see, that is left to decide is how exactly to take off your arms and legs, and your last few minutes are going to be the most horrifying you will ever experience. Sad.

In the next life you will be famous and hundreds of thousands of people will follow your every movement as you lead your fascinating life on their screens, but instead of it being a vindication of your self-worth, of the value of your thoughts and movements and work, it will become your prison, a glass cage surrounded by hooting rubes. The only real value of your actions will be whether they give the neanderthals some kind of instant gratification: the dope rush of terror, pity, love, or laughter.

And that is how you find yourself, in that next and far-off existence, forced to perform ever more intricate and dangerous stunts.

Such as the one for which you will finally cement your name into the boardwalk of the stars, in which you deride and physically intimidate a small child, who of course clutches a pathetically threadbare teddy bear, because you decide you can't stand her irritating mewling. Who is this child in my TADPOLE talk? you demand of the producer, who shrugs. Simultaneously the glass walls of the studio are contracting and warping and rotating so that the technicians and actors inside and yourself the host are tumbled slowly, walking and jumping as the walls and ceilings become floors, and then the whole thing begins to fill with warm water with a creepy biotic burp so that it feels like you've pissed yourself and it's filling up your jeans and socks.

Great, you think, now I have to do this show with them thinking I've wet the bed, and in fact that is how today's TADPOLE talk starts out, with some sneering mother accusing you of being a bedwetter.

How can we trust our children with you, she shrieks, but only so you would notice, a known bedwetter and assassin?

It was too clever, for you were forced first off to defend your reputation as a peace loving non-murderer, which you realized later, too late, left the bedwetting hanging in the air.

You said, I was not in Belarus in 2014, as my declassified file on display in many bookshops in Boston has proven. Next question.

But by now you were a convicted bedwetter, and the toddler that had taken your hand began to weep, probably because you were all in a very scary place, and you kept walking the walls and the pitter-patter of adults talking went on and on, like a washing machine that belongs to someone else that they have placed right next to the apartment wall. Neighbors you have never seen but would murder.

Assassin, smile for the camera, flashes the prompter, and you do, squeezing the little hand, knowing what you have to do next.

Get me down now

Get me down now, said the baby to the mother who was no longer hustling through her list of daytime chores. She lay next to the high chair on her back, no longer worried about anything.

Wah wah wah, said the baby.

It was a truly noisy picture, in that far-away land where pictures move and speak. Imagine such a world, dreamers. What would you say to a picture like that?

Good morning? What are you doing on my wall? And I mean, welcome to my house and all, but I didn't know I was signing up to take care of some kind of pet.

And the picture would say, Is that a gun in your pocket, or is it a carrot, or what is it?

No, see you're taking this all the wrong way, you would probably interject. You could protest that you didn't want to get off on the wrong foot with the picture.

You could say, Lady, I didn't even know you HAD feet, and I did not foresee us having this little spat.

She would reply, Fix me another martini, handsome, with a leer like a woman who has just given you her purse, and though you knew you were not handsome, some part of you would twitch, and maybe you would make a move towards the sideboard.

Gin for me, the picture would bark, and keep your hands where I can see em.

Returning quickly with two gins, slowly, you could say, Are you sure you are really supposed to be at 2319 Eighth?

I know what you did, the picture would coo, clearly

pleased by the gin, and you both getting wetter, and you would shiver and mutter, I'm a girl. I'm a girl! – then just sit back and watch the wall where the picture kept moving, and talking.

Wah, wah, wah, pissed and moaned the baby meanwhile, never stopping, an urchin of just under fourteen inches when upright.

Neither of us was at all sure how the creature would get down. It had finished its meal, a mighty portion of green grocery puree, raunchily slopped, and now it paused in its wailing to observe, from eyes that both puddled and swam, our indistinct forms where we crouched in a place hitherto beyond its conception of audience or review.

We rubbed dour eyes in disbelief and exchanged gasps, for in short we knew that that baby had just conceptualized itself as a star.

Its ruby baby lips pursed and its baby brain rumbled – a decision had been made.

The new starlet rose unsteadily to its feet, clutched once at the air, and got one tiny foot up on the edge of the tray. Its knee strained and slowly straightened, and with a grunt it was up, on top of the high chair tray, tottering and triumphant.

Now, it seemed to mumble to itself. Now, with two feet planted on the brink of fame, of infamy, we cried out and called in an ecstatic swoon.

Waha, said the picture. Waha ha ha ha!

And now all that she had is ours.

Your dreams

Do you always remember your dreams? I asked the professor of the Peoria satellite tech school, in passing, and he lowered the book he had been holding up to the fall, out here where he would be seen, like summer's last sunflower, and mused.

Usually, he replied at length, nodding severely, certain he had the correct answer.

Is that so, I jeered, personally having no memory whatsoever of any of my dreams.

Just last night, he volunteered, now turning his entire sunflower self to gorge as he thought upon the morning glow of a sun that would eat him, did he know, I dreamt I was climbing a staircase inside a tower, and yet I was outside the tower, he tried to begin, and there were these kind of-

No, not those kinds of dreams, I coughed, through my first cigarette of the new morning. I mean the dreams you had before you came to Peoria.

Wrinkled brow – a dream for each crease. Heavy lies the dream.

Sick for the rest of your life

One day you get sick and you just don't get better. It happens to a lot of people we don't want to think about, family members, enemies, pioneers, tribal chiefs, people in the ground. It starts with a sniffle like it always has, sore throat, pressure on the inside of the skull, headaches, shooting pains, so you wait it out. Tomorrow, mañana, the cry, viva! But tomorrow you feel worse, it is hard to lift your arms, your head and throat are throbbing, strange things are now happening to your intestines, and in a freak accident you throw out your lower back jerking a milk carton out of the paper bag.

Two days miraculously you recover, you think, and are seen making obscene jokes in a local pub, but the shooting pains and throbbing in the forward cortex and the hacking persist, and the goo and discomfort when you spit.

The next day is the same even though you ignore the symptoms, the wheezing chest, and your life will continue for all anyone can tell from outside of you and run its course but you will be sick every single moment of it.

Except at the very end it gets really bad, there is a lot of blood and gasping so that you are no longer functional. Imagine dying. But even worse, imagine being sick, really sick, every day for the rest of your life. Well that is a rough slope, it is rocky, but what if it is all you got left.

Here pussycat pussycat

Coming out of the market there were two teenage girls pulling along a dog on a leash but it was a strangely very very unhappy shy dog and when I looked I saw that that was because it was not a dog, it was a cat, a cat on a leash, fighting every inch of the way, creeping, terrified, uncomprehending.

Hey, I tried to say to the girls, though averse to being pegged a child molester, knocked down by strangers, roped in literal chains while being kicked, dragged to town center by men and women who are shrieking PERVERT, doused in gasoline, lectured to out of the local apocrypha, and summarily burned alive on the sidewalk in front of the temple, so I usually do not talk to or even look at kids in this town, but I said, Hey cats don't like that, and when I said it and got the girls' attention the cat took the opportunity to dart off under a bench, the son of a bitch, where tug as the girls would they could not get it out.

Looking up, I saw the rows of vendors and townsfolk watching me from behind their hooded eyes, so I got the hell out of there.

We tried to
rob the same train

We tried to rob the same train on the same day at the same time, high noon. You felled a large tree across the tracks with a powder charge in the same spot where I had already pried up a length of tie that was going to tip the choo-choo onto her starboard, and as the train slowed we boarded together from opposite ends, up both lubbering cabooses, and were both gunned down by the federal sharpshooters squatting in the second and sixteenth cars.

We were dead, clearly, but our boys met in the middle after a gunfight in which the federales ultimately met their end, and a sly child name of Gringo Fuchs made such a sweet argument to the gang of mixed bandits, standing with one leg thrust forward, to divvy up the spoils that he was thereafter made captain of the redoubled force, and went on to conquer the west, cutting swathes through Wyoming, Idaho, and Utah territories, dying only many decades later in a California mansion, swollen feet bathed in luxurious oils by good-looking, well-shoed servants, drawling his last order through a peppermint candy stick, wheezing his last in utter glee.

Goliath

I t is difficult to be so strong on the inside, and brave, not to mention handsome, when they look at you and laugh because to them you appear to be fairly small and skittish, and plain, thought the mouse. He looked mournfully down the length of his brown country coat. He sniffed at the spot of mange, or grease. He nibbled at the mange or grease.

Sighed.

Hopped a couple of steps from the trap caught on the hind leg.

Dirk and Byrnie

Every time I try to decide what I am going to name my sword I get really frustrated because there are so many good options. Of course there are also many bad options that I have already rejected, the most obvious being Sword, Blade, Steel, and The Edge, or any compound noun featuring those words or members of an established European rock band. Imagine naming your sword Deathsword, for example. That would be like calling your dog Deathdog. That would be like naming your child Boy of Death! Stupid!

I have also discarded a long list of adjectives that are too obvious, like deadly, keen, pointy, sharp, and plunging. The only sword for those options is dull.

For several days I was leaning strongly on my weapon towards a compound noun in the Old English vein, something like Manscather or Spitedealer, Mailbiter, Rapterrafter, or Gravedigger. Then that Nordic phase sort of passed.

For one complete week I pondered names that were onomatopoeia for things my sword would do: Hisser, Swisher, Slicer, Dicer, Smacker, Whacker, Slipper, and Ripper. But there was no way I could choose one sound to the exclusion of all the others, so busy was I planning to be with my hisser-dicer.

Then I thought that a woman's name would be appropriate for something as beautiful and deadly as my sword was going to be. Gladys from the Latin gladius, for example, or Luz from the Spanish woman for light, or Priscilla like my guitar.

Eventually I just laid my sword aside and reached for my ivory-handled .45 revolver.

My Steel Slingshot. My Deadly Daisy. My Firespitter.

My Big Banger. My rod.
     Stewart.

Two days after renouncing Satan

Two days after renouncing Satan and pouring my remaining fifth of Cutty Sark down the sink like love after gold, I came down with the worst case of gout of my life, suffered for three days with a palpitating heart, and died alone on my dirty tick, me and my dirty dick.

My friends found out and came over to comfort me in those first few hours but as I no longer drank we had nothing left to say to each other or do together. They sat there for twenty minutes, told me to get well, and then took off for the bar. I never saw them again.

I took up my Bible and began to read, but my Bible believing days were well behind me by the time I had destroyed all my real relationships, career, and body, and as hard as I tried to pucker up for Christ in those my final hours Colossians Acts and Peter but especially Peter only made me stare deeper into the abyss. As much as I stared at the word and willed it to become flesh it was what it was, symbols on paper.

Why had I renounced the Devil?

The pain was exceptional. I was impressed. My right toe and ankle had swollen to eight times their natural size and had to be kept up in the air due to the throbbing. I took some anti-flambé pills, I chuckled, and called out to my mother who had died in 2008.

There was no landline, cellular telephone, or television in my studio apartment, so I just lay there staring at the lines of my own pain as they rippled across the grey ceiling. I had to crawl to the bathroom but even that was too much movement. It raked my leg and back like electricity. My throat constricted and lungs burned and I could feel the blood pumping through my clenched fists and my nose bled off and on and my tongue swelled up and I vomited bile and chunks of half-chewed meat and I could feel the tumor behind my left ear, where she had taken it in her teeth and bit down. I couldn't do the trip to the bathroom again so I just set up a bucket in the corner and that is how I died, in a shitstained, piss-stinking little room, on a mattress on the floor, alone.

Or did I die, I don't know. We are still talking, aren't we?

Her philosophy

When they brought out the kettle of beans we knew the game was up and we would have to sit and listen to her bitch and preach, and when they ladled her portion onto her pewter plate we saw her teeth for the first time in six days as she shucked back the ramshide fleece in preparation for the feast of beans, and words.

For ye may feed the body with the fruit of your labors, she began, overhand spoon moving more quickly than a stiletto in the dancing light of the campfire and stars, yet beware lest through neglect of the spirit ye fall into the ways of the pettifoggers and foreigners.

We pictured the ways of the pettifoggers and foreigners: tumeric in their beans, colorful silks wrapped around their lecherous midsections, and lewd acts performed beneath the spreading trees on altars of stone under the totems of strange and thirsty gods was their soul's carnival, work on this Earth, and grubby pittance.

I'll tell you what, we had been out of Kansas City a good week in posse on the tracks of them pettifogging sons of whores and though we had lost three men and some horses in a skirmish on the banks of the Big Padonia where there had been no good cover we were in good spirits. You might say we were philosophical about this kind of hunt. Inevitably victory would be ours along with the scalps of those that used strange spice to intoxicate our beans and ingratiate themselves with our homemaking womenfolk and cause strange lusts, for which they would be cleansed from the land.

Inspecting her spoon, holding it up for all to see, she

declared, For tis like this spoon, I declare to you, upon which we crawl like ants, on the convex side, which is our world, directionless to our dooms so help mankind if he bottle up his ears to it.

Turning the spoon, she showed us the other side.

Yet the strangers they walk upon the hollow surface of the spoon, she intoned, and they go like shadows through the dark places of the earth, where no light shines, and all thoughts tumble and rumble like a mudslide through a helpless village.

We stopped chewing for one split second, then resumed, mopping our plates with oversized biscuits.

Staggering to her feet she found the main kettle off on one of the cookfires and served herself another helping, hissing something to the Indian woman who squatted over there in the dark by the coals chewing on a cob of corn.

Crucify them, she muttered as she rejoined us around the main fire, and our working mandibles could taste the blood in the sand of the Missouri where it sloughed its way around Weeping Rock and just skidded across the bar for the most part before taking that long plunge down the lazy breaks, rolling on, speaking its own philosophy, and it's a wonder how we can see the daylight in our minds though it is dark and moonless yet on this side of the spoon.

Mrs. Beryl Bell

She arrived at Hacienda Láatsi in a Rolls Royce with two Oaxacan foot servants, whom she required because of the eight trunks stuffed with frilly bikinis, ointments, and bottles of rye whiskey.

Her son stood in the door of the bunkhouse and screamed at her for a very long time.

Go home, Ma, he screamed. You know you are not welcome here. The Revolution doesn't need you, capitalist whores like you.

Rusty's campesino friends gathered around him in the doorway, pulling their suspenders up over the chile sauce stains on their union suits and squinting into the dawn of a new day.

You fight with Rusty, you fight with the pueblo, Rusty barked. Our fight is not your fight, Ma. We are the people. We are the Revolution. We are blood and fire. Go back to your banana company executive son of a bitch bourgeois stepdad motherfucker, Ma.

Gulliver came off the hacienda front porch and pecked Mrs. Beryl Bell on the right cheek, then the left.

Mighty fancy place y'all got here, Mrs. Beryl Bell hummed softly, sizing up Gulliver from the tips of his snakeskin cowboy boots to the cocky angle of his wet combed hairdo, hat in hand, and puffy mustache – dazzling him with one of her most enigmatic smiles.

She barked, Bruno, get these trunks inside, draw me a bath, and pour me a tall sazerac.

You rotten whore, Ma, croaked Rusty Bell, as several

ranch hands got their cigarette fixings lit, but she had already disappeared inside.

A bomb that only smokes worse if you try to put it out by pissing on it

Funelge had the helm as we came screaming through the jungle at 460 knots per hour after a rocky entry and smoking badly from the aft thruster, not knowing exactly where we were except that this was Earth around 16 or 1700 ad deum in the reckoning of that place, well after the great civilizations had flowered and disappeared forever. We came to rest in a body of salt water, flashing light tsunamis across the beach, and after a short reconnoiter I gave our lieutenants permission to exit the ship in their legsuits and roam the streams and dales everywhere upcountry, so long as they checked scrupulously behind every bush and tree before advancing.

'Every single one now, you hear?' I said, adjusting their sabers and plasma pistols with an affectionate scowl.

Yesser, cappin, they replied, struggling with irrepressible grins.

Thus it came about that one band of my roughnecks plunged far into the upper coast of South Carolina, about a mile beyond the others, and got in among a thick stand of cane – What were you doing in the thick stand of cane, I demanded later when they told me their story, were you fucking in there – where with no warning they were ambushed and struck from all directions by volleys of powder bullets and rudimentary lances.

'I'm hit,' cried one soldier, faceplate smashed in and face erupting in puss, like the world's saddest turtle.

You're hit? screamed a second, looking at the grisly flint head of a spear that protruded from his spewing, bubbling chest and antigravity vest. 'I'M hit.'

'Where are they?' our boys called in confusion and terror, above the screams of their comrades, three of whom had been badly spitted, still getting their land legs and handles on the legsuits that gauzed and rocked their perfectly round, featureless bodies like a cup for gorgeous soft boiled eggs. 'I can't see them.'

Fire into the brake, commanded one quick-thinking boy of our company, a child of eleven in oversized legs, taking control of the situation. 'Fire your fusees into the cane and trees to fright em,' he barked, which ten of them did, banging away in random directions.

'Bang, bang, bang,' went the fusees, like gods of thunder.

Not only did the noise fright the aggressors and cut short their offensive, it also seems that a number of our molten shots had actually found live targets, for a great howling arose in the surrounding scrub and brake, and cussing, whether from the injured wretches themselves or friends who witnessed the carnage our men never discovered.

In their retreat, however, their path took our boys past a great old tree, like an oak, and as they approached they were suddenly hit by a volley of powder shot out of its top, and two of our men were knocked down and killed outright, and three more wounded. This infuriated the survivors, as you can imagine, but for the moment they were caught in the open – exposed, deep in enemy territory, on a forbidden planet, impossibly surrounded, and with no place to hide.

'Under the tree,' the clear headed child of eleven shouted, aiming and firing his piece in one smooth kickback motion at a cowboy hat that stuck out from a clump of leaves. Our soldiers, running and hobbling to the base of the oak, found it gave them good cover from the Americans at the top, who could not command the base with their extremely large powder shooters – though they would keep up their yipping and howling.

'Quiet, ye savage sons of bitches,' hissed the boy in his oversized legsuit, aiming a plasma bow that was taller than himself through the tangled boughs and cloaking foliage overhead – squeezing the trigger.

'Bang, whump, thump, crash, wham,' went the firearm, bullet, body on a branch, and corpse striking the ground at our soldiers' feet, in that order. The boy had drawn good aim on one of the malingerers who, despairing of ever killing another space slug, had stretched himself out precariously upon an upper branch of the tree, whence our boy had glimpsed the pinch of his hat, and fired so true that the gloopy ball punched the bad assassin in the face, and knocked him from his roost.

Upon his clumsy accident and crashing fall, and untimely death, the other investors of the stand – the man's comrades in arms – set up a monstrous whoop, and our soldiers heard a great clatter inside the tree, down inside the trunk, so that they were able to tell that the tree was hollow, and absolutely full of southern men. They began to fire their fusees and hip rockets into the tree, but found they could not pierce it, so thick was the trunk on it. Their molten projectiles had no effect whatsoever except to excite the yammering and scrabbling and laughter inside, as though supercharged bullets could tickle.

'Send for the carpenters,' growled the boy, binding the flesh wound of a weeping space pirate with his bandana. 'Tell them we need big saws, axes and drills, lava bullets, a sack of grenadoes, and fire. We're going to get those sons of whores if it's the last thing we do.' Two of our soldiers dashed, yawling on their mechanical legs, into the underbrush to bring word to the ship.

When my space pirates at the ship heard what had happened they were enraged, and armed up, and marched out to the tree in lower-deck armor bearing any kind of weapon they could lay their legsuit hands on whatsoever, and lay siege to the son of a gun.

'We'll starve them out if it takes us a year,' they growled, piling up dirt and logs behind which to crouch and shoot – and eat, sleep, play Go, take shelter from the monsoons, and shit in comfort for literal decades.

The tree was old but tall and very sturdy, the trunk alone rising about twenty-five feet straight up without a branch to speak of, and about four space soldiers in circumference when stood with their mechanical arms outstretched, roughly twelve feet to a soldier. At its top a mess of rotted limbs and half-dead leaves sprouted in a very thick and gangly manner, from which shelter the humanoid militia would rise to take occasional potshots, though they mostly stayed down inside the tree after we murdered their friend.

Funelge had also armed up and gone out to the tree, having the curiosity of a cat, or gypsy, and advised our soldiers to get into the top of the tree and toss wildfire down it, like a chimney, to smoke them out.

'They shall stagger out like bees,' he laughed, 'and then you can have your shooting gallery.'

Others were for bringing up one of our big land cruisers and splitting the tree in two with one or two point-blank rounds from its floor blasters, while still others argued for stacking up a great pile of kindling and burning the tree from its base, which would be sure to make those inside sweat molten bullets, they crowed.

The boy, who had made himself captain of the expedition, decided to follow Funelge's advice, and had a long siege ladder constructed, and propped against the tree, although this was hot work, for the sons of man would appear in the upper branches when least expected and hurl down their missiles, and the big question was who was going to have the guts to go up the ladder on artificial legs behind a steamy faceplate to toss in the wildfire.

'I'll do it myself,' screamed the boy, but we restrained him – easily, with one hook.

'I shall go,' replied one of our foremast pirates, seizing the tackle with which we meant to raise the fire into the top – but got only part way up the ladder before a shower of powder bullets caught him, one striking him badly across the top of one prosthetic shoulder, and knocked him off again.

We pulled him to safety, firing into the top, but the lanky human woodsmen in there just ducked back into the body of the tree.

'This is going nowhere fast,' I giggled, looking up from my charts and meat pies and decanters of blood in my snug little cabin on the mothership. I had opposed the inane project from the beginning, I told them. 'You spent three days just arguing about how to begin,' I chuckled. 'Imagine, baulked by a bunch of men in a tree. Take a big gun if you want to, take five and no more than five floor rounds for the surface cruiser, but don't waste any more soldiers,' I said, playing the part of the schoolmaster, peering over my spectacles. Of course I had no more concern for the souls of soldiers than a jackal for its own photograph – my spectacles contained no lenses. I was just anxious to spend my space gold, and get in between between six of one and a half dozen of another plump strumpet slugs on our next real beaching.

Then the gunner had a bright idea.

'I shall make one of my famous stinkpots,' he said

suddenly, sitting up in his filthy siege trench, and it was a truly noxious thick-smoking slow bomb – a bomb that only smokes worse if you try to put it out by pissing on it, he told us excitedly.

'They would not try to put it out by pissing on it,' we protested.

Just you wait and see, he told us.

So we opened with a barrage into the top from all the fusees and plasma bows our assembled company could bring to bear – you should have heard the dead leaves zinging, and the ricochets off the stubborn limbs – and then sent the gunner in.

Our naked, hushing, stalked eyes followed his form as it crept up the ladder, and the fumes of the stinkpot that swung from a cord. Together they disappeared into the branches, the smoke marking the gunner's progress through the tangled top to the very center, when it abruptly ceased.

'Perhaps he has thrown it in,' mused Funelge, smiling at the thought.

At that moment the gunner reappeared at the head of the ladder – slid to the ground with a flourish of false limbs and a laugh.

'That should do it,' he called, and turned and crossed his prosthetic arms to watch the fumigation.

And watch, and wait, and watch, and wait – for we heard no sound from the tree nor any motion in its top all the night or next morning.

'The gunner has smothered them in their sleep,' we suggested. 'They have choked to death on their own tongues.'

Yet we were wrong – in the morning, as our soldiers already began to drift off toward the ship, and unlimber their fusees and grenadoes, a great chattering and commotion was heard in the top of the tree again, and there was a rain of powder bullets on all our positions.

We cursed, and kicked, swore a cabin boy.

'There seem to be more of them than ever,' Funelge mused.

'The more for us to murder,' snarled the child captain, as evening turned into night – as his trembling lips turned into killing words. 'Bring me a second stinkpot.'

But I stopped him there, for by this time I had come out to the tree to see it for myself.

'You are not sending my gunner up that ladder again,' I told him flatly. 'They are going to grab him, and subdue him.'

'We did it before,' whined the child, now illuminated by the whipping torch I held in one great fist. 'It cannot fail a second time.'

'I shall attach the stinkpot to a long pole,' the gunner explained, 'run up several rungs of the ladder, and toss it into the top.'

Fine, I sighed.

I said, 'Make your second stink bomb.'

Stinkpot, said the gunner. 'It's called a stinkpot.'

It took him about an hour to do, or more with all of us watching, him and his big clumsy gloved fake fingers, and then he had to light it, and slip it into its special sling, and by that time it was too late – for when we get to the base of the tree, we discover the ladder is missing.

'Behold, the ladder is gone,' we said through numb, prosthetic lips.

Where could it have gone to, we stammered.

'They came down the ladder while our backs were turned,' suggested the gunner, 'and carried it off with them.'

See where your stupid ladder has got you, cursed the boy, turning to our crestfallen mate. 'Your very design for capturing them has manufactured their escape.'

Yet he was wrong, for in the morning we saw the ladder sticking up from the middle of the tree, crammed half down the trunk.

'Fools,' we laughed. 'They don't know how a ladder works.'

That's the last straw, grimaced the boy, whose mane had gone grey overnight.

'It's impossible,' exclaimed our surgeon. 'It should go grey only at the root. To go grey overnight is just an adage, and expression, a wives tale. It doesn't literally go grey overnight.'

Yeah, what have you rubbed in it, we demanded, laying knuckles to the boy's scalp back on the mothership, but the boy howled, and clawed, and insisted he hadn't done a thing, and as a matter of fact his mane was always grey after that, no matter how much we dunked him.

'Let's burn them out,' he said, when he had wiggled free, and we set to work chopping like maniacs. We chopped until we had the tree half buried in swaddling dry firewood, and had stood back in satisfaction. Lighting a straw fag from a live coal, the child general took a puff and flicked it onto a trail of gypsum-reduced henequiye he had laid from the central trench. It flashed over the top, spat across the field of battle, and hit the pile of wood with a great roar.

'That should do the trick,' we admitted.

Just as the pile was beginning to catch, however, and starting to crackle and pop, and the men inside beginning to shift uncomfortably in their cowboy chaps, we imagined, there was a great whoosh and hiss and a bisque of steam exploded from the fire and floated across our baffled positions, and we had to cover our mouths plates and gag for air.

The boy general puked through his mask into an open trench, on his hands and knees through the heinous, execrable mist.

We said, 'They have doused our fire with their own urine, as does the lord of darkness.'

Only Funelge smiled as we regained our stature, and composure, and utter dignity.

He said, 'I believe these ingenious native creatures have a tunnel that leads from the tree and communicates with other caves full of their friends, who perhaps – much like prairie dogs – have an entire complex of tunnels and escape holes in these surrounding hills.'

Then he asked me to give him three boys and a sack of grenadoes.

'They're yours,' I said, though generally averse to lending out boys.

Boys in hand, Funelge told the carpenter to drill a series of holes in the trunk of the tree, and to pack them with henequiye, and connect them to a slow fuse, which he himself lit by the normal method, and stood back. When the fuses touched off the henequiye there was a great explosion, that rocked the ground we stood on, and cracked open the tree in a number of places, so that Funelge was able to confirm his theory by pulling the splintered parts of the tree back and reaching his robot hands down in there and feeling about.

'There is a large cave under the tree,' he concluded, with a dashing grin.

'Get your God-damned fake arm out of that hole,' I told him. 'They're going to bite open your space suit, you God-damned lunatic.'

But by this time Funelge and his three men had made a good-sized opening in the trunk and were preparing to go down – strapping plasma pistols and cutlasses to their remarkably wiry body suits, knives clenched in teeth that emerged like hacksaws from the top of their helmets.

'You're not going down there,' I began, but Funelge had already leapt into the hole, following a pair of concussion grenadoes that we could hear puff and blow and punch into the bowels of the man tunnel complex, and he and his boys had vanished.

They were vanished about fifteen minutes, though it seemed much longer to our straining ears, and pounding temples, and in the meanwhile we heard not a syllable of human speech or shot fired in ecstasy – a real worrisome stretch, during which I paced and screamed and brought myself to climax eight times successfully. As I was about to murder a cabin boy, or dog, or destroy my favorite silk shirt that swaddled me inside my suit, the brave souls emerged, choking and gasping.

They crawled from the tree on all prosthetic fours, accompanied by a gush of acrid yellow smoke.

'Thy stinkpot did nothing but teach them how to defend their position, it seems,' chuckled Funelge, sitting in the piss and grass of the battlefield, safe and sound, with a little cough and a little wheeze. 'We followed the tunnel NE from the tree and penetrated to a second cave, where we flushed a group of men into a second redoubt, about over there,' he said, pointing to a nearby hillock. 'There the assassins set a fire that moved down the tunnel onto our position and overtook us, and its smoke began to strangle us, so that we were forced to withdraw.'

We looked at the taffy fumes that billowed from the busted remains of the ancient tree.

'We have to give it up,' I told Funelge. 'These buckskin savages are liable to fight to the last man, and getting them is of no lasting advantage to us now but pride.'

Pride, smiled Funelge, standing at last – brushing clods of

dirt and straw from his maculate black garments.

'Give me leave,' he smiled, 'to try one last thing.'

Robot hands on hips and little else, I agreed.

Funelge called his boys – had two rounds of good powder shot rousted out of the ship, and as soon as the sulfur had cleared from the tunnel he wrestled and stacked them below in the passage as far back as he could, stopping up the way with clay and rocks that he packed in as tight as a wall, and rigged his slow match, and lit it, and stood way the hell back – as did we all.

'Ka-boom,' went the two powder rounds and the man-earth itself.

The ground beneath us kicked and a volcano of dirt and rubble exploded from the face of a far hillock, behind a screen of bushes there, opening a gaping hole from which wafted the jetsam and detritus of bold Funelge's gambit.

'There is your second entrance,' crowed our merry helmsman, skipping forward with a pistol in either clawed hand, and when we got up to it we observed the effect of his peacemaking work: no men, but lots of pieces of them scattered all about, arms and legs and stern startled lips and noses.

'You shot them from their warren like a rabbit from a heavy cannon,' we observed.

'As though from a sort of improvised space age howitzer,' agreed Funelge with a sad nostalgia – trousering his big guns.

For satisfaction of pride, then, and to gain the knowledge of how to raise a siege on a stubbornly defended tree on a planet of men, we wasted the lives of three good space pirates, fifty humanoid warriors in full regalia (hats, boots and spurs), four powder rounds, and a solid month of fair sailing through a benevolent and otherwise unpopulated solar system.

'Congratulations,' I told Funelge. 'I hope you're happy.'

He looked at me – he was.

The Golden Key

'For the last time,' roars the hulking form from the chair one more time. 'Take the sleigh and don't come back until you have loaded it with dry wood from the far side of the mountain. I won't ask again.'

You look out from the worn collar of your winter coat and rub your small mittens together, thinking about the day you fell through the trapdoor into this world of never-ending winter and discovered the people who were your parents in the drafty cabin. The little woman sneaks a glance at you from beyond the kitchen table where she is sweeping. She passes a hand across her smut-stained brow. 'Go, dear!' she mouths urgently, and the fear in her eyes prompts you to slide your bottom off of the stool and drop to the floor. Toddling to the door in your pantaloons, you soldier off into the wind of winter, yanking the sleigh behind you through cresting drifts of snow.

You spend the afternoon rooting in the outskirts of the forest on the far side of the mountain, digging through the heaps of snow for logs and thick branches and piling them on the sleigh. By the time you are finished, your fingers and toes are so cold that you think it best to build a fire to warm yourself before you make the long haul home, and you decide to lay it beneath a large oak tree. As you scrape away the snow from the spot, however, your frozen fingers dislodge a tiny golden key.

Where there is a tiny, golden key, you think, there must also be a tiny chest.

You begin to dig in the spot where the key was lying and soon uncover a small, stout iron chest.

'If only the golden key fits,' you shout in your excitement, no longer feeling the stabbing cold of the wind or the frost in the fur of your boots. 'Surely there is treasure in this box.'

You turn the chest this way and that but see no keyhole.

'How do you open it?' you cry. 'Where is the keyhole?'

Just as you are about to throw your desperately hoar-frosted mittens in the air, you discover the hole.

Concealed beneath a crust of crisscrash ice.

You slip the golden key into the lock and it fits exactly.

Spin the key and the lock clicks.

But now we must wait until you lift the lid to see what kinds of wonderful things are hidden inside.

What is this?

This, the school psychologist says, pointing to her elbow. What is this?

The most clueless boy of them all, touching his elbow, replies that it is his elbow. Put on the spot.

No, says the school psychologist.

The boy hesitates.

So it's my chin, he says.

Very good! applauds the psychologist, the nerves of her face twitching, teeth coming through her lips. What does it do? she asks.

It, the most clueless boy begins.

The entire class is silent, not knowing what the fuck is going on.

It makes babies! continues the voice of Tony, concealed behind the jacket of Lorena where nobody will ever find him except me, as though I gave a damn.

A visual representation
of the human predator

In the texts of the old civilizations of Mesoamerica, of the Mixtecs and Zapotecs and Teotihuacans, for example – and by texts I mean carvings on large rocks, cave paintings, and velum screens – what I take to be the human voice is represented by a straight thick single or double line that curls out of the mouth and down and back towards the speaker's chin at the end of its trajectory like a long tongue. Whether the subject speaks or calls, chants, sings or simply exhales vapors I do not know, but it is clear that the making of the sound or projection of the hissing spit was a significant act.

The comic book hero Spearchucker Bat, on the other hand, a product of post-war culture in modern Mexico and a fusion of the mild-mannered city Indian – object of frequent discrimination by coworkers, strangers, and lanky white women – and a crime-fighting vigilante with superhuman strength and intelligence, normally says specific things that are represented by block letters in Roman script inside a special bubble that emerges from his mouth.

DIE CRABHEARTED VILLAIN, he will cry.

I SWEAR IT WASN'T ME SUSAN, he will moan.

In the comics of Spearchucker Bat the long tongue is used to represent the high-pitched cawing that that hero uses to terrorize and locate his prey, since he is of course completely blind while inside his bat suit.

A terrifying and bloodcurdling way to meet your mouselike end.

Salad Days

There must be a glitch in the program because I have been put into a loop in which I finish the book, get out of my suit and into bed, and then immediately am back in the chair, strapped in and fully dressed, grimacing at the title of the last chapter, and I am forced to read it all over again.

There must be a glitch in the program, I read, because I have been put into a loop in which I have already finished this book, and then am forced to read it all over again, but I have to begin at the last chapter. And I know every word by heart, but have forgotten everything that went before.

There must be a glitch in the program, I read. I have been put into a loop in which I finish the book even though I know every word by heart. The last line is, And I am forced to read it all over again. And I am forced to read it all over again.

If you can hear me, please advise Funelge that there is a glitch in the program. The title of the novel is *Salad Days* but I only have the last chapter. I have tried to read from the beginning but there are no words. I know all the words there are by heart. Please advise Funelge or the assistant to reboot the program. They are forcing me to read *Salad Days* over and over again.

I know every word by heart because there is a glitch in the program. Please advise.

And I am forced to read it all over again.

Battler of Beowulf
A novella

Prose rendering of the third and final episode of the Old English epic, after Beowulf has returned to Juteland from quelling the monster Grendel and his mother. A novelization of Beowulf that follows its strange and problematic source line for line until the end.

Ring-mischievous, tyrannical, a known baby killer, yet to the end of his days a man unconscionably generous with his own, king Highlake bestowed half his kingdom on the prodigal Beowulf with one motion of his skeleton tongue. He essentially made the hero of our epic prince of his realm when he gave him the fabled family sword, in which case it was without even a motion of his lapper – done give him the sword with which he had killed not just babies but mothers and full-grown fathers, because somebody had to do it.

Highlake spoke – smiled proudly and through smoke as always. You have already read what he said.

Rich was he, yet the life of an infanticide like Herod of old, though rife with delectable orgies and unseasonably good stabbings, tends to be both violent and relatively short. This turned out to be the case with Highlake's, too, when it was stymied in the throes of its hearty fifth decade by the very sword he lived by.

'Don't kill me with my own sword,' were not the last words a man like Highlake was likely to have uttered, taunted yet conscious, sprawled in the dying spokes of a sun that refused to go down on that day of his life.

He said, 'If you strike me down now, I shall become more powerful than you can possibly imagine in your little Frisian brain.' They bore Highlake off upon his shield and his son Hard Ginger instantly died in a similar fashion, leaving the throne seemingly, achingly empty.

'Take the throan,' Hygd queen widow groaned upon the casket of her husband, beseeching Beowulf, but that man had rejected the offer – vowed to back Hard Ginger, though the boy was only eight.

'Hard Ginger is king now,' intoned the big hero, turning his back on a pair of legs that had caused many to question their own fealty, and lealty. Queen Hydg stomped off in a fury, but Beowulf was as good as his word – Hard Ginger grew to be a great fighter, and his lacquered blonde hair that was an icon to the god of victory stuck out stiffly in all directions from under his helmet.

Then somehow he died.

'Whoever shall assume power now,' wept the good Jutes, gazing upon the dead lips and nostrils of Hard Ginger, laid out in state as if to see by some miracle whether his heart would not start pumping again – his eyes flutter open and mouth say 'mother' again.

They did not, and Beowulf had to make appropriate arrangements for his cremation and give speeches and then take charge of the rope tiller – the rope of gold tiller of the sprawling Jute master kingdom.

We can't help it – we wonder if Beowulf finally banged the queen Hygd, widow. If he did, it was one of the best times of their lives, and they never regretted it, and they never told a living soul.

'I wonder if king Highlake is looking down on us right

now, wherever he is,' mused the queen mother in her high-pitched mousy little voice, naked next to Norseman. 'I wonder if he judges me for going on with my life and rabbitfucking every last one of his former friends and cousins,' she wept, nude under naegling.

Beowulf did not say, 'Jesus you are queen of the sluts,' because he had already rolled over and was snoring profoundly, and did not know who Jesus was, though all scop bards everywhere agree the noble pagan died worthy of everlasting life in the Kingdom of Heaven.

Beowulf ruled the Jutes for fifty winters and was a battle shield to his people, an old reliable to his allies – a man you would not challenge to a flyting and under most circumstances would avoid in the street even in daylight, when Beowulf was walking a straight line. Beowulf ruled for fifty years of days and fifty years of nights, and then one morning the bliss and cotton-picking fun loving came to an end because of a dragon.

'We didn't quite catch that, a dragon,' you probably demanded in your shrill, impatient voice. 'As in a flying worm with legs?'

'And little grabby arms,' I replied.

Then one night a mighty dragon began to taunt and overpower the darkening Juteland skies, country folk scurrying like ants beneath its powerful flapping wings – housefires leaping like squealing gnomes from roof to roof. The fires consumed children and wives and heavily drunken swordsmen and their pigs.

From sty to sty they leapt, like milkmen.

'Tell us about the dragon,' you begged me.

It was an ancient creature, this worm. It crept and brooded upon a pile of treasure that included swords and big pianos. We do not know where he concealed his stash – his ring hoard, but it lay beneath a stark and stony barrow. The barrow stone he called home and his home was his hoard and his hoard had been his for more than three hundred years. It smelled like him and tasted of him and it was as secret as a nest of voles, highway lost to kin of man and kith of mom.

Yet one day, with the arrogance of the unbaptized and the dumb luck of the helplessly thoughtless, a rat faced intruder entered the hoard hall with his rotten mouth and stinking, somehow bleeding asshole and plundered a golden chalice – plucked it from the pile. I have a pretty good idea who this scapegoat was. He was a man on the run, wanted for a terrible crime. As he ran from the dogs he fell into a concealed pitfall with a muffled shriek, giving himself up for dead as he tumbled down, head over heels, deep into the bowels of the earth.

'Now I am a bog man,' he thought, doomed to die in sucking mud, but he was wrong. His body caught in a root or troll slinky – he fell and landed on dry ground. He lifted his head but could see nothing in the inky dark. He felt around with his itching fingers.

'Why, it's a tunnel,' he hiccupped, thieving hands going up and down the sides of what was surely an orifice carved by a monster the size of a tractor. Deciding not to go back the way he came – crawling forward on his hands and knees, he went left and then right and then left and then right and then left and then right and then left and then right and he reached the great hoard – sniffed air not smelled by man for fourteen generations, and put his hands into a stupendous pile of treasure.

'Big gold coins,' his ingenious brain informed him, but his hands were already through the coins, for he had skidded hard onto the miraculously cobbled interior of the cave and pitched headfirst through the doorway, and his spastic clutching fingers thudded against, fingered, caressed, and finally encircled the gallant sides of a noble chalice – a chalice the likes of which his rattrap mother had never borne to bearm, or lifted anywhere near his bad baby face or greedy little goblin fingers.

'This firebreather won't miss one little goblet,' sneered the abominable hunchback, looking first right, then left – rising to almost equal knees – exiting the cave with a quick gallop and a shallow chuckle, as lucky in an unlit tunnel complex as any fool who uses the same hand to salute his king and clean up after the best night of his life.

Who knows, maybe that was why he was on the run? The poet does not have time to elaborate.

'Won't miss one precious little goblet,' guffawed the mistaken thief to himself, cursing himself to a crispy side of bacon.

ᚠ

Leaving the cave by the front, the notorious slave went directly to the house of his pursuers, cradling the grail inside his scuzzy vest, and delivered it into their clutches in payment for his pardon.

'Where did you find this noble, intricately engraved chalice?' Beowulf did not demand from his mighty throne, turning the precious object in hands that refused to be still or stop killing. Nor did he protest, 'This is no work of human hands, but of ents and giants of ages past.'

He said, 'You are right, slave, this should just about cover the blood price,' with a smile, and the king had the goblet delivered to the offended party. 'This should pay for the housefires you lit,' he may have exclaimed, or, 'This is just recompense for the mothers you insulted the last time you strolled through here with your pants off,' or maybe, 'This completely exonerates you from eating those babies.'

Whether or not the thief had a name we will never know, but we sure as hell can speculate. Go on, talk together about his name. I can hear you gobbling back there. Talk it up, but let me tell you, the goblet robber had fallen into a misfortune, for the very hoard that had saved his life bore an ancient curse that damned its masters to inevitably brutal, violent short lives, and a penis the size of your pinky.

Knowing this, its final inheritor had buried the horrible stash deep under a stone slab with the intention of keeping it out of circulation, and commanded a large boulder to be rolled across the entrance while he was still inside – then laid himself down in a coffin he had prepared for the purpose, and gone to meet his maker.

Or he was metamorphosed – closed his eyes and in the act was transformed into a fire-breathing dragon.

'Now for a little nap,' he sighed, adjusting his coils for three hundred years.

Or that last survivor just died – did the opposite of survive, and the worm came later, snooping in the dark.

In any case, death took everyone in the man's generation and he was no exception.

'I wish to have enjoyment of my gold while I live,' he shrugged as his slaves burrowed out his tomb. Founded on the summit of a great sea wall, it overlooked incessant water – was protected by pitfalls and swinging axes and dripping snake chutes. He said, 'It may be a month, or it may be a day. Take the gold down into the main chamber. You will recognize it by its size and tall marble colonnades.'

Indentured servants hustled into the gaping mouth of the stone grave bearing armloads and chariot loads of gold and goblets, every piece counted and tallied, every last trinket noted and known.

'Where is the lopsided FID MAR you fucking sons of whores?' he screamed. 'You are all going to die, you thieves, you robbing bastards.'

Luckily for the slaves, they were able to locate the lopsided FID MAR and tucked it back into the titan's trembling hand.

'My precious,' he gasped. 'My precious,' he howled, angry at the money.

When the loot was inside the grave baron cleared his throat and declared, 'Take and hold, good ground, this strength of earls, the gold and loot that in bygone times was used to good advantage by men whose character and courage was not lacking, to say the least. Every last one of them is dead now, fallen in battle or stabbed inside his blanket. They had their fun while it lasted – dreamy joy in dizzy high silo. There is none left to swing their big swords now,' he wept, indicating a sword that was indeed too big to be lifted by a modern person, 'or raise this goblet to lips that know the classic war chants, or to prop up this helm, hard under heel.'

The slaves bowed – the skies looked down.

He said, 'They are dead and gone, the ones who knew how to make use of these ornaments and masks – of byrnies that tell their own stories, the men that clashed boards and stayed on their feet through the rain of biting iron. Now their wood and steel shall rot in the ground like their faces.'

The slaves were all outside now. The poet glanced into a sky as bleak and grey as the memory of his mother and of his much, much younger brother.

He said, 'The battle shirt stops here. Never again shall

Bjorn's codpiece or favorite skull flagon venture over the waves as it did, clinging to that hero's tough chest – tossed like a loving toddler over his shoulder in a saddlebag.'

Some of the slaves had known Bjorn – to others his name was just a sound.

He said, 'No more gleebeaming harp music or pet falcons that should swoop and cry,' he moaned, 'taking flight inside a crowded meadhall, lit up on fire and on beer, or the whinny of Bjorn on his pony, clip-clopping into the courtyard.'

The elegist stepped under the stone, faced the slaves, and gave his final order.

'BALEful death,' he exclaimed, the words of Klaeber and a hundred other wordsmiths echoing down the stony sad hall, 'has muzzled me and every last one of my family – sent us down into silent repose.'

The rock shivered and rolled in front of the opening where the man had so recently chirped and palavered like a blond Christ, and the mouth of the treasure pit was closed up.

'What are his instructions for if he changes his mind,' none of the slaves bothered to inquire. There were no such instructions.

The anonymous grief-stricken son of destiny survived a number of days down there, we imagine, sprawled across his gold and baubled corslets, snot and tears dribbling from what was left of his body, but the rest of his words are lost to a posterity that would never hear them. Heartsick, the orphan prince last seen by a slave in a crusty loincloth enumerated the loss of every brother and uncle. Groaning with the horror of a mind under the influence of a destiny that was about to crush him, he pissed away his remaining days and nights, for where he lay day was night and night was night, and vice versa, until he was overwhelmed by death at last – pulverized by the personification of an abstraction he could neither welcome nor in any way escape.

He sunk into death, soul like Turnus' groaning on the inside.

In the gloam of a goat and rooster predawn, pushing himself farther than he had ever gone before, the drake found the headland – brushed the whitecaps where the knee of a country the size of a continent rose from the whitewash. It found the bluff and far beneath it the barrow where it wafted from a milky glow of scree gold where a worm could spew its eggs and nudge them into the speck and loam and finally – finally nestle down.

Its reptilian eyes hissed, heavy body slinking and chunking through air – air it somehow already knew, screwy little fire-breathing mouth chugging like a rhinoceros – like a caboose.

It didn't wear pants, either. It went as nacod and nards out as the day he was pushed from its mother's spewing vagina into the gold-nested crib.

Frodo as an old king the dragon crept onto the fantastic hoard. Alighting on the mountain, sensing without any effort at all every object within a distance of one furlong from its unsheathed, whipping wings – every bee on its clover and every trolling mendicant little porcupine mother and her pups, landing on soft turf she found the grave blown open where it had popped like a pod of peas and spilled bones and silver onto the salt-basted loam of the bluff.

Ducking inside, she pulled the entrance closed behind her with claws that were human hands, we shuddered.

For what man can go into the maw of the cliff and find his

match there, and mate with it, and give it progeny with opposable thumbs?

The smoke that poured from the big nostrils of the rapacious raptor soon vanished, fire under fieldstone. It was not that the draconian fiend stopped breathing, but that the breath stopped coming, or that no one was there to see the vent, not a single wanton rock-chucking shepherd with a flock.

We had to make it all up.

For example: The serpent slides into a hidden mass of treasure. He shivers in an orgasm of greed and greasy love and breathes fire, but not too much fire. He pads a nest of gold and cutting swords in the precise middle of the precocious stone atrium and beds down for the night, because his night is three hundred years long.

He will not enjoy its trove – there is absolutely no benefit he can derive from it. He doesn't need gold and the gold doesn't help, but he definitely likes it. In his mind he trawls the hall – trolls and guards it and counts the little cups and cutting knives and jeweled hilts and I guess there are probably even mounded piles of furs and battle standards in blue and violet that he chuckles over, fabrics pricked with golden thread, and the drake gets onto the corpse of the unfortunate owner of the loot, a five-hundred-year-old skeleton, and sighs – closes its eyes – sleeps for three centuries.

The end.

So the folkscather three hundred winters held the hoard, crafty and big, until someone made the mistake of rousing him from his dreams of gold and – you guessed it – incinerated children and ransacked a cup, a bold bauble that the rat delivered to his man king in the fretless wine house, with which he won his pardon.

'This is a really gorgeous, expensive cup,' Beowulf said. 'You are pardoned.'

The drake's eyes popped open – he snuffled in alarm and rose to his what are these things to his elevators to his legs, from a glorious nap. His claws snapped open and eyes glowed with a fire that could melt hearts through iron, and had.

Sniffing along the wall, grumbling and troubled, the monster came upon the scuffed spot where the thief had tripped and fallen into the dust and golddust of his lair. It was literally only one yard from where the drake's sleeping big head had lain, his incredulous brain concluded. The man had sprawled right into a vast empty space like a toddler – probably would never know how close he had come to ending his life like a barbecue, three calendar days before he was to end his life like a barbecue, mused the infuriated fiend.

Insane jealousy took the worm and convulsed him. Racked with black hate and a trembling spell that shook the caves and was felt as far away as North America (heard of it), the dragon rose and sloughed the chambers – big coils swift under seawings, and sought the mouse that had cheated him in his sleep. It was like when you wake up in the lonely midnight and discover your wife is having rough sex with your best friend and neighbor and bowling partner. Then sudden vengeance comes upon Sven and Maggie – their fun is over, and a veil is pulled over their malingering days, because before they can say, 'Christ it's just a little hanky panky, Tom,' they have heavy battle axes and swords sticking out of their bodies. They are being doused in gasoline.

Such was the reaction of the dragon when he discovered an intruder had taken a piece of his gold. Rising from the barrow, the majestic hearted beast took flight – circled the bluff, cawing and spewing fire in an attempt to flush the criminal and purge the rat dirt from his bones and eyes – from his home.

'There is a fire-breathing dragon circling the bluff,' no one even had to advise the king. The king was looking right at it.

'He is searching for his lost goblet,' Beowulf did not say, though he knew in his bones the moment he had seen it that that mug was bad news. Nor did he say, 'Well maybe we can just give it back.' He knew it was too late for talk.

The dragon circled, swooped, and scorched three glamorous houses with his gawking mouth. He returned to the barrow – hunted like an insane ostrich through the corridors and rooms of the grave for the missing piece. The pueblo would pay, barnyard under bonebreaker. The great animal rose and turned his wicked eyes upon the fragile frosted roofs and gingerbread courtyards of the idyllic settlement our hero Beowulf had made home. For not even their king would escape judgment and death by housefire if the wise one had his druthers, and by druthers I mean grim charcoal remains of human heads and torsos.

The dragon rose and incinerated the town, flames gushing from wanton maw, although none of the murder or destruction could quell the rage in his buzzing, babbling heart. By night he flew and by day he squatted and brooded inside his jewel-speckled nest, smacking about for the precious lost article, furious and cunning. At sundown he would burst from his grave and scorch the falling sky with jetting flames and cremate bonny barns. From far across the horizon men watched in fascinated terror as his black shape rose, bent, and plumed, and the sky filled with an almighty glow that had to be house fire.

'It's a volcano,' said some fool.

'You're a fool,' replied his best friend.

In the morning the worm sought the hoard – entrusted himself to the grave, a sepulcher he turned upside down and backwards and sideways in the throes of a despair that wormed and poked like fire ants in his giant throat.

He puked lava – choked back tears and fizzled hot snot.

'Something is missing,' he hissed, over and over and over and over and over and over and over and over and over and over and over, say that ten times fast. 'Something is missing, is missing, they took it, the rats, the rats, it is missing,' he was hissing.

So he returned to the barrow stone by day – thought with his knowledge of ancient battles and ability to read the minds of human beings and react with stunning speed to any challenge or attempted dint of clumsy rebounding hatchets or broadswords he could defend himself in his lugubrious subterranean redoubt.

On the third night the drake flew circles about Beowulf's gleaming palace as the people – screaming, evacuating and vacating, leaving, stumbling, smoking, trailing licking flames like unwilling recipients of an incarnate Holy Ghost – quickly fled those confines for the acres of gorsy hills on the outskirts of the village. They had a bunker out there, or just cowered in the rubble behind blackened trees and upturned shields and wept.

Behind the fleeing minions the dragon also destroyed the high hall in a terrible inferno. The flames seized many of the slower retirees and children in their rippling hands. They took the proud walls of the gift-stool of the Jutes and kindled them. They melted the gates from the big hinges, the gables from the gold, the faces of old relatives from shining tapestries and upholstered mead bench covers, and the exposed breasts and wet hirsute snatches of the lovemaking sluts embroidered on almost all of the decorations in Beowulf's hall and halls.

'My porn,' Beowulf did not sob, because he was a hard man surrounded by the most beautiful Jutes you could imagine. A man like him didn't need porn, and he was pushing eighty, but he liked it. Watching the spire of smoke and exploding rafters from behind his loyal, hunkering guard, what he said was, 'My gold. What in God's name are they doing with my gold.'

For the dragon was scooping up heaps of cups and bright baubling child daggers from Beowulf's great spilled-open hoard and carrying them away to his rightful silo – snatching from Beowulf's trove in his little groping hands in repayment for the looted goblet and reek of smackass that now filled his precious ancient bunker.

'Sire, your gift-stool is going up in flames,' some God-damned imbecile reported, saluting his king from one knee and a body that was more or less useless to him. 'The drake has consumed your home, the gift hall where you were accustomed to deal rings and give big parties.'

'Give big orgies,' Beowulf did not correct the man. He did not say, 'A sex party is called an orgy, what is the matter with you Humbolt, do you live under a rock or something,' because men live in houses and dragons live under rocks.

Consumed with grief and ripping Job's tunic because his own tunic was a byrnie made of hand-linked iron rings that could not be torn, Beowulf said, 'Why is the creature destroying my town and people? What have we done to him?'

For despite the nagging image of the chalice and leering features of the rat-faced thief he had pardoned, Beowulf could not say for certain why the bad evil had swooped down – why the barn-burner had raised fiery siege to Beowulf's pueblo, a place where peace after pardon is peace.

'What unnatural act of the Christians has aroused him to such a fury,' wondered the great Jute, singling out the only minority in his realm that had no idea what was going on right now, so ensconced were they in enshrining God in symbols – knowing the dragon was a stud with a glance and violent shudder.

His sword thanes shook and wept. Their ring-dealing days appeared to be over, and they shuddered to picture themselves as farmers.

'It is God himself who is doing this to us,' their leader cried, although he was mistaken, for God rules over all things with a love for justice that is like a diamond. In all His acts of violence and reproach and individual attention to detail results the utter destruction of specific, hand-picked buildings – unless you are Sodom and Gomorrah, of course, in which case you are all going to learn to regret all your mind can comprehend in a single instant of overwhelming sulfur, and brimstone that rains into your open mouth.

Beowulf said, 'We have angered the Wealdend God, and He is striking us down with his fire drake, but we shall fight back.'

For who can be struck in his gold barn, even be it by the Almighty Lord and Creator, and not stiffen in his holiday pants and strike back? Easier, I tell you, for a longboat the size of Long Island to pass through the eye of a hurricane.

The ligdraca flame spurter had the fastness, the seaboard-facing bluff silo, the earthward of buff Jute Beowulf son of Edgetheow, ground down with gleed.

With hot chucking rocks blown like boogers from his smoking throat and leather lips he crushed it like candy, and it was gone.

Beleaguered by a flying fire-breathing dragon who spent destruction like it was paper currency (heard of it) and crispy beyond belief, we imagine, Beowulf from his last redoubt called for Carl smith of the gorgeous mane and ordered him to fashion a great shield for the fight he was about to join.

'Not a shield of lindenwood or oak,' said he, 'even such as is often fixed with pointed knobs and reinforced with iron bands that stretch its circumference like a latitude,' because Beowulf was not born yesterday, 1 July 946 AD. Instead he ordered Carl to build him a cheek of eallirenne, he said.

He said, 'Make it all iron, a wonderful stout thick big board of war with padding on the inside for when it gets really hot and rains gobs of molten lava.'

He said, 'Forge me a buckler of all cast iron, and they shall call me Beowulf.'

'You mean, you don't want any wood in it at all,' Carl said, shaking his long locks like this was some kind of picnic – cried the ladies, and swooned inside the fire bunker. 'Just iron, all iron.'

'You heard me, goldilocks,' quipped the ruthless Jute leader. 'Iron on the inside, iron on the outside, like my hard exterior.'

'Like your hard interior,' nodded Carl – nodded Carl's hair. He did not say, 'It's going to be as heavy as a tractor, I hope you realize that.' With one glance at his king and his king's swinging arms you knew the man could lift anything up to and including a house. It was no accident that he was king.

Carl said, 'It will be ready in ten minutes.'

No one was kidding themselves about the valor and physical strength of Beowulf and so nobody was surprised when he refused to take a big army to fight the wide-flying, horrid, flaying terror. They knew Beowulf rarely paid attention to anything he ever did, so great he was, and took meat out of the fire with his bare hands. Heavy calluses covered his body and heart and he did not fear the hour or manner of his own death. They knew the stories, how with his hand grip he had ripped Grendel a new mouth, as though a person could eat through its shoulder, and put an end to his marauding cannibal mother in her own house of spectacle and trophy and purged Heorot of the God-hated race, and made good friends in the process.

Or consider for just one second, they counseled each other from their carefully screened cookfire where they baked potatoes, Beowulf's adventure against the hat wearing Franks, a people who wore their helmets to bed, they chuckled, on the occasion of the tragic death of Highlake king.

'Yeah,' they agreed, 'when Beowulf crossed with his swimming arms holding thirty suits of armor in his hand, and gave them a pretty good taste of their own medicine, which was with blood drinking swords.'

No one said, 'Thirty suits of armor in one hand? That's impossible,' because it happened.

They said, 'Yeah, the hat wearers expected to line up our guys along the riverbank, trembling and naked, and execute them one by one with a battle-axe. Then up rose Beowulf from the winter surf and tossed every man a buckler, belt, sword, and gold-trimmed loincloth, and they butchered the hat people.'

'Hat people, what a stupid name,' they guffawed.

Then McGuire stood and spoke.

He said, 'I do not believe Beowulf took those thirty sets of armor with him across the ocean,' and there was a rippling, explosive silence, as though someone had said the word carnivorous. Fortunately for McGuire, Beowulf was in the latrine, shaking it for all eternity, and heard none of this exchange. McGuire said, 'The song goes *beag*, not *stag*. It was when Beowulf returned from the battle that he carried the armor of the fallen soldiers, both kith and kin. And by swimming hands is meant oars, not literal swimming hands. Beowulf doesn't even know HOW to swim,' said McGuire.

Then Klaeber stood against McGuire in defense of Beowulf and sang.

He said, 'You need to clean your harpholes, McGuire. The scop bard said *stag*, not *beag*. They are two completely different words, ya mother fucker.'

'Oh yeah,' bragged McGuire, stepping up to Klaeber in the smoky interior of all the Jutes had left to call a home, rising to his full five foot two inches and bumping chests with the mighty warrior. 'If it matters so much to you, then why don't you prove it.'

McGuire died a gory death on the end of Klaeber's steely dagger, we all laughed and applauded. McGuire had always been slightly crazy.

For I am told that Beowulf overswam the seal waves and returned to Juteland and the open arms of Hygh, queen and poster girl, a woman with legs that had turned eyes up into their sockets as far away as China and the moon. He returned a lone survivor but having avenged the death of his king and fellows and burnt their bodies as a means of allowing their souls to escape into the clutches of their gods. That is the story he told when he made his remarkable reappearance.

'What happened to the fifty hard men who set out with you in all their fine accouterments from our baubling pueblo and the king whose death would put you into position to inherit a kingdom the size of three – of four Rhode Islands?' nobody inquired, hands upon house swords. 'Did you burn their bodies after shaking the prescribed faggot of twigs and herbs upon the bier and calling upon the agreed-upon gods to take their smoking souls into their ghost bosoms for all eternity, or did you not?'

They said, 'You wrought great vengeance upon the Franks. Fuck the Franks all to hell a thousand times.'

'Now Highlake is dead and I am yours,' crooned the crown queen into Beowulf's blood-splattered earlobes, if in fact he had not been swimming. 'Take me and use me, big man.'

But Beowulf turned down the offer to ride her throne and bounce her babies. He said, 'Your seven-year-old son is now king.'

Why seven years old we do not know, except that most people who survive childhood are seven for about twelve months. There he is at the age of seven, trapped in the poem.

'Look at him,' indicated Beowulf, using the dagger he always picked his teeth with indoors, 'isn't he the cutest?'

Hygd threw a careworn, haggard glance at the fat little piece of shit. Big Red wore a diaper and was picking the wings off a fly. His other hand was inside the diaper. A half-eaten chicken lay before him on a mead bench. Big Hygd sighed, for it seemed like she could never get Big Red to finish a meal. It was ten am, he was seven, and the boy was already on his third pint of mead.

'You have got to be kidding me,' his mother whispered hard, tits bouncing in a combination of lust and fury that had to be sucked and spat, 'this boy is an imbecile and shall never know the secret combination to the rotating lock that guards the Jute hoard, both gold and glory.'

'What is the secret combination,' it did not occur to

Beowulf to quip.

He said, 'This boy shall grow to be a man, and we shall call him Hard Ginger,' and he was right – put a big hand through the boy's shock of carrot top hair. Several years passed, and under the watchful eyes of Beowulf Hard Ginger became a famous swordsman. He learned to kill with style, love with a will to procreate, and rule the hoard of his father Highlake with both passion and the sense of urgency necessary if a man's treasure pile is going to grow, Beowulf smiled.

Yet by the sword Hard Ginger lived and by the sword he died, as his bible indicated he should.

'Ach God it is a death wound,' he cried, looking up from the sword that had transfixed his bowels into the face and eyes of a man he had taken in and given shelter and at his company of ruffian castaways, men who had been in need of help – help he had gladly given. 'How could you do this to me, exile sons of Oht/here, rebels to the crown of old Hrothgar?'

Oht/here took back his sword – turned on his pointy boots and walked back to Sweden, crossed the wide ocean to his home, and in the aftermath Beowulf supported Oht/here's son Eadgils with wigum ond waepnon, both warriors and witherpricking swords.

Why did Beowulf support the man who had murdered his disciple and tyrant pupil? Why did he not swim across the wide wide ocean to Sweden with thirty suits of armor in one hand where the pale king lurked in his ice palace and quell the son of a bitch in the middle of a big banquet, cutting him down in front of a thousand onlookers?

Maybe he was scared, we dared to imagine, or maybe our Beowulf was actually thrall to a foreign king – subject to a dynasty that he knew better than to wrastle with.

'Send them some men, and guns, and they will leave us

alone,' advised the tear-stained exterior of Hygd queen's skeletal face, moving like a shroud through both space and time. The space was a beerhall – the time was high noon. 'Do it, go and make your big nasty dick self useful,' she wept, 'if you ain't gonna get revenge for my boy.'

But Beowulf said, 'Revenge is mine,' calm under a cold eyebrow. He got on a boat, crossed the ocean, and murdered the man who had to die in his ice palace in front of a thousand onlookers.

'It's a death wound,' sobbed fat Eadgils. Or else he laughed, because he loved pain. But more likely he cried. 'Ow it hurts, why did you stick it in my anus,' he screamed.

Beowulf made no reply – ripped the man a new asshole.

These are the battles of Beowulf, and he survived every last one of them except the last one, which is how it usually works. You may survive the first or second clash of swords and fab codpieces or the fortieth or golden fiftieth, but not your last one, the one with your name on it – the one with a fire-breathing dragon in it.

ᛈ

By this time Beowulf had been apprised of the source of the feud and the cause of the enmity and mainspring of the fire-breather's marauding strikes upon a headland that belonged to Beowulf, Beowulf said.

'I know this cup,' Beowulf quoth, holding the baubled goblet between his own two hands for the second time in the same week – for the first time in his astonished life. He looked up at the barrow thief without sympathy for a cheese-eating rat in a look that said, 'You robbed this cup from the treasure mound of a living dragon, a creature that had no bone to pick with us and had been asleep for three hundred years? Are you stupid or are you crazy?'

The criminal was not sure how to respond, so he shrugged his shoulders, a gesture that was not only frowned upon in those circles but under the arching confines of Beowulf's palace (still smoldering, yet intact in the minds and miens of all present in this birchbow, extempore teepee) carried a penalty of death by pulled between horses.

The informer never said, 'I was being chased by dogs, O king, because I am a thief and that is what happens to my ilk, we are constantly on the run from slavers and sword-carrying landowners and frequently fall into blind traps and get speared on the end of renegade pikes but we take it like a man because, let's face it, in a feudal slum like this you can run but you can't pay for a crime by doing time or even by promising fealty and working out your debt to society, that is not how it works here, they are just going to torture you and kill you, so what are we supposed to do?'

He didn't say this – he shrugged and was condemned to death.

Beowulf, eyes glittering from deep inside a sad and moribund skull, a face whose heart knew its end was near, licking its lips, said, 'Take me to the treasure. Lead us to the secret entrance of the trove.'

What methods the Jutes employed to force the man to trudge the alabaster, the dolomite, the basalt, the fetid fern of the scorched escarpment I cringe to say – I shudder to imagine. Beowulf's sword was out and swinging – hands heavy and lazy with irritation and pent-up rage and a knowledge that his own fabled end was near.

Led by a traitor who was already dead to this world, eyes as blank as grey slate – eyes of granite, of rock, Beowulf ascended the bluff with fourteen hand-picked thanes, men who had eaten his meat and snorted his wine and sparkled with the big gaud and killing blades and knuckle brass he had departed into their heart-crossed hands, and wish to die he led them.

It was ten in the morning and they were five hundred and four years old all included. Solemnly they passed a goatskin bottle. What was in the bottle we surmise was sweet mead. They did not straggle but walked sensibly in single file and drank, for why walk across a terrain like a bunch of picnickers when in fact what you have come to do is inflict death and agony on your enemy? Go straight at him in good order and get in there and inflict it, no excuses.

Two goatskin wine bottles of mead – let's make it three. They were happy, grim as hyenas, and eager to die young.

'Hlaew under hrusan,' they exclaimed, pounding its shale foot under man killing bootsies and bodies hung with nothing but hand-me-down byrnies that had caused grown horses to groan, stagger, and die. They cried, 'Mound under morning,' for it was nine am and they had drunk their last drop, bold after bacchus.

'It ain't going to be easy or cheap,' they admitted, staring up the stony slopes. 'But we are sword thanes. Most of the year we lie around in drink and brag and gesticulate with slobbery capons, but now is our time to shine. No one but us can take destiny by a dragon and squeeze out gold and live, if we live,' they said.

They said, 'If we live.'

The Jute king stood in his hard armor and surveyed the bluff out of eyes that were a gateway to his hoard soul, to gold he kept tallied and filed away deep inside where the mettle ran red, and he began to be sore amazed and feel very heavy, and was weary. Then there came upon him an x-ray vision of what was going on under the mountain, and it was fairly accurate –

piles and sprawling orgasms of gold and silver in heaps and horns and drumlins, and whet was his wanderlust. Kindled was his killing pulse so that it throbbed in his sword arm and made it stick out harder than any penis.

By the loud crash of breakers on the headland battle-hard Beowulf exhaled a mournful yet excited gulp of salt air and spoke.

ᚠ

Beowulf mathelode and said, 'When I was young I came through a lot of stormy times, and by stormy times I mean rains of sharp projectiles. I remember all of it. I was syfan wintre old when Hrethel took me from my daddy's farm and made me a soldier – thralled me to the treasure giver and wine lord, in a day and age when mine were arm rings and feasts and all good things, hayloft under hallstel.'

Nostalgic tears leapt from the pages of Beowulf's bible, a litany of hambones and fermented beverages – a hardcore prayer book to the cheeks of hard boiled princesses in their mud wrestling attire and cadenced boasts and daggers that bulged under a petticoat.

He said, 'I got lucky, I guess, knock on wood,' he touched someone's schlong, 'to be treated like a son by Hrethel king – me, beorn between barns, when he lost his own sons in a tragic incident.'

'What happened,' we demanded, ears perking up like a dog's, 'was it a boating accident or an explosion in the hothouse, or did they fall down a shaft onto some nasty spikes and garbage, or sit on a bayonet?'

We said, 'Please say they didn't sit on a bayonet.'

Nothing like that, said a wave of Beowulf's massive death

mitten through the grey sky and sea – said the chunk and clink of expensive armor of big men on all sides where they had circled up, where their heavy breath hung.

Beowulf said, 'The prince and firstborn son of Hrethel king, Herebeald named, was smitten by an arrow fired from the bow of his own brother Haethcyn, a boy whose name meant Wedermarksman. Haethcyn missed his shot – speared his own brother through the neck and lower jaw with a shaft the length of a man and the thickness of a fist. I remember every detail. Blood splattered the length of the tree, so hard had it sprayed from Herebeald's body. It dripped like raindrops from the leaves. Many bad thunderstorms could not get it off.'

Someone said, 'You should have hosed it down with your horse like stream. You and your racehorse,' passing the bottle.

Someone else said, 'We are guessing you and Haethcyn ran into the forest, so frightened you were, so unsure what to do in that situation.'

'Haethcyn tried to lay the blame on you, Beowulf, but couldn't get it to stick,' a third person surmised, recalling his own son of a bitch cousins. 'They thought they could frame you, but they were wrong.'

'Some said I did it,' admitted Beowulf with the ghost of a frown. 'Others said I wasn't even there.'

No one muttered, 'Well were you there or weren't you. Tell us, we're your friends.'

Nor did the Jute hero ever protest in that time before he had land and a boat you might as well call goose-necked, 'You can't shoot a pumpkin off the top of your brother's head,' with a deep guffaw, for he was busy in the barn.

Nor did he say, 'I'll bet you can't do it, Haethcyn, ya pussy. I'll bet you a hundred bucks you'll hit him smack dab in the neck and kill him. Betcher chicken, Wedermarksman, just

Weeds to your friends.'

'How can I miss,' boasted Weeds Haethcyn, who had literally not slept the night before, notching a mean javelin to his hornbow with a foot. 'The pumpkin is twice as big as my brother's goofy, bobbly head.'

'Heh heh heh,' chortled the goofy, bobbly head of Herebeald, getting up against the tree and balancing a big pumpkin on top of his fluttery golden locks, gourd over gore jug – heir under hair.

'So Herebeald was the eldest and heir,' we exclaimed. 'It is clear that his brother shot him in the face in order to get him out of the way of his own inauspicious ascent to power. The sleepless, ever-watchful Weeds Haethcyn knew his brother had to go – was deeply suspicious that he himself would make a better king.'

Beowulf looked me up and down where I pranced in my bard pants and scornfully replied.

'What they were doing out there in the field I shall never understand,' he mused, 'but what's done is done. Their father lost two sons that day – one shot through the jugular, the other guilty of a crime that must be avenged no matter how high-born the manslaughterer, or accidental the accident.'

We screamed, 'It demanded a penalty the king father was unable to exact.'

I said, 'If a brother kills a brother is a crime it follows that a father kills a son is a crime, so Weeds' father Hrethel was in a real pickle.'

Beowulf said, 'He was damned if he did prosecute Weeds for the murder of his eldest son, and damned if he did not. Plus he was in shock and grieving hard. It was as bad for Hrethel as it is for a man already well into his fifties who sees his boy have to mount the gallows to pay for a sin and be carrion for the jackdaw – a raven's delight, and have to sit by, helpless to help him despite all his wisdom and experience.'

'You mean,' I began.

'You're talking about,' exclaimed the gem-studded sword thanes from their buckles and straps, straightening from the circle. Vultures wheeled and gobbled overhead. The mountain trembled underfoot.

'That's right, you know the man,' winked the old Jute king, and although we were all picturing a different event, we had the right idea. He said, 'You know how he remembers his son in the morning, brooding upon the boy's passage into the gloomy nethers, a place where you do not want to go. Screaming into dank grey air, fists clenched as tight as they will go, he neglects the hot soups and goblets of summer mead his thanes frantically thrust at his senseless, listless fingers, and the outhouse and tables and floors are a mess.'

We said, 'He takes the boy's image off the wall and caresses the lovely flat neck of parchment. He kisses the etching, and it seems for a moment as though the beorn is back in his arms – alive, laughing, smelling of fresh grass, a dimwit.'

'Picturing the gallows tree, he chokes down his breakfast,' many thanes agreed.

Beowulf said, 'My uncle killed my uncle with his bow and arrow and this sunk their father into a stupor of grief so profound it reminds me of the bottom of the seal road where the muck just belches and heaves – where every movement of the sword is slow and your enemies attempt to shriek but die helpless and mute without the opportunity to plead for mercy – without the satisfaction of that rite of passage.'

I pictured a regular battle, but behind every warrior was a second warrior without any swords or anything whose job it was to restrain the thanes with weapons from moving at a normal speed so that it would look like they were moving neck-deep through nasty slop, and was flabbergasted.

Beowulf said, 'Hrethel was like the father who can not see past the death of his firstborn and pines away – looks no further for an heir to command the barns and be captain of a world of gold. The man refuses to eat or drink – no longer bothers with the latrine. He looks upon the wine silo and sees a wasted life. He sees generations of glorious victories and cunning housefires pissed away with the execution of a single barnyard prank.'

'The old man groans,' we replied, sensing our cue like it was a cue stick in the abdomen. 'He scans the expanse of his blustery fort hill and staggers through the empty stables and guest rooms – stares into the dusty ratshit nursery and into the dead boy's forlorn room where the mark of Herebeald's noggin still blasts the bolster.'

'Now just look at it,' he moans, 'my fine hall and hallstell, in which the riders sleep in a windy bed and the hearth is cold and the cornices crumble. Now it is nothing more than a tomb for the hale and fallen.'

Beowulf said, 'It seemed a lot bigger without any furniture in it. There was no shouting and scrambling in the courtyard or harp music in the halls or pitter-patter of servants' feet. The cages had all been opened – all falcons flown the coop.'

The man's vacant eyes search the corridors, confounded another day in a row in his hope to glimpse one living person in human skin or mottled feathers, or combination of any man or beast with whom to speak. With difficulty he rises and gropes his way to his couch. He croons an old song.

'It's a big bed, wide fields and generous battlestead, this home,' he sings. 'It was better shared,' and he dies in there.

ᛒ

The child Beowulf was taken under the wing of the powerful battle master Jute Hrethel, and was placed in the yards to play with Hrethel's own sons Herebeard and Weeds Haethcyn when they got bored, and they terrorized the countryside for a number of years until the day that Weeds accidentally shot his brother Herebeard through the nose and tympanic membrane with a spear the size and shape of a taut, thawing python, and that firstborn son died.

What was Hrethel supposed to do, exact vengeance on his own son?

Instead of this he threw up his hands, gave up fine wines, women, hunting, and human speech, stopped breathing, and died. His land and hoard went to his second-born son Weeds, who was promptly assaulted on all sides by enemies.

'Who is it?' shouted the terrified, crouching form of Weeds Haethcyn through the burning attic window, addressing a mob of men with drawn swords that ranged below in the slop and fumble of the main courtyard. 'Why are you burning my house down?'

'We are Ongentheow,' replied the Swede, a tall man in dashing pants who rode a rearing charger – who proceeded to clearcut a semi-circular swatch of charred farmhouses and crunchy beer benches and bloodstained byrnies and skirts through a Juteland that would take a hundred thousand years to heal. 'We are Ongentheow,' said their army, shaking both pikes and bucklers.

'I am Weeds Haethcyn son of Hrethel,' exclaimed Weeds in reply from the back of a sturdy mount – for unlike his father, he had not cut out the pastries or sweet wines or rich cheeses.

'I'm not hungry,' his father would groan, 'why did you kill your brother?'

'More for me,' yukked the young Weeds, a boy who wore diapers well into his twenties, reaching for the plate with both hands. 'Are you going to finish your wine, pops?'

For Weeds or, more accurately, his proxy the noble Highlake, had returned to exact vengeance on a land pirate who had taken advantage of Weeds Haethcyn's disreputable youth and the disorder of his sophomoric administration to plunder and pillage him like there was no tomorrow.

Except there was a tomorrow. That was the big problem for Ongentheow.

'I am here to take back what is mine,' screamed Weeds in front of an army of thousands – repeated his proxy and general Highlake in a voice much better suited to war than the king's.

'Yeah,' said the king in a squeaky voice. 'Come down out of your tree fort before we have to burn you out.'

'So you want to marry my sister,' mused Weeds Haethcyn, king, stalking solemnly before his throne, but with hands clutched behind his portly self sometimes slipping from the knuckles because they could ju-ust reach – stealing a glance at his sister and playmate Hygd. 'That would make us, what, brothers?'

'Brothers in law,' replied brave Highlake, not amused to have to wait on this weak little prancy-pants fratricide. 'We would be brothers, but not by blood.'

'Never by blood,' he vowed under his breath.

'What are you muttering?' squeaked the king, but he would never know.

Weeds said, 'Brothers, but not by blood,' turning it on his tongue very slowly, biting a soft pink finger through one half of a pair of lavender satin gloves. His mind did not work extremely quickly, to use a rhetorical device, and he often repeated what people said in order to buy time while he focused. He flexed his ingrown jaw, anus clenching and unclenching somewhere under all that fabric like the mouth of a landed trout.

Turning decisively at the end of one length of his throne dais, Weeds declared to Highlake, 'You can have her. She is yours,' he said, gasped his sister off to one side where she was trussed and waiting.

'Take her to the longboat,' growled Highlake to a thane, for he and his people did not share the scuzzy, strange-smelling apartments of Weeds Haethcyn and his people, or ever spend the night in them. 'You shall not regret your decision, Weeds Haethcyn. I'll expect payment in full before sunup on the third day.'

Weeds giggled inside his clothes and shivered, pleased that this big handsome man knew and used his nickname. It was as though they were already brothers.

'Don't you fret, you big Viking,' cooed Haethcyn, mouth the exact shape of a you know what. 'I'll bring the treasures to you myself, and we can map out our raid on the Swedish land pirates over a nice dinner,' he called, because Highlake was already out the door.

When they landed on the shores of Swedish pant boots Ongentheow with their mighty fleet of heavy-armed goliaths, whose wives and buttermilk girls had refused them sex for thirty days and thirty nights to get them good and fighting mad, Weeds preferred to stay on the beach and set up a base camp near a source of good water and let Highlake go on ahead.

'I'll catch you up,' lied Weeds Haethcyn to high Highlake. Weeds was directing the placement of mirrors and couches and sultry furnishings inside the broad, tall, plank-floored tents. Outside a fine drizzle plastered the manes of the waiting horsemen, accoutred and straining for blood and war and the cozy insides of unwilling teenage Swedish girls – of Swedish boys.

'You can't stay here,' protested the strider Highlake, feet planted so far apart you could see craters on the moon between his legs. 'If anything happens to me or our main force you are a sitting duck out here. They are going to wheel a hundred and ten degrees west, trample right down the beach, and hit you in the mouth like a bag of dicks.'

'First it's ducks, then it's dicks,' scoffed Weeds, sticking a big pink finger into – wait for it – a perfumed ear and turning it clockwise, then counter-clockwise. 'I'll be there, you'll see.'

Highlake galloped off with the main army, leaving the king to prance and pirouette along the torchlit water and debauch his body in every imaginable combination of garters and stockings. Meanwhile Highlake hit the unwary Swedish countryside and its scattered, weakly garrisoned outposts with a swiftness that literally stunned the pants off them. He sent them reeling headlong in flight into their main redoubt, fifty miles inland, the doors of which the natives got closed just as the first heavy sex-angry Jute fists started pounding on the wood.

Meanwhile the main Swedish force, having struck west from the snow castle with the intention of dismantling the boats and main dump of the intruders, wheeled a hundred and ten degrees west through forests they knew better than their mothers, marched straight down the beach under the comfort of a three-quarter-full moon, and hit the cavorting Weeds Haethcyn and his soft boys in the mouth with what felt like a bag of dicks.

'My mouth,' cried Weeds, sinking to his knees and eating a face of sand – dying beneath the stroking sword of high-panted Ongentheow, who sniffed and looked around the love tabernacle and was probably the first person in history to hear rock and roll.

'Let's get out of here,' he growled, and made like a tree.

ᛈ

In the morning, after sacking the great citadel of the inland pirate and Swede the dread Ongentheow, and receiving word from a fleeing bareass of the unremarkable death of Weeds Haethcyn, the ring proud warrior Highlake retraced his march of the previous week and fell upon the slovenly Swedes where they lay debauched in the clotted blood and smoldering remains of tide-drunk visiting boats and their dead keepers, and massacred them to a man.

Two days previous:

'Oh my God, tell me how he died, tell me what he said, was he in much, much pain?' Highlake did not whimper, upon being presented inside the ransacked snow fort with the shivering Jute survivor and learning of the death of what amounts to a brother.

He said, 'You, asshole, how did you come so far – and by far I mean how did you run fifty Geat miles over hill and dale through the snow without any shoes on, without ever thinking to clutch a single biblical leaf to your privates?' demanded the man who was now in charge.

'Weeds' final words were-' began the poor messenger.

'Tell me,' interrupted Highlake in a tone whose firmness is legendary, tangible, and historic, 'and try to concentrate for one second. Tell me straight, what activity there was in the camp of Ongentheow at the time of your precipitous departure.'

'There was a revel in the tents,' wept the messenger, one hand creeping in front of a pair of sadly frostbitten balls and a cock that was a sure goner. 'A great party, a party you could write a n-'

'They were raping your friends,' Highlake interrupted, never one to get into unnecessary details with a girlfriend or sword thane. He hollered to the hall in general, 'Get my charger and put the shiny saddle on her. We're going to surprise them in a state of celebrity,' he allowed himself an unwonted chuckle to say – was serious again one split second later.

He said, 'They think they know me.'

The sounds of horses being strapped with gold and iron stirrups rang through the clear air of the despoiled mountain redoubt.

He said, 'They don't know me.'

In a rambling mood, Beowulf spoke.

He said, 'Then I heard our kinsman and ring-giver and high thane Highlake surprised the Swedes when he came upon them where they had Haethcyn's men pinned down in the forest off the beach – king Haethcyn's purple body still warm in its boots, boats upturned in the surf and flitting flames.'

We said, 'Ongentheow's men rose from their cots and beers, as was their wont, and fought hard, but doughty boar helm Eofor cornered the Swedish king in the morning and they scrapped it out in the gasping sand.'

Beowulf said, 'Then the Boar, as we called him, cleaved the old king's helmet. It slipped and banged off his face. The furrow in his skull was visible from a furlong away. I was far out at sea, swimming hard, yet I saw it. Eofor cut down the king – the battle bled him. With an arm that knew its business and did not hesitate in the thick of the fray – muscle memory cut him down,' we murmured.

The terrible Swede had fallen, noticed his thanes, and in the aftermath both victory and loot was in the hands of the Geat storytellers.

Beowulf thought of gold and said, 'I repaid Highlake's gifts – always went in the first row in battle and stood by his side. My killing is compulsive. You have seen my collection of brain-purpled, empty helmets and breastplates, and truth be told I will probably always have to be the first in a battle line as long as this longsuffering sword does not shatter against something really hard, like something from another world – not forged by man, scalelike,' he damned himself.

Knock on wood, we all should have said, but we were silent – stood in awe.

Beowulf said, 'Later I killed the man who killed my ring-giver – Dayraven in his fluttery black garments. He was unable to take much enjoyment of the plundered chest metal of high Hyglac after I ended his days,' chuckled the big white mustache upon the doughty lips of the trusty beer thane, upon that famous bluff, 'not with the bite of the sword, as you might imagine, but with my wrestling hands.'

'No,' we did not aver, 'yes.'

We said, 'Tell us how you did it with your wrestling hands.'

Beowulf said, 'I squeezed Dayraven's night riding bonehouse – throttled his torso so that his heart bleated and farted and shut down. Then I ripped off his arms.'

'You did not literally rip off his arms,' no one deadpanned, spraying sweet mead from a mouth that would never utter blasphemy. Nor did anyone say, 'So it wasn't just Grendel and his she wolf that you quelled and quashed in their own chosen mode of combat, and the sea worms you cleared from whale roads and misty inlets, you bad boy, you didn't stop there – you have been fighting and shredding armors from shrimplike thanes for the past fifty years of this life, and still have the body of a forty-year-old,' we said – we thought in our secret hearts.

We said, 'Murmur, murmur,' for it was clear to everyone in that middle yard that Beowulf was capable of tearing a human being to pieces with his hands. Mothers were careful not to pass him their babies when he was distracted, and to greet him with a shaken hand was the nearest thing to an automatic car wash we had.

Beowulf said, 'Then the murderer's heart's blood spewed onto the waiting ground out of his new pair of assholes, and victory was mine.'

ᛈ

For the last time Beowulf spoke. Turning to each in turn he greeted his men – one by one, his hard helmhumpers.

Looking again up the mountain, Beowulf said, 'Now with hand and hard sword shall I fight for possession of the hoard. If the manscather rises from his burrow I shall win glory, which is why all of you have to stay back and let me fight. The fight and the glory belong to me,' he said, we all cried.

We wanted to go with the big hero – we feared to do it.

Beowulf said, 'Nor would I use a sword, but rather fight like I did with Grendel, in a loincloth – with nothing but my reaching hands and heavy, straining thighs.'

'Your hands are your weapons,' we admitted.

We sighed and said, 'But the drake has such little hands. It would be difficult for any man to come to grips with a dragon in the usual way.'

Beowulf assented.

He said, 'If I could think of any other way to come at the foe, I would leave my sword and codpiece in the bunker and venture against him as nature intended – butt cheeks straining, knuckles cracking, nothing fancy. Yet it is not for him to join combat otherwise than under the whelm and spleen of a hurricane of flapping and flame, as we well know.'

We said, 'The flapping and fire with which he has already flattened many of our largest houses.'

The valiant company gazed down the hill at the incinerated village, choking back grief and anger.

Beowulf boasted, 'There is only one reason I am still fully dressed, having both board and byrnie. But you shall see I won't retreat a single step from the old wall. God in his wyrd wisdom shall decide the outcome.'

We assented – we yeasaid.

Beowulf said, 'You gentlemen stay here below the bluff with your war shirts on, awaiting the upshot. I and I alone can take this fight to the dragon and win the gold, hot gold, booty gold, good gold, or else fall in the encroaching flames and die a terrible death.'

There was silence as everyone together pictured his fall in the encroaching fires and terrible death.

Beowulf stretched his neck and said, 'Or else the fight shall take your old friend with the application of a terrible wound, and by terrible wound I mean third-degree burns over more than ninety percent of his body.'

There was silence as our minds struggled with the idea of death and the life hereafter.

Beowulf broke the silence. He said, 'I mean fourth, fifth degree burns over more than ninety-nine point five per cent of my body. I am talking about human barbecue, where there's nothing left but a pile of blackened ribs and goo.'

'Like in a bad house fire,' we marveled, picturing Hrethel's first cousin – picturing Eofor's first cousins and mom and most of his bickering aunts.

Beowulf smiled sadly at the word house fire.

'Like a house fire inside a house fire,' he snorted –
scorning all fate. He turned to face the open grave.

We said, 'Cheers!' – stayed well back below the bluff, with
our best breast covers cinched tight.

He went up then, hard under helm, buckler over boot –
mounted the bluff to the crag open crypt. He went alone – not
like a chicken. He was near the top before the heat hit him. It
hit him full in the lips and eyes and scorched him dab in the
bare nipples where they kissed his hard-forged war shirt on
the inside.

Breasting the rise in his metal war sark and not much else,
Beowulf saw the blasted grass and wilted hibiscus by the tomb
mouth gnash – felt the wistful reminiscence of battles past. The
wall at the top trembled with the passage of heavy air below.

'What is that wall?' wondered his sword thanes, squinting
up the hill. Is it the face of the grave entrance, or the outer face
of one of its pillars? Is it a wall made by the original master of
the hoard, who used his mind to command slaves, or the very
wall of the mountain? Or is what we are talking about a wall
of climbing fire that would consume their ring giver and wine
friend like a son of a wench?

Beowulf, a man who had survived hundreds of battles,
looked directly into the shimmering heat of the stone archway
– made up his mind to plunge in.

'Guffaw,' spurted rippling fiery tongues of liquid nitrogen
from the entrance – shot out like a spider on fire from a
malevolent furnace – flowed in a river along the crest of the
mountain. Far below we watched in dismay – cowered deeper
into our armor and bard tights, trimmed with balls and bells.

'Gush, whoosh,' spewed the flames from the precipice, tossing and sputtering smoke. Beowulf's thanes lost sight of the form of the brave hero. Where was he? they cried, retreating behind rocks – falling back into the treeline and hiding their faces.

Then the voice of the Weder Geat roared – Beowulf's battle shout boomed like thunder weather from a blue sky. It echoed into the cavern and rebounded into the salty air.

'Out, vile manscather,' screamed Beowulf, chafing at the injustice of the fact that it was too hot in the hole for him to charge directly down it and confront the beast on his own terms, as he would have done had it been underwater. He must wait, he realized, and to wait was something he could not abide.

Beowulf's voice resounded in the barrow – sang bravely under the grey stone.

Under the wall it shook and tumbled, the angry speech of man, both stichic and strophic. Like a robber the itchy, scratchy syllables got on top of the trove warden's gold and skipped and skittered and pounced, awaking old memories and buried hatred. It was too late to beg for peace now. Smoke boiled from the catacomb door – Beowulf smiled a grim smile – raised the knobs of his shield to meet the oncoming foe.

They flashed in the light of day.

'There he is!' some tomfool cried from far below. It was me, nothing visible of the poet but one eye, so well was I camouflaged down there, so forest green in my tights. 'He's alive!'

Then the hero's thanes saw something flash at the summit. It was Beowulf's sword, drawn in a hand that gleamed like an icicle – like a piece of lightning – like the white billy goat on the opposite ridge that faces you across a chasm.

We all fell further back down the hill and took cover anywhere we could from that goat – from that ice saber and the clash of titans about to shake the mountain. Two titans, I sang, though clearly one much larger than the other, that we feared would soon blowtorch the hillside with human barbecue and scattered implements of war.

Beowulf swung his great iron shield into the attack. The drake, sorely offended by the light dashed into his eye of green and gold from the boss and spit of the battle orb, rose from its squatter's cave. It recognized the shield as a shield and the man to be a man and suspected a cunning advance in technology – yet damned all torpedoes. It rose on its coiled backside and charged into open space, oozing the snot blood of war and scruff of generations of gelatinous knights like a hornless snail on all the rocks and soil where it passed.

'He is blinding it with his marvelous shield,' crooned a God-damned asshole.

Another asshole sang, 'Now the hero draweth forth the flashing ember from its sheath, and raiseth its sharp sword edges,' as though we did not have eyes – as though Beowulf did not already have the hand-me-down brandished ten feet in front of his man-sized – not to say coffin-sized – form, as though any coffin would be needed on that day in his life.

In that second both of the ones who intended to fight the other to the death hesitated – both man and serpent felt horror of the other, and an awful chunky flood of stomach acid flooded the backs of their throats, as it was ever since the incident in Eden.

In the flash of what must have been measurable time – a coin, a coy look, a bead of perspiration – the serpent coiled and launched its sturdy but remarkably taut form at the good Geat. He flew at the boy behind a bossy shield, biorn under barrow, and struck him.

Beowulf stood firm in the rock hollow in his shirt as the dragon lunged against the man's tractor-sized, Aeneus bun of a shield, on which were engraved just the words SICVT MORIRE, plus an entire history of Vikings too complex to repeat.

The worm went burning to its destiny, sparkling like a meteor, and the shield lasted longer than Beowulf expected. It lasted longer than the drake thought possible, also, in a world in which for the first time it was not Beowulf's luck to survive in combat or win wyrd glory but to cope through the final drastic minutes and look a losing battle in the death pig eye and go down in a fen with an arm wrenched off, crying for his mother, as we all must.

If pigs could fly and Beowulf could have chosen the moment of his own death, his iron clipper would have protected him for more than two and a half seconds in that fight, and pigs would hunt men.

You choose.

A great shower of sparks and pieces of iron shield rained down on the position of the Jute hero's sword thanes and friends where they crouched below the mouth of the rock where the giants fought where the ocean spray sang. High above, in plain sight of all the townspeople's corpses, Beowulf raised his hand but could not grapple with the fen and fairyland monster with his bare knuckles, so he struck the drake with his giant sword.

Did Beowulf not try? We watched with horrified expressions as the great green-gold coils of the ancient sea thing rose above the mountain. Beowulf could not be seen because he was under the mountain somewhere. Had he got into the burrow and been rummaging through the wonders of a thousand years of piracy and black avarice, the sneaky rinck, nimble of foot for a man of his size? Had he found a new sword, a sword with which the trove's own keeper could be quelled?

Our eyes and mouths narrowed and bloated and drooled.

'He is grappling with the croc and platewing smoke demon,' cried a Jute fool. 'He has her and is swinging her!'

But he was wrong, unless he was talking about Naegling, Beowulf's sword, a weapon he had taken off the corpse of a man he had recently slain, a brand that shouted 'I am going to naegl you' every time you plunged it pommel-deep into the torso of a man whose day it was to meet his fate, eat an iron breakfast, and die. Beowulf liked his sword. Now he swung her as hard as she had ever been swung into bone, except this bone was on the outside – the skin and flesh and organs pumping beneath remained intact and in that order.

'Krung,' shuddered the blade, shattering into a thousand pieces. Beowulf looked at the broken hilt in his hand in disbelief – groped at the wall behind him and for the first time in his life considered taking one step back.

The drake, infuriated because it was no stranger to thieves and their intentions, rose on its limber coils, beak gaping and bubbling with translucent napalm. Thunderclouds had gathered – far below we saw a great light through the hastening mists, and were sore afraid.

ᚠ

Naked as a person with no clothes on, Naegling failed Beowulf, as it should never have done. Almost impossible to believe and even more difficult to say, the hero gave ground – sallied back from the grundwong grey rock, and tumbled onto the ridge at the top.

I recalled the events of the previous evening as I turned on my pointy heels and fled – tumbled, scissored, sprawled, scrambled, raced down the hill into the smoldering remains of a dark age Jute village.

'Even if all these should fall away and abandon thee,' I had sworn to my liege and ring lord, drunk as I was and desperate for a ring friend, 'I shall never leave thee.'

'You shall all abandon me,' Beowulf swore through his gnarly stained off-white beard, glaring around the cookfire at the friends and thanes he had bought with gold and cunning murder, 'before the cock crows three times.'

As I ran I heard the cock crow – recalled the challenge – did not give a damn. I ran for my life, and everyone else ran with me.

Reaching the village, we found some substantial cover and returned our gazes to the bluff – observed the wings and back of the horrid worm pulsing and beating against the sky, like it was fucking a hole up there. Its great neck rose and throbbed one time – a great stream of fire hit a patch of the mountain about the size of a man, we cried – we wept.

'Where is Wiglaf?' called out one of our numbers suddenly. 'There are but ten of us cowards. Where is the eleventh, the shock top son of Walstein, the little guy?'

'Where are you, little guy?' we called in utter horror, picturing him up on that mountain – alone, trembling, afraid for his life, about to die.

'We have to go back for him,' declared one of the bravest cowards, tossing his best cape over his shoulder like it was a big bunch of parsley. 'We have to find him, wherever he may be. We can't just let him die up there on that mountain.'

Yet I disagreed.

I said, 'You're wrong, ya bastard Jute. I mean, go if you really feel like you have to go, to salve your conscience or whatever you have left to call your dignity, but my opinion is that the Walstein boy can take care of himself. He has two legs for walking and two arms for punching and he volunteered for this mission just like you and me.'

The other man opened his mouth to reply, but our conversation was interrupted by the crumbling, rippling, jolting occasion of the dragon taking flight. We had to batten down the hatches.

'Whoosh, whoosh, whoosh,' went its great wings, flattening trees in a radius of a hundred meters, where a meter is like two cubits.

Meanwhile Wiglaf, son of Walstein had scorned to run with the others – stood tall on the hill as we cowered, then looked hard into our backs and discarded shields and lucky pants as we fled from the embattled bluff. Above him the dragon rose into the sky and roared across the waters where the surf crashed with its little fists. It soared the rocky beach, summoning all fury. On the peak a lone man stood – a man who had been a king and a champion now staggered under the remains of his smut-stained armor.

'This man has literally made me rich with his gifts of gold and land and lush haciendas,' screamed Wiglaf through clenched teeth, despising the skin and thudding guts of his craven comrades. 'I can't abandon him now, in his hour of trial and defeat, after having sworn to stand by his side in good times and bad – after eating his barbecues,' we winced, in our secret hearts not approving his Jute humor, smirked Wiglaf, 'and drinking his fine wines and fucking his sisters,' we did not gasp – did not shudder, did not splutter.

Wiglaf, son of Walstein's, hand shot out – gripped the slender lindenwood where it lay in the scree. He got it and rose, bone under buckler, and charged up the bluff.

The dragon circled and crashed back onto the mountaintop. It stood – inhaled – exhaled. It spat in furious indignation, searing the side of the peak with suffocating, petroleum-based vapors.

Wiglaf son of Walstein mounted the mountain – drew his hand-me-down, the birthright of Eanmund son of Ohtere, a man Wiglaf's father Walstein had quelled in blood and robbed of his mail shirt, brunfagne helm, boots, and an ent sword that looked like it had recently fallen from the stunned clutches of a Goliath of modern times.

'It is not quick, clean work to have to kill a nephew, the son of your brother,' were the only words Wiglaf's father Walstein ever uttered on the subject of having killed his brother's son and stripped that boy of his armor. He did not speak of the feud – it was unspoken of.

'Hey dad, why did you-' taffytop Wiglaf once blurted out around the council fire.

'Smack,' went the hand of his mother or uncle or some guy who was always there looking out after the little guy.

'Thou shalt not speak of it,' hissed a bible from the lips of a clutter of unholy men.

Unholy men we may be, they grunted over their lambchops and beer, but men with a roof over our head and food to eat at the end of a day, they chuckled. Their glittering eyes shifted in the half dark to see who looked at them or breathed their air. Their murdering thoughts dwelled with deep satisfaction on the newly wrested byrnie and greaves and twisted hilt that lay blood-splattered and winking in the corner of their murder shanty. It was theirs and they would keep it, they swore, and the day would come when they would teach their sons to fight with them and their sons would raise the son of a bitch above their heads and bring the gun down with a mighty stroke to sever arteries of men history would later claim could not have been killed with landslides.

'When you are old enough, boy,' grimaced the already fifty-something Walstein from a throne he himself had made, gripping the arms of shy, skinny, eight-year-old Wiglaf in his preposterous meathooks, 'you shall take the giantkiller and all the stacked armor you see that rests behind my royal chair that I use as currency, yea even the pretty ones you yearn to stroke that I tell you you can't you have to wait, Wiggy, your day will come to stroke them, and it shall be yours, young carrot-top.'

'Can I have just one byrnie now, to play with and run around in?' begged the little son of a goblin, bitching and moaning.

'No,' shouted his father, thrusting the boy roughly to the dirt floor of the hut where he lived and commanded. 'Your day shall come, my son, mark my words in a bible that is your brain and yours to mark and scribble in, but you must wait. Today is not that day.'

And he was right, for once. That day would come, eight or ten years later on a bluff the size of a mountain versus a dragon the size of a dragon. It would be his first and greatest battle, perhaps his last.

Looking down, Wiglaf would stroke his iron nipple, raise his ginger freckles into the kicking dust, and follow his lord into the fateful fray.

Wiglaf charged up the hill at a gallop on his gangly, mismatched legs.

ᚠ

Wiglaf spoke to the chicken-livered sword thanes who had precipitously fled the battlefield and his big sad heart cried inside him like a bleating goat.

He said, 'I remember the promises we spoke in the spacious and luxurious confines of the beer silo under the influence of alcohol and stunningly perfumed women and their thumping orifices,' he exclaimed in real anger. 'I recall you took the king's arm bands and hand-me-downs and love and said you would be there for him in his hour of need, and stand with him, and fall with him. You swore. He gave us rings and you promised him loyalty, and now you run like men of the bog. I see some of you even crawl like bog men,' he sobbed – he laughed, through bitter tears.

'You are young, Wiglaf, you haven't seen a man's brains splattered across the broad side of a wine-yellow shield yet,' no one was there to answer. We had all vamoosed.

Wiglaf mathelode.

He said, 'Beowulf handpicked us for this mission because we were the best. We glitter harder, sing louder, and speak braver boasts than any thanes he has ever seen in his life. We impressed him with our bully swagger, he gave us rings, we pledged our allegiance to his cause with helms and hard swords, and now you run.'

No one said, 'Well, Beowulf said he was going up there by himself to take care of the job alone. He said he didn't need any help,' because we were long gone.

Wiglaf said, 'Heaven bless him, he tried to do it all by himself,' wept the little ginger. He cried, 'But what would you be if you didn't help the man who helped to make you what you are today? How could you go home to the smoldering remains of your father and mother – and mothers and boast that you had done your best, snapped on your war shirt and pig helm and charged straight into the glory behind your mandryhting folk shepherd, if you had not?'

No one replied.

He said, 'Come on, ya tomfools, scop bards in swirly pants. Rise up and join me. Join the fight while the fight's still hot,' and by hot he meant 1,165 degrees Fahrenheit.

Girding his loins and cinching up his fat white nipples through a shirt that was for generations to be famous for the mysterious blackened pits like stained double raisins tangled in its hand woven net, he cried, 'This is the day our lord mentioned when he said in my hour of need you shall help me.'

For Beowulf had said, 'Take this gold and booty as a payment plan for your future assistance against grimm gledegesa.'

Instead of saying, 'What is grimm gledegesa, prophet father,' the aethling crowd seethed and sighed, reaching with their grubby, cummy fingers for the gold rings their lord was distributing, and 'greed.

They had said, 'Anything, anything great ring giver, give me give me.'

Wiglaf scorned the memory inside his conscious soul.

He said, 'It's not right to return to our hamlets and houses without having first quelled the demon that flies by night – not good, when here we have him finally outside of his cave in broad day.'

'We can't do it, our swords will shatter against his steely breastplate,' no one protested, casting a panicked glance over their shoulder at the doughty knight Wiglaf in his pants of iron, who neither cringed nor cowered.

We were long, long gone.

Wiglaf said, 'For the things he has done Beowulf does not deserve to be abandoned by his own people in a battle whose issue is in the balance.'

Turning his face to the twilit sky and hovering foe, he said, 'Sword and helm, byrnie and battle shroud we shall share, king Beowulf,' slamming home his helmet with a hand that was about to become extremely famous, and glittering.

The firedrake never knew where the second man came from. When he alighted and encountered not one foe, but two, and the second in accouterments you could not have tailored to look more suited to the boy's noble thighs and his slashing, picturesque forearms and boots, he almost swallowed his own flamethrowing tongue.

'I am coming, Beowulf, hold on,' Wiglaf did not scream. Without a word – with a determined glint in his codpiece he mounted the steps to the dragon's lair – waded through the smoke and flotsam to the side of his staggering ring friend.

'Beloved Beowulf,' I cried, reaching the top and glaring into the rind of blackness in which the concentrated object of my hatred must now be lurking, I suspected. I spoke for Wiglaf. I said, 'There there, old thing, up on your feet now,' and helped the giantkiller onto his noble legs. He had been cawing and weeping into the blackened earth. I said, 'Jesus Christ, look at you, Beowulf. Weeping and bawling like a little baby. Do babies go to war, Beowulf?' I chuckled, and gave what can only be described as a shrug. 'Do they go to war and then cry?' I wondered out loud, prancing in my frilly panties underneath all my gear, as only I would ever know. 'Do they go to war and lose and then cry about it?'

The great king rose with my help, shaking. He shook his grey locks – finally focused his eyes on my metal helm. I slapped him hard – hard across the mouth twice.

Wiglaf said, 'Beowulf, king, stand and meet the hostile foe – bend your mind to the task at hand, dragon killing. I am with you now and together we shall overpower the fiend and free the middle yard of this curse.'

Beowulf did not say, 'Is that you, ginger lad?' He knew all hope was lost. With the words the firedrake charged from the billowing thunderstorm – blossomed out of darkness in an ecstatic chundering plume of fire and molten chunks of Roman coin.

'Cover up,' cried the young carrot top, shielding big Beowulf with an arm of shirt mail and one lindenwood bolster about the size of a cauldron lid.

Improbably they took the discharge of flame and advanced, first under the cover of the blasted remains of the king's shield, then behind the standard wooden shield of the brazen youth. The drake belched fire to itself, reared on its coils, and tried to bite the heroes in their faces and necks. Yet too nimble were they, with their parries and hard knuckles, and the fiend could find no flesh in which to sink his furious fangs – fangs you could have hung a tire swing from.

Behind one of these shocking encounters around the shields the battle king got his second wind – channeled for a moment the strength and daring of his younger self, a self that had slain sea eels in the raging streams of underwater rivers and (why not) pounding lava.

Raising the sword Naegling in one hand, he drove it with all the fury of a tornado against a tree into the very noggin of the serpent, between the eyes.

The head retreated into the smoke – the sword went with it.

The blade lay in shards upon the scorched terrain of the blufftop, but the point was impaled in the dragon's full-grown skull.

'He has killed it,' many onlookers concluded, snapping their fingers, but they were dead wrong.

ᚹ

Beowulf was always breaking swords – daggers – skull

mugs – platters of mutton and veal, and ripping his pants bending over or sitting down. So strong were his thighs and hands that he frequently woke up after an orgy to find himself the only one left alive.

Beowulf used to have a kitten – then he had a dead kitten.

So it should come as no surprise that when the great Jute king lifted the brand Naegling and drove it into the face of the dragon the force of the blow was so crude and rippling that the ancient weapon shuddered, shrugged, and shattered into a thousand pieces. Only the tip lodged in the skull of the monster remained intact, a head that you can bet money and horses, was precipitously withdrawn.

The dragon withdrew – the crippled hero staggered forward with the support of the sandy-haired youth, still intent on becoming master of the gold under the hill.

Beowulf and Wiglaf went right at the beast, one shield in front. A third time the firedrake reared and roared and uncoiled, striking with its searching fangs, and this time Wiglaf was splattered with blood, for the monster's snapping jaw had closed on Beowulf's neck. It clamped down on the part between the nape and the brain, above the metal collar but below the helm, and clung there, its imbecile eye inches from Wiglaf's tender bricktop brow.

You or I might have been startled and screamed, dropped our shield and sword and skedaddled, but the noble ginger took everything in stride, as was his destiny – strode past the face of his enemy and thrust his ent sword deep into the chink between the dragon's plates where you could see its organs swill and push – and killed it.

Ignoring the big throbbing eye, Wiglaf did not waste a thought about the hand that gripped the sword that he had drawn and was about to plunge into sloshing, scalding prehistoric guts. The hand, scorched almost beyond recognition in the act, would be an object of comment and stupefaction for the next fifty years, every time Wiglaf produced it from its sash, as he would at birthdays and weddings when he recounted blow-by-blow the action of the fight against the dragon that once ruled the hill.

'Tell us the one about the dragon,' the children would cry.

'The dragon that once ruled the hill?' Wiglaf would chuckle, hand around some meat platter slut.

'No, the other dragon, stupid,' the children would shriek with laughter.

Wiglaf went down on the drake – thrust his epic liverspurner deep between the heaving plates where they gaped open above the shocking penis. He sank it in to the hilt, though it cost him an arm. Hot lava shot onto Wiglaf's sword hand and boots, but the fire spluttered in the jaws of the monster. The fangs relaxed on the neck of the king, and released him.

Leaping to his feet, Beowulf drew a battle dagger from his boot and with one motion cut the serpent in two – dealt the fiend his death blow. That is how you kill a dragon, with verve and panache and a friend who arrives at just the right time to back you up.

It was Beowulf's final act of glory – but he was singed nearly beyond recognition.

ᚢ

The roxy youth lay the badly burned hero onto the bluff at its snub peak. Far below we strained our eyes and hearts to see.

'He'll live,' someone predicted, meaning the eponymous hero of our story, Beowulf, but that asshole was wrong.

'Your neck and head wound is purple and bloated from

the poisonous fangs of the biting worm,' Wiglaf did not comment as he lay the king down, bracing the big Jute in his arms – weeping, spitting.

Laying the considerable form against a comfortable rock, he said nothing – went to investigate the deep tomb, to touch the gold and quell any other worms he could find from a warren he intended to keep and have.

'This is no work of human hands,' Wiglaf marveled, passing his steely glove across the massive stone pillars and rammed-in hand-chiseled grates – gazing upon a trove that spilled like gravel from a mighty ceiling onto his charry boots at the bottom where he stood in his pants and male underwear.

In the middle was a high throne. Wiglaf strode to it – touched it – turned and sat on it.

He gazed out across the expanse of the eorthreced barrow barn. There was no sound but the wind outside the face of the great wall – the creak of the boy's harness as his neck moved now left, now right. He observed the great columns that held up the mountain. He looked upon the flying stair with its steps three Roman paces high – saw how they commanded the width of the hall at its foot. He observed the upright stones that flanked the hall that served as columns, and watched for smoke or movement down the file, good hand upon his atrocious pommel.

There was no movement – no smoke. Wiglaf lifted one leg and farted hard, as was his right. Reluctantly he lifted one leg, then the next – rose and returned to his ring lord.

ᚱ

Blinking in the bright light of day, Wiglaf knelt by the gold giver's crumpled form and pulled off his helm.

Removing the attack helmet from the scorched, chopped

face of his king with a delicate motion, hopefully Wiglaf did not have to hear the folded skin of the man's scalp or ears snap or locks of hair rip from the inside of that valiant accoutrement. He laved the scorched features of the hero with water he produced from a cool mountain rivulet.

For his part Beowulf felt no pain. His eyes focused on the vultures – on the clouds. The rain had gone away. The loss of his ears would never be commented on in the centuries following his heroic last stand. For a lesser man it would have been impossible to speak under those circumstances, from blasted lips welded together like pieces of putty, but Beowulf mathelode through his open wounds, knowing his days as a human were over.

He said, 'You have been like a son to me, stripling redhead. If I had had children of my own they would have inherited my armor and boot knife. Let it be you instead. I have been king of a state eight times the size of New York City for fifty winters and part of one summer. No one fucked with me because I was the most dangerous person anyone had ever met, yet I never abused my power, never terrorized the weak or went back on an oath sworn over mead. Though my body is dying, my mind is filled with memories of my mothers and father and the descent into the witch cave of which you have heard me speak, and above all my glittering possessions. I believe God shall take me into his sky in glory and Abraham receive me into his bosom.'

'What in the name of Christ would you do in Abraham's bosom,' no one exclaimed, picturing things better off not pictured. They hummed and prayed to a god that received men's souls in the form of smoke, which is why it lived in the sky, because smoke travels upwards.

Beowulf said, 'Go down under the grey stone, boy, and root around in the worm hoard, rufous little Wiglaf. Run your blonde fingers through the coins – pick out a nice chalice for yourself. Make sure there aren't any little dragons snorting and smoking amidst the rubble down there. No mother dragons,' Beowulf half killed himself laughing, remembering Grendel and the aftermath. Again we shake our head at his attempt at humor. Beowulf said, 'Bring some of it back up here so I can gaze upon it before I die, both gold and jewels the size of grapefruits – of muskmelons. Go, run, stout boychild. You know what you have to do.'

Rising from the seared and smitten form of his king and hero, spry Wiglaf sprang across the fallen burning corpse of the dragon in his net of rings shirt and glistening pants. He dropped through the stony spans that marked the entrance of a grave the size of ten beer silos, and went below – down, far down the stairs, under the roof of the bluff.

Halting in the doorway of the great hall, eyes reflecting both the gems and glitin gold, he saw dagger hilts that looked back out of empty eyes. The wide floor was utterly strewn with treasure, we realized, tongue flicking from our reptilian mouth. The boy stared and ogled, and not in vain. The light that originated in the trove flashed and rippled off the walls. It shone upon the boy's gawking features and his future, in which he had his good hand around the tight waist of someone else's high falutin daughter.

Wiglaf did not stammer any fool words whatsoever – he was born for this day.

Nor was it just another pile of looted denarii, mind you. There were tapestries hung from the walls, of grim faces in old battles, vials containing mysterious liquids, goblets standing as though abandoned in the middle of a party, cups upright upon fine teakwood dining room sideboards, and mummified princesses and piles of tables of pitchers and meadcups, all those that were not crushed into fine powders by the furious roaming coils of their last guardian.

Wiglaf gazed upon the fine powders and potshards and death and saw that everything was buried in dust and just thrown around in a jumble and apparently covered in a saliva that had lacquered over the centuries.

He picked out a big chalice for himself, wrapped a pile of truly good-looking gold coins and variegated sapphires in a hankie, stuffed them down his expensive shirt – the one that protested with big hard nipples, and went back to greet his lord and wine friend.

Looking back into the hole we saw dead faces from the inside of rusty helmets, arm rings fastened to crunchy humeri, human rib cages pinned to the walls by cruel stakes, spiders slipping through cobwebs that swung and reached.

We saw a veritable working parable against the temptation to put gold above staying alive.

'It's curst, this lot,' Wiglaf – spray of red – did not whimper.

He told himself, 'Sinc eaðe mæg – gold on grunde – gumcynnes gehwone oferhigian, hyde se ðe wylle.'

On his way out he looked up and saw it – the homespun source of light, a great eallgylden standard a hundred yards across. It swung above the vaulted doorway of the horde – darling of the drake of the hundred years. It dripped of, what is this stuff, honey? wondered Wiglaf, charred fingers remaining where they were, by his impossibly strong thigh.

There were no more monsters down there, confirmed the shaggy dragon slayer, looking left, then right. Wiglaf and Beowulf have killed the last remaining specie of the hate race, smirked the kid – freckles going everywhere.

Wiglaf checked and confirmed that the dragon was not in the lair. Its massive corpse smoldered outside the entrance in plain sight of the town and God, but the boy had to be certain. He went down the big steps into the mound – peered into the deep corners of the grave. He looked behind pillars and climbed to the very top of the heap, and he did it with his sword out.

'There are no dragons down here,' he did not growl. He did not want to make new dragons with a heedless barking mouth. He knew there were no monsters. It was just his bully pride that demanded he poke around in the dead criminal's mundbora house – chase the shadows, and cleanse his worried mind.

Wiglaf stood before the great stone sarcophagus and paid his respects. Like Saxo and Klaeber and so many others before him he marveled at the size of the lid – wondered how the giant who made this tomb had survived the flood – if he had been buried in his richest garments, with his most costly ten wheelbarrows of treasure.

The spring chicken pried at the lid of the sarcophagus, but the lid could not be budged.

Wiglaf gave up – turned to go, went.

Wiglaf strode into the sunshine and knelt at the king's side. He revived the old man with a splash of water he produced from a pocket and an armload of gold he shoved under the liege's dancing eyes. The eyes followed the gold – lit upon the golden fabric. For around his shoulders Wiglaf bore the great standard, as well, the plundered light and glory of the trove that he had dropped from its poles high up on the wall.

Far below we saw the flash of the flag on the mound and our hearts cowered inside our puny chests. We thought we recognized the slough and sick fallow glitter of a dragon's back, and cried out.

'He has a mother,' wailed one nincompoop.

Plundered then was the sly work of giants. It was the work of several hours in the day of one man's life. The bill that had already cut down the bane barnfire nightflyer, its edge was of iron. Wiglaf hurried with his arms full of beautiful objects, wondering in his hard chest if his lord had already succumbed to his awful wound, or if he would return to find the famous friend still kicking.

He hoped beyond hope, bearing gifts in his hand – he panted and prayed.

Emerging from the barrow – stepping straight out of the mountain, the hard ginger laid eyes on the charred and bloody form of his king. Beowulf's mighty chest moved – one blackened finger twitched and was still.

With water Wiglaf revived the ailing warrior – with water and the sight of gold he did it. Beowulf's eyes snapped open. They glittered as he gazed upon the blondie and the treasures in his hands. He looked with insatiable eyes and mathelode aloud. They say his pupils changed color. I have heard that this is because the old dragon possessed the king's body for a second, then released him. They say the king's eyes went taffy yellow. They say Beowulf blinked and overcame the ghost of the goblet master. They say the drake entered Beowulf in the demon smoke that trailed from the wreck of the great body and attempted to take control of his arms and legs and thoughts and cunning tongue. They say that he would have been better off to try to enter Wiglaf, who still retained his major motor functions and would soon be a walking, talking, policymaking ring-giver.

They say many things. Some are true, others unconfirmed.

The man's old wordhoard – the breasthoard broke like an inevitable sphincter, like a mouth with the tip of a word, and there was no stopping it. Tip first, a sword emerged from Beowulf's lips, we thought, and daggers and stones would be soon to follow.

Beowulf spoke across the gaping, wheezing wound in his chest. Battle sad, he let his eyes rest upon the plundered gold.

He said, 'For the trappings and ornaments of gold I give thanks to the sky king. With words I say it, glory be that I was able to win this mad hoard of gold for my people before the quelling day took me. I bought it with my old life and bony body.'

Looking deep into Wiglaf's soul, Wiglaf later claimed, Beowulf declared, 'Take care of my people, young ginger, brave graverobber. I can no longer tarry here.'

'That means,' Wiglaf later explained to a crowd that included his own mother, 'coming from a man with no male descendents who is king and about to pass away, and by pass away I mean die, whose life I had saved,' he boasted, 'that I am now king.'

'Hail noble Wiglaf,' we cried, going down on one knee – reverencing and hullabalooing.

Beowulf mathelode and said, 'Take the hempen tiller of this proud Jute nation and her fields, stripling blond, lands that would easily cover more than half the state of Vermont, and drive her like a son of a bitch.'

The figure was not lost on Wiglaf – he knew all about hempen tillers, and driven sons of bitches.

Beowulf said, 'Command the shield thanes to raise a great barrow upon the bluff at her brine-blasted tip, a mound and lighthouse to tower after you torch me, that shall serve as a reminder to my people of her greatest hero.'

Beowulf said, 'Off the whale point, young rutabaga, and the seafarers shall call it Beowulf's Barrow, they that pound and drive the flood from far away places in their blunt and snippety little barks,' Wiglaf exclaimed, charred remains of his crimson cape fluttering in the headland breeze.

'Burn me with this crazy treasure by the seaside upon a great monument of earth and stone,' Beowulf commanded, closing his eyes upon that picture, 'þæt hit sæliðend syððan hatan, Biowulfes biorh ða the brentingas, ofer floda genipu feorran drifað.'

Then, removing the golden collar from his neck, the mark of his mandate and symbol of his accrued power, Beowulf gave it to Wiglaf. Unstrapping his byrnie and atrocious codpiece with trembling mundum, he told the boy to take his armor, it was his now, and use it well.

'Take and enjoy the use of my arms, blond lad, for you are the last of our kin, the only remaining heir of the Waegmundings,' said Beowulf, Wiglaf did not start in surprise to hear. He smiled grimly – took the neck ring in hands that knew no other answer – fastened it around his big, pulsing neck. It fit.

Beowulf said, 'Wyrd fate has taken all my family into the bosom of God's death, them in their strength of days – and I must follow.'

He said, 'Ealle wyrd forsweop, mine magas to metodsceafte, eorlas on elne – ic him æfter sceal,' and died, nose thinner than a crochet needle.

'Ic him æfter sceal were his parting words,' confirmed Wiglaf, stony face and shoulders already godlike in silhouette against the falling night.

Of all the things Beowulf could have said, he said that, we worshiped.

'Ic him æfter sceal,' we sang.

Beowulf spoke, seeking the hot and keening pyre, soul choosing to bare itself of its great body and seek judgment beyond the whelming fires of this battleground.

Tears sprang into our eyes – leapt and gurgled and splashed out of them, streamed and crackled down our faces through the crud, we knew. The king was dead and soon we would burn him under stacks of gold upon a barrow no one could ever mistake for another man's inferno, and we were not bragging.

ᚠ

It was difficult then for Wiglaf, alone on the hoard house ridge, to stand between the battered smoldering remains of king and earth drake and look upon the horrible ring hoarder – gaze into the ruined smoldering corpse of a worm driven down to dust by the hacked-up, battle-dinged product of a smithy's anvil. But he did. He stood tall over the scene of wreckage with his iron edges in triumph – in his famous byrnie and ring-bound helm and royal neck ring and pants that no one could fault. No more would the far-flyer burst through the night and rain showers of drizzling, crackling napalm into babies' cribs, for his cadaver was the handiwork of the battle savvy, as the battle savvy knew.

Wiglaf flashed a weary grin that creaked and cracked, or it was his battle shirt that made the sound, for the blond boy's face would never again move with emotion.

'Ahem,' I cleared my throat and spoke.

I have heard of few men who have slain dragons, I declared. Even those ringmail heroes who are successful in everything else often fail to kill a fire breathing serpent – to charge through the black space with raised shield, shove into the frying heat and grapple with the fiend. Even fewer ever get the opportunity to plunge their goblin hands into the dragon gold and stir up the fire king's silo with either hondum or mundum – not if they come face to face with a woken, walking worm.

'We have to admit it,' we said, 'it was a damn good thing we kept our distance well downslope.'

But would it be worth it? we wondered, cowering behind rocks and blasted trees. Beowulf paid for the liberation of this trove with his life, nor do I know if I have ever heard of a firedrake who would not fight for his stash to the bitter end. This dragon under the Jute mountain, for example, did not call for a truce when Beowulf called him out of his hole with unmistakable intention.

'Nay, never,' replied Klaeber, grim under bard garb.

Up there in plain sight young Wiglaf strode the mountain. We remarked him on the peak with his sword at rest, and we crept from our ditches in the thick wood. We took our tall spears and began to pick our way back up the hill to the top, although we stalled outside the grotto. It was like we were outside a chapel, anxious to get some religion, but some young new widow had not quite finished in there yet.

We put creepy eyes to chinks in the weathered planks – picturing her in our own armor, slapping us hard across the weathered hips, and lips, and iron nipples.

At the top the hard ginger fought like a widow with his emotions – with the happy greed to be king and rich for life, and with the welling grief to have lost both wine friend and king.

'You alive in there, slender blondie?' no one called out to the boy. We were filled with shame, standing in our bright armor and juggler's pants, bearing linden shields and dangerous boot knives and regret and disrepute. Wiglaf had bent down and was trying to resuscitate the dead king with water from a jug – from a mountain brook.

'You're okay, you're okay,' he crooned, patting Beowulf's

cold dead cheeks with frantic hands.

'Hold on,' we cried out, seeing the coast was clear – no double-dealing Franks, Frisians, or galloping Swedes on the horizon. 'We're coming, young ginger. We're coming!'

When we came upon the roxy youth, Wiglaf was slumped and reposed by the shoulders of his lord. We screamed – recoiled with almighty horror from the great body of the drake, with its translucent wings folded crooked under its heavy fallen trunk and one pterodactyl claw dragged eight meters through the dirt in the middle of the sacred grotto.

We looked at Beowulf and saw a dead man, face composed but as stiff and cold as it was going to get before we lit it on fire. We looked at Wiglaf and began to speak, but stuttered, sure the words would come – they did not.

Looking up, Wiglaf saw us and reached for his sword. Then his arm relaxed – in a gesture of scorn that caused us to take a step back and reach for a tree.

'Too bad,' he spat, struggling to his feet to speak, the doughty youth. Getting to his feet the carrot-top said, 'Too bad the king made such a bad mistake when he gave you the armor and treasure you took, in which you stand and fidget now,' he shouted. 'When you rode his mead benches on your complacent fat cheeks and took his gold and reached out with your grabby hands for his gifts and brass knuckles. They are only the finest weapons in the entire world that he gave you. From the king's best trunks, and look how you've gone and repaid him.'

We grimaced to countenance Beowulf's crumpled form. Our lips moved, but no sound came out. It was awkward, a word with two double U's.

Wiglaf said, 'All the beer. All the accouterments.'

In our minds we pictured the sweet autumn mead and the

accoutrement. With sheepish looks we appraised our coward friends. We looked good.

Wiglaf said, 'It was all wasted on you. You took everything with you when you ran. You were supposed to take the war gear into the fight, not into the forest.'

We came up with no reply to this. We knew the woods he meant.

He said, 'Of course our lord was capable of fending for himself, just one man and his sword, alone when what he really needed was studs at his side with expensive weapons in their hands, but it was not the proudest day for your lord and liege. It was nothing to write home about,' Wiglaf laughed – scorn in a mouth full of teeth, we mentioned in adoring tones.

He said, 'It was nothing to weave into a tapestry or bang out on a sharp, hefty hand-me-down.'

The dragon smoked like a hot peat roof – smoke puffed from the dead king's armor and blew straight into our superstitious eyes. We moved to the left – the smoke followed us. We ducked to the right – it came back at us and filled our mouths.

Wiglaf shouted, 'I could do almost nothing to help the king, though I tried. The most I could do was slow the worm down for him – strike it once with my sword, which caused the fire to splutter for one second in his face and snake brain. It turns out that that was enough for your king.'

'Who killed this dragon?' we did not demand, being in no position to demand – being beggars, not choosers.

Wiglaf said, 'When I stuck my big sword in, at the moment in which I lost the hand you probably do not now recognize, that gave the king a moment to get his bearings, he rose up in his smoldering mail shirt, and he slaughtered the slithering grundwyrm with his dagger. With his boot knife he did it,' swore Wiglaf, motioning to the fallen king.

We followed the movement of his hand, as we followed any moving object. We looked at the dead worm, eyes and throats stinging with the smoke and reproach – saw that the king lay motionless. We found it impossible to believe that Beowulf had killed that thing with his little letter opener, and did not remember how Wiglaf's hand had looked before.

Someone said, 'He was born a hunchback and cripple like Richard the Third,' but that was years – centuries later.

Wiglaf said, 'Our lord slew a dragon with the help of one loyal thane. Now imagine if all of us had been there to help him. We'd have made quick work of it, wouldn't we have?'

We all nodded like disreputable toddlers – clutched our penises and moaned.

Wiglaf barked, 'If we had surrounded him, hacking at him on all sides all together, our king would probably be alive right now, would he not?'

We shrugged and gripped bark, the doughty ginger towering over us, somehow.

'Yes,' we chorused eagerly. 'Yea, he would uv.'

Wiglaf said, 'But you ran away.'

No one denied it because Wiglaf was right, even though it was the first time we had ever heard him speak. Gleaming from a golden collar we were suddenly able to identify – with a wrenching feeling in our bowels and crestfallen chests, Wiglaf said, 'Your days as sword thanes are over.'

He didn't gloat or boast, pronouncing our doom.

He said, 'You know that from this day you and all your kin are cut off from ring dealing and treasure giving and access to the high benches and the right to own land. When people find out what you did – what you failed to do, that you'll be outcasts, wanderers, you and your dirty kith and wives and the filthy generation that spawned you.'

Wiglaf stood exhausted in hot armor in a grove of cherry blossoms. We exchanged glances and in the glances were silent questions: Could we murder this taffy-haired sprig and make it look like an accident? We could take credit for coming to Beowulf's aid and slaying a dragon, something that is extremely difficult to do, an act of true strength and valor.

Our red rat eyes narrowed in the thinning smoke – noses twitched, hands moved to our blue scabbards.

At that moment, looking down the bluff, we saw that the townspeople had emerged from the rubble and a clutter of warriors had gathered at the bottom of the hill.

'Wiglaf has slain the dragon!' rose their cry. 'The deserter scum have emerged from the trees!'

Wiglaf turned to us where we shivered in our battle garters and said, 'You'd be better off dead, you flouncy butter cakes. Better for any man to die in battle, gagging on his own blood for the worst thirty – worst sixty seconds of his life, than to live as a wanderer – as an orphan, a son of Cain.'

Up galloped a spear thane from the village – surveyed the smoke and damage.

'Go quickly,' Wiglaf told the horseman. 'Spread the word of this day's work in battle.'

The redhead stepped back to guard the armor and remains of the eponymous hero and the tons of portable gold that rested – that breathed several flights down a nearby hatch. We looked as he sat in mourning above the fallen king as the cowards and gawkers slipped into the underbrush – talked about it, but gave it up as impossible against a man as cunning and strong as young Wiglaf, king eager of the Jutes.

Then Wiglaf told the rider to fly – report the outcome of the morning fight and call down into the secret cave where the townspeople were crouched in fear and uncertainty, a lot of them carrying shields but sad about the fate of their king. Would Beowulf come back to them, staggering under an atrocious armload of arms rings which he would distribute at a big feast, for here was much burnt swine and kindling for a bonfire, and there would be much mead and the swead melody of the scop bard that would weave new exploits to old bars, or would their king fall and die on this last day of his life, and the dragon rule the skies for all time?

'He fell and died,' reported the horseman, tearing at a shirt that refused to rip, 'on this the last day of his life. Now hath the lord of the Jutes, the hope of the Weders sunk in the sleep of slaughter, the worm's doing. It was next to impossible for Beowulf to wound the creature with one single upraised sword.'

'We are all doomed,' moaned the people, but they were wrong.

'You are wrong,' retorted the proud messenger, 'for the drake no more rules the skies. Beside the body of the king crouches Wiglaf son of Walstein,' we thought we heard him say, 'a carrot-top who champions the person and armor of the fallen liege and lord and gloats upon the chastised form of the far-flyer, that he hath quelled.'

He said, 'The dragon is dead, and Beowulf ring-giver is dead, and as you know what remains is to scrap it out for our very lives against the surrounding tribes, people lord Beowulf has spent the last fifty years subjugating and humiliating, especially the Franks and Frisians and Swedes,' declared the man – both messenger and prophet on this occasion. 'When they find out that Beowulf has fallen the Swedes are going to drive at us like we have been messing with their women.'

Sheepish looks were exchanged between a number of men who had been messing with the women of the Franks, Frisians, and Swedes. Looking into each other's bloodshot eyes they remembered the fight against the Hetware instigated under Highlake, when that great marauder got a fleet of heroes up the river onto Frisian sand but was promptly overwhelmed by a strong column of allied Franks and Frisians who launched their attack from the trees, riding hard. The king fell among those land troops and his forces were utterly routed, although Beowulf fought a valiant rearguard action with thirty sets of armor clenched between his wine stained teeth.

Together let us picture his swimming hands and be glad.

'After that, things were not very friendly between the Jutes and the continental tribes,' we surmised.

'Truer words were never spoken,' replied the messenger from his high horse.

He said, 'You can say that again.'

I opened my mouth to say it again – was interrupted.

'The thing is, I do not expect any diplomacy or trucemaking from the Swedes,' the messenger shouted. 'We all know how Ongentheow cut Haethcyn down at Ravenswood – how with a slight of hand he quelled the brine-sly king and raped his wife and chased the survivors into the trees.'

'With his host he surrounded the sword-weary,' we agreed, 'and pursued the hacked, bruised, and thoroughly discouraged Jutes into the forest they call Ravenswood.'

It was called Ravenswood because it was full of ravens, we winked.

We said, 'The wood was full of ravens because it was completely littered with exposed human corpses. They exposed the corpses there on purpose, so that the ravens would come on for the carrion.'

We said, 'They charged – we retreated. We retreated into the trunk of a great round tree in the center of the witching grove where Ongentheow besieged us for the length of the night, threatening to sacrifice us in a cruel manner on the gallow tree in the morning.'

'When we get our hands on you,' screamed Ongentheow from his battle horse, picking his nose with a dagger that could cut ice and effortlessly shave a forearm, 'we gonna put you on a cross and cut you open. We gonna expose you for the birds to peck at and pick at to pieces,' he said ten times fast in Swedish, with a cutting blade wedged deep up one nostril, galloping on a horse.

'Yet at dawn Highlake's horn rang through the grottos of the forest,' replied the messenger, eyes filling with love as he looked deep into our swinging thighs and bells, 'and they recognized it to be Highlake by his yelling manner of entering a fray, and king Highlake cut through the allied host and freed the soldiers from the beleaguered oak.'

We said, 'All that you say is the almighty truth. We like the look of your mouth when it speaks of glorious deeds. It looks good. We could almost kiss you.'

'Stay where you are, foot soldier, now is not the time,' replied the proud envoy with a satisfied chuckle. 'Lo, stout Ongentheow saw the writing on the wall – knew Highlake and his seamen were capable of carrying off bearn ond bryde, both women and children, and he skedaddled into the hills before the Jutes had time to regroup.'

'You are correct,' we sang, strumming our catguts in full gusto. 'The assassin turned tail and made a desperate thrust with his army in the direction of his Swedish ice castle, but was cut down on the way.'

'Made to stay,' resumed our mounted idling angel, 'the blonden haired king. Wulf came upon him first, sword upraised, and was promptly struck in the face with Ongentheow's slashing broadsword. It glanced off the helmet, but blood poured from that Jute's raunchy scalp under the hair.'

'So you don't want to fight hand-to-hand like a man,' bellowed the incredibly tough and good-looking Wulf, a son to a man named Wonwred, for it was clear as Ongentheow turned to face Wulf with his sword in his hand that he didn't want to wrestle.

We said, 'Ongentheow drew his sword, advanced, and cleaved Wulf's face through his mask like a watermelon on a stump, and the Jute had to stagger back and sit down and die.'

The golden hermes assented.

He said, 'But unluckily for Ongentheow, it was two against one, and their swords were flashing like lightning sabers.'

We did not say, 'What is a lightning saber, is that something you just made up? Is it like a sword made out of lightning? It is a figure you use to describe something that looks like lightning when it reflects light in motion? Is it a sword that cracks like thunder and rumbles when it pounds the shields and benches of its enemies?'

We said, 'At the sight of his fallen brother, the blade of the Wonwrethling, Eofor boar helm, swung and chopped through the Swedish king's astonished shield, fist, byrnie, and face, moving like a lawnmower. The body of the man who had killed his brother was torn and fileted by the giant killing sword in the hands of the giant killer Eofor, and no one ever blamed the Jutes for ganging up on the Swede in battle. It was going to take two full-grown men to get to Ongentheow.'

'The folk shepherd Ongentheow bowed down,' said the herald, 'and one soldier plundered the unconscious dying body of another – iron byrnie, hard hilt and helmet he snatched, to boot.'

We said, 'To prove that he had killed the Swedish king, Eofor bore these big accouterments to Highlake, where Highlake was sternly directing the execution of prisoners and arranging for all the women and girls to be distributed amongst his sex-angry sword thanes.'

We said, 'Yes, you are correct. Highlake took the treasure in his hands and promised to make Eofor rich when they got home, and he made good on his promise.'

The herald said, 'You are right. Returned to Juteland, Highlake presented Wulf and Eofor and the corpse heir wife and kids of Wulf an ofermaththum of rich booty, both interlocking gold rings and a hundred thousand units of land.'

'Essentially ten Rhode Islands,' explained the crier, 'although the exact quantity and acreage of treasure and land doesn't matter, for it was title and gold earned in battle, to which no man could ever raise an objection.'

The courier said, screwing up his mouth with the dignified satisfaction of a man who was about to drop a bomb into a dam from a hot air balloon and eat fish, 'Highlake also gave Eofor boar helm his only child, a daughter, as homewarmer and wife.'

'Yes,' I agreed. 'So all of that is the enmity to which you refer.'

'This is the kind of feud and enmity that I am talking about when I mention the Franks, Frisians, and Swedes,' our messenger declared, speaking from a mouth that glittered with false teeth. This man carried his bank in his gums, and slept with a dagger under his pillow, we knew, and was sometimes difficult to look at in broad daylight, he smiled. He said, 'In short, the Swedes are going to attack us when they learn our king has died – to seek our hoard and hoardhall.'

No one said, 'Don't call it a whorehall.'

'That is why time is of the essence,' we gawked. 'That is why we must burn the king's body, and burn it now.'

'That and because it is going to be pretty ripe before morning,' said our interlocutor, a locutor, 'carrion after conflagration.'

'Carcass after combat.'

'Cadaver after copulation.'

'Cranium after caterwaul.'

'King after killing,' cried the big talker. He said, 'Haste is best, that we deliver the ring giver to his pyre, and drape him not only with a single portion of his treasure but also with the gold of the hoard from under the grey stone, yea the untold coins bought with the king's own grim life the fire shall graze upon and devour.'

We said, 'The blaze shall pounce on the cursed trove. Let no man snap those arm rings on his burly biceps or shock top virgin adorn her delectable cleavage with a neck ring or a nipple ring from the worm loot.'

'Sad at heart and without showy baubles pinned to our bodies shall we trudge to the funeral,' cried the crier, 'now that our battle king has laid aside laughter, merrymaking and dreamy joy. From this moment forward be spear gripped in cold morning mundum – raised in handum, nor shall the harp be beaten like a kind of dinner bell, but rather let the voice of the black raven announce his intention to eat to the eagle, mounted on the cloven chest and open neck of a battle dead soldier.'

'Yet he won't get the opportunity to eat our king,' we declared, grim and sure, 'for we are going to burn him all up.'

'Burn him all up,' sang the herald – sang the crowd.

'Release his soul to the gods where they crouch in the clouds, into their billowy bosoms, into their bosoms and beaks, praise be to Jesus,' and his word for Jesus was Sky.

Thus did the soldier bear us the bad news, nor did he varnish the truth. The host arose – climbed out of their fire bunker – clambered miserable and chilly under the bluff, weeping and screaming, to see the remarkable mess left of the fight in the grotto.

Lacking a sawol life soul, the ring giver lay on the bald face of the sandy moraine, we saw. We looked and confirmed that he had died a death that not many would ever repeat, grilled like a shrimp inside his own armor by the pluming heat of a creature few would ever have the good luck to look at close up and live.

We had that good luck, we congratulated ourselves – but cautiously, with low voices, like a conspiracy.

First we inspected the dragon. We had no choice – it was impossible not to look at it if you strode the bluff path that day in this life. The thing stretched across the ground like a mighty beached whale – humped and motionless above the corpse of our fallen leader. It was thirty feet long. It was at least fifty feet long from tail to teeth, we swore, and it took three men with their arms outstretched to measure the circumference of its belly – five men, we guffawed – ten, twelve men.

'Should we bury it?' someone said as we stood in awe above the butchered fireworm.

'It is smoking,' we replied. 'Everyone knows that dragons melt down in their own heat when they are punctured. They are like banked coals when they lie like that, covering their own gnarly furnace. It is only a matter of time now before the dastard fiend bursts into flames and starts to burn down.'

'Yeah, stupid, dragons cremate themselves, everyone knows that,' someone else shouted. We exchanged glances of true affection and high fives.

The courier said, 'Do not worry about the dragon, slender youth. This night flyer has flown his last lyftwynne sortie upon the yards of middle earth – already enjoyed an end to its eorthscræfy gold silo where it coiled to launch itself against the pueblo.'

He said, 'He lies dead upon the crest of the ridge – upon the hump of the bluff he inhabited. He has strutted his last crocodile pace beneath the bowels of the mother upon which we men pace and pray.'

Spilling from the mouth of the grave stood cups and pitchers, golden disks and hand-me-down swords, rusty and eaten through as though they had lain in the earth's bowels for a hundred – for a thousand winters. It was gold of men of times past and bore a curse that kept the hoard from the hand of any mortal.

'I got in there and saw it. It has a magic light of its own so that the entire cavern is full of glittering light, and of course I knew I shouldn't have but I couldn't help myself, I reached out and tried to run my hands through some of it. It was fabulous and glittering, everything that flashed was in that hole. I couldn't help myself. I had to,' ribbited the mortal.

'So that is why you have frogs now instead of hands,' we chuckled wryly. We knew it had to be something like that, for in olden days men buried their treasure in the ground and protected it with powerful incantations, so that no mere mortal could reach his picking fingers into the old hoards, unless the god himself gave him leave to open them. Those robbers would die of heart attacks and instantaneous poxes or come out with ravens where their hands and penises used to be.

'So that is why you have a gerbil now instead of a penis,' we mused drily, running a hand through our shock of blonde moustache. 'Why did you stick your penis into the cursed gold hoard?' we shouted, saying cursed with two syllables.

'I don't know,' wept the unfortunate thief. 'What am I going to tell Hilda?'

But Hilda was a virgin, what was she going to know?

'Hilda won't know the difference,' we shrugged. 'It's the gerbil you should worry about.'

The gerbil looked up at us with big, frightened eyes.

'Everything will be fine, little buddy,' we reassured him, petting and smacking him a little until he relaxed and drooped into a restless slumber. 'You rest now,' we told him, knowing how much hard work lay ahead of him.

Our bright eyes returned to the spill of ill-gotten gold and it was clear to us as we gazed upon it that the jealousy of its warden had all been in vain. The firedrake had destroyed our king – vanquished one man out of all the men in the world, and what a man! For that he had felt the vengeance of Wiglaf, wræc under weall, wrecking ball with a sword under a seawall top the fell wrecker erroneously had counted on to shelter him from his doom.

We tore our eyes and minds from the stretching, mounded corpse of the drake and surveyed the panorama of the flattened mountain top. It is always a mystery when a man is going to die, but the mystery had been solved for Beowulf on that day when he shouted into the cave with the intention of calling a fire-spitting snake out to battle on the slopes of his town. For the lords of yore who sunk the gold hall in that whale cape goddamned the man who set foot in its corridors forever and to hell. Nor did our bulky hero find out how or why he was going to die until the very flames and barrow curse enveloped him.

'Damned be the man who lays a finger on our smutty diamonds,' the lords had screamed, sacrificing an unblemished virgin on a flat rock with a quick thrust, 'and cursed to wander as an outcast the yards between the barns, confined to idol-fanes of demons that bear the face of goblins, and when he dies let him suffer for three days and three nights, and when he goes down under the shades may the hell manacles hold him with their fiery bands until the day of final judgment.'

Yet we protested, 'Beowulf had not even laid eyes on the treasure that bore the curse. How can you say he will go down under the shades and be tangled in red-hot shackles for all eternity because of the words of one angry druid?'

'He never meant to touch the gold,' someone cried, in anguish. 'Our king only meant to quell the plague!'

Wiglaf raised his shining locks to us where we struggled with panic and superstitious pandemonium and mathelode.

He said, 'To wander the middle earth is the fate of many men, and so be it for us if we be cursed for what our king has attempted. We tried to stop him, but he would go and meet his wyrd destiny and greet the gold ward, not content to let the freak worm retire to his caverns and remain there until the end of time.'

The end of time – we pictured this. Many eyes flitted nervously to the great sundial where it was mounted by the gallows tree, and blinked.

'Yet our lief king burst open the hoard,' cried the redhead. 'Grimly he gained it.'

Wiglaf said, 'If there is a curse it is on me,' we gasped, stepping back as from an infectious kiss. The youth declared, 'I went into the barrow and gazed upon it all, the rich furnishings of the silo, after we had taken care of business on top here, at a price that was not sweet in a place where prices have different flavors.'

We said, 'The price you mean is the life of a king.'

'The price was the life of a sweet prince, and his loss bitter,' exclaimed Wiglaf – a man who had everything to gain from Beowulf's death, and yet mourned the fact with a bleating heart.

He said, 'As quick as I could I grabbed a great armload of treasure from the hoard and brought it up to my king, damning my soul to hell, though you see my hands are still hands and my codpiece bears the future within its grand contours. That is the treasure I brought him,' Wiglaf son of Walstein said, indicating the spill of goblets and gold rings by the boot of the dead king. 'He was still wise to me and conscious and said many things – emptied his considerable word hoard into my capacious ear and memory for all time.'

We murmured and sobbed where we stood and kicked. 'That was a king,' many moaned, recalling his turn of phrase – the timbre of his war voice – the way he ripped apart a chicken.

'What did he say?' we cried. 'Tell us, for the sweet love of Sky.'

Wiglaf said, 'He greeted you all, each and every one, old and alone and in terrible grief, and ordered you to erect a barrow the size of a barn on the hill where we are going to burn him, a monument to the memory of his work in these yards, and that it be a tall, glittery one.'

Wiglaf's voice fell – killer's eye cast on the mouth of the dark grave.

His voice said, 'Follow me now, under the mountain if you dare, and you shall behold with your own eyes the wonder under the wall, the heaps of rings and broad gold. I shall lead you.'

'Who, me?' I said, looking left – looking right.

I did not say, 'But I don't want to spend the rest of my days a wanderer, die a hundred deaths to make my peace, and then be God-damned for all eternity to hell just for the pleasure of looking at a pile of ancient buried treasure.'

Wiglaf said, 'And we aren't just looking. We're going to despoil the trove of the spawn of a far-flying bitch who did for our king. We're going to take every last ring he's got, and we're going to do it with smiles on our faces.'

Wiglaf smiled. His mouth twitched, and then he smiled.

We tried, too, and just managed.

Tossing our shields into a reputable pile, and standing our spears together, we girded our loins – followed the torchbearer down the gargoyle steps into the old lair, throwing caution and most of our clothing to the wind.

Seven chosen men went under the evil roof – entered an enemy house. They went behind Wiglaf, son of Walstein. The carrot-top said, 'By the time we come out bearing gold and treasures and everything good that sparkles and twinkles and glitters, I want you to have the bier ready for the Divine Service.'

People looked in shock – through both smoke and debris.

He said, 'When we emerge from the belly of the enemy house we are going to raise the body, carry it out to the whale promontory, and lay it on the pyre.'

Nobody said, 'Then we're going to torch the sucker,' because they were Jutes, not bastards.

Wiglaf gave the orders, turning in what was left of his pants.

He said, 'Prepare the pyre wood, faring far afield to get it, princes of folk as ye are, for the good man. The fire shall consume him, though it starts out as a single flame, and shall take the captain of fighters, a man who frequently endured the iron showers of arrows and heaving javelins and clanging gangplanking broadswords.'

He said, 'Even when the bolts got in between the bucklers and went straight for the bullseye, and by bullseye I mean crotches and open armpits, featherbound and fus after arrowhead, he was always strong.'

They went directly into the mountain after Wiglaf and did not have to draw straws to determine who would go first. They were all eager to get their hands in among the precious plates and stones and rummage through the goodies in a free-for-all like you can't even imagine. They did not regret the fact that it was going to be easy as picking up sticks.

Free of remorse or fear of ancient spells, they gutted the cave of its ancient treasure. If they felt queasy at the prospect of their hands turning into puffer fish or any guilt at all they never showed it. They filled the tunnels and deep chambers with laughter and grunts of deep approval, and their sexes were stunning in the torchlight.

It grew darker and darker down there until the only light was from the lonely torch in the hands of the hilderinc. The light from the hoard and grand pianos steadily diminished until you had to squint and feel your way along the walls.

'Is that everything?' Wiglaf demanded, sword hand akimbo – bow hand a kinked bow. 'Bring me every last penny. Leave him nothing. Pillage without mercy,' he said, and didn't have to ask twice. They left him nothing – showed the fuming dead drake no mercy as they stripped the walls and floors, levered open trunks, shoveled gunny sacks and haversacks and bibs and pockets full of coins and goblets and harpsichords.

Gold-greedy eyes feasted on the plates and piles of the mathmas loot that they dumped into the grotto.

When the last sestertius had clinked and fallen into the light of day, Wiglaf directed the clan's attention to the worm.

'It's stopped smoking,' they exclaimed. Placing timorous hands on the gigantic scales they said, 'He's cold.'

'I am afraid to say it,' Wiglaf lied, not afraid in the least, 'but this loathsome corpse is not going to bury itself.'

After a hesitation of just three seconds, the Jutes put their shoulders to the great dead serpent, rolled the great worm to the edge of the sea wall, and pushed it off.

'Holy shit, look at it tumble,' they exclaimed as the drake's body paused, then lurched and slipped off the high cliff. Giving a long half cartwheel through the mist and blasting waves it landed with a crack on the rocks below. The rinc warriors and alliterating, four-beat poets watched as the tide lifted the hoard shepherd and warped its body off a continent – green-gold coils under grey wash of water.

And that was that.

ᚠ

After looting his castle and playland, committing it to a dark pitcher than a seaworm's maw, they tumbled the firedrake from the edge of the cliff and watched it fall. It fell heavy and dead into the sea and sank through the surf and washed away. It was now food for the fishes, we remarked, its great cranium home for the fishes and plaything for those that walked upon the floor of the ocean.

For who can walk upon the floor of the ocean, and not stride through the causeways of bones formed from the carcasses of many such great creatures, syllicran wiht?

There was a dray in that place, a vehicle we used to call a wain or farm cart. It was extremely tall and large and had great wheels, for it would carry the gold, and gold is very heavy. So heavy was the gold they placed in the dray that it took countless animals to draw it. Maybe fifteen, maybe more, who can say? It went fully loaded.

Fully loaded the wagon lumbered toward the hrones naesse bluff that loomed like a landmark by the sea. On top they lay the body of the aethling Beowulf, ashy from battle – grey from loss of blood and multiple scorchings and from being dead.

A great procession conveyed the cart to the headland where the whales were accustomed to spout and cavort, and there they raised the great pyre out of firewood, stacks of blood-hardened shields, boar helms and bright byrnies, according to the king's final instructions. They lay the prince in the midst of a collection of armor that had cost many arms and legs, laughed the Jutes, recounting the fallen heroes who had relinquished each piece. We frowned at the tasteless Jute humor, so foreign to our own sensibilities – pursed our farmwife lips – but said nothing. The air was full of weeping and praise.

'Light it,' commanded strong Wiglaf, tears and snot carving cuneiform corpses through the soot around his eyes and snub nose, and there on the brine-blasted brow on the bluff where the boats came and bobbed the battle-bent built a great fire, the greatest you ever saw. Woodsmoke stood out from the treasure-decked pyre. The crackle of twigs and roar of the flames and howl of keening toddlers could be heard for miles around.

Then Beowulf caught fire – his bonehouse broke from the hot heart and burst into a towering sheet of flame.

'Good God,' we screamed, falling back onto our considerable backsides, for the plume rose fifty feet into the air, scattering ducks and faint retainers. It was visible for five miles out to sea – for five leagues as the gannet flies, and despair rose in the hearts of all onlookers. We realized our own grief, our lord's final ruin, our mondryhtnes cwealm.

A Jute woman brayed a dirge for Beowulf, her hair in a bun. But she talked mostly about herself, how she feared the days to come, the brain eating sword frays and clash and clatter of hosts and her humiliation and death in the inside of a slutbarn where its chains came out of the walls.

Her torture and final death, she sang, torture and final death.

Meanwhile the sky ate Beowulf's smoke – heaven swallowed him whole. The pyre burned until nothing was left but a twisted mess of iron shield studs and woven war shirts and char-blackened codpieces, the leavings of his famous brass knuckles.

Then we got to work – then the Weders spent ten days and ten nights mounding up a great barrow of stone and earth upon the spot, a beacon that would be visible far across the waves. It was fifty, a hundred feet tall. It was two times as wide. Around it went a wall, and inside they piled the treasure of the dray, rings and brooches and everything the seven with Wiglaf had looted from the worm's burrow. They let the earth take the gold under her smothering breast, and there it sits today – gold on ground's greote.

When the barrow had been raised, around it rode twelve horsemen bemoaning their king. They were going to eulogize his earlship, praise his earthly accomplishments, mention his courage, and say a few words about the man. It is a good thing to remember your lord and battle chief when he leaves his body and goes into the arms of his Maker in the form of smoke, and to treasure him in your heart.

They said, 'He wære wyruldcyning manna mildest ond monðwærust, leodum liðost ond lofgeomost,' and they were right.

END OF COMBAT!

Captain Singleton

A novella by Colin Gee

Loosely adapted from The Life, Adventures and Piracies of the Famous Captain Singleton by Daniel Defoe

William Walters

Off Barbados in the Caribbean Sea, 1705
13°33' N - 60°22' W

How we ever did murder -- Truth becomes mixed up with fiction -- The modest terms of William Walters, a peace-loving Quaker -- The canary sings and it's for us -- William saves our asses with a syllogism -- Our hide-away -- Mister Harris has a sorry run of luck and dies -- A mighty storm -- We refit, reconnoiter, and reconsider

Stories had been circulating as far off as England and France of our activities in the West Indies and criming indulgences there, and although tales of our brutal, brumal bloodletting were greatly exaggerated, and immensely popular – especially when we would tie prisoners back to back and roll them down a plank into the sea, screaming, to drown, the French and Anglos were whispering in the wharfside pubs, they said to shut their children's emaciated yowling over supper – they were no lies.

'Daddy, I'm still hungry.'

'Shut the hell up or Captain Bob will come and take you away, and eat your fingers.'

'All eight of them?'

Yet I became angry when these new stories came to my ears through conference with prisoners or new recruits, for though it was fiction, it made us look soft. We were hard-boiled pirates, not thespians, and cruised under no flag but the force of metal and self-made fear, having no other warrant.

There are things we did that would chill the marrow of lesser buccaneers and stop the hearts of grown men, and give all mothers white hair, that we performed without a thought.

William Walters I took out of a sloop we intercepted near Barbados. I was charmed not only by his calm manner but by his constant, droll commentaries, that would cause us to double over with mirth and chagrin, and he was a big man, to boot, who could probably handle himself in a fight, we suspected, though that remained to be seen.

'Don't kidnap me, Captain Bob,' he winked with deep satisfaction in his eyes, 'not without the signing of a contract that says this doctor was removed by force, good neighbor, kicking and biting, with his instruments and wigs torn off and taken before him, screaming for help from his struggling yet incapacitated captain, all of it made law in ink or blood, whichever suits thy preference,' he laughed, stepping across an actual puddle of blood and fecal matter, he smiled, 'by the master of this sloop and every member of its company.'

You do that for me, he told me in a raunchy undertone, and I shall go anywhere with thee.

So I made the document and showed it unto William, and he with a little nod of assent and a smile is content, and I forced the master of the sloop and the whole company to sign the document – or else be tied back-to-back and lobbed into the aqua-marine waters, a fucking surefire method to die.

When they all had signed I made a big deal of trundling old William up out of the brig, and of trussing him, and tossing him like a bag of potatoes into the longboat, and cussing him too, though I warned my men that they must not strike him, or be God-damned, an order they were very careful to obey. When we had brought him on board my pirate ship and his sloop had slipped over the horizon, all chaste and hobbled, and

I had untied the doctor and showed him to a cabin and give him back his things, and thongs – these are yours, saith he, I realized – and Harris proffered him a good thimbleful of rum, we told him that we had some conditions of our own.

'Name them, friend,' he smiled, declining the thimble.

We told him, look, Quaker, that if he was going to work for us he was going to share with us on equal terms, and be one of us, for that was the pirate code.

William looked us up and down, noting our gold nipple rings and tattoos of talking parrots.

'Heavens,' exclaimed William, noticing with a smile that Polly wanted to fuck his mother, and replied that he would do good service to thee in role of surgeon, or doctor – thee being his word for me – but that thou knowest he was no fighter, and must take no part in a brawl.

'I can no more do violence to a man than whore to that strumpet,' he quipped.

We all followed his gaze to Lieutenant Harris, who had been caught at an awkward moment, he realized.

'By a brawl he means a battle,' I explained, redirecting the attention of everyone on board with my deep young voice, and majestic curtsey, 'and the boarding of prizes, and personal use of a pistol and cutlass, and probably cannon, I imagine.'

'How about ship guns,' I asked, with a gleam in my eye. 'Big guns.'

'Absolutely forbidden,' replied William – smiling ear to ear.

'It is forbidden of his religion,' we surmised, slapping one thigh.

Well then.

'Yet surely you may take part when it comes to doling out the money,' we laughed, to our relief, clapping him on the broadcloth back – a question, William Walters, for your listeners.

'Nay,' said he, only that he would take what was necessary for his subsistence, which was very slight indeed.

'Only what I need to stock my medicines, ointments, and instruments,' winked William, and three wives on two continents and their children, we suspected. 'Nothing excessive, such as gold chains or flashy earrings for me.'

Thus William avoided both horns of the pirate dilemma, one as infamous and deadly as it was imminent to us in those days of magenta red trousers and violent blue skies: by neither volunteering for the cruise, so said his parchment, nor fighting at our side, vouchsafe for which would his milky white hands and unruffled cravat and bear testimony – though we swore he could have made himself captain of us all had he been of the mind, or said a single word. As for the lot of us, as cheerful and oblivious to danger as we were, the smooth-sailing days were about to come to a shocking, blood-splattered end.

In Cold Blood

Bahia de Trujillo, Caribbean Sea, early 1706
15°55' N - 85°57' W

Our cruising so long in these seas began now to be so well known, that, not in England only, but in France and Spain, accounts had been made public of our adventures, and many stories told how we murdered the people in cold blood, tying them back to back and throwing them into the sea, one half of which, however, was not true, though more was done than it is fit to speak of here. –Defoe 157

'Two of them,' swore the informant or rat, a white wharf pimp we often confided in and slapped upside the head of while moored at Honduras.

'Three,' swore his girl Frambuesa. 'Three men-of-war, coming for you from England.'

We lurched slightly from the buffet of her foul cock breath.

'Impossible,' we didn't swear – we knew it was entirely likely.

We said, 'Look. Are there two of them or three of them?'

Frambuesa and her pimp exchanged glances of mutual disdain.

'Threeow,' they said at the same time. 'All we knows is is they is several. Engish man-of-war, rounding Jamaica as we speak.'

Holy Mother of God, I didn't say – it was Mister Harris.

He said, 'Holy Mother of God, Jesus and Holy Trinity.'

Trinity raised her head feebly from a sack of biscuits.

'Trinidad,' put in our own private canary, exchanging a bag of gold coins, we supposed, for his own fucking heart, 'not Jamaica.'

'Jamaica,' insisted the slut who may or may not have also been a wife to a man we called our bitch, before pounding off into the avalanche of casitas and casotas of old Trujillo – though it should be drunk, we guffawed – rocking the fucking pier so that we had to grab onto each other, or be tossed onto the rocks.

'Jamaica it is,' sighed our rat, eyes dull as his pride and joy vanished into the nethers of the night with a sailor I knew would never make it back in time, for we immediately high-tailed it to our boats and Admiral Wilmot gave orders to heave-ho and put on as much cloth as ever we dared.

'Put on as much cloth as ever we dared,' ordered Admiral Wilmot. He said, 'Give the old heave-ho.'

'Ron DeVoo is at Santa Marta,' he instructed us, using only Dutch code, 'or failing that, at you know we both know where.'

And you know we both knew where was where we ended up, several weeks later or older, while the English fleet moved upon Campeachy, where all pirates go when they die, well in our wake.

Ha ha ha, we laughed, when we learned how far upwind the English hound dogs had bayed.

'Bayed, as in put in to port. Put in to a bay,' Admiral Wilmot chuckled weakly from a cot, straining to raise the heavy bottle a last time to his sleeping lips.

'Bayed,' I corrected him, reshuffling the deck of cards and putting everything – my revolving pistol, its atrocious pills, the oversized cards, the IOU's, and both our monies – into a pocket of the waistcoat I wore over my bare chest on Tuesdays, 'as in howled, barked into the air,' but it was just more breath wasted on Wilmot.

At Tobago we put our heads down for a time and waited. It was an actual desert island, and there we had constructed our pirate fortress years before, that in fact was more like a shantytown of camouflaged huts and little privies than a redoubt for defense – for we feared no interference.

'From who or from whom,' we would belch with drunken laughter, lying back on piles of furs and silver cups and oriental scimitars, and oriental women. 'The tide? The rabbits? The fucking rabbits?'

And old William would sit in a corner and smile, watching everything – observing every last detail, but always with half an eye on the roads to the harbor, and his daffy cuffs.

'Excuse me, young pirate,' he addressed me suddenly in his soft and laughing voice – the voice of a kind of waiter, of a priest in his rapture, a chaste monk in his gloaming, 'but I believe our friend has found us.'

We looked and saw what William called a friend: a forty-gun English man-of-war, stripped for action, standing in upon our cove.

Yet no one had to run anywhere, so well disguised was our lair with snarling surf and rocky precipices and visions of cannibals with shaking lances along the cliff tops – and palm fronds and sticks and mud, that she never saw us.

'We're not going in there,' said the English swabs, chest-first, turning the prow of their longboat from the heaving entrance and nosing along up the shore to the place where they would later build a resort and private golf course – where the sand was soft and fluffy and the surf was kind.

But I warn you, all that was some months afterward.

In the meantime, as we lay in rut in Tobago the captain or sweet muffin of the brigadine, our last-most powerful ship, fell ill – or fell off the poop deck onto some heavy rocks, or fell in love and pined away, or lost in a duel which I attended, which of the above I never could say – and died and my long-time companion, friend, and lieutenant Mister Harris was nominated to her helm as Captain Christ to you, he declared.

Bravo, we cheered, and wanted to cross to big Brazil, and thence to Africa and up Madagaskar for an honest-to-God prowl into the Indian Ocean.

'But my ship is too small,' whined Mister Harris, now that he'd had a chance to look around inside and take her out for a spin – who was bleeding from an open wound in the forehead where he kept repeatedly ramming into low beams and hard forehands. 'I shall cruise a mote more here with my hardy men and see if I can't capture a larger ship, that shall take us to the rendezvous. I shall go off on my own, and meet you blokes at the appointed time in Africa. In China.'

That's a really really dumb idea, William Walters told him.

'You're going to get your ass handed to you,' he said, words of a true but unpopular prophet. 'Then you're going to get run under a sea jury, a mere formality to the Royal Navy, and after that – in a very few short hours – you are going to die, strung up by your neck from the yardarm.'

We all looked hard at Mister Harris in agreement – though we had no intention of hurting his feelings, short as he was.

'The yardarm,' he mimicked in a real falsetto, turning in a circle. 'Of what yardarm dost thou speak, Quaker?'

One day out, it came to us later, Mister Harris and his

brigadine and men were run up on, out-maneuvered in a cat-catch-mouse game of a cat is going to catch a mouse, volleyed upon, smashed to one side, knocked upon, and cut to pieces piecemeal by one of the purported English men-of-war. In short, let's not bread-and-honey this thing, they had their asses handed to them, explained William in his patent, soothing voice.

'I warned that young man not to tempt God's will,' he said with a big smile – for he always said God's will when he meant what he had just told somebody.

As for my old pal Harris, word was that he died in the brig in chains, actually choking to death on his own frustration before they could hang him. Mister Harris' lieutenants were all put on special exhibition in England for a time, then hanged for pirates in front of a crowd as a warning to the youth, William assured us when we learned of it.

'How do you know so much?' We never asked him.

We said, 'Rest in peace, Mister Harris – you taught us all we knew. All we know. How often the student outlives the master,' we said, lying again, and many similar platitudes, knowing in our heart it was not in our furniture to accept captaincy of a twelve-gun brigantine.

It was not only Mister Harris or his conscience who met with big problems when we sailed from Tobago and parted ways – for it was a bad moon, we knew, and a worse hangover. Admiral Wilmot and myself set a course for Brazil, but met nothing but water, and one night were overtaken by an overwhelming storm that moved us a hundred miles in one of the many wrong directions, and separated our two ships, taking away from both most of the sparring and rigging and washing away much riff-raff from the ropes and head. It could have been either tragedy or comedy, as luck would have it, for the moment the typhoon hit Admiral Wilmot was astride my boat, in my cabin drinking – guzzling, woozling – whiskey and brandy and mixing it with a strange fragrant tobacco from Tobago (toboggan in English, but tobacco in every other sense), we seemed to remember later, to his chagrin.

For a captain separated from his ship is like a head separated from a body: the body may survive for a short time, but the head must live on in anguish and helplessness for the rest of its mortal life.

'My ship,' Wilmot bawled from my taffrail, clinging with superhuman hands as many midship and foremast pirates flew screaming through the air into nothingness – into chill dark wetness, into the abyss that was our giver and mother, Wilmot reaching out to the ghastly space where he sensed his men battling off the bow even though I told him to hang on, for hot God damn, Wil man. 'My beautiful baby, *Wilmot*,' he cried, we realized, hearing the pet name of his ship for the first and last time.

The winds and seas finally subsided after a long, frightful night, and we made such way as we could, pumping like midshipmen on a Goan strumpet for three days and three nights, bleeding like ulcers on a Christ all Friday, Saturday and Sunday, and made it back into Tobago – in through the dicey rocks on the right tide, and set about making repairs, especially to some very tall masts that had cracked and carried overboard in the gale or gales. We fell back onto our jeweled mattresses, into a handful of grateful middle-eastern princesses, and that was when William Walters turned to me and said, 'Excuse me, young pirate,' with a gleam and a shake in his smile I knew was excitement.

But if you have been paying attention you already know what happens next.

Trinidad, My Dad

Trinidad, West Indies, early 1706
10°22' N - 61°01' W

Captain Wilmot trips and falls ill -- Timber on Trinidad -- Frambuesa recommends tall ducky merchant ships for our piracy -- Patience and impotence tempt us upon a night chase -- The wisdom of William -- We waste and board the merchantman and are content -- We sail further S than ever before

Now a second captain aboard a ship that could have only one, we both realized, Captain Wilmot saw the thunderclouds and heavy lightning on the horizon – read them as clearly in the jagged lines of my brow and brass knuckles as in the nervously cocking and uncocking hammer of my small-arm locker pistol, and he immediately came down with the influenza and was bedridden, only calling out messages if solicited, which in fact he was not – just crouching in there in the half-light and sipping on my brandy, I knew, but spilling nothing on my books or rough-housing strumpets.

Captain Wilmot let me have the weather deck and my dignity – I let him have a cabin and his life for the time being.

Only once did he emerge from his door, reeling drunk, and begin to shout orders, but he was hustled quickly back inside by William with the help of some half-clad bitches.

'Now now,' we all heard William say quickly, in a remonstrative but cheerful tone, you mustn't et-cetera et-cetera.

Having jury-rigged a topmast to carry us along for the

time being – the time being early, the night a child, we would always joke, laughing into our sudsy drinks – we dashed across to Trinidad and put some men discreetly onto the backside of that fine island, where they have a tall spruce forest, and they cut us a stout mainmast that we hiked and swung and coaxed into place with ropes and straining sweaty biceps that shone in the bright and only true sun. We resolved to make a second attempt upon Brazil, but our faithful spy Frambuesa pulled us up short.

'Captain Wilmot's ship was seen flying across the full moon two nights before last,' she did not inform us, knowing better than to feed us that malarkey. Nor did she say, 'Your buccaneer companions have been captured, tried by kangaroo jury, and shot in the face.'

She couldn't speak – her mouth appeared to be completely full of food.

'What do you want,' we demanded.

'Spit it out,' we cussed, perhaps the only time she'd ever heard the phrase. 'Tell us everything you know,' we said, stepping back as she spit out most of what appeared to be the original Satan.

She said that, even as we spoke and fumbled with her buttons and drawstrings, the Portuguese merchant fleet – a fleet of a hundred sail or more – was preparing to weigh anchor from All Saints Bay on the western panhandle or love handle of Trinidad, and make for old Lisboa, she moaned.

'Mais de cem barco,' she gasped. 'Mais de oitocento marinheiro.'

'More than hundred ship,' we mused drily. 'More than eight hundred sailor,' we expectorated.

'How does she know this,' we didn't have to ask – we already knew how she knew eight hundred sailors.

'What does Frambuesa know,' lamented her pimp, instantly at our side, though he had been warned to keep to the lee rail because of the state of his trousers and weepy bladder. 'She has neglected to tell you about the cannon.'

Cannon, we laughed. We too have cannon.

'Don't stand next to our bare feet,' we hissed.

'Suit yourself,' wept the wharf rat, to our dismay, but he turned out to be correct as to the strength and disposition of the armada. Riding close in to shore to get the advantage of the wind, we said, and surprise, said William, we saw the flotilla emerge and saw warships among them, mingling with the merchantmen, so that we balked, we cursed, and had no opportunity to snag anything.

We rode anchor and tide for some days more in the road to All Saints, however, knowing how desperate men were to get to Brazil and exchange pants for britches, and this time both luck and weather held.

'Sail! Sail ho,' called our crow's nest lookout.

We made directly for the stranger, who turned and fled with all sail due E – directly into the ocean. We chased her all afternoon and evening, gaining on her furlong by slow furlong, until the sun was down, and darkness fell upon the deep, wrote Moses.

'Friend Singleton,' smiled our merry Quaker, coming up to me where I stormed and screamed on the weather rail, 'what are you doing?'

'Well,' I coughed, startled to admit it, 'I am chasing yonder boat, that I mean to strafe with my cannon and small arms, board with hooks and grenadoes, and plunder.'

'I see no boat yonder,' replied William.

That's because it's night, I told him.

'It's there, trust me,' I growled. 'You just can't see it. That is how it works.'

'Mercy me,' murmured William with a long, soft chuckle, 'I beg thy pardon, friend, but I do believe our circumstances have been reversed – that today is thy day to be Quaker, and me the hardcore pirate.'

The hardboiled pirate, I corrected him.

'What are you saying,' I grimaced, eyes everywhere: the helm, the sheets, the bitts, the butts, the bells. 'You are the Quaker.'

'Ho ho ho,' explained William, 'yet I am not the one running from a fight.'

What do you mean, I screamed, looking at him for the first time with my bloodshot eyes, and hilt of a saber like a you-know-what. 'You are always fucking teasing me.'

'I am not teasing,' William said in a voice that was both cold and sober. His words froze me in my pants – I stopped and stared. 'I tell thee,' William told me, 'the boat thou thinkest thou chasest, that bears gold to feed us and make us rich, is not out there,' he motioned off the bow. 'I guarantee you that she has tacked and turned back to All Saints Bay. That is, after all, where she is going.'

He sniffed indifferently.

'Yet if thou durst not fight,' he said, 'and hath turned Quaker, I cannot detain thee.'

How can a pirate be a Quaker, I scoffed.

'Fuck you, William Walters,' I said.

At that moment Captain Wilmot burst from his quarters in the incident of drunken shamefulness which I have already related, screaming not to hearken unto the Quaker, that the Quaker is leading us to our own deaths, the Quaker this and the Quaker that, we laughed, and his foolish weeping brought us round.

'Fuck you, Wilmot,' I screamed – I smiled with a quakering,

simping mouth, as William and a dozen half-clad vixens wrestled Captain Wilmot back into his cabin, and kingdom.

'Put her about,' I called, to the astonishment of all my men, who could not follow a conversation.

Hands aloft, we turned and crowded back the way we had come, and by dawn were lolling beneath the narcoleptic forts at All Saints Bay, just beyond range of her patch-eye guns, you can bet, sails reefed and spars down to make us out like a drowsy zambra – like a lazy trawler, and a real late sleeper. I ordered the men to arm themselves and get down the hatches out of sight and wait for my signal.

In half an hour up come the little barkie, sure as William had foretold, toddling towards the mouth of the bay and our open jaws, neither expecting nor recognizing us in the haze of dawn.

'Show them our colors,' I barked, as the merchant crossed idly within gunshot, and our great black flag fell from the jack with a thump and a great cheer rose as our men poured from the hatches at my sign, mounting the ropes like dire monkeys and loosing the sheets. Wheeling sixty degrees on our fulsome anchor, throwing out our big guns, we fired everything we had from the waist – for when I shoot, it's always from the hip. The merchantman, raked from bow to stern with our flying projectiles, flew up into the wind and swung under our sights in the smoke and commotion and cries and his colors shivered and came down.

There was no time to waste on congratulations, torture, rape, or executions, however, for as we were nudging the prize with our sprit and grappling her to our corpse-black fanny and boarding her and subduing her single marine, the first shot from the cannon of the fort fell forty paces starboard with a terrible geysering splash.

'See here, Pirate Singleton,' laughed William, approaching me as I directed the looting and very limited sodomy, entirely ignoring the many such shots that were splashing harmlessly into our larboard, starboard waters. 'Dost thou expect the proud Spanish to sit idly by while we plunder her boat in broad daylight within range of her harbour?'

Following the extrapolation of his wink, and finger, I noted the commotion aboard the three Spanish men-of-war moored within the spanky interior of All Saints, and easily guessed William's meaning.

'You mean we had better skedaddle,' I said. My eyes narrowed in their sockets. 'You are talking about running away.'

'Well,' William replied with a smile, 'if thou allowest yonder ships to weigh anchor and get under sail they are going to be here in just under an hour,' he estimated. He said, 'And then we are going to die. Now I never have pretended to know thy business, young captain, nor tell thee what to do, but if thou art willing to listen now I do believe we have only two options.'

What two options are you talking about, I snapped.

'Tell me about the two options,' I said.

'The first,' smiled the Quaker calmly, 'is to cut and run immediately, as any reasonable person would do in your situation.'

We are not reasonable people, I replied.

'What's the second option,' I said.

'The second option,' William replied, face transfigured like Moses, 'is to go in after the motherless sons of cunts and hit them so hard they never knew what happened.'

I looked at William in astonishment. You mean, I said, enter hostile waters in a solitary sloop with an exhausted crew and attack three superior naval gunboats in broad daylight, I said.

'You want to attack those three massive warships,' I cried

incredulously.

'Yes,' smiled William, the grin spreading across his face like mashed potatoes. He scowled – his eyes twinkled. 'Get in there and hit them hard, and finish the job so that they never know what hit them. No letters home, no rumors, no witnesses.'

A terrible, wrenching doubt or intestinal cramp crossed my face and life.

'I don't think so, William,' I stammered, finally. 'Stow the loot below decks on the double,' I commanded my men and mateys, and lieutenants and gun captains, 'and cripple this lug so that she has to row if she wants to make the next tide,' I laughed, indicating the prize merchantman, that in fact was yielding up none of the things we so fervently coveted in this life and world – gold, silver, pearls, ivory piano keys, precious oriental goblets, or even one single female woman. 'Take her cannonballs and bullets and powder and hardtack and beeves,' I belched, turning my face to the rising wind, 'and good sailcloth and anchors, and set her adrift. We're going to give these hair lips the slip,' I claimed, getting it right the first time, fast.

I said, 'We're going S – further S than ever before.'

Grim as death under a sky that twinkled and darkened, deep in the bowels of the ship someone hummed and chuckled – it was me.

Cry Me A Rio de Janeiro

Rio de Janeiro, April or May 1706
22°57' S - 43°07' W

William the Quaker comes to me with a kind of smile: Friend, says he, what does yon ship follow us for? Why, says I, to fight us, you may be sure. Well, says he, and will she come up with us, dost thou think? Yes, said I, you see she will. Why then, friend, says the dry wretch, why dost thou run from her still, when thou seest she will overtake thee? will it be better for us to be overtaken further off than here? Much at one for that, says I; why, what would you have us do? Do! says he, let us not give the poor man more trouble than needs must; let us stay for him, and hear what he has to say to us. -Defoe 164

Sailing fast and true S by nothing but S, we laughed, we made Brazil in two days and were nudging into the aching, open mouth of the bay of Janeiro when we saw the Portuguese men-of-war.

'Forty-six guns,' we had to admit, wantonly inverting the six and four to everyone's confusion forever, 'and the first under full sail with unmistakable intentions.'

There is no other way to varnish it, my friend: we turned and ran, trusting to the speed and airy cheerful gamboling lightness of our craft and dam Fortune to save us, and the gut-lugging brain of one motherless orphan – me.

Yet the first warship must have been a marvelous sailor, or else we were all drunk and doing something banefully wrong – always a possibility when I think back to those days of bathtub grog and Caribbean skirts and bonfires along the beach – for she gained steadily on us through the midmorning and afternoon, and if it had not been for eventual night she'd have caught us, and learned us. When that night finally fell we doused the lights and tacked into the great maw of the black Atlantic, using a tack everyone knows about, but few dare to employ. We meant to shake our pursuers, who we expected would continue on the weather course we had run throughout the splashy, plashy daylight chase.

They did not. They were deeply suspicious Portuguese, we realized, and had guessed our trick and tacked too – when daylight broke they were closer than ever before in their lives. The good news, if there ever were such a thing, is that they were now only one.

'Now we can destroy them piecemeal,' William chirped, apparently eating an apple.

'We love to fight,' I concluded, knowing it would be a fight to the death, with no quarter given. 'For we are cutthroat pirates,' we truly knew, 'and they are the Portuguese navy,' the very lowest of the low – scoundrels and cowards to a man, with orders to murder those outside the law, and a pox on their crotch.

'You don't say,' stammered two of our newest recruits, shrinking inside their pantaloons.

'A pox,' we confirmed. 'On their crotch.'

No, they said. We mean you don't say we're pirates.

'You never told us,' they whimpered, clinging to their shivering ratlines.

'We told you,' we told them. 'We said that if you join us, you are automatically pirates.'

They told us there had been some kind of big

misunderstanding; that they had never even suspected we were that kind of can't of can't uh of canting crew; that could they leave now.

Yes, of course you fucking can, we told them. Rio de Janeiro is a short swim in the direction we just came from.

'Go,' we indicated.

'Friend Bob,' began William, finishing his apple and tossing the core after the two deserters, 'it appears the people in yon barkie desire to talk to us, or am I mistaken.'

Don't use that intonation with me when you are pretending to ask a question, you sassy Quaker, I said.

I said, 'They do indeed,' pacing the deck like a young lion, I assure you. 'They mean to speak to us in the only language they know – in iron and fire.'

'Dear me,' laughed our jaunty Quaker, wiping apple juice from a grinning chin. 'If that is the language they use, I suppose we'll have no choice but to reply in kind.'

'That is our intention,' I growled – by our meaning my. 'We are just busting for a fight,' I grinned – by we meaning me.

William watched as I made two more rapacious turns, eyebrows doing somersaults of unadulterated anger, and said, 'Well?'

Well what, I fucking screamed.

'Well what, William?'

'What are you waiting for?' he said. 'That boat wishes to talk to thee, and it's downright unkind of you to keep her in the lurch.'

Captain Wilmot staggered from his cabin at that moment, ill with brandy, and shouted or barfed up to and upon us.

'The Quaker is right this time,' he choked, and puked. 'Let's turn and claw them before they can get their feet under them,' for by feet he meant keel.

I looked deep into Captain Wilmot's eyes, and knew that he was drunk.

'That's exactly right,' however, beamed William from beneath his black hat – from behind the screwiest little white ascot. 'Hit them now and hit them hard,' he chuckled, with grit in his satisfied smile.

I gave the orders: we luffed and wheeled hard onto on the starboard tack and, as we meant to hit them on our port side I said, fuck it, put all the guns on that side of the ship and we'll punch a hole in their God-damned futtock.

We drifted down towards the powering sixty-gunner in a state of cold excitement, all hands at their stations, even Wilmot petrified against a barrel like some prehistoric porcine entity turned to stone in the act of being throttled by a suddenly conscious, malignant vine. The Portuguese, seeing our intention to fight, attempted to sheer off, and he opened up with several guns, whose projectiles bounced harmlessly around our ears. As we came up I threw the wheel hard over with a vicious movement, and a loud grunt, at the same time giving the command to drop the freewheeling skysail, which swung us onto their quarter, and we opened with all the metal we had, pouring in a cracking, smashing, crunching, bewildering double broadside that took the Portuguese Navy right in the teeth. We could see great splinters of wood, loose cannon, arms, legs, and geysers of blood and snippy guts flying through the smoke – through the middle of what had recently been a house and workplace for four hundred tits.

The screaming came to us across the water, we cheered with open throats.

For our part we received very little fire, the Portuguese being unable to train more than two or three big guns on us, and because as the ships had struck and become entangled, and they been in a state of utter panic and confusion since the very beginning, the fancy nancies, we had them like fish in a barrel without any water in it.

'Crash, pound, kazam,' thundered a second and third broadside from our waist, slamming the big Portuguese repeatedly like a diminutive john on a portly, sad and slightly rocking hooker. 'Boom, dum, chubum.'

All this time the voice of the gunner was audible on the gun deck, ranging and shouting along our hotsome, snazzy line of swabs and muzzles.

'What is your friend doing?' called an also stunned and rapidly sobering Captain Wilmot. He had lost the bottle he always had in his hand or tucked into his yellow and crimson sash, and was pointing to the forecastle through the din and flash of small-arm fire that filled the forward shrouds, where the unmistakable form of William was in the mix, bullets flying around his expansive wainscot, Wilmot's bottle in his hand.

He was directing the men, encouraging them with shots of brandy as they lashed the enemy sprit to our own and prepared to board.

'Friend Bob,' he called after one moment, traversing the waist in great strides to speak to me – standing calmly at my side and indicating the gaping holes we had punched and mown through the enemy's hull; the cowering shapes we could make out crouching in there, that aimed their little guns and were immediately scythed down by our own incessantly firing pistols and muskets, 'now that thou hast spoken with thy neighbor, and he appears to have opened his door for ye, why dost thou not enter?'

I looked at William with love in the face of a serial mass murderer.

'Boarders,' I cried, and our men swarmed the nets and rails of the sixty-four-gunner with our men screaming and firing behind. They charged through her waist and lower decks, pouncing after hand-rolled grenadoes and sniping fire from our own shrouds. In a matter of seconds we had cleared the enemy of all upright and living adversaries – the few who had been alive to stand there in the first place, and the cry for quarter went up from the Portuguese wheelhouse, and her ensign went down and hit what was left of her blackened, bloodstained, splinter-strewn deck.

'Looks at this bloody fucking mess,' we laughed.

The pirate cry went up – the wounded were busy being clubbed to death by my sailors. I knew it – William knew it: we had just taken a sixty-four-gun ship with nothing but a sloop of eight and twenty, and our own daring and brazen good luck.

'I hereby make me captain of the prize,' I interrupted Captain Wilmot, 'and Wilmot shall be promoted to helm or till of the little sloop. We are now on equal terms, Captain, except for the fact that your liver is no longer able to process what your body requires for you to live.'

Captain Wilmot's eyes swam in their yellow juices – he nodded and slouched back to his cabin.

Of the surviving Portuguese a good number of them joined us, and the rest we marooned on a godforsaken desert island after taking all their clothes.

'Trust me,' I told them, 'you won't need your capes and wigs out here.'

Please sir, they begged me, don't abandon us in this primal state.

I told them to look about them and to tell me if they saw anyone with clothes living on this island. They turned and looked at the naked cannibals that peered out at them through the shivering fronds, with licking lips, and had to admit that they did not.

'No,' they said.

But they begged hard for a couple of ancient muskets and some powder of dubious origin to defend themselves and bang up some food, claiming that they could not go long without meat.

Here, we said.

'Here's your dumb muskets,' we cussed, dumping them onto the sand and standing back with disgust inside a pair of queasy pants.

'If you start to eat each other,' I warned them, 'I will come back and personally skin you alive and eat your testicles,' I coughed. 'And eat your faces,' I said quickly.

They promised they would not eat each other, not so much as a finger or arm, and we left them there – all except some of the most grievously wounded, that we dumped into the deep Atlantic to fend for themselves.

'We have no use for prisoners,' I told William. His mouth opened and closed.

It was his job to save their lives, yet he failed in this instance.

Captain Wilmot argued that we should stand back in toward the river of Janeiro and take the remaining man-of-war while the cards were down, blood fresh in our nostrils, and luck on our side.

'Luck is on my side,' I corrected him. 'Your side is full of shadows and uncertainty,' I informed him, turning over the last card he had. I exchanged glances with William, who smiled from the pure, untarnished joy of breathing air. I gulped hard on a mouthful of rum – we glared at the pirate Wilmot.

'Friend,' William told me, 'as to this matter of standing in after the second Portugee, I should never wish to tell thee thy business, but is it not to make money?'

Money, I said, and lots of it, in all kinds of denominations, by any means.

'Gold and pearls,' I assented greedily, refilling his glass with lemonade.

By any means, he mused. But preferably without a fight.

He said, 'Is it better to get money by fighting, with the risk of possible bloodshed, damage to thy bark, loss of partial or entire sailors, and the chance – however remote – of capture, trial by kangaroo jury, death by hanging, and Hell, or by not fighting?' he asked.

All of us together at the same time pictured a row of literal kangaroo jurors. Boards creaked omnipotently and water splashed omnisciently. Captain Wilmot farted faintly – a soft undulating hiss that he was helpless to prevent.

I told William I supposed it was always better without a fight.

'We always pursue peaceful methods of robbing the innocent blind and dumb and stuttering,' I admire, I admitted. 'It's all fun and games until you take the life of someone's friend, in the wise words of the Grecian bard,' I guffawed. 'Until you fuck a friend, friend,' I gulped rum.

This was exactly his point, explained William, in his dry and rhyming way.

'And what advantage – money advantage – dost thou gain from attacking a sixty-four-gun man-of-war? The infamous brick gold? Pearls? Silver dubloons?' he asked.

I told him that he had a point.

'It is true that men-of-war do not usually carry a lot of money on them,' I said.

'Take for example the great piles of gold and pearls and Persian silks we took from this latest man-of-war,' William suggested.

I protested that we had taken none of those things.

'This is something to consider,' he smiled back, and I turned to Captain Wilmot, who was just sitting there in his usual drunken idiot stupor.

'We shall sail to the river de la Plata,' I told him, summing up everything William and I had been discussing in one tidy little phrase. 'We shall ply there, and become as fat as cows on the Spanish shipping out of Buenos Ayres,' I assured him as he sat and wheezed, eyeballs goggling out of his apoplectic skull, 'and have an easy shot overseas at the Cabo de Bona Speranza and our rendezvous with your ship,' wept Wilmot, 'and finally eat us some of them gamey black cattle they have on Madagaskar,' I said with my lips, and thus ended our fracas with the Portuguese for the time, and we entered a period of waffling and quibbling, and lying about, and looking about before making the crossing to the East.

William's Dream

Nosy Mitsy, December 1707
12°54' S - 48°34' E

Our friend William, of whom I have said nothing a great while, had a great mind one day to go on shore, and importuned me to let him have a little troop to go with him, for safety, that they might see the country. I was mightily against it for many reasons; but particularly I told him, he knew the natives were but savages, and they were very treacherous, and I desired him that he would not go. –Defoe 194

Captain Wilmot, who to his own chagrin insisted on calling himself Admiral Wilmot, came down with bad seams and had to put into Mangahelly or some other damned place to refit, where he claimed we up and vanished, and afterwards threw a long tantrum about it, claiming he had sailed half round the world in search of us.

'You did not,' we laughed.

'Did so,' he spluttered.

We shut him up with his share of the two hundred thousand pieces of eight we had got, as you shall find out, and the following story.

'We disappeared because of a rumor and a dream,' we explained. 'The rumor was true – the dream was true.'

Everything was true but our Portuguese peter.

The rumor had it that a European ship had gone aground on one of the islands off the western shank or foreleg of

Madagaskar, where we too happened to be lying in a secret cove waiting for Wilmot on rendezvous, upon an island called Nosy Mitsy, when William came to me and said, 'Friend, I would go ashore to see the country.'

The country, I replied. What country. This place is no country.

I said, 'Why, William, why.'

I said, 'This island is full of hostile tribes of meat maneaters. They meet people to meat people,' I punned in something close to despair. 'They enjoy looking into their victims' eyes while they cannibalize them. They frequently force their victims to eat parts of their own body before they finish them off, which the victims are desperate to do, because they have also been starved for days. They take three days to eat a single man,' I continued, 'keeping him alive with transfusions of his own blood, or that of his mother and sisters if they can get their hands on them.'

I was making all of it up – I was terrified of losing my main man, my boy, my oracle – my Quaker, my joker.

William replied that he fully understood the dangers, and for that reason wished to enlist a small band of cutthroats to assist him, for he always said cutthroats when he meant shipmates. Then he said he wished to explain himself, for he hated to bother me with such an inconvenient petition.

Inconvenient is right, I told him.

'What explanation could you possibly give me,' I spat.

'I had a dream,' William told me, 'in the night. Such a terrible, mystifying dream that I have been unable to sit still since waking, and think I must satisfy my curiosity about it, for it has to do with this island.'

Well, I said, what was the dream, for chrissake.

'What was the dream, William,' were my very words.

William said he dreamed he had gone on shore and gone up into the hills where he and his boys had discovered an old mine.

'You went into the old mine,' I prompted.

Yes, said William, with thirty of his boys, yet the mine went up rather than down, though they were inside the mountain. They bore torches and drawn pistols, and the wind howled through the shafts, and they went up on a rickety ladder, and sometimes the rungs would snap, and it was a very long way down.

'I was thinking about something else, for some reason,' he said, gripping his hat between fingers, 'when we come to the top of the ladder and enter a strange room. There we happen upon a line of priests in robes, filing out of a door to our left. They are very tall pale men, old men with white hair and they look at us. Out of the corner of our eye we see they are looking at us.'

'So they looked at you,' I said.

They tried to look at us, William said, 'but we were invisible.'

I said, 'Nothing.'

He said, 'Then we notice there are beds in there, with shapes under the covers. Two white heads peek out, two very old white heads,' William told me, the heads of two old men. 'And the funny thing is, we knew they were dying,' he said, 'but they were happy. They had been strong and important men. We knew this, although they were very weak now, and had just received their final, God what was it, a communion?'

A communion, I said. 'What's a communion?'

'Their hearts were singing,' replied one transported Quaker.

'They were pumping and thumping,' I nodded.

Said William, 'They were thrilling and filling. The priests saw us in the doorway with our swords and torches and stopped and looked, and looked again, but then they realized they were out of their minds, there was nothing there, and they ignored us. The two old men were alone with us – happy, ignoring us. They closed their eyes and became very still and small, and I thought it was like I had killed them by thinking, Old guys, you going to die.'

Well, William, I told him, you did.

I said, 'You were controlling everything. It was your dream.'

I said, 'You did kill them.'

I don't know about that, William replied, with a shell shocked glance.

He said, 'We backed out of the doorway and closed the door.'

He said, 'That was when we saw that the door was red. The whole mineshaft was painted red, and we went up it on a staircase that went round the corner from the door.'

'Great,' I told him, taking a big fat swallow from a muddled arrack – from the fat hand of a little tart with grease around the ears, the way I like im.

'Thinking back on it now,' insisted William, glancing at the strumpet in disbelief, 'I realize the door the priests had filed out of could not have existed. I looked at it, and touched it,' you cat, I thought, said the whore, he whispered, 'and it was nothing but a sheer rock face on the other side.'

He touched his face with one hand – with his hand or the hand of a fat little tart. I had never seen William look so agitated – I immediately got up and began rummaging in my locker for that good brandy, that good old port, that fancy Goan rice wine – a good, fancy anything.

Seawater slapped my dainty little window.

William told me they counted, they continued up the stairs.

'We reached a hall with wood panels and wood floors and went past several rooms,' he said. 'A room to the left had benches with strange stains on them, coiled with tight loops of rope. I passed very quickly because I thought there was someone in that room. I thought they prepared the dead bodies in that room.'

'I thought they made their sacrifices in there,' I said.

William said, 'So I did not go inside.'

I raised my glass to William's decision in his dream of the previous evening.

'Cheers,' I said. 'If you ever find yourself back there, don't go into the room on the left.'

William shot me a look of horror. Me and the strumpet looked back in self-satisfaction – inside a sunlit and early afternoon.

'Do you see where this is going?' I asked her, but she shook her head.

'We walked by three bedrooms,' William wept, 'two on the right, and one on the left. Right, left, right. I do not remember what was in the bedrooms, only that they belonged to old men who had lived there for a long time. They were at the end of their lives. Their lives would end in a couple of days, tops,' he said.

Here, drink this, I told him.

'Quaff it down,' I said, because you're giving me and the strumpets the gnarlies.

William looked at me – at the strumpets, now more than half a dozen. His hand reached out and took a silver goblet from my pirate clutch, a clutch that loathes to relinquish a full glass, but did.

He took, but did not drink.

'Down the hall,' he continued, 'I entered a large room that I took to be a cobbler's workshop. The passage ran all the way through on the left. To the right the room opened up into a small atrium. Beyond that ran another long passage. In the middle of the room there was a high chair with leather upholstery for shining shoes. I looked down and I was barefoot,' he cursed.

How could you have forgotten your shoes in a dream like that, I guffawed.

'I tell you again, William, it was your own fault you had no shoes on,' I said.

'I looked at the walls and there were nondescript tools hanging from pegs on the wall,' our Quaker continued. 'Beyond the atrium was the treasure.'

It sounds like a cobbler's workshop to me, I said, 'like a shoemaker paradise.'

'What treasure?' I shouted.

The treasure we were there to find, whispered William.

I drank deeply, and the magic elixir hit my kidneys like two malevolent fists. I gulped hard – William went on.

'On the far side of the atrium,' he said, 'was a bed and on the bed was a creature that was very sick, with a man's body and a round bald skull with a large round mouth full of pointy teeth. See, this one was going to die today. It was in the final stages of the disease.'

'You looked at him,' I said, 'and knew all this.'

'Yes,' agreed my Friend. 'The creature saw me and sat up. It was so happy to see me that it propped itself up on an elbow, and the shape of its mouth changed. It became triangular, closed. The teeth disappeared and thin red lips crept out and a single fang or bone spurred at the lowest part of the face where the chin would be. The mouth and teeth dilated from the fang.'

'So you are not talking about something that exists in this world,' I demurred – disappointed.

William looked at me.

'Everything exists in this world,' he said.

I see, I told him, drinking down my drink. 'Now you're making sense.'

William looked at my drink. He said, 'I take a step towards the creature and ask it how I can get out of the monastery. I assumed we were in a monastery, though I knew it was a mine. So technically I lied.'

Your eternal soul, William, I chuckled.

I said, 'Your salvation and personal honor.'

William said, 'The creature was agitated when it heard my question, but happy. It began to writhe its body. The body was grey now with large sucking cups and it shimmied down the bed and tried to maneuver onto the floor.

' 'Down the hall,' it told me – eagerly, indicating the passage on the far side of the atrium that ran past the bed, toward the treasure I knew I needed. Yeah for real, was my first thought. I knew it wanted to eat me, or have me, but for some reason I went around the shoeshine chair and walked towards the hall.'

'Then what happened,' the tarts and I said in unison. 'Tell us quickly, for the love of God.'

'The creature was in front of me in the blink of an eye,' said William. 'Its teeth had disappeared but its mouth was wide open. The chair had closed the passage behind me, or the petrified forms of my boys, I am not sure. I wasn't sure what had happened to my boys. There was no time to look back. I tried to step back but I couldn't.'

Then it ate you, I guessed.

'Then you woke up,' I said.

'Unfortunately I did not,' William replied. 'I saw that the body was humanoid. It was large, twice my size,' we realized, seeing William stand and pace at six feet plus in his stockinged feet! He said, 'and it had two heads. Above the bald skull head was a second head, the head of a knight in a heartbreaker black helmet, in a black scarf. I couldn't see behind the visor but it was moving in there.'

'You don't say,' I didn't say.

Nor did I say, 'Two heads are better than one.'

William's lips moved silently, searching for words.

He said, 'I put both of my hands into the creature's mouth to see what would happen.'

Well why in the fuck did you do that, I said.

I said, 'You crazy fucking Quaker.'

'Its teeth flared out again,' breathed my friend, 'and bit down softly, like a pet dog, but as benign as it felt I could feel it was trying to get me down into its throat. I tried to pull back but it got me by the shoulders with its human arms.'

You writhed to get free, I said.

William said, 'I writhed to get free.'

My glass was empty – a noon sun shone strong through the main cabin window.

' 'Can I have the green one?' it asked,' said William, 'opening and closing its mouth, smacking on me and spraying saliva. 'Can I have a whole bowl full of the little green ones?' said the monster,' said William.

I sat back.

'Well what is it supposed to mean,' I said.

'That's what I intend to find out,' replied William, fixing me with an eye, straightening nearly to his full height. 'As I writhed in its clutches, I turned my head and down through a little window I could see the shape of your ship, riding in the cove.'

That means nothing, I laughed.

I said, 'Your mind is playing tricks on you.'

'I had just awoken,' said William. 'I could still feel the fingers of the creature on my sides, when the coxswain come bursting into my cabin, and he proceeds to tell me the very same dream, from start to finish, down to the very last detail.'

'You mean-' I began.

'Yes,' replied William.

I said, 'You had the same dream last night.'

William said, 'Putting our heads together,' winced the party sluts, 'we concluded it was also at the very same hour.'

I think you had better not go ashore, I told him.

'Don't go into the old mine,' I said.

'Yet the coxswain tells me he went around the creature,' William mused, 'and got down into the gold mine, and found the treasure.'

And made us all as rich as gods, I breathed.

'And made us all as rich as gods,' said William.

Jesus, I breathed. 'I thought *I* loved gold.'

Take your volunteers, I replied, 'and two good pistols, but don't be long.'

William paused, bowed stiffly, and went out to choose his guns.

Bullets Over Nosy Mitsy

Nosy Mitsy, Christmas 1707
12°52' S - 48°36' E

He told me the last night he had a dream, which was so forcible, and made such an impression upon his mind, that he could not be quiet till he had made the proposal to go; and, if I refused him, then he thought his dream was significant; and if not, then his dream was at an end. –Defoe 389

I had never had much use for dreams, considering them more proper to the race of priests than pirates, or even a discreetly buccaneering Quaker, but the thought of the dream gold began to weigh on me like something heavy and glittering, so that my breathing changed and there were shooting pains in my temples and chest, and I saw stars and slithering margaritas.

I told William he could have his little troop of cutthroats and go.

'Choose well,' I said. 'The men are mustering in the waist.'

William chose best: he took fifteen of his most awesome boys, and fifteen of mine, which made them thirty-one tough fuckers of a mother, as in the dream.

'You may be tempting fate,' I warned him. 'You don't want what happened in the dream to happen to you in real life.' But William only smiled, because he wanted what happened to him in the dream to happen to him in real life.

He left in the morning, rowed the cove and put ashore in

the middle of the beach – disappearing into the trees, and that night we saw his fire upon the mountain, the prearranged signal that all was well, and on fire.

They went down the far side of the mountain the following day, they later told me, into a pleasant valley that spread along a stream that ran right out of Nosy Mitsy into the sea, but were only several furlongs down it when they were badly startled by the discharge of a European firearm. His boys hit the dust and bit it and strained their ears in that position for a long time, counting blades of grass, but heard nothing more – got up and moved forward through the clumps of grass and clutters of disreputable trees.

When they neared the mouth at the bay or inlet they were in for another surprise, for there they found the remains of a great ship wrecked upon the bar, a boat of European make that sat bone dry in the sand at low tide where it had crashed and flopped.

'They must have been drunk out of their noggins,' William's boys exclaimed, walking all around the beast – checking its portholes and hawserholes, and busted spars and walking through her ragged flapping sails.

William, striding onto the strand and pausing for what was almost the last moment of his life to observe the cant and lines of the monster, sniffing the breeze as was his nature, nearly had his head taken off by a bullet that whizzed past his ear. Following the report and smoke of the shot with a casual eye, he ordered his boys to unload on the vicinity of the report, which they did with zinging, sizzling bullets that punched and tore into the foliage of the far side of the river. Immediately, with a holler and a leap, a dozen men jumped from the trees and ran towards down the shore, waving their arms and muskets, and our boys said they were Europeans, cease fire!, though it was difficult to see if they were Dutch or French, for they were upon the far side of a stream.

'Those are the very drunken fools that crashed their ship,' someone muttered. 'Want to bet they're French?'

'I'll take that bet,' someone else said. 'What we are dealing with here is a smut of Holland ease.'

Meantime our boys had got a white shirt up on a pole, and were answered in kind by the motley strangers, who put a boat in the water and pulled across the inlet toward William's cutthroats. And how sweet it must have been for the cutthroats to discover not only that the strangers were not French or Dutch but English, and their own countrymen, but very old friends! For these were the very men from the ship that Captain Wilmot had lost during his epic binge on my boat at Tobago, that we had intended to meet on rendezvous in this selfsame Madagaskar, and the stranded boat was his lost ship.

There was much clapping of naked, sunburnt backs, I can assure you William told me, and cries of happiness, he narrated me to narrate to you, and their story was as follows. Having survived the typhoon, and upon making fall at the rendezvous on Madagaskar and finding it deserted, and after waiting some time there in absolute boredom, they had heard some rumor of our depredations on the Arabian coast and sailed that way intending to overtake us, when they had fallen in with the grim pirate Avery, we all shuddered, and having no further word of us promptly joined that pirate and his crew of buccaneers and had roved and riven with them all this year gone by, taking dozens – hundreds – thousands – of prizes richly laden with pearl and gold, and one mogul's daughter.

'Describe the mogul's daughter,' our boys demanded, and did they ever.

'Now how about this here wreck,' said William.

They told him that they had been sailing down back on up to the rendezvous to see if they could not, would not chance upon us there, when a great storm had forced them to put into the cove where they now squatted, and smoked, and the gathering seas drove them upon the spit, and they lost their ship to Nosy Mitsy.

'You were drunk as bats,' our boys said.

Well, replied the others. That depends on your definition of drunk as bats.

'Not totally drunk,' they thought.

Drunk as bats, smiled William. It means blind drunk.

'Drunk as in you cannot see to walk,' he told them.

'Ah,' said Wilmot's former crew. 'In that case, yes – everyone was drunk as bats except Wilbur.'

Our boys looked over at Wilbur: slender and balding, he wore a pair of cracked spectacles and a carefully darned shirt, sported no tattoos, and was sitting apart from the others examining his collection of seashells.

What's his story, William wanted to know.

'I am worried about Wilbur,' he lied.

'It was a terrible storm,' Wilmot's men hurriedly put in, to change the subject – they had no idea what was wrong with Wilbur, either. 'We heard that Captain Avery, too, lost his ship in the hurricane, and was driven upon some rocks.'

How in carnation did you hear that, smiled William.

He said, 'But you are hopeless castaways who have been hiding in the jungle for the past three months. Who told ye of Captain Avery?'

'A little bird,' Wilmot's men almost laughed – still giddy from the fresh tobacco our boys had given them, with open and proffering hands.

No no no, they thought. We won't say that.

Yet what they said was even worse.

They said, 'We saw it in a dream,' and fell into a gloomy silence, like a tunnel that goes only in a circle.

William picked tobacco from the inside of his lip. His eyes were bulging out of his face.

'You were inside an old mine,' he prompted. 'In search of treasure.'

Wilmot's men glanced at him sharply.

'No,' they stammered. 'We were in a big ship, being pinned onto a nasty reef.'

The wind breathed in the skittering dry palms – the mood passed. Wilmot's men pestered William to go with them, to see the jungle fortress they had constructed with their own hands, and there William met the rest of the survivors, about a hundred and sixty, all about various tasks. Wilbur was with them and went directly to his corner, where he appeared to have been building a new ship. It was already four stories high, remarked one of William's boys.

'It's an honest-to-God launch,' he blurted out, as Wilbur went red.

William shushed his boy, and they were able to move on.

The fort was built against the mountain and protected by an earthen redoubt on the seaward side that Wilmot's men had topped with sharpened stakes, for show, and into which they had sunk firing slots for the big guns from their ship, that they had hauled up and emplaced there, and these commanded the approach to both cove and camp. They had latrines and running water from a crick and at the very back of the encampment was an abandoned mineshaft.

William looks at it, he tells me, and lays both hands on his pistols.

'Let me guess,' he told Wilmot's lost crew, eyes mere slits

of Quaker black, with a glance and nothing more, 'that is where you keep the treasure.'

How did you know, they sneezed.

'Sorry,' they said.

Yes, they told him. 'It's an old mining shaft,' they explained for some reason. 'We have the gold and pearls in there,' and the bones of one mogul princess, they neglected to mention – assuming William had already guessed it.

'Follow me,' William snarled to two of his two boys, and the three of them disappeared down the shaft, cutlasses drawn, spitting back cobwebs, wind howling through their hair. I stayed outside, obviously – but was told that after a short time the passage inclined up, as in William's dream, and William found himself at the bottom of a rickety old ladder.

He looked up it, foot on the bottom rung. It went far up into the mountain. It disappeared about at the height of a brigantine's mainmast lookout. It was pitch black up at the top. William pictured the hole his fifty-eight-caliber dueling pistol would make in anything he met up there.

There was a slight scuffling in his rear.

'Not that way,' Wilmot's men called, beckoning to my Quaker. 'It's down here.'

William looked up the ladder. He paused and leaned back.

'Come on,' yelled the men, eager to show off their loot. 'There's nothing up that way.'

Reluctantly, William took his foot off the bottom rung – turned and trotted down the tunnel after the men.

At the end of the shaft they stepped out into a very large chamber and William and his boys stopped in their tracks – and surely the tracks of many other pirates before them – for they had never seen such quantities of gold and jewels and human skulls in one place before in their lives.

'And this is chicken feed compared to what Captain Avery has, wherever he has got to,' Wilmot's men exclaimed with a grin.

'This is a lot of gold,' said William, turning a bejeweled dagger hilt in a trembling palm. 'People dream about gold like this.'

Wilmot's men chuckled, and then led the way back out.

I never asked William if he had gone back to the ladder, or put his hands on it, or gone partway up it, or gone to the top of it, or seen what was up there, or if it had been the same as his dream, with the priests and the two dead men and the bedrooms at the top and the tools and the thing, nor did he ever mention it. While all this was going on I was pacing the deck of my pirate ship on the far side of Nosy Mitsy, cursing and dying of a case of the nerves, bottle of black rum in hand, wenches banished to the surgical deck on pain of fedth of frendth of death, I spluttered.

'Where is he, where is he,' I muttered, speaking as usual to my bottle, my lieutenants realized. 'Where is that Quaker?'

At that moment a strange sight met our confabulated eyes: a small ship's boat making its laborious way along the shore or haunch of Nosy Mitsy, my men cried, with William in the prow and fifteen of our best boys with him.

'My God, they have decimated him,' I thought, and when the boat had pulled within hailing distance I shouted, 'Where are the others? What have the cannibals done to the others?'

William laughed. He called out, saying that they were all alive and in good health, and told me everything that had happened.

The next day I sailed to see Wilmot, who was still screwing around at Mangahelly with his bottom, to bring him the news, while William took the sloop around to the wreck and got the castaways off, with their chests and furnitures and gold and jewels and pants, as well as one curious object I discovered many years later, rummaging through William's things after a book or some papers he called for, for all the world like a visor off a suit of armor, I swear, as black as night, of one piece like a rock, with curious figures etched into its face like tattoos – that I cast into the Thames upon the first opportunity, as you can imagine.

Withdraw Thy Person

Nosy Mitsy, February 1708
12°52' S - 48°36' E

In a word, all the force Avery had at Madagaskar, in the year 1699, or thereabouts, amounted to our three ships, for his own was lost, as you have heard, and never had any more than about twelve hundred men in all. –Defoe 398

We found the living dire pirate Captain Avery cast away on a desolate strand with his men, and all his treasure intact.

'Give me a ship,' said he.

'Nay,' we never could have brought ourselves to mutter.

Nor could we bring ourselves to mutter, 'Well what did you do with your other one.'

We said, 'Here, take this one.'

William could not believe his ears – he had to depend on his eyes to believe it.

Let me begin again.

We joined forces with Captain Avery after taking him off a long beach, I wrote, licking frequently at the tip of my shuddering quill, and agreed to give him the Spanish frigate, with all its sails and masts, and shift ourselves into the Portuguese or formerly Portuguese man-of-war, we who were somewhat too few to sail all of the many boats we now had at our disposal, anyway, Avery paying us the round sum of forty thousand pieces of eight for the frigate, plus a pirate curtsey, for he was rich as Theseus.

What is he doing, said William through numb lips.

'He is doing the pirate curtsey,' we explained. 'All the kids are doing it now.'

Get rid of it, William blubbered. 'I don't want to see it.'

His boys, who always surrounded him, died of laughter, one after the other.

The frigate, plus our sloop and man- or maniac-of-war, we said, was all that Captain Avery counted on in that year of 16 or 1799, or seventeen or eighteen hundred, the turn of a new century for him – for us all – no matter what you read in other accounts.

Now that we were all shipped, and fabulously wealthy, Captain Avery suggested we build a pirate town right there in Madagaskar, yea on Nosy Mitsy.

Not Nosy Mitsy, said the chalk-white features of William's quaking face.

He said, 'Anywhere but Nosy Mitsy.'

Yet the pirate Captain Avery would describe his pirate town.

It shall be called Averytown, we winced, he began.

Why not Bobville, I told him.

'How about Wilmotsburgh,' I laughed.

Captain Wilmot raised his head momentarily from a drunken swoon.

'Wilmothburrh,' he smiled, thinking he was already there, before his head thunked back down on the table or what is this thing, a horny prostitute.

'Averytown,' Captain Avery said with a benign smile. He said, 'We shall build a great parapet,' speaking apparently to the parrot on his shoulder, 'or outer wall with ramparts and slits for archers and redoubts for the cannon, cannon we shall transfer from the ship – or the hell with it, we're rich, we'll buy new cannon, big guns, and implace them on the ramparts,' he cried.

Great, we replied. Sounds perfect.

'Polly wants to fuck your mother,' said the parrot.

'The outer wall shall be enormous,' continued the man who now considered himself our admiral, shirt unbuttoned to the navel, 'for it shall contain an entire pirate village with shops and houses. We'll have butchers and grocers and cobblers, and a pub on every corner,' he giggled, beard literally sopping up his beer, 'and one church in which we shall worship the true god.'

Mammon, we all cried together, thumping our mugs on anything handy – on top of both tables and whores.

'A church to Mammon,' confirmed the pirate Avery, 'and its convent shall be a bawdy-house, and its priests shall be everyman.'

Amen, we cried – we barfed.

'And we shall have mansions,' said Captain Avery, in his mansion already in his mind, 'every one of us his own mansion, and there shall be a large clubhouse or castle keep in the midst of this pirate town, and there shall be a series of secret, underground tunnels leading from mansion to mansion, so that we can visit each other any time we want, and each of us shall have official keys to its various doors, and in the very middle of the underground complex we shall install our vault.'

The vault, we whispered, eyes wet – tongues dry.

'Tell us about the vault,' we cried, desperately, wantingly, wantonly.

'The vault shall be twenty fathoms deep and fifty fathoms wide,' exclaimed Captain Avery, 'and shall be lined with our treasure, including both gold bullion and jewels the size of living children,' he cried, 'which shall ever increase, and each man shall have his share, and have the right to go to the vault any time he wants and swim in the gold.'

I don't know how to swim, we did not say.

We said, 'Righteous. Yet you are forgetting that we are infamous pirates, and are bound to come under attack by the fleets of English whose mercantile shipping we have been harrying, and susaning, if we set ourselves up like a blarney target and operate from one single location,' we said.

I suggested that if what we wanted was a change of circumstances, or even profession, that we become farmers.

There was a wrenching, catapulting silence, into which Captain Wilmot farted – short, fiery, wet.

Farmers, spat Captain Avery. 'Did you say farmers.'

He said, 'Do you think you are looking at a fucking farmer,' he said.

'It is good land for a retirement of the sort you imagine,' I told him – knowing the land and contours of its shores intimately, like a blanket – like the inside of my first vagina. 'Yet only if you mean to settle down and live peaceably,' I explained, without recourse to the plundering and pillaging and raping to which you are – and by you are, I mean of course we all are – accustomed, and addicted.

'There are cows and goats there,' were my very words.

Captain Avery made no reply to my suggestions – he changed the subject, and would not talk to me about his plans after that night. He did, however, enlist Captain Wilmot in his schemes, and I was able to obtain his purpose from conversations with that man – for Wilmot intended to help found the pirate colony with Avery, and to pirate from that land base a bit longer, until he had sufficient money to look after his retirement, and he always blurted out anything that was on his mind after no fewer than two lagers.

Enough money, I said. 'You mean even more money than you have right now.'

'Yes,' replied Wilmot, gazing with affection at his slumming ship, where she rode at anchor like a deadly gull. He said, 'When I have enough.'

I told him he probably had enough already, or how was he supposed to know when enough was enough.

'Are we talking hundreds of thousands of pieces of eight, or millions of hundreds of thousands of pieces of eight?' I asked him.

'I wish to go ashore in Egypt, and go overland to the Mediterranean,' he swooned, ignoring all my sensible questions, a third beer nestled between his hands, 'where I shall ship myself home to England as a passenger on some small vessel. I wish to give up this dangerous, pirate life and enjoy my winnings while I can.'

You can't just give it up, I told him. It's not that easy.

'Just looking at your eye patch, peg leg, and complete lack of modern clothing they will know your entire history – and then they will hang you,' I explained.

'I shall guise myself,' Captain Wilmot told me with a triumphant gleam, into his cup.

'Even if you think for one second you don't stink of pirate,' I told him, 'the probability of you escaping capture and slavery at the hands of the Turks in the strait of Babelmandel is virtually a hundred to zero.'

After this last comment Captain Wilmot stopped speaking to me, as well.

I am a dread pirate, he told me, shaking what was left of his hair as though it were the mane of a lion, or stallion. He said, 'I go wherever I wish, with whomever I wish, and do whatever I wish.'

Fine, I belched, as he stormed off to join Captain Avery and his people, taking all his trunks and furnitures and considerable fortune. In the hours and days that followed, though I offered him his choice of either the sloop or the man-of-war, he refused to take either, instead making what could have been the most terrible decision of his life, had I been of a mind to quarrel, which was to take off with all my carpenters, and force them to build him a fourteen-gun brigantine there upon the shores of Nosy Mitsy.

I looked across at him strutting on the sand over there in his loincloth, or sometimes nothing at all, and felt deep sorrow for my carpenters – yet was unwilling to risk bloodshed with men I considered my brothers. It may have been the orphan coming out in me, or the queasy rumblings of an incipient religion.

When I saw that their work was nearly complete, I took the sloop and the big ship and all my guns and weighed anchor – my men with me heart and soul. They loved my bravado and way of ripping into a treasure scow, and would have rather parted with their own bodies than part company with Captain Bob in that year of 16 or 1707 or 1708 or 1607 or 1608 – or 1609.

Managing to snag back several of my carpenters, for we were all under our own law, and governed by our own charters, Wilmot had no choice but to admit, I saw, I gave orders to set sail.

We never even said, 'Goodbye.'

I heard later that Captain Avery went on to establish his pirate colony, though it was of course much less impressive than the one in his description. Instead of a wall with a moat around it they had a bamboo stockade by a shallow crick, or shall we say a place where water sometimes seeped across the ground; instead of grand mansions, huts with earthen floors; where the church to Mammon should have stood, they had a crude rock altar on which they would copulate and eat feces; and where the promised vault should have gone, there was a cross that marked a spot in the ground in which was buried a single chest.

What was in that chest only I now know.

What happened to Avery and Wilmot is another story altogether, too long to tell here even if I cared to say. Christmas is tomorrow, so happy Christmas and a good New Year to you. Inform your children we'll see each other there if they're bad.

With Me In Command

Bay of Bengal, July 1708
9°72' S - 79°45' E

Our men were so pleased with my forward, enterprising temper, that they assured me that they would go with me, one and all, over the whole globe, wherever I would carry them; and as for Captain Wilmot, they would have nothing more to do with him. This came to his ears, and put him in a great rage; so that he threatened, if I came on shore, he would cut my throat. –Defoe 201

Parting company with Wilmot and Avery, and taking command of both our ships, for all I cared, I sailed us – though by no means ever single-handed – up big Africa, and we crossed by the Maldives to Malabar and rounded Ceylon where we sighted three English East Indian Company ships not only barging the strait with their bows deep in the wash, but pushing for home like their hearts were in their throats.

We shivered our braces, losing several sailors, and turned and squatted for them in the road, hoisting one of our many flags of a nation, maybe Portugal, I now chuckle, at the last second dropping our roger with its silver crossed daggers and skull, and pounced.

The first reaction of the oncomers was almost of audible laughter, as they drew up in a fighting line and stripped for action, we swore, and came directly at us.

'We'll show them what we do to declared pirates where we're from,' those brave Englishmen said, not mistaking our lack of colors.

Yet when they come up a little further, and got a good look at our tonnage, and could really see our weight of metal – or maybe it was the looks of us that spooked them, the dangling locks of hair and gnarly beards twined with bits of bone and voodoo crosses stuck through our bare and tattooed nipples and lips, and us men or women for all you could tell from the distance of eight insanely herky furlongs – they turned and ran with the wind.

We feigned a chase, but then fell away, for I knew it would be a hard run and an eventual fight, for they were English, and we were confident of easier, richer purchases in those waters, in those glory days.

And we were right. The following day we come upon a sail off the cape they call Kanyakumari and pondered her, for she had the wind of us and could easily slip into one of the three hundred thousand little inlets and cricks in that part of low India and escape if once she saw our teeth or caught so much as a whiff of our cock breath.

We said, 'Cut her off on the landward side, Captain Gordon McCann,' the captain of our feather-sandaled sloop. 'You can if anyone can.'

So the sloop drifted down and slipped between the prize and the nefarious cricks. When the stranger saw her intention she tried to dart in, but it was too late: she was cut off by the sloop and gunned into – pumped into – until she gave up way, slowed, and came to under a white and bloodstained peter.

'It could have been worse for you, you know,' we told her, meaning plunder, full arson, rape and everything rape implied in those latitudes, and massacre to the last man. 'It usually is.'

Please don't kill us, they laughed – it was their last laugh.

'Ha ha h-' they began.

'Slap,' went our ring-studded fingers.

She was a little hardbody of ten guns, we said, when finally we strode her deck, coming at last upon the smoke and scene of combat like the hero of our own novel, touching both taffrail and poop, Portuguese-built like so many others, yet both Dutch-handed and Dutch-handled.

'She is fucking drum-tight,' we whispered, hands still on her, and contained so much gulf pearl and spices and lace that we did not give a damn whether she had once upon a time contained people.

But it was the sloop under Captain McCann that had the real rummaging of her before we came up, we observed by the furtive penises of his men, and their private chagrin, we cried. It was all written in her log – the long entire voyage from Batavia to Persia and successful speculation there. The log read in its entirety, in a sloppy, almost illegible longhand:

'Which as is her official log, Her Mayesties Mercanteel Fulano of Oh Porto, befitted, captain Dutch Henry under his own protestation and pilot Dutch Richard and master Dutch Bill; cargo NO SILK UNDERDRAWERS, naught but spice and pearl and lace and sundry monies, so save us God, shit they are coming for us we have to abandon ship now, SOS,' read the log that was placed into my clutching, needing hands. It was sixty words long, contained two hundred and seventy-nine characters, and stunk of the sour wine preferred by Captain McCann and his first and best lieutenant, Cam McCandlesticks III, and the cabin boy they shared between them.

'Where are the crew,' I immediately chuckled, glaring into their beady black, terror-dead eyes and wine-stained little urchin. 'The frilly lace and underwear you can keep.'

Hearing my words – observing my profound anger – they produced the crew from a net they had been dragging behind the ship.

William, coming on deck at that moment and seeing the bedraggled, gasping forms in a wet mess on the softly pitching planking, looked down at them and was very still.

'Look at these miserable human beings,' I told our merry Quaker. 'Whatever are we to do with them. If we release them and give them back their little ship,' I said, 'they shall make their way directly to the Dutch factories and rat us out. Look into their rat eyes and see for yourself.'

Well, replied William, you surely cannot release them – as many blue eyes looked up and blinked at him for the first time in their lives, from a full and squirming net. 'If they shall turn rat.'

We have no choice but to throw them back, in that case, I guessed, 'or am I wrong.'

'Yet a Dutchman swims like a fish,' William smiled, 'and all my men say the same. There is no use in dumping them in the ocean.'

Your men, I did not splutter. So now your boys are men, I had to bite my tongue and last remaining parrot not to scream. I looked over at his men, who were no longer boys. They no longer slunk and giggled – they stood and gambled, using dice fashioned from human teeth.

I said, 'Well, we can't very well pickle them up with the herrings,' but immediately regretted my careless quibble, for pickling them up among the herrings turned out to be a hilariously fun prospect for most of my crew, and almost instantly, in the blink of a waning day, I was presented with a number of empty man-sized brining casks.

All of this occurred on their derelict deck in the dawn of a setting sun, I once wrote.

The Dutch in the fish net began to wail and moan – they

had noticed we were drinking hard. I immediately saw the man they would pickle first, a red herring with a taffy beard.

You, Redbeard, I called to the red herring, who was sticking out of the net on my side. 'Speak to your men, and ask them who shall join us, and be pirates.'

Fourteen hands and several legs were immediately thrust from the net.

We blinked with real pleasure.

Yet one must not simply say pirate to be a pirate, William explained to them – with the patience of a Christian god, in a language only they could hear.

'You have to undergo the initiation,' he told them.

What are you telling them, I said. William ignored me.

Redbeard asked him what the initiation entailed.

'What meanest thou, initiation?' he spluttered with respect in his outthrust fingers and right leg, still wondering if they would survive even if they were not put back into the water.

'Thou shalt find out when we cut off thy manhoods,' squeaked one of my prominent midshipmen – whose initiation had been extremely irregular.

Twelve Dutch hands and all the Dutch legs immediately returned to their places inside the net.

'Please kill us,' Redbeard told me. 'Do it quickly.'

And my men were all for this, but William calmed them down by having the Dutch removed or dragged off from line of sight, belowdecks, and by cracking several barrels of my finest personal wines, and passing out silver doubloons – by saying, 'Hey hoy, ready cash from a willing Dutch cow.'

Our men laughed until they were red in the loins and gambled themselves into a drinking state.

Meanwhile I interrogated the prisoners in the privacy of

a lonely king – of a man already more pirate than orphan.

'Look, Redbeard,' I said to them, 'You can't go to Ceylon or Kanyakumari or the Maldives because the Dutch are going to talk to you and find out where I am and then send a flotilla after me, if that is also a word in your language,' they nodded, 'and are going to blow me out of the water, which can never happen.'

It's literally impossible, they agreed.

'In our times it can not come to pass,' they said in a Bible full of love and pity.

So what I can do for you is to maroon you on Madagaskar, I continued.

No please no not Madagaskar, they wailed. 'Pretty please no.'

I looked at them in stony silence. Back in my day, I did not begin.

'Redbeard,' I said finally, with restraint in a Bible full of wrath and carnage, 'I can maroon you on Madagaskar, or any other place you can point out on a map where the Dutch will have no contact with you for at least three months. Because I am on a mission,' I explained with studied, learning patience, and as I write this I can tell you that that mission was going to be completed, come hell or high water.

'Anywhere but Madagaskar,' replied Redbeard, but our interview was over. The Dutchmen were saved, I spat out into open water, striding my poop in a bloody dawn. It was November of 16 or 1708. The fish were jumping, I was rich, and the man at the helm that leaned like an ancient up on the spokes had just turned fourteen, or a hundred and fourteen.

Pickle Them Up
With The Herring

Bay of Bengal, July 1708
9°72' S - 79°45' E

While William and I were talking, the poor Dutchmen were openly condemned to die, as it may be called, by the whole ship's company; and so warm were the men upon it, that they grew very clamorous; and when they heard William was against it, some of them swore they should die, and, if William opposed it, he should drown along with them. –Defoe 205

It was now essential to dispose of the evidence of our crime.

'Shall we burn the little Dutch vessel, or run her upon the rocks?' I asked William.

'Those are the only two options,' he mused. 'Or else you could blow her up.'

'Waste of powder, methinks,' methought, after allowing visions of the frail Dutcher going sky-high in a glory of smoke and series of crunching explosions to shudder and flash past my eyes and throbbing life and fully erect penis.

Yes, he nodded William, though clearly balky at letting a chance like this go by. 'I should crash her against the rocks,' he smiled, pointing at the tremendous surf that tumbled against the high seawall to windward, and I gave the order: foresail with tack at the masthead, helm over to starboard right side, and push her off.

We stood with the Dutchmen on my man-of-war as their ship sped away, unmanned. There were tears in their eyes – in ours, nothing but delight and curiosity. What would happen to the little boat? Would she strike the rocks at the base of the cliff and be smashed to smithereens in our full sight, as we hoped, or would she veer like a prodigal and fall onto an inconspicuous reef and go down in sections?

Suddenly Redbeard gave a great start, and he shrieked something unintelligible into the aura of my captain's halo.

'What is he saying,' William, I asked the softly smiling, wheeling Quaker.

'It's Moppins,' explained William, as Redbeard began to jump up and down in circles and clutch at his tawny hair. 'They forgot to get Moppins out of the brig.'

Who the fuck is Moppins, I wanted to know.

I said, 'We didn't see anyone in the brig.'

'She's trapped in there,' wailed Redbeard. 'Oh God, we have to stop the ship.'

The little barkie, already miniature against the sky and growing smaller with every passing second, and inch of wind, began to pick up real speed now. It flew like a gamboling fish over the slappy waves and leaden troughs, heading as true as a darling for the cliff face that destiny had put there for her.

'It's too late now,' I said grimly. 'Moppins is about to mop up big India.'

William turned to me and said, 'Let me take the sloop. It's not too late.'

It's too dangerous – you'll put yourself and your men at impossible risk – I can't lose you, William, truelove, were all things that flashed through my mind.

'Do it,' I said.

William called to two of his men and, having given the order for the sloop to sloop alongside our bustling big gunner, and shear us close, they gave a flying leap and got aboard her, already making good way.

They tacked into the wind to get room on the Dutchman, then came round hard on her tail, though we thought they would hang up for a moment in the maneuver, but they got her round and swooped down on their quarry like an Icarus from the wall.

We placed our fingers into our mouths and bit down hard.

Two furlongs from shore we saw them close with her and, after an agonizing pause, observed forms leap across the water into her chains, as they sped closer and closer and closer and closer and closer and closer and closer and closer and closer and closer and closer and closer and closer to the hard and foaming rocks. At the last second the sloop sheared off, and moments later both vessels shivered, luffed, clawed, slowed, hung, and pulled up into the wind.

Coming up shortly, we saw exactly what a close thing it had been, I swore to all my calf gods and damaged wives, for they swam in blue water not a furlong from the towering, sharp, loudly crashing wall, we shouted above the roar and heave of the water. I immediately went aboard the Dutchman with Redbeard and my personal bodyguard, where I found William standing on the main deck, hands on his hips, as calm and smiling as a constable.

'Good work,' I told him.

It meant, Never again.

'There is no one in the brig,' William reported, looking at Redbeard with a big grin. 'It's completely empty.'

No no no no God, wept the Dutchman. 'Moppins!'

screamed Redbeard, rushing below deck.

'It is some kind of ambush or distraction,' I muttered, and ordered our men to stand ready with cutlasses and pistols – signaled our ships to check the prisoners – scanned the horizon for the flotilla of Dutch-gunned frigates that would bear down on our sweet, well downwind, candy asses. I stared at the stranded cliffs that towered from the coast and waited for the Dutch cavalry to gallop up and start lobbing bombs, or the natives in secret cahoots to shower down a rain of death-be-damned spears.

None of these things happened. After five minutes Redbeard emerged from a hatch, big smile splitting his fuzzy chin like a man-eating plant. In his arms he held a fat purring tabby cat with a white spot on one ear.

'It's Moppins,' explained William, faint amusement playing around his mouth and heavy pistols. 'Moppins was in the brig, after all. We saved Moppins' life.'

My eyes slit like daggers – my jaw set like a bank safe snapping closed on a couple of pranking toddlers. A low growl began somewhere in my throat, and continued as I gave my next order.

'Put the Dutchmen back in the Dutchman,' I called so as everyone could hear me, 'and roust out two kegs of that good gunpowder.'

William stroked the cat for good luck, gave me a glance, and shrugged to show I meant it.

Amboyna

Banda Sea, Dutch Spice Islands, August 1708
3°33' S - 125°35' E

Preparations for our next project -- We sail to the Spice Islands, and get in among them -- Dutch from Amboyna -- Their version of the incident at Amboyna -- We murder them

For years or centuries I had been licking my wolf chops at the prospect of getting in among the Spice Islands, and ripping into them with my canines, and hitting them like a sack of heavy bricks, the bricks being fists and cannon, and one doughty Quaker – and finally I got the chance.

What was the particular allure of the Spice Islands, you ask, that lay irrevocably in the clutches of the scurvy, heavy-gunned Dutch? Nothing more than the world's exclusive traffic in nutmeg, cinnamon, and cloves, I scratched excitedly onto the parchment, eyes goggling out of my skull because of nutmeg.

Nothing more than the brick gold and pieces of eight and sundry European goods necessary for purchasing that kind of consignment, I informed my men, because we love gold and silver and European goods.

'Cheer,' they replied.

I thought so, I chortled into my small beer.

We weighed anchor and beat it out of the Bay of Bengal, flitted through the Straits of Sunda, dodged by Kuala, and edged past Java – in short, slipped straight into the Maluccas, or Dutch Spice Islands, like a shiv into a two-handed whore.

There we met with some small storms, and on course a whoreson great number of islands and reefs, a great embarrassment to our pilots.

'We are chagrined,' they would shout, turning the helm hard over, meaning that we were on the weather side of some very sharp rocks and about to die.

Yet we opted not to die – we steered instead for Manila, where the great weight of the spice traffic was bound, we assumed, and we were right. Not a day off Banda we took a Dutch junker that carried sixteen tons of nutmegs and some excellent little britches, and didn't put up as much as a fight.

Where are ye out of, we demanded, in nothing less than sterling Dutch, in our newfound state of blessed wealth.

'Where do ye come from?' we barked.

'Amboyna,' they replied. 'THE Amboyna.'

Not THE Amboyna, we actually asked them.

'You mean, you admit to being the same motherless sons who tortured and belittled twenty-odd English East India Company English, men with recourse both to court and king, and stood upon dry ground, and done thrown their corpses to the sharks?' we gasped.

'You are our slaves,' they replied.

What, we said.

'What do you mean, we are your slaves. You are OUR slaves,' we told them.

'These are Dutch waters,' they replied in nothing but Dutch, if I can recall anything at all in Dutch. We looked across the gay, gunpowder haze of nothing but a broad, Indonesian sea.

What in the fuck are you fucking talking about, we asked them. You are our prisoners.

'These are not Dutch waters,' we told them.

The Dutch captives merely smiled – told us to tell that to the bumpy, lacerated English bodies they had recently dumped into these same Dutch waters.

'Tell that to the twenty men we just tortured and murdered, and dumped into an ocean that belongs to us,' they chuckled softly.

You say what, we repeated, with both stupefaction and repetition.

They repeated what they had just said. Then we nearly heard the following story.

'Aliens came down,' they told us, creatures from a distant planet, 'and occupied our bodies.'

Occupied your bodies, we repeated – William by this time leading the interrogation.

'They are lying,' he smiled, squeezing and patting their bodies.

'Are they still in there?' we shouted, admittedly stepping back – throwing open a porthole to shine more light on the Dutch.

'They were inside of us,' they replied, 'but have recently returned to their own spheres.'

Why did they inhabit you, we demanded. We said, 'Why did they even enter our world to begin with? And how did they ever enter our world?'

'Our world is not your world,' laughed the hardy Dutch. 'Chuckle chuckle chuckle. You shall only confess under torture.'

'They are insane,' concluded William, standing up and brushing off his tidy black pants. 'Throw them to the sharks.'

'First,' remonstrated our captives, 'allow us to tell our story.'

'No,' replied William, and over the side they went.

Meg, My Nutmeg

In among the Banda Islands, October 1708
4°35' S - 130°01' E

It is not possible for me to describe, or any one to conceive, the terror of that minute. I thought myself doomed by Heaven to sink that moment into eternal destruction; and with this particular mark of terror -- viz., that the vengeance was not executed in the ordinary way of human justice, but that God had taken me into his immediate disposing, and had resolved to be the executor of his own vengeance. -Defoe 213

I would have been glad and willing to shell out major Spice Island dollars, which were pieces of eight, for the kind of clove and nutmeg available in those climes, in those palmy days of man bite loincloth, but my men absolutely refused to pay for anything. Why pay for it when you can just take it, they would snarl, as I reached for my purse, though in much lesser English.

'Grrrrr, garrr, snarl,' they would say – and everyone involved would know what they were talking about.

'Have it,' the cunning natives would tell them.

The Dutch on their diminutive craft would say, 'Take everything you want, just spare our wives.'

Where are your wives, our men would growl.

'Not our wives,' you dumb shits, the Dutch would stammer. 'Our lives. Spare us our lives.'

Where are the wives, our men would growl.

I would have to turn my back on the scene, but – whether

by hook or by crook, or by the grace of God – we got our spices.

Thank God, and praise be to us.

'The sloop,' cried Pajama my brave lieutenant, pulling up his pajamas, and getting them on forever. 'They have signaled a sail – two sails. Nay, yet, even three sails have they signaled,' he eulogized.

Well when are you going to write your fucking novel, I told him.

'Full steam ahead,' I cried emphatically, anachronistically, impossibly, aloud.

Yet this nearly cost us our bark, and bucking skins, for as we steamed on, all sails full of atrocious, snarling wind, we found ourselves in the midst of snipping, creamy rocks, and felt our bottom crash upon the very sand, and thought we saw the floor of the ocean rear up like a snarling pig.

'Right full rudder,' I screamed, but I was mistaken – our rudder had been knocked askew, and we were powerless to turn the boat. 'Reef the sails,' I cried, growing even larger and angrier in this state of emergency, 'and let our skysail carry us through.'

I laughed to myself – already writing my book of poetry, noticed PJ Bottoms with a sinking heart.

You're lucky, I told him. 'You are watching history in the making.'

We all always watch history in the making, he did not retort – his mouth was fixed in an open scream. It was a close thing, and we were lucky there was an island at hand, for we were taking in water at an alarming rate.

Work them pumps, I said. 'Pump for all you're worth.'

'Take us into that little cove,' I told them, which they did – we limped in, and came to anchor at exactly the last second, and began to unload our guns and gold and massive bacons and barrels of mead, and strumpets in a hurry, that left without proper goodbyes, which alleviated the flooding.

'Erect eighteen little tents, or hell just one big one,' I ordered my men, 'into which we shall unload our goods, and victuals, and thus free the lumbering bottom of its load,' I sneered at Pajama Bottoms, 'and then we shall beach this bitch, the butcher, and effect repairs.'

PJ knew I was parodying his way of talking, and writing – I could tell by the way he mooned and sighed, and by his crestfallen shoulders and the blood trickling from his right ear.

'Hey, Pajama Bottoms,' I shouted, hooking one thumb into his diaper, or what was this thing, his sweatpants. 'Hey, PJ, don't feel bad,' I told him. Pajama Bottoms looked for one startling second directly into my eyes, for the first time in his life, and realized he was pissing himself.

'I take back what I just said,' I stammered. 'You are a disgrace. Go ashore and look after Mamsy and Taffy and the other sluts.'

Mamsy and Taffy and the other sluts sighed audibly from the boat that would carry them to the party. They knew what Pajama Bottoms was like at a sleepover.

'Her bottom is very foul,' we exclaimed the next morning, observing the Portuguese man-of-war where she lay still and lighter than ever before in her experience upon some hard, dry sand, – upon nothing but the island which I have already mentioned. 'We must needs scour it. You,' I said, 'must needs scour it.'

'Bottoms, reporting for duty,' cried PJ, stumbling from the bigtop with his shirt clutched in front of his necessaries, and undignitaries.

'Not you,' I barfed – me, faultlessly dressed in just knickers and gold medallions. 'When I call you, you'll know it,' I informed this badly mistaken man, who had fallen into the sand at my what are these things at my feet. 'Now go away.'

We watched Bottom's bottom as it went, sobbing somehow.

'I'm not entirely sure he's going to make it,' I confided in my other lieutenants, who were shaking their heads in sadness.

When the God-damned sloop came up, and found us in our pirate cove, we invited her, too, to join in the festivities.

'Come on up here,' we shouted. 'Lieutenant Bottoms is swabbing the boat by his lonesome, and rubbing coconut oil all over her bunting,' we realized with something like horror.

And they unloaded the sloop, too, and ran her up on the beach alongside our big frigate, and Captain Wilmot got out and looked at everything and exclaimed, 'I would expect nothing less from a man like PJ,' he guffawed.

Lieutenant Pajama Bottoms glanced up from his work and tried to smile.

'Don't stop,' we warned him. 'Don't smile.'

And it was also a warning for all the other sluts on that beach, in that marvelous year of 16 or 1708 or 1808, when men were men and whistled while they worked.

In that place we constructed quite a little fortress, I admit. We dug a moat and erected a great stockade around our bigtop, and emplaced our guns there, in nifty little redoubts, and topped it all with a kind of mesh of dry thorns, and we had passwords that everyone had to memorize in order to get inside.

'Is this where the party is happening?' some God-damned fool would blurt out.

'What party,' we would hiss in reply, through the grate.

'THE party,' the numbskull would say.

'Do you have the password?'

'Jonestown,' the invariable reply.

'Ha ha ha ha,' was our only response – for that is the oldest password in the world.

'The password,' we would whisper, 'is Octogenarian.'

'Octuh guh uh what?' they would always – always try to say.

'No no no,' we would have to reply. 'Octo. Gee. Narian,' I would curse, naming my own age to a month if it was a day. 'Octogenarian.'

'Octogenarian,' they would repeat, and be shunted into, onto, and unto the party.

After staying on that island a space, or spice, however, and getting cleaned up, we decided to continue on our roving ways, and sail for purchase among the Chinese in the waters of forbidding Formosa, William our jolly Quaker having rejected the notion of cruising against the Europeans.

'They know thee, and shall fight thee,' he explained, and have very little money, pointing out that the Chinese, on the contrary, being closer to home, would invariably trust to good luck to get by.

'But the luck is mine,' I marveled, nodded William.

'The luck is yours,' he concurred.

Thus to Formosa.

And we were lucky, though scared halfway shitless by a number of bad bolts of lightning, one of which struck our mainmast in a SW gale, upon which we rolled and rowed, I exclaimed, and burnt a number of men so badly that they could not speak again, and had blisters upon their foreheads and lips, and mothers, and eventually had to be brined.

I can not even describe the moment of the blast, more like a broadside than any weight of metal I have ever felt, or seen, for I was admittedly passed out drunk in my cabin at the time. Yet I believe the accounts, for I awoke in the aftermath to see with my own eyes the men that fell shrieking into the sea, all charred and writhing.

'Where is the enemy,' I roared. 'Point your guns at the

enemy.'

Nay, insisted William, placing his hand on my gasping chest, as was his habit, 'there is no enemy but God and Satan.'

Point all your guns at God, in that case, I screamed, puking black blood and what looked like green beans and most of a goat off the windward rail. I was shaking and terror filled my soul and shoes somewhere. It was truly the first time I had ever thought about God, or what I had had for dinner the night before.

'I am dying,' I told William, he guffawed lightly, with a cool smile.

'Yes,' he agreed, looking at my puke and stool. 'As your physician, not only of the body, but of the everlasting soul, I can't even begin to advise thee.'

It's that bad, I wondered, as despair touched me with its saucy fingers, and stuck.

'I don't want to die,' I wept.

William felt sorry for me, but said nothing.

'It's guilt you are feeling,' were words that came from his Quaker black black.

I feel no guilt, I screamed, into the wind and rainy spray and air.

'I have done nothing,' I blabbered. 'I am not an aminal.'

'You are not an animal,' chuckled my best friend, with a soft and wheeling grin.

'Not a aminal,' I blubbered, falling into his arms, and weeping for the first time since old Lisboa.

The ship took no damage from the hits upon its masts and ropes and sails – we assumed the men absorbed it all, we laughed, raising our glasses at ten o'clock next morning.

Full of grog and love, and confusion, and terror, and grog.

Ceylon

A chase and our honest terms -- Our men make free with women of foul temperament -- A narrow escape -- Cooler heads prevail, and they are mine -- A desperate hurricane -- Stranded! -- The story of Commander Knox -- William's plan -- Conversation with an old Dutchman

Never forget that beneath our mascara and gregarious exoskeletons we too were made of flesh and blood. Thus we found ourselves in the process of procuring meat and drink as we carved up and down the shores of Java, but were in fact on short rations, having only managed to capture some dozen hogs to pickle, and were wary – though unafraid – of going ashore at a major port in our shirtless, lurching state. We had just taken on some screwy river water for drinking, and begun to soak the pork for lunch, when we spied a sail bearing down on us hard from the NE, and said to each other, well now if it ain't one thing it sure is another.

Suspecting trouble, only able to imagine she had friends with big guns, for she would run at us with all the sail she could bend, we weighed anchor and tacked coastwise to get the wind of her, which we just managed to do.

Cleared for action, we let fly our heavy, flapping black flag.

'Holy Jesus, mother of Mary,' swore the unknown interloper, shivering her braces, and tacking with the wind, never having expected to meet a pirate in these waters, in broad daylight, and the chase was on. We caught up with her presently, being pretty good sailors ourselves, if I do sail so myself, and sent a hard, round, iron postcard across her bow with just one word on it.

'Belay,' said the ball, whistling through actual shrouds, and our friend luffed up and sent a boat across.

We sent the boat back. 'Take down your colors,' we insisted. 'First strike your colors, then presume to speak to us.'

The boat returned to the mother ship, a Dutch one, yet the colors remains aloft.

'Bang,' spoke my favorite gun again, and we could see all the Dutchman in her jump, yet the colors did not move.

Fucking God damn it, I swore, and ordered all our godlike guns run out.

'On my word,' I screamed, 'give them everything you've got.'

At that moment her longboat came off again, this time with her captain in the stern, and with a shiver her flag came slowly down.

'Hold your fire,' I wheezed, although tempted to blow her out of her own element.

'What we seek is vittles,' I explained to her captain, after he had offered me his sword – when I had graciously refused to take it. 'Though there is something funny about you, sailor, I like you. You shall sail with us, and go ashore with our men at Batavia, and procure meats and sweet arrack for us there, and then you and your men shall be free to continue on to, on to, to. Where art thou bound?'

We don't know, the Dutch captain almost said, and was a mere boy in my eyes, I saw. He said, 'To Acatpulc. To Austral. To big Form. Too big Formasa.'

To big Formosa, we mused, incredulous eyes hovering above a mouth red with the blood of our own enemies. I motioned to the substantial Dutcher, swaying in blue water, knee-deep at a cable's length, in the very ocean at our feet. 'Son, are you sure this is your boat?'

His pleading eyes looked up at me and I told myself I didn't care.

'Sweet arrack and meat,' I repeated. 'That's all we want.'

Sweet arrack you can have, replied the Dutch captain, 'and the six hundred bushels of rice we have on board. Just don't touch my men.'

Touch your men, we chuckled, looking the son of a bitch up and down for the first time in our lives – as with new eyes. 'Or are they not men.'

Their captain or captains looked into my eyes, and quick words, and trembled, but swore that they were men – his men.

'You sure you aren't a bunch of footloose dykes,' I did not ask him – did not ask her – did not care. My job was to feed my people, and I had a soft spot in my heart for mutineers, be they girls or boys. I said, 'Give us your rice, and arrack, and go with us to procure beeves, and I swear not a man among you shall feel our black peter.'

She wanted to ask what my black peter was, whether it was my name for my jolly roger, but good thing for her she did not. I waited two jiffies, hand on my everlasting sword, then turned on my heel and left her.

She returned to her men, who sailed with us at gunpoint to the port at Batavia where the captain and her small lieutenants went ashore with our striding dudes and haggled for beeves, and got us eleven nice cows, which they had butchered and salted and casked, and I stuck by our agreement, forbidding my men to set so much as a cat on board their ship.

'If I find out you have been setting our animals on board the ship of paradise,' I warned them, 'I will shoot you from a cannon.'

And by shoot them from a cannon they realized I meant shoot them bodily from an actual cannon, and they knew the one I meant.

'You were right to forbid communication with the ship of small girls,' slurred William, after having personally tasted all eighty-five barrels of arrack to check for poison, as he claimed. 'It would of been a bloodbath. They would of rizz up in murder us all.'

I thought you were a teetotaler, William my good friend, I smiled.

I said, 'William, Jesus, go lie down on your sweet cot. We can't have you be seen like this. What if one of the men needs an amputation?'

'Let them eat cake,' guffawed William, as he was led below.

We let the Dutch boat go when our supply was complete, gazing after them with blinking eyes, and sailed for Ceylon, where we touched and rode anchor for a number of days while we took on yet more water and yet more pork. I had avoided a sad scene with a boat of innocent young women, but on Ceylon my men made me pay for their days of abstinence and false memories of Dutch thighs in hot ankle-deep bilge by going on a mad, degenerate spree.

'I never even saw it coming, William,' I confided in William afterwards.

How could you have, he replied. 'There are not words to describe those Ceylon women.'

'Homely,' I suggested. 'Of foul temper.'

Homely and foul-mannered and recovering lepers, he

replied, 'and four-legged.'

'Not actually women,' I said.

Ambushed, betrayed! were the screams we heard, the first clue that something was amiss on shore. I sat up in my hammock and told William to arm his boys – to cut out those damn fools on shore, and to leave no man behind.

'Do it now,' I winced, reaching first for my sword, then for my grog.

'You fucking morons would stick your dick in a God-damned clock,' I reprimanded my men, as they leered and guffawed in the aftermath. 'Those are the trashiest, smelliest, nastiest women I have ever seen – and I have been all over the modern world,' I boasted. 'Those ladies would stop a parade in Paris.'

'Women,' chortled a few of the boys, thinking I thought they had fucked women.

I never was able to find out exactly what our men had done to those people, whether fucking had anything to do with it, but it must have been something bad, something unprintable or else entirely illegible, so drunk and mad I was when I scribbled it, for they were promptly attacked by four hundred extremely angry gentlemen, all shaking spears and makeshift clubs. Fortunately William acted quickly, crashing the beach with twenty of his trustiest boys, and was able to rescue our embattled platoon, that had been cut off from the water and were on the point of being overwhelmed. Even so, the survivors had been nicked about and were convinced they would die, for they had heard that the arrowheads and incisors of the Ceylon guerrillas were poisoned.

'They say the old men poison their teeth when they go into battle,' they moaned.

Now that makes a lot of sense, we replied, with scorn in

the full face of an offshore breeze.

'I can't feel my leg,' wept a sailor, lying in the bottom of the boat. 'It's the poison bite.'

That's because you only have one leg, William smiled. He said, 'I took the other one off the coast of Malabar in 16 or 1707 after our infamous action with the Dutch sloop, where your ankle was crushed beneath the recoil of a big gun, do ya remember, and the leg mangled beyond saving.'

No, it's the other leg I can't feel, the man gasped.

But he was wrong – his other leg was fine, and none of them had been infected.

'Seventeen wounded, and one dead,' reported William.

Did he die of a hemlock arrowhead, I inquired.

'No,' laughed William. 'Rather from drinking an entire barrel of sweet arrack in the aftermath, and bursting wide open.'

Gruesome, I said.

I said, 'Gnarly, friend William.'

You're telling me, he grinned back. 'I'm actually in here to get the mop.'

We pulled out of Ceylon and thirty or so truly rough-looking ladies, though our men argued long and hard to go back ashore and get their vengeance, as they called it.

'It seems to me that the score is actually about even at this point,' I quipped, tipping my pirate hat back on my gregarious, attractive blond curls – squinting into the waist. 'You raped their women, they inflicted some light carnage on your persons, nobody died. Except Steven. Even Steven.'

We want to inflict carnage on their bodies in return, our men grunted, and flexed.

'If you did that then they would have to go to your port of residence and rape your wives,' I explained, with patience like a sequel to the Book of Job. 'Why is this happening to me again? See, in that case things would be lopsided, and it would be their turn to hurt you.'

Raaaah, graaaaarh, replied our men, looking for something to break and throw.

'Get back inside,' I told the cabin boy, who had just poked his scrawny little neck out the roundhouse door.

In the end William convinced the men that it would be fruitless to pursue their idea of revenge here, reminding us all that our work was to extract money from the weak and sailors short on powder, and shorter on sail, and on minors; that the very folks they intended to murder were insufferably poverty-stricken yokels who did not wear clothing, whose only concept of currency was love and a chicken.

'You don't want to go on shore and force them to give you their love,' he laughed – Quaker humor, we suspected. He said, 'You don't want to have to pay for their chicken,' he chortled.

The men sullenly agreed, and we rode N, the way the bottle pointed, chaste by no big regrets.

Quakers!

Surat, India 1710
17°33' N - 72°56' E

I come now back to my own history, which grows near a conclusion, as to the travels I took in this part of the world. We were now at sea, and we stood away to the north for a while to try if we could get a market for our spices; for we were very rich in nutmegs, but we ill knew what to do with them: we durst not go upon the English coast, or, to speak more properly, among the English factories, to trade; not that we were afraid to fight any two ships they had; and besides that, we knew, that as they had no letters of marque, or of reprisals, from the government, so it was none of their business to act offensively, no, not though we were pirates. –Defoe 538

A further doubt: is saying you owe someone an apology the same as apologizing to them – saying the words I apologize, I am sorry, I was wrong and unhappily drunk, forgive me, say you still love me, tell me I have a fighting chance, baby, please, I am yours, as a friend of mine supposed, writing to say he owed me an apology for a (slight, gambling) debt, but without ever writing the words, in fact moving on immediately to prate about his family, and business, and the paydirt and weather in Virginia, as though mentioning his debt were the same as begging for his life back, and my forgiveness?

'I am writing this to apologize,' the son-of-a-bitch scribbled in his big loopy cursive. 'Blah, blah, blah.' In the old days I would have called him out right in front of his greco-pillared plantation, in front of all his slaves, and shot him down in his own gravel. Let him thank his stars I am no longer that sort of man, that I am a new man.

Yet let him not tempt the old one.

Deep at sea, leaving the barbary coasts of the Malabars far behind, astride our touted poops, upon a cream-dark wake, we contemplated means by which to transform our nutmeg and allspice to hard cash – even if hard cash meant in part the favors of a credible transvestite or passable theater boy.

'A rose by any other name,' we quipped.

We said, 'We would accept sexual favors for our nutmegs, if there were that much sex in the world,' but there was not.

So we looked to trade, but were forced to admit that after more than ten years as pirates we could not talk or behave like ordinary people.

'The English in these latitudes are not liable to attack us, gararrrh, bearing no letters of marque, id est, of reprisals from the English crown and invested powers,' we explained, using mostly Latin to express our thoughts, 'and seeing that we are a mighty, bustling, fifty-odd-gun dreadnought with blood on our hands, and lust in an Ethiope-dark countenance,' we menaced, 'they shall give us no quarter.'

Agreed, we said. We said we have no fear of them, per se.

'Yet they will be a-talking, and carrying news of us from factory town to factory town all up and down this coast, even unto the Dutch in their Malabar and Spice Island redoubts,' we confirmed. 'In short, we must go over to the Portuguese,' we concluded.

So we sailed upon Goa and Marmagoon, and touched land there, and put into a hidden cove somewhat S of Surat and her chubby Porto factories where there was good, deep water – where we would disguise ourselves and our boats.

'Friend,' William said, coming to me in my cloakroom of confidence, 'let me have Surgeon Mephistopheles and the old pilot, and half an hour, and thou shalt never say thou hast not reaped thee three good Quakers.'

Reaped me three good Quakers, I said.

'Good William,' I cried, 'are you telling me you are going to instruct these men in your secret catechism, and that I shall examine them?'

What are you talking about, William, were my very words.

He said, 'I shall never catechize them, dear me, no. Indeed that might prove a great danger for the entire ship,' he smiled. 'No, I shall merely dress them as Friends, and correct their language, so that we appear to be three – not one.'

A trinity of Quakers, I shuddered, when next I gazed upon the old pilot and Mephistopheles and the original William, presented at the taffrail in a row, all black pants and waistcoats and busy, almost flippant white cravats.

'You are William,' I guessed.

A horselaugh – nothing more.

I turned on the third in the row.

'You are William.'

His beard fell off.

'Father, Son, and Holy Ghost,' I remarked, kicking a swab, I admitted.

The real William smiled, and went direct with his quakering trio aboard the sloop, which we stripped of all her big guns and ornamental woodwork and flare, of which she had but little, and disguised of her splinter and small-shot scars, of which she had a considerable bunch, and painted a decent color.

'Smash,' went a bottle of good arrack across her starboard

bow, and with that sacrament she was jesused the *Amiga* – shifted with a mogul's hoard of cinnamon and spice, eighteen hand-picked men, and the jaunty good fortune of God's favorite Quaker.

They sailed immediately out to sea, coming back upon the headland of Salsat by the great factory hard by Surat, and lay there – rocking – within full sight of the colony.

'Cxu ivi deziras fisxojn?' inquired some native fish peddlers from a longboat they stood and rowed, calling across the swells to no lesser a man than William himself – or one of his body doubles. 'Ni havas fisxojn, panon, kaj sukojn, se estas ke ivi dezirus.'

How dare you offer to fuck, suck, and spank me, William did not cry, drily – he understood all languages, including the trite, sour, daffy ones of old Goa. He replied that yes, he should very much indeed like fish, and bread, and above all juices, and would pay them in full at once, and give them good silver to take him ashore, to boot, if they could, in their jolly skiff, friends.

'Thus I was able to go ashore without the knowledge of the factory men, and introduce myself covertly to the sleaze and solitary contours of their innermost pubs, where I promptly presented myself to some Englishmen as live there, Company men but businessmen on their own *account*, as well, if you catch my drift. If you get what I am driving at,' he said.

William, I told him, you are talking to the world's greatest pirate. 'If it is speculation or a heavy swiving you are talking about, I am your man.'

'So they were willing to do a little trade on the side,' winked he – though they were not in the market for so much tonnage as William had aboard.

'So you did not unload the entire package,' I despaired,

kicking out – flailing out.

'It is so much cinnamon and spice,' cried the Englishmen, upon William's discovery of the entire contents of the sloop. 'We shall have to indulge Danny and Tompkins in the deal.'

Who are Danny and Tompkins in the deal, deadpanned William, slamming the bar hard with his mug of frothy pineapple juice. The Englishmen indicated two shady customers that frolicked in the corner of the establishment – rectangular, stucco.

'What do Danny and Tompkins want with thirty-three tons of nuts and cloves,' demanded William, already knowing what we all knew – that they intended to ship them into the strait of Babelmandel where they would be worth their weight in anything Danny or Tompkins could possibly imagine.

'And they have very good imaginations,' winked William's Englishmen.

Give me Danny and Tompkins for surety, Williams told them, with a shudder, and a couple of good pilots, and at midnight I shall steer the cargo up the creek you have indicated to the rendezvous, and unload the entire parcel.

'And is that what happened,' I asked him.

In terms of money, replied William, we are as rich as bankers – as Theseus, as you would put it.

He said, 'They paid me thirty-five thousand pieces of eight in hard pieces of eight, plus these two ogreing diamonds, which I was content to take.'

I took the diamonds in my hands like boobs and squeezed them – and wept.

When the transaction was complete, William invited the men aboard the light, the prancing sloop to dine, 'And you thee'd 'em and thou'd 'em till you got 'em so drunk they could not see to piss into the scuppers,' I suggested.

Precisely, smiled one foul little Quaker.

'They went all around the ship asking my boys who we were, and where we come from, and what our business was, but our boys said not a word, for I had learned them to bear tongues of lead, and pull sullen faces.'

What have you done to them, Danny and Tompkins had to bite each other's tongues not to ask.

'Very presentable,' they coughed. 'Presentable, presentable,' they giggled, hands all over each other.

William told the merchants that we had a second sister sloop that lay in Marmagoon with a similar cargo if they were interested, he said he said.

'There is more where this came from,' were his very words.

Danny and company were so eager for William's nuts and spices that they would have bargained with him for the sister sloop's consignment on the spot.

'This is not just drunk people talking,' they shouted, words carrying far across the lagoon into the bushes and trees, and rustling banana fronds. 'We'll buy your sister's sloop's consignment, sister sloop and all, with hard cash in advance.'

William replied that he could not speak for his sister, who was a very stubborn, hard woman, with tattoos up the Yazoo, they shuddered, nor promise that she had not already unloaded her goods at a profitable advantage upon another coast, or factory outpost, or black market or some other market, or even just capsized because she had so much heavy loot on board; but that he was willing to go and speak to her, and give her their offer.

'Please, yes, please, God, go, go now,' they begged him, which was how he came to be narrating me the story of Danny and Tompkins.

I said, 'So you want me to go down to them with the rest of the cinnamon and spice and unload it onto their taffy banks.'

Yes, thought William, looking up in surprise.

'Nay,' he replied, looking down, thumbing idly through a Bible – swinging in a hammock with one big stockinged foot upon a plank. 'For though they scorn not to traffic with stolen goods, they should truly weason to bespeak an actual pirate, or take a single daffy iota from his bloodstained, criminal fingers,' he read – St. Matthew chapter five, verse eighteen.

I stood back and surveyed the wreckage of William's words.

'Go on,' said I.

'Rather,' continued he, standing in all his clothes and indicating the bouncy, pouncy sloop, 'I shall paint the sloop pink with black stripes and rig her with a square sail, much different from the ones she been known by, friend, and christen her the *Prima*, or *Lady Cousin*.'

'Or *Cousin Lady*,' I suggested.

'Or *Lady Cousin*,' he continued, ' and shall put big Ralph into her as captain, and thus we shall show Danny and Tompkins the sister sloop they want so hard, that they shall weep to see her.'

'Sounds like the perfect cheat, you goofy Quaker,' I assented.

Having painted her pink and black, and squared her rig, we put the perfect load into that little sloop, filling her to the gills – in fact emptying the man-of-war of all her sundry packets and parcels but the gold and jewels and guns and last best remaining strumpets, swapping this cargo for some considerable tonnage of arrack and rice and fruits and meats that William had procured at the Surat factory – the man was never still; he hardly slept, and rarely rested – and William sailed big Ralph and the last of our nuts to his fence, having very favorable weather, and was successful in unloading of it all.

'Thirty-three, thirty-four, thirty-five thousand pieces of eight,' counted Danny and pissing-his-pants Tompkins into the hand, as it were, of William Walters, Quaker, acting as supercargo and formal procurer for one Captain Singleton, and doing it all above the table and in plain view of the world, we laughed, and laughed.

'The *Lady Cousin* is a fine if small bark,' the merchants remarked, 'er, barkie. We like her better than the *Amiga*, if you don't mind us saying.'

Not at all, smiled William, running not only pieces of eight but also dozens of good hard diamonds through his busy fingers.

Did they give him the diamonds, I asked him?

'I took what they gave me,' he told me.

'Not at all,' he said, fixing Danny and Tompkins with his cat's eyes – for the first time using words that they could hear, Quaker friends at his elbows like apparitions.

Danny and Tompkins froze where they cavorted.

'Thank you, Bill Walters,' they stammered, clutching behind them for the rail – taking the long fall backwards into their boat – calling out faintly to their men to pull hard for shore, as if their lives depended on it.

'Their lives did not depend on it,' I told William, looking up with a slight giggle, but seeing him there with the diamonds in his Quaker hands, it came to me like the dove to disciples that I had possibly spoken too soon.

To Thy Truelove Be True

Surat, India 1710
17°33' N or so - 72°56' E or so

Well then, says William, I would ask, whether, if thou hast gotten enough, thou hast any thought of leaving off this trade; for most people leave off trading when they are satisfied with getting, and are rich enough; for nobody trades for the sake of trading; much less do any men rob for the sake of thieving. Well, William, says I, now I perceive what it is thou art driving at; I warrant you, says I, you begin to hanker after home. –Defoe 280

Now we were really as rich as a man could be, we concluded, but when I passed the word to weigh anchor for Nosy Mitsy, our most natural rendezvous and secret fortress and de-facto home, William took me aside and said he wanted to talk.

'As long as the talk involves two (3) bottles of good arrack,' I replied, thumb stuck jauntily into my purple sash, gazing huskily off the starboard larboard – thirsty after so many words.

William's eyes blinked – a tear flashed down his merry cheek.

I gulped and stared in this belief.

Why William, I told him. 'William, Jesus, of course. Come into my great cabin,' I said hurriedly – hating to see a grown man cry, or look at a map in confusion.

'I know thou hatest to see a grown man cry,' William

began, 'and the thing about the map,' he continued, that he did as well, and explained that he wished to speak to me of the future, of our prospects, but said that if what he was about to say should offend me, he begged me to promise I should never bear him a grudge for it, or tell any of the men.

I swore to him very heartily.

'Also,' he added, 'that if thou dost not agree to my terms, and plans, that at least thou shalt do thy most to assist myself and my new doctor friend to accomplish them.'

You and your new doctor friend, I did not repeat – my mouth hung fire, like a wet pistol.

'What doctor friend,' I demanded.

'Our young doctor Mephistopheles.'

'But he's a whining little dipshit.'

Please don't talk about him that way, William implied.

He said, 'He is a true Friend.'

I thought of many ways of killing William's new friend. William with friends? How could William have friends? My knees were weak – I placed a hand on a very large chest of treasure to steady myself, and blinked through foggy eyeballs at our jolly, sullen, vaguely gay Quaker. I thought I could keep Mephistopholes alive for a number of days before he succumbed to loss of blood and major organ failure, or the giant python I would wrap around his face and neck.

'I agree,' I replied, after a pause in which drink both splashed and frothed in my cup, and gargled in my dumb throat, and my soul went missing. 'I shall do anything for you, William Walters, but you can never leave me.'

Shit, thought William Walters.

He said, 'I do not intend to leave thee, unless it is thy own wish.'

So I promised him.

'I swear,' I said. 'You have the word of a pirate.'

William turned to me, planting his shapely legs on the stout knees of my atrocious gunboat, and spoke.

My first question, he began, is whether you think you have enough money yet.

He said, 'Whether thou thinkest thou hast enough hard cash for thy investments, and designs.'

Designs, I said. What designs.

'I am going to hole up on Madagaskar with a covey of whores and a literal flowing night and day river of whiskey,' I told him plainly – a thing I already knew he already knew. 'And when I say night and day, and literal flowing river of whiskey, I mean it is going to gush across the ground twenty-five hours a day,' I explained, very carefully. 'Not two or three fingers of whiskey,' I screamed. 'A literal, flowing, river, of whiskey,' I said.

'By designs – and investments – what I was driving at,' replied William, getting one hand firmly around his arrack, or bastinado of drink, where it would remain for some time, 'was whether thou hast designs on leaving the *accounting* trade, now that thou hast made thyself as rich as any Greek or Roman.'

'Ho,' I mused, now that I thought about it for the very first time. I admitted, 'I do begin to hanker after home,' picturing home: a massive castle at the top of a very difficult jungle bluff that had a lot of guns sticking out of it, with bare-chested maids running hither and thither along its corridors in nothing but skirts and stockings and high black heels without any underwear underneath, moving at top speed between the polo field and the pantry in response to my five-shot sawed-off revolving blunderbusses, and those of my friends.

'I do begin to hanker after it,' I confirmed.

Ah, smiled William, leaning back upon the piled heaps of

pearls and decadent calicoes that were both blankets and bedsheets to us. 'Of course it is natural for any man to pine for home, after a time.'

I looked at William, and had a sneaking suspicion we were not talking about the same place.

What do you mean, home, I asked him finally.

'As you may or may not have heard, I have no home,' I said. 'I was bought by a gypsy in a London back alley and raised in an orphanage by a schoolmaster, not in a family by a mom. This is my family,' I said, indicating my ship and men, and the Mom on my arm. 'You are my family, and Madagaskar is as good a home as I got – as I ever could get or ever ask for.'

'Why,' said William, taken aback – like the man who thought you had brought him flowers, only to discover they were for his son, 'art thou not an Englishman?'

I speak English, I replied.

I said, 'I was born in England and raised there til the age of six, but the sea was my school, and it is everything I know. I have been back to England only once in all my grown life, and on that occasion they lied to me, took my money, beat me and left me for dead.'

William pursed his lips. I knew he was about to say something.

He said, 'Hast thou no friends or family, in that case?' It was the rhythm of the sea that night that drove the talk. We waited – he said, 'No cousins or chums that wait for you?'

None, said I.

William took up his arrack in its saffire-plugged skull and gulped it down.

'Come,' I said, pouring from the pitcher again and again and again and again and again and again and again and again and again, 'tell me why you have sequestered us in here. I know you aren't finished.'

But William mumbled only, 'It is nothing! If it is as you say, all my plans are finished.'

Out with it, friend, I clapped him – him, upon his Quaker black. 'Even if not for me, I have sworn to help you and your friend, and you always speak the utter truth, and even when you lie it is extremely entertaining. So spit tit out. I did not choose this pirate's life, and might even leave it if I could quit it.'

'You could quit it anytime you liked,' cried William – said a wistful glance about the cabin.

'I just don't want to,' I shrugged. 'Or I don't know how. What else is there?'

'There is indeed something else,' said William's bloated, claret countenance above his necktie – white and blithe, and as shifty as his own lips and tongue. I could have sworn I saw tears fill my friend's round, brown eyes, and I laughed in his face.

'You are talking about death,' I chuckled into my own formidable glass. 'Well, let me tell you, friend, when we die we die, and that is an end to it.'

'Do you never think about death?'

'To think about death is to die. I would rather not spend my life dying.'

By my own logic I realized that to think about sex was to have sex – my mind spun, for I was furious that somewhere someone could be fucking me just by thinking about fucking me.

I hurriedly placed an utterly chinkless chastity device upon my cods, and loins.

'They that never think of dying,' said William, after observing my frantic activity, and screams, 'often die without thinking of death.'

I laughed, picturing the eight hundred years I had left in me.

I said, 'Who said we were supposed to die, William. Who said we would not live forever.'

Drink more, flashed William's eyes from a skull demented from the fear of God, I thought, and hellfire, and conscience, and a deep and queasy inner grief. His Quaker face was screwed up and he spoke to me between breasts – between breaths.

'Friend Bob,' he said, and I confess that for the first time in my mangy, rangy, murdering life on this earth my heart broke in me when I looked into his blubbering blind nose. 'Friend Bob,' he cried out, 'think of what comes after those eight hundred years, be thou Methuselah himself.'

A solitary tear escaped a treacherous eye – words caught in my throat, for my heart was in my throat, and nothing else would come out.

I had to gulp, and paw at my eyes.

I reached out to embrace my friend.

My friend, at that moment, looked up with a grin.

'When I said something else,' he laughed, suddenly as cool as a cucumber, 'I was not talking about death, but about repentance, and clean living.'

You son of a bitch, I cursed him, to his face and nose, and eternal future.

I said, 'You lying fucking Quaker. You closet Quaker.'

But I was wrong – William spoke with affection in a face pocked with powder explosions and sliced with the sabers of many of my battles – saddened by both sin and syphilis.

I said, 'When have you ever known a pirate to repent.'

'I have known one,' William replied at once. 'On the gallows.'

Thanks for the kind wishes, I snarled, 'but I shall never hang – nor sing.'

Indeed I hope not, replied our grim Quaker – now pacing, now drying his eyes, for when he wept tears he wept real tears; now sighing, now adjusting his cravat – now pushing his finger distractedly into a cage of canaries.

I said, well, how could we repent and still be cutthroats and marauders.

'That would be something,' I exclaimed, imagining a double life full of both drunken strumpets and churchgoing wives and wives and drunken wives and churchgoing strumpets.

'We must quit being pirates, if we are going to live sober,' I drank. 'We shall do it tomorrow.'

William agreed, but said nothing – he was so transported by joy, and his favorite beverage in the world, that for the first time in his life he was at a loss for words.

He said, weeping, 'It all depends on you,' said his shrugging, mumbling mouth.

Command me, I told another man for the first time in the history of words. 'As I have commanded thee up to now, so shalt thou command me henceforth. How shall we escape this pirate's life?'

Easy, quipped our merry Friend, straightening on his drinking cot – as merchants. 'Wrap your gold and jewels in a discreet bundle and hide it in a cask,' he told me.

'It won't all fit in one cask,' I replied – knowing that much for certain.

Then put it inside ten casks, William hissed. 'Put it inside of twenty casks, for these casks are going with us on the sloop to Babelmandel.'

He said, 'The caravans shall arrive in a fortnight to the

strait,' in a loud voice to me, upon the quarterdeck, 'and we can easily unload our cloves and purchase powder and shot for our proximate cruise, and rice and arrack,' cheered the men, and William bullied me for a long time in public until I agreed to go with him.

'You must go,' he breathed, like a lover, 'else there shall be no order among the men.'

The men looked at us and agreed.

'I shall not dress as a Quaker,' I warned William.

Just put on a shirt, replied my concierge, 'and take out a couple of those earrings.'

This done, I called a meeting of my senior officers and boys, who were to remain with the hulk, our pirate fastness, the man-of-war, and we made our rendezvous at a secret location upon the Arabian coast in fifteen days, or failing that, at Nosy Mitsy in thirty, or failing that at the Madagaskarian mainland sometime in the next anno Dei, assuming some Greek tragedy had befallen either the sloop or the gunboat, gods forbid.

Arrangements made, we sailed into the teeth of Babelmandel, and got through into the gulf and made Bassora or Balsara, and rode there for a week or so, and we unloaded our bales and cloves, and William placed our own effects inside a house that we had rented there on the sly. We were ashore with twelve or fifteen of our men, including Mephistopheles and a man he said was his best friend.

'Your best friend,' said William, clearly shocked.

'Yes,' whined Mephistopheles. 'A true friend.'

Fuck your true friend, rang William's blood in his eyes and lips. I am your true friend.

'Fuck your true friend in the eye,' he almost said, but in the end he said nothing.

'Run along down to that jolly boat,' he instructed a local boy, where we could see our men milling and guffawing and making obscene remarks to passing ladies, 'and deliver them this letter.'

The letter said, 'BOATSWAIN THOMAS, We are all betrayed. For the love of Jesus get off this shore with the boat and the men, or you all are lost. Captain Bob, William the Quaker, Surgeon Mephistopheles and the so-called friend of Mephistopheles (me) are captured and beheaded. Actually I managed to get free before they cut off my head. I have hidden myself and shall venture to escape overland. As soon as you are on board, weigh anchor and slip harbor, and sail for your lives, for they are coming for you.'

The letter concluded, 'Your friend, the friend of Mephistopheles.'

Thus I died, beheaded, in old Arabia.

Our bosun, taking the missive in his great and horny hands, and perusing it but once, being a man of great reading, leapt with the remaining men into our boat and rowed for his life for the sloop. Before morning they were gone, and we would never hear from them again – and I write this more than a century after it happened.

Turning our eyes to big Arabia, and our heavy bundled treasure, we exchanged relieved, perplexed glances – looked at the spot in the harbor where the sloop no longer lay. Blinked, but she was gone.

Seignior Constantine
Lexion Of Ispahan

Bassora, Arabia, 1710
29°51' N - 48°25' E

Nay, says William, the answer to that is short. –Defoe 291

Thus shed and shucked of our underworld friends, and criminal gunboat, we set ourselves up in that town as Persian mechants, dressed in silk and crimson robes, and wore our beards as long and pointy as men humping after a star.

'That's it,' we pointed out – but we were wrong.

We agreed never to speak of our affairs but in the open fields of an evening, where we could never be overheard, for those were days of fear and reckoning, we knew, once we had got our land legs under us and were able to look soberly about, and look to see, and assess our state and lives and pasts and futures.

'I want to kill myself,' I told William, upon one such stroll, gripping my hair and beard in my hands, and wringing fingers. 'I am tormented by grief, and dreams.'

Tell me your dreams, William said quickly.

He said, 'I too have dreamt of Nosy Mitsy.'

Of course you have, I replied. 'Of course you have, William. That is your dream. My dreams, on the other hand, are of blood and murder and money.'

'Tell me,' cooed my friend.

'I am,' I said, 'tormented to think that everything I am and have I got thanks to the suffering of others.'

William was surprised, for he had only walked out with me to discuss his thoughts on transporting our loot overland, and getting back into England without suspicion.

'We may yet hope for God's mercy,' he mumbled.

There is no mercy without repentance, true repentance, I cried.

I said, 'God looks at us and he doesn't see our tattooes that say Mom. He sees our bloody gold.'

True repentance, William said quietly, not quite following me. 'What do you mean by true repentance, in your busy, heathen mind?'

True repentance requires we give up what we have gained by dishonest means, I told him. 'Otherwise how could a man's conscience be clean – get clean?'

'You mean, give back the gold and silver we have stolen,' deadpanned one funny Quaker. He laughed out loud, tossing a clump of grass to the wind. 'That would be impossible. For starters,' he chuckled, 'we would never in a hundred years be able to track down all the people we have robbed, even if they were still alive.'

Which they are not, I confessed. 'Most of them died immediately after losing their money.'

Exactly, smiled William. 'You see, you are worried about something that does not even concern us.'

I disagreed.

I said, 'We must throw our money into the strait, or abandon it in our rented house.'

Nay, chuckled William, eyes as tight and porcine as a priest's, 'to do that would be to give it to men – to fish – who have no more right to it than a baby raised as another man's baby,' he said.

Are you talking about orphans, I said.

I said, 'No more right to it than we do ourselves,' I said.

'It is true what you say, that we have no right to what we have stolen,' mused William. 'Yet you surely do not deny that we have possession of it,' he said.

I did not deny that we had possession of what we had, I told him.

'What are you driving at, you batty Quaker,' I shouted.

William said, 'If we have what we have, we must say it is because God wishes us to have it. For only God gives, and only God knows what circumstances He has prepared for us to dispose of our wealth in honest – in philanthropic ways, even to help the victims of our very own *accounting*.'

I love it when you say *accounting*, I screamed. 'Fuck fuck fuck fuck. Fucking fuck you, William.'

William said, 'Be calm, Captain Bob. God and all women love you.'

He looked over his shoulder, scanning the clearing and crummy huts, but we were alone. Yet even with William's comforting words my conscience would not be quiet, and I kicked through a mess of dandelions.

'I hate myself for a dog and a thief,' I cried, and though we broke off our conversation then, I had no thought for days afterwards but to shoot myself through the head with my pistol.

'Where is my pistol,' I screamed, rummaging through many treasure chests in the back room where everything important was kept. 'What have you done with my fucking guns.'

'Whatever do you want a gun for,' quaked our merry

Friend, as I confronted him about my missing weapons upon the dusking fields, far from earshot of any meddling snoops.

'Give me my gun,' I replied, 'for I have determined to shoot myself in the face.'

Shoot yourself in the face, laughed William.

He said, 'Why, what will that get you.'

'It shall put an end to my miserable existence,' I told him, trigger hand akimbo on my silken robe, and nothing underneath. 'Give it to me. GIVE IT TO ME.'

'Fine,' replied William, blinking into a gorgeous sunset, 'but first tell me one thing.'

I almost said, 'Shoot.'

I panted, 'I'll tell you.'

'How are you so sure the next life will be any better?' William asked.

I was not sure – I swore.

'God damn you and your quakering lips,' I told him. 'I can't take it anymore. I am beyond help. Last night I—'

'Last night you what.'

'Last night I dreamed that the devil came for me.'

The devil, repeated William. 'What did the devil want with a person like you.'

'My name.'

Your name, thought William. 'So you said, I am Bob Monoklino of Ispahan.'

'I said I am Bob Singleton,' I said in a loud voice. 'Then do you know what the devil asked me?'

'What did the devil ask you then.'

'He asked me what I did for a living.'

'So you told him you were a Persian merchant in Babelmandel on business. That your name was Monoklino,' said my only friend.

'Wrong,' I said, 'I said I was Bob, Bob Singleton, a thief and a murderer and a pirate, and should be hanged.'

'And then you shut the fuck up.'

'Then I cried out violently, screaming it over and over in my sleep, and woke up.'

'Here is your pistol,' said William, handing me my pistol. 'You need to do us all a favor and shoot yourself now, Captain Bob, pirate, before you get us all hanged.'

I looked at him in astonishment – in a Bible full of maggots and shit.

What, I spluttered, taking the heavy wrench between my fingers and gripping for the rope.

'Why do you say that?' I asked him.

'Why,' William grimaced, 'you are a menace to us all with your fucking nightmares and confessions. You have to die, Bob, to save the rest of us.'

I saw his point – I raised the gun to my temple and cocked back the big hammer.

'You are right, William,' I wept, baring my teeth. 'I am a menace to myself and my friends.'

Don't be an asshole, William said, knocking the pistol from my grip as I squeezed off a round – that soughed and zwanged off through the knee-high barley. 'Ask forgiveness of God, for Chrissake,' he told me, 'knowing full well that thou hast already changed thy life, and do what thou canst in this world while you still live.'

I looked down at the pistol in my hand, and for a moment I could not remember whose gun it was or what it was for. My eyes blinked – William talked on, and on. After an hour I gave the gun back to him. He blinked and thanked Jesus – quickly primed and charged the firearm and tucked it firmly into his waistband, with a glance all around the barley field, deserted and blowing in a full-grown sunset.

'We shall go by boat to Bagdad,' he told me, 'with a cargo of Chinese bales and spices, and cross by caravan to the Levant, where we are going to make a killing, and thus cross over to Scanderoon, Cyprus, and get into Venice, where we shall live like kings,' he told me.

And he was right. We made a killing after crossing the desert, though I cared little at the time, being in a dumbfounded stupor, and suicidal depression. Yet William watched out for me, and carried off all our transactions with one plomb, and a tidy little moustache, and got us into Italy on a little packet with more money in the world than ever before – than anyone ever before.

'This is the house,' he told me, as we drove in beneath the archway, trailing our own caravan of mules and wagons piled high with trunks and effects. 'Here we may stay and pass as Armenians,' he explained, looking around the courtyard in grim satisfaction, 'as long as we never speak English.'

I looked at William from beneath a heavy cloak – from behind a full beard and out of sad and listless eyes.

'Mi ne falas persianan,' I told him with a dry guffaw.

'Mi sepas,' smiled William. 'Mi sepas.'

We remained in Venice for three years, living as brothers and gentlemen and in great ease and respect and discretion, speaking only Persian in the street, careful to conceal exactly how rich we were, which in any case no one would ever have believed. How could they have? We were richer than the Pope. Yet still we hesitated to be known as Englishmen, lest we be suspected or recognized by some stray son of a fucking dog out of our previous lives, and professions.

'I do not know if I shall ever see England again,' William confided in me one day, as we lounged upon a balcony at teatime in our silken drawers, 'but I should very much like to try.'

Why, I replied, whatever kind of zany scheme do you have in mind now, William.

'Tell me what the plan is,' I said, sipping something loudly from some very fine china.

'I have a sister and an uncle living in London,' William admitted. 'Or I suspect still living. I shall write to them, with your permission, Captain Bob, and inquire after them, and if they are there I should like to send them a little money, for they have always lived in Squalor.'

Squalor, I mused. 'Don't know it,' I said.

I said, 'I readily assent to your foibling scheme. Write to them, using your nom de guerre Seignior Constantine Lexion of Ispahan, and be glad on it,' I drank to.

William did so and drank, too, and one month later he received a reply.

'We thought you were dead,' wrote his weeping, transported sister, 'murdered by pirates in the West Indies,' explaining that she was alive and well, though widowed with four children; that she kept shop in Minories (not Squalor) and thus eked out a living; that she had enclosed five pounds, in case brother William be in need of clothes, or food, I smiled.

'Or a five-pound whore,' I could not help but interject.

But William wept when he read the letter.

I said, 'I never knew you had a sister. Is she your real sister?'

'What shall I do for this poor woman?' William cried, shewing me the letter and the note for money.

Do, I snarled. I'll tell you what you are going to do.

I said, 'You are going to return her her five pounds, and send her five thousand more, and instruct her to sell her little shop and take her munchkins into the country. There she shall buy a big house on a large estate, and wait for further instructions,' I said – as though struck by lightning.

By Jove, William whispered, looking me up and down.

He said, 'By Jupiter, Captain Bob, I cannot send her five thousand pounds. All the money we have belongs to the both of us, and I feel I should be robbing you of your share.'

My share, I smiled. I said, 'Let me tell you about my share.'

Leaning in, I whispered something extremely dirty in his ear.

William straightened, stiffened, frowned, and smiled.

'Thou shalt live without keeping shop,' he wrote in his next letter, 'and say that Uncle Katzen is taken ill, and must be moved to the country; that thou hast invested thy earnings in a country house to be rented to lodgers,' and William's sister was no dummy. She took the money and followed William's instructions to the letter – to the iota.

In her next letter she wrote that she was waiting for us, if we should ever wish to retire from our lives as businessmen – for I had begged William to tell her about me, to say he had a business partner and good friend, who was like a brother to him, whom he loved.

'Actually, don't say brother,' I said. 'And don't say loved, or love. She might get the wrong idea. Tell her about my buxom pantaloons,' I panted. 'Tell her about my jaunty chin and flashing teeth, and send her five thousand more pounds. We are going to make that widow rich.'

William smiled, and scribbled dutifully, and we made his sister and her family as wealthy as the Catholic Church, and she importuned us on a weekly basis to come home to her.

'Come home to us, cousin Constantine,' she wrote, 'and bring cousin Captain Bob Monoklino with you.'

The following year we shaved off our beards, bought western suits, and moved with all our appurtenances upon

London and the country house where William's sister tended her babies and gardened, and rode upon the ponies we had instructed her to purchase, and sipped at fine sherries in her seventeenth or eighteenth century underwear, and there we became her foreign cousins.

'I love you,' she loved me, that autumn, after William and I had settled in and returned to a life we had thought we could never go back to.

'Marry me,' I replied.

'Oh, Captain Monoklino, take me,' she screamed.

'We shall speak only Italian in public,' William and I swore, 'and always live together, and never leave each other, and always use the same barber, and be brothers.'

'You don't have a sister, do you?' William asked.

'Se mi havus hermanino,' I replied with a wink, 'sxi estus via, nur via.'

I said, 'If I had, she would be yours, cowboy. All yours.'

We laughed heartily, standing on the Persian rug in our slippers and gowns – chucked our empty glasses into the fire.

And now, friend, having told you absolutely everything, including a full confession of my life of crime and mind of sin, and my current whereabouts on the outskirts of London, and hopefully amused you a little, I shall have to kill you.

Without more ado,
CAPTAIN BOB.

YOUR END

Colin Gee is founder and editor of The Gorko Gazette, teacher and writer. His poetry can be found in the chapbooks fear of sleep (2023) and All you want (a series of lies) (2024). His third novella Lips will be published in 2024. Originally from Wisconsin, he has been in Mexico since he got there.

www.ingramcontent.com/pod-product-compliance
Lightning Source LLC
Chambersburg PA
CBHW020336010826
48970CB00012B/1336